Promises after dark

by

Kahlen Aymes

TELEMACHUS PRESS

PROMISES AFTER DARK

CoverArt:
Designed by: Kristen Karwan
Cover photo by: Scott Hoover Photography
Cover model: Colby Lefebvre

Published by Telemachus Press, LLC
http://www.telemachuspress.com

Visit the author website:
http://www.kahlenaymes.com

ISBN: 978-1-941536-70-4 (eBook)
ISBN: 978-1-941536-64-3 (Paperback)

Version 2014.11.12

Printed in the United States of America

10 9 8 7 6 5 4 3 2 1

Acknowledgments

Special thanks to my *Super Friends:* Vi Keeland, Penelope Ward, Julie Richman, S.E. Lund, J.L. Mac, Kelly Elliott, Liv Morris, Kailin Gow, Heidi McLaughlin, Aleatha Romig, Sandi Lynn, Ilsa Madden Mills, T.K. Rapp, Kimberly Knight & Crystal Spears. I love you bitches so flipping hard! Thank you for all of your support, love, and, (ah-hem), inspirational pictures. :)

To the many blogs who post, pimp and feel so passionately about these books, I couldn't do it without you! Thank you! Thank you! Thank you!

Thank you to everyone (blogs, authors) who organizes and invites me to the events and gives me the opportunity to meet my readers! You ROCK!

My street team: Kahlen's Angels, Team Ryan and the Peppy Pimpers! Thank you for always having my back!! <3

To Jennifer Singh & Amber Hayden ~ Heartfelt thanks for all you do! Group hug! xo

Heartfelt thanks to my agents: Elizabeth Winick Rubinstein and Shira Hoffman of McIntosh and Otis Literary, NY, NY.

And Especially...
To my readers... Thank you for the support, love, tears and amazing words you offer to me on a daily basis. You humble me and I adore you! <3

Olivia ~ As always... Hugs and Kisses. xoxo

Table of Contents

Promises
after dark

1

You & Me

DR. ANGELINE HEMMING sat in the leather chair across from one of her regular patients, listening to her drone on about her abusive ex-husband. The desperateness of the woman's situation should have held her focus and she admonished herself, shaking her head a little to bring herself back to the conversation. She'd heard the same story on previous appointments, and though she was sympathetic to her patient's plight, she also felt frustrated when the woman stayed in a situation that didn't change. Besides, Angel's mind was filled with her own personal fight to push aside her fear of being hurt and to just dive headfirst into the amazing feelings she felt for Alexander Avery. Her heart told her he was amazing. He was everything. Her head told her he was a huge risk. But, she didn't want to concentrate on that.

She counseled people for a living and was having one hell of a time practicing what she preached, and the irony was not lost on her. Alex had been nothing but wonderful and her heart was lost to him, but there was still that irritating niggle that picked at her, telling her to keep her eyes open and her feet firmly on the ground.

She was frustrated. She hated worrying, hated doubting even one little thing when it came to Alex.

She was drowning in her relationship with him, though she was afraid to trust it one hundred percent. Angel wanted to. Badly... and maybe, she was nine-tenths of the way there. It was incredible how well the two of them connected mentally, and of course, physically... She was giddy and floating, her heart full and mind filled with him, but there was still a moment here or there when his phone would ring or one of her patients would talk about her womanizing boyfriend when her heart still clenched.

Angel loved everything about Alex and looked forward to every second they spent together; he made her feel beautiful, sexy, insatiable; utterly and completely intoxicated; loved. He made her feel empowered by the way he craved her. He was still very much the man in the relationship, but she sensed he was just as much a slave to the attraction as she was, and at times, there was vulnerability in his eyes when she wanted to kick herself for even a second of doubt. She closed her eyes at the thought. *Damn it!* She would kick her doubt to the curb and leave it there if it were the last thing she did!

The hours apart from Alex dragged, and she found herself constantly checking the clock on her desk, her phone, and email. Even though her schedule was chock full until the end of the day, she longed for his touch, his words, the way his eyes caressed her, and their conversations.

She brought the woman's words back from the sort of muffled, subconscious place it had been relegated to and blinked. Normally, Angel felt this type of session wasn't the best use of her expertise and just a different version of the shit she dealt with on the radio show. She'd much rather be putting sex offenders behind bars, but her soft feelings for Alex, and the freshness of the relationship still hanging precariously on the precipice, gave her a more empathetic view of women whose hearts were hanging in the fragile balance. Angel's cynicism had become somewhat diminished, but her logic didn't come to a full stop. Her brain told her this woman was doing very little to help herself out of a bad situation, but had now fully acknowledged that you don't choose whom you love, and how much it hurts to walk away from someone who'd become your entire world. Even when you fought—every inch of the way, clawing and scraping—hoping not to fall in so deep that your heart lay open and defenseless. Her own vulnerability made her acutely aware of the pain of those around her; the perfection of her situation with Alex screamed how fragile it really was. And rare.

"I know I should take the kids and leave him, but I love him so much," she cried, her words breaking. "He's good to me in many ways, and he never hurts the children."

"Maryanne." Angel sighed sadly, trying to temper the tightness in her chest and the bluntness of her words. She wished she could reach across the desk and take the woman's hand. *Of course, your husband is hurting your children. How can you not see it?* She thought, her jaw tightening as she swallowed but making a conscious decision to soften her tone. "If he hurts you in front of them, naturally, they're hurt. Horribly. Watching their mother being beaten and berated is abuse as well. I know you see the situation isn't good for any of you, including your husband. He needs professional help."

Maryanne nodded and blew her nose loudly into a tissue. "I know. I've managed to hide the fact I come to you. I tried to tell him, but he put his fist through the wall in our bedroom. He doesn't want to come to counseling—he sees it as admitting he's doing something wrong. He can't admit he has a problem."

"Admitting it is the first step to recovery. If he can't face it and want to stop badly enough, he won't." Angel looked sympathetically at Maryanne as she spoke. "For the sake of your kids, you need to. You have a responsibility to take them, and yourself out of the situation. You don't deserve being beaten or made to feel bad about yourself."

"I know that's what you keep saying—"

Angel interrupted her. "Because it's true. No one deserves what he has done to you."

The woman's face crumpled again and a sob burst from her chest. Angel's heart went out to her on one level, but on another, she was frustrated with repeating herself and with her patient's refusal to do anything about her situation. Abuse victims were made to feel worthless; like they somehow asked for or deserved what was done to them. That was how abusers manipulated and kept the victims in the situation long-term. She sighed aloud.

"I'm going to have my assistant give you information on Harmony House. It's a safe house where you and your children can stay free of charge until you get on your feet. You'll be able to take a step away and think things through; they have counselors there, and it's safe."

Angel buzzed her assistant, Liz, on the intercom and asked her to get the woman the Harmony House address and contact information, and soon after, the session ended. She had an hour for paperwork on another molestation case, but at least with this one, the perpetrator showed classic signs of a pedophile, so she could make solid recommendations and a substantiated profile that would put this one behind bars.

Her afternoon progressed at a snail's pace, and her last appointment was a woman who was raped in the underground garage of her apartment complex. At least, on this occasion, there was DNA evidence, and it was an open and shut case. The hard part would be helping the girl get through the terrifying fear that now paralyzed her so she'd be able get on with her life.

Angel couldn't help but shudder at the memory of Alex's car being vandalized in the garage of her own building and how she'd almost been raped and killed under Mark Swanson's hands inside her own home. Now, it was natural that she would want to get away from that condo, but she wasn't sure if she was ready to move in, lock, stock and barrel, with Alex as he insisted. They'd both gone through so much to get that bastard arrested and charged. Still... he was out on bail, so Alex and Angel would remain on edge until the trial was over.

Alex's shoulders got tense whenever Swanson's name was mentioned in the news or in conversation between them or with Kenneth. His green eyes would skirt to Angel's face to gauge her reaction, yet trying to disguise his own, but his demeanor was tense. She could read the worry behind his eyes despite his attempts to act unconcerned, and she was certain he was equally aware of how petrified she was, in spite of her bravado.

Cole, Bancroft, and the others were still following her everywhere, and even though she protested, she knew better than to argue with Alex. She would lose anyway, and secretly, she was glad to have the protection.

She'd learned two lessons well. One, Mark Swanson wasn't one to give up easily, and two, Alex was a force to be reckoned with on many levels. He would have his way, especially when it came to Angel. The thought caused a delicious shiver to run through her entire body.

Her phone buzzed in her purse as she made her way out of her office. In the hallway outside, Cole was waiting, leaning nonchalantly against the wall, dressed in dress slacks and a dark gray turtleneck sweater.

Angel smiled wide as her eyes skirted down to his finely polished shoes. Alex was certainly beginning to rub off on Cole. His strong jaw was lightly covered in a day's worth of stubble, and the sweater accentuated his broad shoulders.

She felt bad. He was with her so much. Alex worked him like a dog, and the only time he had off was when Alex was with her, because Bancroft was tailing Swanson. She'd seen Cole send appraising glances in Becca's direction on the few times he'd seen her. Angel decided when things settled down, she might have to have them both over for dinner. Alex's lackluster opinion of Cole was changing, and Angel could see the changes herself. She trusted Cole implicitly now.

"What?"

"Nothing." Angel shook her head and smirked. "I was just thinking you clean up well."

"It's still not a suit." Cole shrugged and grinned back. "I'm still kicking and screaming in regard to that."

"True, but it's a lot closer. You look good. It suits you."

"Have a good day, did you?" Cole asked with a sly grin, taking her coat from her and holding it so she could slip her arms inside. It was fall, Chicago had turned colder, and today a light mist had been constant all day. Angel's shoulders shrugged a little as her phone buzzed again.

"It was okay. Glad it's over."

"You gonna answer that? Sounds like little brother has a rod up his ass," he remarked wryly.

She laughed and laced her arm through Cole's. "Maybe, but he'll live. He didn't call or email me at all today."

Cole pursed his lips then chuckled. "I see. So, now he's being punished, is he?"

"Not exactly." Angel paused for a beat when the notion she was intentionally punishing Alex hit Cole. She wasn't one to play adolescent games with men, but his lack of contact stung, despite her logical brain assigning a laundry list of reasons why it could have been impossible for Alex to spare a few minutes to call or email. He did run a multi-billion dollar company. "At least, I wasn't trying to."

"No?" Cole's eyebrow shot up, knowingly.

"No. But I don't need to be a pushover, either." Angel bit her lip as Cole opened the door to the black Lincoln sedan he was driving. Her brown eyes glinted with amusement as the door was closed behind her, and Alex's brother walked around the front of the car and slid behind the wheel. Cole glanced at her as he started the car, his smirk telling her what he was thinking. Angel kicked herself mentally.

"Right. That wouldn't be like you, and you were both working. Alex has some big deal in Sydney he's trying to get done without actually traveling there." He stopped, astonishment flashing over his strong features. "Did I just make an excuse for him? Un-fucking-believable." He shook his head and rolled his eyes.

A laugh burst from Angel, and she shot him a look.

"Seriously, maybe he didn't call, but he's been all over me. Trust me, you were on his mind all day."

"Really? Is he pestering you to bring me out to the house? I told him it's too far to go during the week. I have too much work to do to commute that far."

"Is that the only reason you don't want to go?" Cole pointed to their left, in the direction of the building where they both had apartments, silently asking Angel if that was where he should take her. Alex would have his ass, but he'd rather beg forgiveness than go against what Angel wanted. When she nodded, he pulled into the stream of traffic and accelerated. "Alex mentioned you were moving in together."

"Oh, he did, did he?" Angel's brow furrowed angrily, and she huffed at Alex's presumptuousness. They'd discussed it for five minutes in bed, once or maybe twice. "He's too sure of himself. It hasn't been decided for sure."

"He's worried and in love." Cole cringed and gave Angel a look that said he couldn't believe he was buying into that sappy shit. She dipped her head and smiled softly, her fingers nervously fiddling with the straps of her purse. "Never thought I'd say this in this lifetime, but Alex deserves a break, Angel." Cole paused for a few seconds, clearly considering his next words carefully. Angel glanced his way and waited for him to continue. "He's always been in control, and he can't accept when he isn't. He doesn't know what the hell to do with himself, and he's floundering a bit. It's kind of funny to see him act so out of his element, but this Swanson thing has him in knots. He's more relaxed when you're with him."

Angel grinned broadly. "Thank you, Dr. Phil."

Cole chuckled. "Don't you mean, Dr. Hemming?" he retorted.

Angel's expression sobered. She felt an easy camaraderie with Cole, and he could shed some light on what Alex was thinking. "Alex scares me as much as Mark Swanson. I'm trying to let myself just go with the flow, but his track record doesn't include long-term. And I even understand why, but I'm already—" She stopped and looked quickly at Cole.

There was a stall reserved for him in the parking garage, and Cole pulled into it. It was cold so he hesitated before turning off the engine. "Forgive me, but you'll never know if he can make it to long-term if you don't give him a shot. His relationships end when he wants them to." Cole flushed and shot a glance at Angel, instantly regretting his choice of words. She looked pensive as she bit her lip. "He never fails at anything, especially something he wants. It used to make me want to beat the crap out of him when we were kids. Trust me. He's in this. *All* in. There are things I could say to prove it, but Alex wouldn't thank me for sharing. Is it necessary?"

Angel shook her head. She didn't need proof. She felt Alex's commitment in his actions, and when they were together, his touches were reverent, his kisses passionate and worshiping. His intensity, not just in his protectiveness but his possessiveness, was a big part of what worried her, even as it thrilled her. She knew she could trust him with her life; he'd done more than enough to prove it. She'd accepted she loved him, accepted there was nothing she could do about it even if she wanted to, but her mind still cautioned, even as she silently acknowledged she was way beyond the point of no return.

Her skin warmed and her heart started to thump each time she remembered the passionate plea that had ripped from Alex's chest, almost as if he were unwilling to admit his feelings to either of them; *"I'm in love!"*

He hadn't formally proposed, their relationship only a few months in, but he had mentioned making babies with her. She didn't want him to rush anything and would have questioned his sanity if he did mention marriage. They were having an amazing time together. She just wanted to live in the moment, and God knew, to throw any expectations out the window. Yet, her heart just about jumped out of her chest as she remembered his comments about Jillian, surprised by the overwhelming want she felt at his words. Even Alex lost control sometimes. He had when he'd admitted his feelings, but also in his jealousy over Kyle and Kenneth, or when he'd almost beaten Mark Swanson to death. Chills danced over her skin… Alex could have killed the other man so easily.

The phone in her purse started playing his ringtone. No longer accepting of having his texts unanswered, Alex had called instead.

Angel pulled it out and answered Cole in the process. "No, it isn't necessary." She pushed the answer button and spoke into the phone. "Hello?"

"Hey," Alex responded, the sigh that followed the word clearly indicating he wasn't expecting her to pick up. "I thought you were still working since you hadn't answered my texts."

"Cole and I were just talking about you."

Alex hesitated and Angel could physically feel his need to ask her what it was about, yet he didn't.

"Greaaaat." Alex's tone betrayed a hint of annoyance. "So, what are your plans?"

By now, she and Cole were climbing out of the car and beginning the walk toward the elevators. The air was cold in comparison to the warmth inside the vehicle. and her breath created a fog when she spoke. "We just got back to my place."

Cole pushed the button on the elevator. It dinged as it arrived at the garage level, and the doors slid open. Alex sighed heavily. Angel could hear his frustration; her mind conjuring an image of him running his hand through his dark hair impatiently.

"Okay. I guess I'll catch a quick workout, then I'd like to see you. I might stop by my place and grab clothes for tomorrow before I come over."

She knew he'd say he wanted to see her and that it wasn't his choice he hadn't been in touch all day, even before Cole confirmed it. Angel could sense he was bristling as the unspoken question hung between them. He was wondering why Cole hadn't delivered her to his estate as he'd wanted, but he didn't ask permission to come over. They would be together, regardless of where. Angel bit her lip.

She could have easily reassured him she was only picking up clothes for herself before allowing Cole to do as his brother had asked, but the issue was more than one night and needed more conversation. Angel decided to bring it up when they were together rather than confronting him on the phone. Besides, she missed him and wanted to see him as badly as he obviously wanted to see her. Needed to see him was more accurate.

"Sure. How was your day?" she asked.

"Busy, but slow." Agitation laced his tone. "I'm leaving the office now, but give me an hour or so and I can bring something for dinner. Unless you want to go out?"

Cole placed his arm over one of the elevator doors to keep it from closing as Angel went inside, then he followed, pushing the third floor button.

"No. I'd rather stay in. I'm tired and Cole said you might have to leave town?"

"I'm trying to avoid it."

"Let's just watch a movie or something." Her mouth lifted in a wry smile in anticipation of a teasing remark regarding what the *something* could be, but it didn't follow as she expected.

Instantly, Alex was on edge and concern filled his voice. "Did something happen today?"

"Nothing out of the ordinary. I'd just rather stay in, especially if you might be away for a while. I want to talk to you." Mostly, she just wanted Alex close by. It didn't matter where or how, but she was still Angel, and she still didn't want him making plans for her without checking with her. Not as a matter of habit, anyway.

After they'd both declared their love for each other in the emotional and vulnerable aftermath of the concert for the Leukemia and Lymphoma Society, they'd both had to face the inevitability of their togetherness and spent all of the following Sunday secluded in Alex's apartment, mostly in his bedroom wrapped up in sheets and each other's arms. It had been magical and surreal, and Angel had to close her eyes and just let it sink in. They'd made love multiple times, not letting go of each other, even holding hands while they cooked or ate, and unable to keep from making love when Alex followed her into the shower.

But, as Sunday night turned into Monday and the real world began its intrusion into their idyllic little bubble, the insecurity she hated nagged just below the surface. The only thing she knew of his previous relationships was what she'd learned early on. Had his heart ever been breached? Was that more of a reason for his "arrangements" than his busy schedule?

"I want to do more than talk." His mood lightened. Angel couldn't help but smile, her body reacting immediately to the meaning behind the words, even as his teasing demeanor finally kicked in. "It feels like years since I've touched you."

"Mmm… for me, too. I'm still sore… um, from the weekend," she stammered, realizing that Cole was privy to the intimacy of the conversation. The ride upstairs felt endless but the elevator doors finally opened on the third floor. With raised eyebrows, his lips twitching in the start of smile, Cole wordlessly took the key that he carried with him out of his pants pocket and put it in the lock on the door to her apartment. When the door opened, Angel went inside, turning around to give an embarrassed smile and wave at Cole before he closed the door behind her, and went to the apartment he occupied on another floor.

Alex listened for the sound of her turning on security and putting the deadbolts in place at the same time he laughed softly. The sound was so sexy as it vibrated over her skin in a physical caress. "Now, that's what I like to hear from my girl; too bad Cole got to hear it."

"You might not think so later when we can't have a repeat performance."

"Well, Dr. Hemming, maybe seeing you is enough. You said you just wanted to talk tonight anyway, so that will fit into your plans."

"I never said I *just* wanted to talk." She made her way to the bedroom, swapping the phone into her left hand so she could shrug the right arm out of her coat. She flung it on the bed then kicked her high-heeled navy pumps off into her walk-in closet. Alex started to chuckle, and she couldn't help teasing back. "I also said I wanted to watch a movie." When Alex huffed in mock sarcasm, she added with a grin, "But that has its risks. I might want you."

"The truth is, I might be out of commission in that respect, too. I don't think I've ever had a sore dick before."

Angel burst out laughing at the same time Alex did. "Oh my God! Really?" She proceeded to undress, peeling off her dark navy wool crepe suit and fuchsia blouse, giggling so hard she snorted. "Is it all red? I mean, more than usual?"

He laughed again, harder. "Shut up. At least I can walk without looking like I pulled a muscle."

"Oh, I'll pull your muscle like you wouldn't believe, then you'll stop teasing me," she goaded, smiling still.

His soft laugh filtered through the phone. So sexy. "One can dream."

"About me pulling or you teasing?" Her tone was lilted.

"Both. But, I'll *never* stop teasing you," he said, the sound of his low chuckle vibrating through the phone.

Happiness filled Angel as she peeled off her stockings and kicked out of them on her way to turn on the water in the shower. The water rushing began to echo off of the marble tile, and Alex could hear it easily.

"And, I'm never going to play fair. You'll remember that in about ten minutes."

"Ugh!" Alex groaned but with amused laughter. "I'd be disappointed if you did, and I can only imagine."

Angel grinned, leaning over to test the temperature of the water under the spray. "You won't have to imagine," she quipped happily, tongue-in-cheek. "I'm naked and just about to take a shower."

"That is my cue to get off the damn phone and get my ass to the gym. The faster I get that done, the quicker I can come over and teach you a lesson."

She laughed again, letting out a huff. "Humph! You're still under the impression you can teach me anything? Delusional, much?"

"I'm sure I can think of something. Baby, I adore this, but I really have to go. Darian is ringing the other line. I'll be there as soon as I can. I can't wait to see you."

"Okay. Me, too." She smiled softly as her heart leapt.

Alex was handsome, amazing, and mind-blowing, and while he made her feel safe, she was more determined than ever to get past the worry that he might eventually end things. *Go with the flow, remember?* she reminded herself with an exaggerated sigh. She'd have to take it one day at a time, trusting his and her own feelings more as time went on. So far, he hadn't disappointed her. Not even once. His next words proved it again.

"Love you."

A gentle smile tugged at one corner of her mouth as her heart swelled.

"It's okay, you can say it… you won't melt." His voice was coaxing, like soft velvet or warm honey oozing over her skin.

"Maybe I want to. Melt, I mean." Her soft laughter echoed his.

"I can arrange that."

"Okay…" she bemoaned, as if the admission was utter agony. "I love you."

"I know," he shot back without hesitation, his tone loaded with cockiness and sex.

A smile lit up her beautiful features and made her eyes dance. "Asshole."

Alex burst out laughing at her dry reply, and Angel ended the call, intent on making him squirm.

The room began to fill with steam, and despite her current state of euphoria, the atmosphere still made her skin crawl. She couldn't help but think of the attack from Mark Swanson, which began in a similar situation and just weeks earlier in this very room. She shuddered slightly and thought about locking the door to the bathroom, but she didn't want to let the bastard have any more control over her than he already had. The security on the entire building had been stepped up, and Angel knew she had to get her life back to normal. She tried to push it from her thoughts and get her mind on better things.

She held up the phone, which she now lovingly thought of as *Alex's,* to take the half-naked picture she intended sending to torture him. She held a fluffy white towel in front of her, covering just enough but leaving the curve of her hip and bottom visible as she turned at a slight angle in the mirror. Her hair was mussed and hung long down her back. The image would be hazy, but it would be enough to get Alex going. Her cheeks hurt from smiling, though she did her best to put deliberate pout on her lips and a sultry look in her eyes as she took the shot in the mirror. She warned women against doing this all day long, but teasing Alex was too exciting to resist. Besides, she trusted him never to share something so intimate, no matter what might happen between them.

She sighed, setting the phone on the counter and dropping the towel to her feet and climbed into the tub, the warmth from the water seeping through her skin and muscles. She closed her eyes, anxious for Alex to make his appearance.

*****

The teasing image of Angel's almost naked form saved securely on his phone, Alex decided to forego his workout and declined Darian's invitation to get a drink. His muscles needed exercise but he'd already pulled his phone out six damn times, and he couldn't wait to get to the woman he couldn't stay away from. He could breathe easier whenever he was on his way to be with her. He was anxious. Always anxious, and while it felt fucking amazing, it was disconcerting at the same time.

As much as Alex wanted to sneak in and take Angel by surprise, he didn't want to frighten her, and she wouldn't be expecting

him so soon. She was still on skittish, and he could see her visibly
relax whenever he came home. A small smile curved his mouth as
he realized it didn't matter where they were, home was wherever
Angel was, even though she would be with him at his estate if he
had his way.

He couldn't believe how much his perspective had changed.
Four months ago, if anyone had suggested to him he would take a
180-degree turn, he would have told them to go fuck themselves.
No longer did he work into the dark hours of the evening without
a thought to the time. When work delayed him now, he was itching
to leave, glancing at his watch every few minutes and practically
barking at anyone who kept him in the office.

He'd asked her to marry him in a half-assed sort of way, but
he wanted, and needed, it to be official. It was iffy because Angel
was already balking at moving in together, so he could only assume
she'd be even more adamantly opposed to an engagement this
soon. The first thing on his agenda would be to meet her father
and introduce her to his parents. They'd seen her the night of that
charity thing, but didn't actually get to meet her. For the first time
in his life, he was aching to put a woman in front of them and for
them to love her as much as he did. Earlier that afternoon, he'd
asked Mrs. Dane to find the best jeweler in the city. He'd sent her
on jewelry acquisitions before when he'd been trying to calm the
ruffled feathers of Whitney or one of her predecessors, but never
for something like this.

"What am I buying?" she's asked matter-of-factly.

"Nothing. *I'm* buying."

"Oh. Is it your mother's birthday?"

"No. I'm buying an engagement ring."

Mrs. Dane's face showed surprise and she quickly tried to
mask it. Certainly, that was the last thing she would have presumed
her young boss to purchase. Alex couldn't help but notice the
raised eyebrow as the woman busied herself by picking up the

financial documents Alex had approved for her and she began fiddling with the edges. He felt uncomfortable, and the silence compelled him to explain when usually he wouldn't have given a thought to what his assistant was thinking. "Um, nothing too gaudy. Elegant."

Her mouth opened then shut without a word, and she'd stared at Alex as if he were an alien from outer space. One thing was certain; it was out of character for him to spend time researching diamonds and educating himself on why one was better than the other. He'd spent a few hours on it and he'd found gems online, however, he'd want to choose this himself. It had to be perfect.

When she still didn't answer, he'd looked up from the contract he'd been going over to find her stunned into silence. "Tell them I want perfect and one-of-a-kind, and I'd like to come in before the end of the week." She stood there for several seconds before she finally nodded and went to do his bidding, her surprise now mixed with something akin to pride.

"Forgive me, Alex. This may not be my place, but it's not for that Whitney woman, is it?"

He let his breath out with a smile and until that moment, he'd been unaware that he wasn't breathing. Mrs. Dane was his subordinate, but he valued her opinion on many levels and they had a mutual respect and fondness for each other that went beyond professional. She was more like a favorite aunt or young-ish grandmother, and he wondered if she'd heard Angel's show and would know who she was.

"No. We stopped seeing each other months ago."

"Thank the lord for that," Mrs. Dane shot out with a snort and then paused. "And so soon, you are ready to propose to someone else? I know it's not my place, but—"

Alex held up his hand. "No, it's fine, Mrs. Dane. I realize that in the past my romantic choices have left something to be desired, but it's different this time. You'll just have to trust me." He winked at her slyly.

"She's in it for the right reasons?"

Alex's heart warmed at the older woman's concern. "She is. I sound like an idiot, but you'll approve."

"See that I do," she said in mock sternness and got back down to business. "Now, a diamond or other precious gemstone? More traditional? Vintage or contemporary in style? A solitaire?"

Alex considered his options carefully, knowing a big flashy engagement ring would mean nothing to Angel, but damn if he didn't want to make sure the world knew she belonged to him. And he wanted Angel to have no doubts about his feelings or intentions. Their time together was always incredible, but he could sense part of her was still bothered by his past relationship rules, and Alex hated that she was feeling anything but absorbed in him. More incredibly, he wanted her to be sure he loved her and in no doubt he was completely committed.

"Um, I don't really have a clue about style, but definitely a diamond. Something classic. As I said, understated and elegant. I want it to be as flawless and individual as she is. Excellent cut, and colorless."

It was obvious that Alex had done his homework and showed that he was indeed serious. "Does this perfect young woman have a name?"

A smile slid over Alex's mouth, making him even more handsome. "Angel. Her name is Angel."

"That's quite beautiful."

"I agree."

The older woman could practically see the love radiate from Alexander and felt happy that the young man, who she thought would miss out on love had finally found it.

"I'll set something up. It might take a few days, sir. It's rare jewelers have such perfect diamonds on hand. Especially, large ones. Any particular shape?"

He laughed, despite him self. "Something that not many women have, but it doesn't have to be huge. Angel wouldn't want that."

"That's excellent." A brilliant smile split across Mrs. Dane's face before it faded when she realized she may have overstepped. "Um, I mean, I'm happy that—" she stammered and then composed herself. "Yes, sir. I'll set up appointments with the three best and have them come to the office. I'm sure you don't want to be seen in the stores?"

"Excellent as always, Mrs. Dane. And, I appreciate your concern."

The woman's smile returned. "Yes. You should give me a raise."

Alex laughed out loud as she left his office and closed the door behind her.

So, as absurd as it was, Alexander Avery was going to propose, whether Angel was ready for it or not. Months ago, he would have scoffed at the abstract possibility, but now, he was chomping at the bit to make sure she belonged to him. At least if she married him, he'd get her under the same roof once and for all, and he was goddamned tired of arguing about it.

It wasn't that he wanted to control her; he liked the push and pull they had between them. It was fun and sexier than hell, but he wanted to know she was safe, and living together would put his mind at ease. Until that cocksucker, Swanson, was behind bars for good, he wouldn't relax. As it was, he could think of little else, and his gut constantly burned with worry. It would have been easier if he'd killed Mark Swanson the night he'd attacked Angel. God knew, he'd wanted to, and it wasn't the first time he'd considered it could have been self-defense. At least, he'd be able to breathe.

Alex sighed as he walked into her apartment and closed the door behind him, carefully disarming then rearming the security system. He almost dropped the pizza box he was balancing in the other hand. He groaned inwardly, hating that his thoughts were consumed with thinking about that fucker. He hated how Swanson was still able to get into his head and under his skin, and worse, he hated that he could still frighten Angel.

A small lamp in the living room offered the only light other than the blue glow cast from the flat screen TV mounted across from the sofa. It appeared Angel left it on one of the news channels but was nowhere to be seen. Alex glanced around the living room then took the pizza into the kitchen and left it on the counter beside his car keys.

"Babe?" Alex called, rubbing his jaw with one hand and meandered down the hall toward Angel's bedroom, loosening the knot of his tie then pulling it free from his shirt. The fingers of his left hand pushed open the door, and he peered inside while his right hand opened three of the buttons on his white shirt.

Her suit jacket was lying on her bed, and he could hear the shower running behind the closed door of her en-suite bathroom. He kicked off his shoes, unbuttoning his fine linen shirt the rest of the way to push it off and fling it carelessly on the bed, followed by his T-shirt. He quickly unzipped his dress slacks and pushed them with his boxer briefs down and to the floor. He used his feet to pull the expensive slacks free of his legs then left them discarded on the floor with his socks. He walked to the bathroom completely nude.

When Alex slowly opened the door, the steam flowed out around him like a cloud and heat from the room rushed over his skin. Angel's bathroom was large and decorated in soft shades of coral, sand, and cream, with a big whirlpool tub in one corner and a glass-enclosed walk-in shower along the wall opposite the vanity. The air smelled of her shampoo and perfume, and though the door and walls of the shower were fogged over; the delicious outline of Angel's curves and the curtain of long dark hair down her back were clearly visible. She was humming softly, her iPod docked in the device built into the wall.

He smiled to himself. Angel raised her hands to her hair, her breasts lifting as she did so, only enticed him further. Her eyes were closed as she moved to rinse the long dark strands free of shampoo. Alex's cock was already swollen erect and had been since he'd made the decision to join her in the shower. His eyes roamed further down her womanly form, knowing that, as always, her skin would be smooth and free of hair. Even as the fire of desire surged and more blood pushed painfully into his erection, his mind briefly wondered if it was a man or woman entrusted with the intimate task of waxing Angel's body. Jealousy tugged at him as he envisioned another man having such open access to her intimate secrets. He decided that was a question he would be posing to her very soon.

It would be exciting to sneak into the shower with her, but it would scare the shit out of her, and that was the last thing he wanted. He moved closer and kept his voice low.

"There's something in there I want."

Angel turned, surprised and wiped at the steam on the glass, her expression softened as their eyes met and held. She smiled softly; so alluring and tempting, Alex almost licked his lips. Her eyes pulled from his and ran down the length of his body as he opened the stall door.

"Wow, that was fast. I thought you were going to the gym," she murmured when her gaze landed on his erection, "and that your dick hurt." A short giggle burst from her chest until she quelled it to a sly smirk when he pulled her roughly against him.

"I want you more than the gym. Yes, it hurts, but in a different way," he said honestly, his eyes intense and locked with hers.

As soon as the glass door closed behind him, it took Alex mere seconds to slide his arms around Angel. He turned, lifting her against the ceramic tile in the corner with one smooth movement, the water flowing behind him, her face now level with his. The multiple showerheads were a luxury and rained from every direction. Angel's legs automatically wrapped around his waist, her fingers curled into the muscles of his shoulder, and then slid into the hair at his nape as it was quickly saturated. Alex slid his palms down her body as they both stared into the other's eyes for a brief moment.

"Are *you* sore, sweetheart?" he asked.

She stared at his mouth mesmerized, as liquid heat rushed through her lower body, making it begin to hum with need. "Even if you were going to split me open, I'd still want you."

His heart thundered within his chest. "It's sometimes too much. I love—" It seemed the most natural thing to tell her that he loved her. The words, now said, wanted to tumble forth, and this wasn't the first time he'd stopped himself from repeating them. Alex reminded himself he'd just said them on the phone less than hour before. He knew she needed more than the words. She needed proof. Only his actions, and time, would accomplish that. And, he also acknowledged that saying them aloud too often made him equally vulnerable "—that we can't get enough of each other."

Angel nodded, two fingers of one hand finding their way to his lips then into the side of his mouth. He turned his face so he could suck them into his mouth and she gasped. "This is so much better than the last time I was surprised in the shower."

Alex shook his head almost imperceptibly then kissed her fingers. Then his mouth sought hers, hovering just enough to speak, his hot breath mingling with the steam. Angel sucked his exhale into her lungs, unable to help herself. "No. Don't think about him. Focus on me, baby. We'll make a better memory in here. You and me."

Angel's pink tongue appeared and slid over her upper lip. Urgency throbbed between them; Alex's eyes dropped to Angel's mouth, and his hips anchored her to the wall. She swallowed. "You're right. It's just us."

Alex finally took her mouth hungrily, his tongue plundering into the dark recesses, tangling with hers, and she let him, eagerly answering his need with her own. His hands beneath her bottom and thigh began to explore soap-slickened flesh, seeking the warmth and wetness he knew would welcome him. Angel's hips surged toward his body, seeking Alex's probing fingers, aching for the fulfillment only his body could offer.

He groaned into her mouth when one of her hands raked down his chest between them and grasped around him, gently rubbing and pulling on his dick, worried she'd hurt him, that he might be in real pain. Alex pulled his mouth from hers as he sucked in his breath then let it out in a rush, his chest rising against the swell of her breasts.

"God," he ground out, his hips pushing his cock more fully into her hands. "It's okay, Angel," he said, reading her thoughts. "Jesus! I always want you so much."

He shifted, hoisting her higher, both hands wrapping around her breasts and holding them so his mouth had easy access to the hard buttons of her nipples. He loved her and being with her was profound: better than he'd ever imagined sex could be. He wanted to worship her, but he was rock hard and throbbing. He felt if he didn't bury himself within her in seconds, he'd burst.

Shivers shot through her under the magic of his tongue and lips as he teased and pulled at her sensitive flesh with his mouth. Finally, she succeeded in positioning his cock at her entrance and arched her back greedily seeking, but his position only allowed her to take in his head part way.

"Alex, please... now."

She didn't have to ask twice, and in the next instance, his hips pushed forward and thrust deeply into her. Skin slipped on skin, and soft moans turned into panting breaths. Even though he was embedded deep and moving in deliberate precision, first slow then hard, burying himself balls deep, Alex couldn't get close enough, her needs driving him on as much as his own. Angel was lost in sensation; her eyes closed, and her fingers clawed at the muscles of his arms and shoulders as he drove into her over and over again.

"Mmmm…" she moaned, squeezing around him, her hips surging against his, wanting Alex to feel her as much she did him. He reached up, his hand clamping onto her jaw and his mouth hungry, gnawing at and sucking on hers as he bounced her against the wall over and over again. His kisses and movements were voracious, leaving her in no doubt of his desire or excitement.

"Uhhhh… Fuck—nothing feels as good as this." He groaned against her lips, only to resume his ruthless onslaught, his mouth demanding and hungry as he took what he needed.

Emotions, born of desperateness, flooded her heart until she physically hurt. He was here, and he was real. When they were together like this, she had no doubt he was as committed as she was. Alex was getting close, and it became Angel's mission to make him come apart with an abandonment he couldn't control. It was only love that spurred her on, making her want to give him unspeakable pleasure, and she admitted that it would kill her if he could feel this with anyone else—before or after her—ever in his life. It was debilitating to know she was just as helpless, and yet, somehow, exhilarating to need his touch so much… even as his body claimed hers and they were all wrapped up together.

"Alex… God, yes!"

His speed increased as if he couldn't help himself, his hand sliding across her shoulder and down her arm. Threading his fingers through hers, he lifted Angel's hand above her head and pinned it against the wall, his open mouth over hers, his breath panting in time with his thrusts.

His muscles coiled and he pulled out of her abruptly, his forehead coming to rest on the tile beside her head as his eyes closed.

"Uhhh, Uhhh, Uhhh…" Alex's chest rose and fell roughly as he struggled to gain control, and Angel's eyes flew open in the same instant he stopped making love to her.

"What is it? Are you okay?"

He took one more deep breath and let her legs slide to the floor of the shower. "I'm perfect," he murmured against her temple. His green eyes burned into Angel's concerned face. "Everything's perfect." Alex leaned down and brushed his mouth softly against hers. "*You*—are perfect."

Her mind raced. *Why did he stop?*

Alex kept his body close to hers, his dick still fully erect and pressed into her hip as he grabbed two towels and wrapped one around her body and draped another over her wet head. His hands were gentle as he pressed the plush material into her hair and squeezed the strands within its folds to absorb the water. Angel stared into his face, watching his expression, her breathing shallow.

"Why did you stop?" Her hands splayed out on his solid chest, loving the curves and contours of the hard muscles under her hand. "I wanted to make you come apart."

He pulled the towels closer around her then scooped her up bridal-style and carried her effortlessly into the bedroom, wordlessly pulling back the covers and laying her down. He stood, open to her view, his eyes caressing and possessive. The towels soon pulled free of her body; Alex's hands began to follow the path of his eyes over her shoulders and down her arms, sliding up her stomach to ghost over her ribcage then cup each breast. Angel's skin exploded in goose bumps and she shivered, but not from chills. She sucked in her breath. He was so intense and beautiful as he studied her body. When he finally joined her on the bed, his hand slid down over the curve of her hip to hoist one slender leg over his strong hip.

"And you will, but I don't want this to end," he said seriously, his eyes blazing over her flesh. "You intoxicate me."

"It doesn't have to end. We have all night. Make love to me, Alex." Her hand slid to his and she pulled it to her mouth. "Make love with me all night," she repeated softly, taking his middle finger into her mouth.

Alex closed his eyes, his heart swelling inside his chest and more blood pushing into his cock. His breath hitched. Fuck, she excited him more than anyone ever had, but that wasn't even it. He wanted to make sure she understood. He ran the tip of his nose down hers, and his lower lip nudged hers. "I intend to, but I mean, I don't want *us* to end. I want you in my bed, my body inside yours, to give you so much pleasure you can't form a coherent thought. But more, I just want you with me. Next to me. I want to take care of you, to protect you. Always." His eyes opened and locked with hers as he stilled. "I need you to believe you are the only thing that matters to me now. The *only* fucking thing."

Angel's eyes burned as his words washed over her, causing her to gasp aloud. His tone was serious and insistent, and she trusted him more than she'd ever trusted anyone. Unable to speak, Angel turned her face into his neck and shoulder, her throat aching as emotions left them both reeling. She was ready to give him anything he asked, her heart and soul soaring.

"Yes," she finally whispered, her voice cracking with the effort.

Alex sighed deeply and settled down into the cradle of her body: he kissed her, his movements ruled by his feelings. He nudged her chin with his nose, wanting to prove it, to erase any doubt. "I mean it, damn it. I've never meant anything more in my life."

Overcome, Angel's eyes flooded with tears and her hands slid up and fisted in his wet hair. "I believe you," she breathed out. Pulling his mouth closer, she silently begged for more of his kisses, her body arching as he slid back into her slick heat. Alex was determined to leave her in little doubt of his feelings as he pushed into her body and invaded her heart like no one else ever could. His hands were worshiping and reverent as they played her flesh like an instrument, his mouth staking his ownership and his soul burning its brand on hers. He evoked no refusal and no denial as he made absolute love to her.

Every time he touched her, it was perfect and earth shattering; stunning and staggering. Angel knew she couldn't fight it anymore and didn't want to. She was completely and utterly lost to him... and he to her. "I love you, Alex."

2

Maybe I'm Amazed

ANGEL LAY AWAKE in the darkness as Alex slept, pulled closely against his body, a sheer layer of sweat still on their skin. She really was sore now, and he was finally exhausted. They were both always so hungry for each other; it was exhilarating and still surreal. This need to be close, to have his hands exploring her body and his mouth on hers, was overwhelming.

She was anxious just to touch him or talk to him, and in some ways, it was debilitating, just as she'd feared it would be. The first time he'd touched her, she'd known how it would end. But it felt so damned good. Just looking at him could steal her breath or choke her up. She might as well enjoy it because she couldn't protect her heart anymore. If it ended, it would fucking hurt—like nothing she would experience before or after him—but not to experience the splintering, intoxicating ecstasy that was this man would be nothing short of tragic.

Her eyes widened in wonder at the evening's events. Once Alex laid her down, they hadn't left the bed. Time passed as he languidly explored her body with his hands and mouth; she wasn't sure how many hours and didn't care that she had to get up early

for work. She didn't want to lose a precious second of the night
with him. They'd made love a few times; the spaces in between
were filled with gentle touches, sighs, and soft conversation so
deep they'd forgotten to eat. She inhaled deeply, the scent of his
skin overpowering the faintness of his cologne, now a mere rem-
nant after the shower. Her stomach rumbled loudly.

Alex's arms were tight around her, her back plastered to his
chest, her bottom firmly against his groin, and a big hand cupped
one of her breasts. Even in the throes of sleep, he was possessive.
It was sheer bliss. She didn't know why she let that scare her earlier
because now it just felt amazing and safe, like nothing could hurt
either one of them as long as they were together.

Her fingers traced up and down his forearm, the muscles
strong beneath the soft, downy hair. She could feel the tiny pricks
of his whiskers poking into her shoulder. The skin of her chin
would be red from the hours and hours of kissing him with his five
o'clock scruff, but it had been so delicious, she didn't notice the
pain. The kisses were always so perfect, whether they were in passionate frenzy or slow, deep sucking. A shiver ran through her at
the thought, even though heat from his body infused and merged
with hers in a fine sheen of shared perspiration. She knew she'd
probably find red scratches on the inside of her thighs and stirred
at the memory. His insatiable need for her made her just as wanton
and abandoned. She felt sexier than she ever had in her life.

Alex was incredible, and as she lay in the quiet contemplation,
enshrouded by the night and his strong arms, Angel relived every
amazing night with him. Each time he touched her, she could do
nothing to resist, instantly melting into a puddle even as she tried
to take control. She was still stunned by the force of nature that
was Alexander Avery; he commanded every room he walked into
and every woman who wanted him. And as Angel had teased him
before, that would be every one of them with a vagina, and some
without, she acknowledged with a low laugh.

Angel's air of confidence and the way she carried herself now was learned but had become second nature. She knew she was attractive to the opposite sex, but she was still shocked that Alex would want her with such voracity. It turned her on immensely. Before him, she wouldn't have wanted a man to be so dominant, but with Alex, it was who he was, and it felt right somehow. She knew she could still be herself, push back on him, and he'd welcome it. She smiled into the darkness. The fighting was as much a turn on as the touching, and she knew he loved it, too. He might take from her, but only what she shared willingly… and she sensed it meant more to him that way. Taking was easy for him, but he'd proven that night he made her choose he wanted her to want and to want to give. And he did; Alex made her want to give everything she had in her to give, and he'd proven again and again he would give in equal measure. Maybe even more.

"What are you thinking about?" Alex's groggy voice murmured softly in her ear, his hot breath washing over her shoulder. His arms tightened, his lips finding purchase on her shoulder in a series of soft, open mouth kisses that dragged along her skin. She shivered in his arms, her body reacting as always.

"You." She wanted to know about the others. She knew about Whitney and his emotional detachment from her. But she came off as a bitch, and it was no wonder Alex wouldn't fall in love with her. Were there others he was like this with?

"Alex…" Angel began. "Being with you is incredible."

His embrace tightened and breath rushed across her neck as he bent to gently kiss and suckle the sensitive skin. "Mmmm… I agree," he whispered. "Amazing."

This was so perfect; she didn't want to ruin it by asking directly. She knew he'd be pissed if she wasn't careful. "For me, it's—"

"It's what?" He probed softly, still continuing his sensual assault on her neck and shoulder, brushing his nose along the cord of her neck before resuming the soft sucking along it.

"It's never been like this with anyone else."

He paused. "It better not have been." He'd considered her relationship with Kyle many times, and he'd wondered about it, but it was unlike him to probe his women about their pasts. It never mattered before, and he'd never once needed to know. Before this.

When she didn't respond, he continued gently. "I've thought about it to. I hate picturing anyone else being with you like this."

Angel closed her eyes, and her heart swelled at his words. She inhaled deeply enough for Alex to feel her body expand in his arms before she shook her head twice. "Yet, it's hard not to."

"Yes. I suppose it's inevitable to wonder when you care about someone. It's human."

"Maybe you should do my job."

"Okay." He huffed softly. "Why aren't you sleeping yet?"

After a beat, Angel answered softly, knowing it was an admission. "I'm scared to sleep."

Alex paused, resting his chin on her shoulder, considering how to comfort her and ease her fears about that bastard, Swanson. "Mmm. I'm sorry."

"For what?" Angel was surprised by the apology. "For telling Cole to deliver me to your house without talking to me first?" she teased.

Alex ignored her amusement, thinking she was brushing off her fear. "No. For not killing Mark Swanson when I had the chance."

Angel gasped as the conversation suddenly turned serious. She turned in his arms, needing to see his face, reaching out to cup his stubbly cheek. "Don't say that." She shook her head adamantly. "I'd never want you to live with something like that."

His green eyes flashed almost black in the darkness. "I don't want you to be afraid anymore. He'd be a memory and we could—"

Her hand slid from his cheek into the hair at the side of his head and then further back. He closed his eyes in pleasure at her touch. "We still can. He's a bug on the windshield of our lives. It's you—" Angel stopped. She wasn't sure if she should tell him how deeply he affected her. He had to know, based on how she reacted to him, but telling him was another matter.

"Me, *what?*" Alex asked in a low tone.

"It's you I'm scared of. I try not to be. It goes against—" Concern and bewilderment flashed across his handsome face at the same time she struggled to voice her feelings without seeming like a weakling. "You can hurt me a million times more than Mark Swanson ever could."

Alex's eyes grew wide even as his brow furrowed. "Stop," he said with one shake of his head. "I thought we were past that. Don't I show you, in no uncertain terms, that I'm in this? I just said it again. What more can I do?"

"Nothing. Don't get upset." She tried to soothe him. "I fight with myself about it. I don't mean to think about it, and I know I just need to let it go. I'm working on it. You've been nothing short of amazing... even if you're an overbearing ass at times." She grinned at him, her fingers still threading through his hair in steady rhythm.

Alex sighed heavily, wishing she didn't have any doubts about him. "I've never given two shits about anyone before, but this is different. There is nothing I wouldn't do for you." His voice was low but insistent. His hands slid down her arm to her naked hip under the sheet, and began to knead her flesh.

"I know. I'll stop making you say it."

"I'll say it as often as you want. Angel—" Alex began.

She placed two fingers on his mouth and then kissed him softly, trying to coax his response, but when he resisted, she knew he would not acquiesce until she gave him the answer he needed. "You don't need to," she whispered against his mouth.

"You can be as provocative and beguiling as you want, I will not let you distract me until I'm sure you accept how committed I am. And, once and for all, you trust me."

"It isn't your fault I feel this way. You've sort of become this... drug that I can't get enough of. My feelings leave me vulnerable, but it's nothing you've done, and it isn't that I don't trust you. You said it. It's human and it's a precarious place to be. A place I promised myself I wouldn't be again."

Alex's hand tightened a little when Angel said the word again. He knew all about precariousness and unfamiliar vulnerability. He sighed heavily.

Angel frowned and lifted her right shoulder in a half-shrug. "I have to accept it and deal with it. Loving you this much, it's just the way it is."

Alex bit his lower lip as the ache in his chest eased a little. He gently cupped the side of her face, his fingers pushing a tendril of her hair behind her ear, as his intense eyes studied her. His thumb brushed her chin while his fingers tangled in the long hair at the back of her head. He stared into her face for a moment, fighting with how to convince her, once and for all.

He abruptly rolled her onto her back, pushing his leg between hers and allowing his weight to press her into the mattress. Angel saw him swallow, and his eyes burned into hers; she could feel him getting hard between her legs, his hips pushing the proof into her.

"Do you think I'm any less addicted? I can't wait to see you; I think about you all the time, obsessed with protecting you and possessing you. I have this insane need to pleasure you until you beg me to stop and my name falls from lips that are swollen from my kisses. I want you to forget everything but me... to make you forget anyone else you've ever been with. I need to mark you, to own you body and soul—" he paused when Angel's brow shot up in mock reprimand, but still, he could see her defiance battling with how she felt. He smiled softly, letting out a small huff, then continued to bare his soul. "—until you'll never want another man to touch you. Never again. Because if you let that happen, I'll be destroyed; it will literally *kill me*. If anything happened to you, I don't know what I'd do. I can tell you I love you, but it's not enough to explain it." His chest pushed into hers as he took a deep breath, and she could feel his heart pounding above hers. "I'm— *fucking consumed*."

Angel's amusement fell away in an instant, and she gasped; her arms and legs wrapping around him, fingers fisting lovingly in his hair. Her eyes became luminous, filling with tears, and her throat ached with emotion. Again, he left her speechless, and she struggled to say something. Two tears tumbled from her eyes, first one then the other rolled down the sides of her face to land on the pillow behind her head.

Alex smiled gently and kissed her three times, once on each corner of her mouth, then more lingering in the middle of her mouth. She nodded, her mouth coming alive under his, but Alex pulled back, brushed her hair back on both sides, and used his thumbs to trace the tracks of her tears. "I didn't mean to make you cry." A small smile tugged on his lips. "But, do you get it now? No more doubts. We're going to do this."

"Yes. I promise. I never want this night to end. Being with you feels too good. I think that's what scares me the most."

Alex exhaled through his nose, a full grin allowing a flash of white teeth. Maybe, finally, she'd understand.

"As long as that's all it is. It's madness. To want you again when we're both sore and exhausted—to feel this empowered and yet completely at your mercy is nothing less than *madness*." He nibbled on her mouth with a series of teasing kisses, using calculated movements of his hips to press his cock against her, slide it along her clit, and then pull away.

"I am sore, but it's turning back into a throb," Angel moaned softly against his mouth. She was writhing beneath him, her hands pulling at the flesh of his arms and back, only to slide down to his ass and pull. "Alex—"

He chuckled when her hips started bucking beneath him, and she reached up to get his mouth. "Fuck, yeah, it is. But we might pay for it tomorrow, sweetheart." His teeth pulled on her lower lip, and she glared into his face even as her body begged his.

"I don't care. Do I have to tell you I want your big dick inside me?"

He laughed softly and stopped moving and playing with her mouth so he could look into her face. Amusement danced in the green depths of his eyes as they met her dark brown ones. "Now *that's* romantic," he taunted. "I know it drives you crazy, baby. You don't have to say it." An arrogant smile tugged at the corner of his mouth as he teased.

Angel's eyes widened and she huffed out a small laugh. "Um, yeah. You drive me crazy, all right. Though, I think I'm pretty adept at working you up, too, so can we just—" She couldn't help but join in his laughter. Angel's hips surged against his, increasing the pressure and rubbing her slick heat up and down his erection until Alex's breathing increased.

"Just?" He prodded and smiled down at her softly, moving against her again, eliciting a low mewling moan from deep inside her chest. Knowing how much she wanted him only increased his desire. When she lifted her hips to line up the head of his cock with her entrance, Alex couldn't deny either of them for one more second and thrust in deep, causing Angel to bite down on her lip.

"Just what?" He filled her to the hilt in a sudden movement that caused her to gasp. He didn't move, waiting for her response.

Angel moved her hips, grinding against his, using her inner muscles to squeeze and milk a response from him. Alex clenched his teeth against the urge to echo her movements as pleasure shot through him. "Just tell me."

"Uhhh…" He groaned as his head dropped, and his eyes closed in pleasure. Resisting was too extreme an effort. "Fuuuuck." The word sounded wrenched from him. "Just say it, Angel."

"Fuuuuck," she repeated with a velvety chuckle and continued to move on him, determined to get him to give in. "Satisfied?" She quipped. Clenching around him, Angel smiled wickedly.

Alex laughed but pulled out all the way, hovering above her, and she pouted. "Hardly. You're such a little shit!" He sat on his haunches, his legs spread to anchor his position, and he grabbed Angel's hips and pulled her forward, hard, onto his cock and she hissed. "Okay, you win—this time."

He used slow, long thrusts, grinding hard into her clit and pubic bone. He could see himself sliding in and out of her, and it drove him nuts. He was reminded of the first time they were together after their first date at Tru. Angel reached up to hold him to her, but he was beyond arm's length. He was teasing her until it was on the verge of torturing her. Angel knew what he was doing and decided to inflict a little torture of her own. Her hand slid up her own body, cupping her breasts and then tugging on the nipples, sultry, passion-glazed eyes meeting his as he continued to move on her. Angel bit her lip and waited for his response. His eyes fell, hooded and darkened with increased desire, as he watched her. The guttural sound deep within his throat told her how she affected him. Still, he didn't stop his slow torment—in and out, in and out—nor did he increase his pace, content with the slow building of the incredible pleasure. She reached down to touch herself, but Alex pulled her hand up, and away. It was hotter than fuck to see her do that, but it would send him over the edge, and he wasn't ready for it to end.

"I want us both to win. More. I need more, Alex."

"I know what you need." He grasped her hand and pulled her up until her chest slid along his. He wrapped an arm around her hips, pulling her closer, getting as deep into her as he could. His movements slowed, and his tongue slid up the cord of her neck. Angel's back arched, her head fell back, and her fingers dug into his shoulders. Alex winced even as his balls tightened, and he got closer to the edge. "And I'm going to give it to you. God, I'm so deep like this. It feels amazing."

One hand gripped her chin as Alex brought her head down. His mouth plundered then gentled, leaving Angel trembling in his arms. His muscles coiled and tightened, and he felt her thighs start to shake. He kissed her again, his tongue laving hers in between nips and tugs.

"Now, what was it you were going to tell me?" Alex insisted against her mouth.

She sighed, wanting to deny him nothing because he would give her everything in return. And, because more simply; it was the truth. "I'm all yours."

Alex's mouth latched onto hers then, and he kissed her over and over again, deep penetrating kisses that fueled the fire between them. Angel's fingers tightened in his hair, and her body sucked hard on his.

Alex reached between them to brush her clit with his fingers as he exploded inside her. "Come on, baby." He groaned as his body continued to jerk as he poured into her. "Baby, I want you to come, Angel."

Soon she was unraveling around him, convulsing and trembling as he pushed her over the edge. He watched her face as she came, hard. Alex had been with several women, most of whom acted out the screaming, porn-star-esque scenes when they came. Angel was silent except for soft moans and panting breaths. He realized all of that was unnecessary. All he needed was this woman calling his name and clenching around his cock to transport him to a place he'd never been; her fingers pulling him closer, winding in his hair as she rode out her climax against him. His head turned and he pressed a kiss onto her temple.

"You are so damn beautiful. It hurts to look at you."

She was left heaving in his arms as she struggled to regain control of her breathing. Alex lay down on the bed, his hands still stroking her flesh wherever he touched her, his own breath coming out in heaving pants as he pulled her back against him.

"You're mine, too, you know," she murmured.

His eyes were closed but he smiled. Love had become a welcome marauder in his life, and he was happy as hell at her words. She couldn't see it, but she could feel and hear his amused huff. "Yeah, yeah. Whatever."

Angel laughed and snuggled into his embrace, her head resting on his chest. "You want me to own it; I'm fucking owning it."

His soft laugh echoed hers as he wrapped both arms around her. "No doubt about it," he murmured happily as they both fell into an exhausted, sated sleep.

3

Compromise

THE WEEK PASSED much the same as it started. Alex and Angel spent every night together in the city, alternating between their apartments with Cole and Bancroft accompanying her the hours she was separated from Alex. There had been no trouble, and she was starting to get annoyed with the entourage. She could sense Cole getting antsy and bored as well. Who wouldn't, with the same thing over and over, day-in and day-out? Bancroft and the others were all business and followed her around like the *Men in Black*. She felt ridiculous.

Tuesday night, they were both exhausted from their sleepless weekend sex-a-thon that had spilled over into Monday, so they agreed that abstinence, while it didn't make the heart grow fonder, was called for. Still, the air around them vibrated and each was acutely aware of the other's presence.

Alex glanced up from his laptop, his anxious eyes always searching for her. He was working on the contract details Mrs. Dane would add to a deal for a property he was trying to acquire in Monaco. He should have finished it at the office but brought it with him, for no other reason than he wanted to get to Angel as soon as possible.

As hot as sex was between them, they were content to just talk and hang out in each other's company, teasing or baiting each other. Alex's eyes followed her as she moved around him no matter which apartment they stayed in, whether she was doing laundry at her place or making dinner at his. Every once in a while, she'd run her fingers through his hair or he'd take her hand to kiss the inside of her wrist without saying a word. Alex was still in awe of his need to be close to her. They didn't make it an hour without touching each other, and he reveled in it. So what if it was out of character? Being with her felt fucking amazing. *She* was fucking amazing.

After dinner, Angel's phone rang, and she went into the other room to dig it out of her purse. "Hello?" Alex's ears strained to hear who might be on the phone. "Hey, Kyle," she said softly, going back into the kitchen to continue the conversation.

Alex flushed and his stomach clenched. He groaned inwardly. He'd just told Angel to stop worrying, so why the hell couldn't he do the same? His skin crawled and jealousy blazed, even as he argued with himself. Alex's chest expanded painfully with his deep intake of breath, and he ran a hand over the stubble on his jaw. He pushed the laptop away impatiently and leaned back in his chair.

He tried to justify that the burning in his shoulders and neck came from hunching over the damn thing for the last two hours and not the fact that Angel's ex, who was clearly still into her, was on the phone. Alex told himself, over and over again, that Kyle wasn't a threat, yet he'd seen the other man's face when he looked at Angel and heard the tone in his voice when he spoke about her. The primeval part of him roared and had his caveman ownership of Angel shoved into overdrive. It was a lack of control and he despised it. He didn't like feeling threatened, and he didn't like that his logical mind was unable to quell the tightness in his chest. He hated it. *Fuck.*

In reality, though, it was simple. Love breeds insecurity, and insecurity went against every confident bone in his body and everything he knew about himself. But, Alex acknowledged it was the nature of loving someone, of opening up your heart and spilling your guts on the floor at their feet. It was the quintessential giving away of power. When you love, especially in this all-consuming, gut-wrenching way, there would be the possibility of pain... even the absolute certainty of it. He snorted and ran a hand through his thick dark hair again. He even felt irritated to consider the possibility she might be swayed to leave him; let alone for some stupid fucker who'd cheated on her. It dawned on him that Angel's insecurity echoed his own and he understood. She didn't want to doubt any more than he did... but it seemed unavoidable. He sighed again.

In general, men don't dive into sappy, revealing discussions about past relationships, and Alex, being Alex, was even less likely to do so. Mostly, because in life before Angel, he didn't give a shit about who had come before him and spent zero time worrying the woman would ever end the relationship. If, on the off chance it would have happened, he would've simply shrugged it off and not felt the slightest twinge of regret. There were always others. *That was B.A. Before Angel.* A lot of things were B fucking A.

A sardonic smirk slid across his handsome face, and he shook his head at his thoughts. Part of him didn't want to know any more than he already did about what went on between Angel and Kyle. But, a bigger, masochistic part—deep down in his gut—wanted to know every damn little thing. It was a searing need to know how deeply she'd felt, how far she was invested, how long they were together, and how hurt she was when he cheated on her... and, if there was a snowball's chance in hell she'd ever want him again. He rationalized he was just sizing up an opponent in preparation for battle. *That* he could relate to.

Anyway, he is one stupid cocksucker, Alex's mind railed. *She couldn't want him now.* Kyle didn't deserve her if he'd do something as brainless as hurt her like that. Alex huffed again. But, if Kyle was a moron, what did that make *him?* Hadn't he almost done the same damn thing with Whitney? Thank God, he hadn't been able to cash that check. And, Kyle *had* snapped Alex out of his jealous rage with a dose of his much-needed reality. He didn't want to like the guy, but he had to be honest; it appeared he'd learned from his mistake and put Angel first.

He shook his head in disgust. What the fuck was he doing thinking about this crap? That was over. *Long over.*

Kenneth Gant, on the other hand, Alex didn't see as a threat. Kyle might be because emotion had been involved and Alex was quickly learning that emotion was a selfish, greedy bitch. He glanced toward the kitchen again, hating that he couldn't help himself. The mere fact that Angel left the room to speak to Kyle in private ignited his anxiety.

He was lost in his thoughts, work forgotten, when Angel came back into the living room and sidled smoothly onto his lap. His arms came around her, and he looked up at her as her index finger slid down his left cheek. She was here with him, in his arms and Alex's heart began to unclench.

"You look so serious. What are you thinking about?" Angel asked quietly, a gentle smile playing on her mouth.

The words welled up in his chest, as he willed himself not to speak. All he wanted to do was ask why the other man called, but he didn't need to look like an insecure asshole. Angel bent to kiss him, first his cheek and then softly on his mouth. His mind was working, so his response was distracted.

Angel pulled back and looked into his face, summing up his expression. His eyes didn't meet hers, and she knew his wheels were churning. She smiled gently. She could ease this worry so easily, but it was somehow endearing and cute the way he was jealous, and he didn't know how to process it. It put his emotions on the same playing field as hers. Her hand cupped his cheek, trying to bring his mouth into more-active play. Her heart thumped inside her chest.

"Hey—" she began seductively.

Finally, Alex couldn't help himself. "What'd he want?" he blurted out.

A short laugh made her jerk in his arms. "Shhh… just kiss me."

Angel's reluctance to tell him, while it sounded teasing, only pissed Alex off. His hands closed around her upper arms, and he held her away, preventing her from continuing to kiss him. He scowled at her. "What's so damn funny? Tell me what he wanted," he demanded, eyes flashing angrily.

Angel smiled openly now and shook her head. "Nothing!" she protested. "Apparently, they've had some interest from a record company. He wants me to come back to the band."

Alex's brow furrowed further. "That's not nothing."

Angel's head fell back in frustration. When she snapped her gaze back to his, she was resigned. "It is to me." Her expression twisted derisively. "What part of 'Kyle and I broke up because we wanted different things' did you miss, Alex? I'm not going to change careers."

"Is his deal contingent on you?"

"If it is, he needs to get better at negotiation."

Alex's mouth thinned in irritation at the confirmation of his worry. "So, it does. Why can't you just tell me instead of making me pull it out of you?"

"Because it's fun," she said simply then bit her lip playfully. A teasing smile tugged at her mouth.

"It's fun? Why don't I agree?"

"Oh, Alex. Come on."

"Maybe you should do it." As much as he didn't want her around a man who was still in love with her and would pull no punches to get her back, it was better than having her work with criminals who had no conscience about hurting her.

"I know you." She rolled her eyes. "You'd just worry about other crap."

"In a different way. You wouldn't be in physical danger, at least."

"Right, but you know I'm not going back to the band!"

"You said that before. Before you reconnected with Kyle. Before you were almost raped and killed." His words weren't loud and expletive, but the serious tone told her everything.

Her eyes softened. She saw the concern and love in his eyes and wanted to comfort him. Angel snuggled further into his lap, her hands closing around his, and began running whisper-kisses along his jaw as she chose to ignore the latter part of his comment. The light stubble that shadowed his skin tickled her lips. "We haven't reconnected! Not like you mean. One conversation can't change the course of my life." Her tone changed to softly coaxing as she spoke against his skin. He could feel her warm breath.

He didn't move. "Won't it? Are you sure? One conversation was all it took for my life to change irrevocably."

Angel pulled back to meet his eyes. "Well, me too. But it wasn't the conversation. It was you."

He stared at her unflinchingly, and she was equally unwavering, brown eyes locked with intense green ones.

"Alex, really?" she goaded gently, a giddy smile spreading across her face. Still he was stoic and clearly uncomfortable. "I have to admit it makes me all kinds of happy that you're jealous, but why?"

"We are still new, and you have history with him."

"So? You have a bigger dick."

He tried not to smile and didn't quite make it. "I'm serious."

She cocked her head and pursed her lips. "So am I."

"Angel, stop kidding around."

"Okay, should I worry that you'll run back to Malibu Barbie?"

"No."

"Just like that. No? No question. That's it. Just, *no*."

Alex's thumbs began to rub circles on her hips as his hands spanned her waist.

"Yeah, no. Whitney lacked substance, and I wasn't in love with her. You were in love with him."

Angel couldn't deny it, but why was his word law and hers in question? She had been in love with Kyle, but it was like comparing a spring shower to a hurricane. She tried teasing to make him feel better. The great Alex Avery was feeling anxious.

"I'm not supposed to worry when you bed-hopped across Chicago, but it's okay for you to think I'll run back to Kyle? Someone I haven't been with for more than three years?" She pushed against his chest angrily and tried to get up, but his arms held her fast against him. "If you think so, then why are you suggesting I start playing with Archangel again?"

"Cut it out."

She poked him hard in the chest with her index finger. "*You* cut it out! Maybe she fucks or *sucks* better than I do. Wasn't that her *job*?"

Angel widened her eyes to make her point. She pushed her boobs up with both hands, letting them bounce back in place, then batted her long lashes at him in her best airhead impersonation. When he just stared at her, Angel cocked an eyebrow at him in question, trying hard not to smile. "Well?" she questioned and started singing a breathy, bimbo version of *Stupid Girls*.

Alex paused before he finally grinned, his white teeth flashing against his tanned skin. He was so beautiful; he stole Angel's breath. "You put her out of business."

Angel was dressed casually in those sexy, holey jeans Alex loved and a burgundy shirt that emphasized the curve of her breasts and left the top swell of cleavage open to Alex's burning gaze. He bent his head to ghost his mouth over the top swells of her breasts, his hot breath rushing over her skin. A shiver skittered over her skin, and she stopped pulling away from him.

"Some business," she scoffed.

"It was." Angel jabbed him in the ribs and Alex howled. "Hey!"

"Well?"

"I know. Being insecure doesn't sit well with me."

"Let's not fight about big dicks and who sucks better. You don't want me to doubt you; so don't doubt me. Deal?"

Alex's face sobered, his hand moved up to push an errant tendril back from her face and behind her ear. "It's hard to argue with your logic, but I do wonder since you loved him."

It was Angel's turn to pause, still straddling his lap as she considered what he wanted her to say.

"Are you saying you want to know what it was like between Kyle and I physically?"

"And Kenneth because he was recent, and I've met them both," he said without pause, taking a tendril of her hair that was on her cheek and threading it behind her ear with a gentle hand.

"Seriously?" She tried to sound nonplussed.

Alex raised one eyebrow and nodded. "Against my better judgment."

"*And* mine."

"Though it's my nature to be fully aware of the competition." Alex's eyes shot to hers and demanded she explain.

Angel sighed, knowing that male pride demanded she state the obvious. It was endearing that Alexander Avery—lover extraordinaire—would worry that any other lover would surpass his prowess. *Ever.* Angel realized it revealed he really did love her, and her heart filled, allowing any residual doubt of her own to disappear.

"Well…" she began, "Kyle was like a jack hammer—kind of all over the place, and Kenneth was like white bread."

Alex's lips twitched then put both hands up in front of him. "Fine." Angel was a strong woman and he couldn't believe she'd be with anyone who didn't please her. She was with Kyle when they were younger, so maybe, but not more recently with Kenneth. She would have communicated with him if he wasn't taking care of her. Alex felt sure of it. "You don't have to tell me." He couldn't comprehend that any man, faced with someone as beautiful as Angel, wouldn't want to make sure she was satisfied and panting for more.

Angel shoved her hand against his shoulder. "It's true!" Alex's wry expression told her he was skeptical. "It is. Don't ask if you don't want the answer."

"I just would think that—"

Angel interrupted him in a quiet voice with her eyes cast down and her hands twisting together in her lap. "That it would be all that deep digging and slow adoration like sex is with you? No one is like you."

"Babe," he almost groaned, pulling her against his chest. He turned his head and slid his mouth along the curve of her neck, kissing and sucking as he went. He shifted her, pulling her tighter against him, and her arms lifted, fingers threading through the hair at the sides of Alex's head. A dangerous position, considering they'd agreed to take the night off from lovemaking, but he wanted to be as close to her as he possibly could. "Thank you. But, it's because it's making love. Not sex... but it's not always slow," he murmured against her skin, his face buried in the silken curtain of her hair.

"No, but it is a lot. I know you want to take care of me."

"Always. I hope it shows that I love you."

She nodded and her throat tightened. As much as she tried to tamp it down, it wasn't like she hadn't imagined him with Whitney and the ones before that, wondering if he was as amazing with them, as adoring, as he was with her. How could he not be anything but who he was? She pulled back, holding his head away from her with her hands. She wanted to know. She knew she should just not ask, but now it would eat at her until she knew.

"Alex?"

His green eyes were piercing as he read her thoughts.

Jesus, I'm a stupid idiot! Alex berated himself.

Now she'd be wondering about all the women he'd been with, just when she said she wouldn't worry any more. Whitney, and a few others in his past had asked, but he just shut them down, telling them his life before they'd met wasn't their concern. He'd never understood why it mattered, but looking into Angel's sullen eyes, and with his own burning jealousy, he knew it did. Finally, with her, he understood.

"No. I don't want to do the goose and gander bullshit."

"Too bad. Is how you're with me, just how you are?" She persisted. "Sex, in general?"

She swallowed hard, not wanting to ask, but he'd opened this can of worms, and God damned him, she was only human.

He could see her throat move and her eyes begin to glass over, and he wanted to kick himself. "No. I wasn't invested."

"I'm not asking that. I believe that emotionally it's different. I'm asking how it was physically. You're such a considerate lover. I mean, I—"

"Not even close, Angel," he answered quickly. His tone lowered and he softly threaded his fingers in the hair at the side of her face, resting his forehead against hers. He wanted to communicate how he was feeling, not just say the words. But he knew the words he chose would be important. "Before, it was just about the act of getting off. It meant nothing to me, beyond release. I'm in love with you. I make love to you."

She closed her eyes, and one traitorous tear fell. Alex bent to catch it with his lips and kissed her cheekbone, then her mouth, gently sucking on her lips and teasing her mouth open with the tip of tongue.

"I fucking hate that this even matters to me. I hate that I'm acting like those weak women who call the show, and I just promised not to think about this shit, but I know men, Alex. Either they are so self-centered that the woman doesn't matter or their ego demands they satisfy. So I'm sure you—"

"Your theory would also apply to Ken and Kyle, right? It's true, but so what? I promised I wouldn't lie to you again, so yes, I prided myself on... *that*. But it was irrelevant, other than it was one less thing for them to bitch about." He could feel her stiffen in his arms and lean back, straining against his arms as if she wanted to create distance. "Baby, don't pull away. Angel, stop. Fuck, I can't believe I brought this up," he chastised himself.

They were adults—healthy adults—and Alex was a virile man, more virile than most. It would be naïve to think he wouldn't satisfy his women 100% of the time, and Angel was anything but naïve. Logic told her they both had past relationships, and though she didn't expect that he'd be celibate; but knowing how intimate they were together, she didn't want to think of him entwined with anyone else, feelings or not. She shouldn't be hurt by something that happened before they even met, yet her heart burned and tightened in anguish. "It's okay. I get it. We've both..."

He shook his head adamantly and pulled her close again. "No, Angel, we haven't done any of this before. How it is between us, is not like anything before us. I was like a robot and pleasure for the woman was an obligation. With you, it's the objective, and I won't have you thinking otherwise. The way it is between us—you shouldn't ever wonder."

"I think we should both stop wondering and worrying," she murmured.

"Agreed. We're together, and if I have my way, I'll never touch another woman again. And no one takes what's mine. Okay?"

Angel's hands lifted to his shoulders and slid around his neck as he nuzzled into her. He felt good. Warm and loving, his scent engulfing. Safe. "Does that mean you'll never get jealous again?"

"Fuck no, but I hate it."

"Mmmm, I can tell. I promised myself I wouldn't let doubt ruin us. So let's just promise no more secrets, and if we have doubts we won't let it eat at us. We talk it out."

"Yes, well, the next time that happens, you can bet I'll keep my goddamned mouth shut."

"I'll believe that when I see it. You have no reason to be jealous."

"You did leave me. Twice."

Angel pulled back and looked directly into his face, a little crinkle appearing above the bridge of her nose as she frowned. This was good. Talking was what they needed. "I know. But, not because I didn't love you. I loved you... that's why I left the first time. I didn't want Mark Swanson to hurt you. That's all it was. I just couldn't bear the thought of something happening to you."

He shifted beneath her and took both of her hands in his, threading their fingers together, his lungs felt ridged, unable to expand. "He could have killed you."

"This isn't about him, Alex. Don't sidetrack me."

Alex knew she was right, and he wanted to concentrate on her. It pissed him off because that cocksucker was still in his head, and he would be until he was behind bars. "My point is we're stronger together."

Angel nodded. "I know that now. But, I was scared... and professionally bound to keep it to myself. It was so hard to try to convince you I didn't want you."

Alex wondered if that professional ethics bullshit would still be in place after he was her husband because, illegal or not, he was damn well going to know what the fuck was going on with her. "I knew you wanted me. That's why it fucked me up so bad."

"I was heartbroken. I almost suffocated myself with a pillow to keep from screaming. I sat in my closet and cried."

Alex's eyes softened, and his thumb rubbed back and forth over the top of her hand tenderly. "Oh honey. It was so needless and so unlike you. All you had to do was tell me, and I would have handled it. I was already working on taking that motherfucker down, anyway."

"Ah… which leads to the other side of the secrets. Do you want to be the pot or the kettle?"

"You were so stubborn. It felt like I had no choice." Their eyes were locked together and didn't waver, neither of them moving a muscle other than his thumb over her skin. "So now you tell me everything. Professional ethics bullshit notwithstanding."

"Yes. No more secrets."

"Finally," Alex teased with an overly exaggerated sigh. He smiled when a giggle burst from Angel. *Finally*.

*****

"Anga!" Jillian squealed loudly into Angel's ear as she squirmed on her lap. "Are you coming for my birfday?"

Angel and Becca had picked Jillian up from Becca's parents' house and trekked to Chuck E. Cheese's in one of the western suburbs after their Saturday morning workout. True to form, Jillian was stuck to Angel like glue, giggling and shoving the atrocious pizza into her mouth.

"Of course! I wouldn't miss your birthday! Who's coming to your party?"

Angel had spoken to Becca about it and she already knew that a week and a half from now, there would be a big party. She was helping plan it, complete with face painting, balloon animals, and dress-up activities. It was a little over the top, but Angel insisted on helping to pay for it. The little girl would be three, and they were inviting some of her pre-school friends, their parents, and of course, Becca's parents.

"You, Gramma and Pops, Amanda, Sally, and Miranda! Mama says we'z is gonna be peencesses!" The chubby pink cheeks were rosy and more pronounced as she smiled, and her blue eyes danced. Angel adored her and ran a hand down her blonde curls, kissing her head. Jillian held a piece of pizza up with both hands and took a bite.

"We are?"

"Yep!" She chewed and tried to talk at the same time.

"Jillian, don't speak with your mouth full," Becca reminded, her blue eyes meeting Angel's dark brown ones. She hadn't seen Angel this happy in a while; maybe never. She was glowing, her eyes sparkling, and her smile had been constant all day.

Angel wiped at the corner of Jillian's mouth with a napkin and smiled happily down into the little one's face.

"Princesses! Wow! That sounds exciting! Which one do you want to be?"

Jillian thought about it for a while, her lower lip popping out a bit. "Uh, Cinderella. I yike her. She has yellow hair yike me."

Angel widened her eyes and nodded. "Oh, that would be beautiful! I think we need to go to the salon and get our hair and make-up done, shouldn't we?"

"Angel, the other little girls will feel bad if we do that."

She hadn't thought about that, and she certainly didn't want to hurt anyone's feelings. She shrugged. "Okay, I agree. I'll just ask Lauren and a couple of the other stylists to come to the party and we can do it there."

"That's too expensive, Angel."

"Shush. My girl is having a birthday!"

"You spoil her."

"Only on her birthday!"

Becca's eyebrow shot up. "Yeah, sure."

Angel laughed, and Becca examined her friend's features.

In the days since Mark Swanson had attacked, Angel had been vulnerable, and Becca was shocked at how beaten up she was—her bruises were starting to turn yellowish as they healed. Becca had seen her, but Angel had refused to allow Jillian to see her with a full-blown back eye and bruises to her cheek, neck, and chin. Those were just the visible ones. Becca knew there had been more.

"How does Alex look?"

"His shoulder was pretty banged up, but he's taking it like a man," Angel said with a soft smile.

"As if there were any doubt." Becca's eyes twinkled mischievously.

The women had always talked a lot about the men in their lives, and Becca was happy to see Angel with someone like Alex, but there were still details she wanted to know. Angel was the best friend she'd ever had, and she wanted to see her happy and settled. She was always so into her work and worried about other people; it would require someone as charismatic as Alexander Avery to pull Angel out of her self-preservation mode. Angel needed someone who was as strong, maybe even stronger, than she was so she could allow herself to be vulnerable and trust unconditionally. Her own past wasn't peachy keen either, and both of them had relied upon the other to get through some serious shit.

"So?" Becca prodded, picking up a piece of the offensive pizza and sniffing it, then wrinkling her nose. Children were everywhere, and the place was loud with music, screaming kids, and the various clanging, beeping and bells from the electronic games that lined all the walls.

"So, things are good. I'm trying hard not to be a typical, whiney female. It's hard not to worry, when…" Her voice dropped and a wry expression crossed her face. She shrugged.

"When you love someone so much," Becca filled in the blank with a cautious look on her pretty face.

"Yes."

"Hallelujah. Amen!" Becca's mouth twisted wryly. "It's about goddamned time you admitted it!"

Jillian held out both of her hands toward a sippy cup filled with soda, her little fingers waving at it in silent request. Without thinking, Angel reached forward and handed it to the little girl. "What?" Her brow wrinkled. "I told you very early in that Alex was unavoidable."

"Yeah. But you were so guarded," Becca answered. "So this is it, though?"

"Uh huh."

"Uh huh." Becca eyed Angel with skepticism. "You're not going to run away or sabotage the relationship? Because, even though I thought he was going to just be good sex, I can see that you're different. Softer now. He's totally got you."

Becca's words sent a thrill through Angel. Yes, he had her, all right.

"Don't go getting all mushy or philosophical on me. I admit I've been struggling, but I've seen Alex struggle too. It makes it more real, and I believe this is different for both of us."

"I'm just glad you finally decided to give him a chance. I didn't want to have to kick your sweet ass."

Still clinging to her cup, Jillian looked up. "Tweet ass!" she shouted out.

Angel's eyes widened and snapped up to meet Becca's as a snooty looking woman and an older lady from the next table gave Angel and Becca a disapproving once-over. Angel and Becca giggled; Becca coughed and tried to remain somber as she corrected the little girl, and Angel covered her mouth with her hand to hide her smile.

"Sweetie, only mommies can say that word."

The little girl frowned, unsure what her mother was talking about. "No, Mama! Anga, too! I hear-ed Anga say it, too." Jillian's face was so innocent and matter-of-fact as she gnawed on her pizza, and it was even harder to hold the laughter at bay. "She say'd it ayot!"

Becca laughed because she couldn't help herself, and Angel was the one trying to stifle the laughter. "Angel will stop. Your mommy is right, Bean. Grown-ups say stuff they shouldn't sometimes. But not sweet little girls, like you. Okay?"

The little head bobbed up and down. "Kay."

"Good."

Becca watched the interaction between her little girl and best friend. Angel would be an amazing mother someday, and it was a blessing she had finally found someone who was a mental and emotional match for her. Didn't hurt that, physically, he was a god. Becca sighed ruefully. Maybe someday she would have someone she could love like that. She'd seen Alex's brother, Cole, a few times when he was with Angel but only made small talk with him. He was attractive in a big way. They obviously had great genes, though he wasn't as polished as Alex.

"I'm surprised you don't have your pack of followers with you this morning," Becca observed as her thoughts took her to the obvious. "How'd you manage that?"

"Alex was with me, so he called off the dogs."

Becca's face twisted and she frowned. "Yes, but he's not with you *now*."

At the same moment, Jillian squealed and wiggled off Angel's lap to begin running from the table. "Zander! Zander!"

Angel's eyes caught sight of Alex walking toward them, even bending to scoop up Jillian and tossing her gently in the air; he still oozed sex, muscles working under his clothes.

Jillian giggled and screamed in delight. "Momma and Anga are there!" She pointed in their direction, and Alex's intense green gaze landed on Angel's. She could see he was not happy with her, though he hid it well when he spoke to Jillian.

"I left him a note telling him where I'd be."

"He's gonna be hot. I mean… he *is* hot." Becca's eyes took in Alex's messy hair shoved underneath a baseball cap and his unshaven jaw before roaming over the midnight blue fitted V-neck T-shirt and expensive jeans. His biceps and chest muscles flexed as he tossed Jillian again. "But he's got to be pissed!"

"I'm sick of being tailed. I love Cole, but the others get on my nerves. I feel like I'm in jail." She watched him with Jillian and something inside her chest clenched. He was so perfect. Every woman in the room from twenty to seventy-five was gazing at him as if they'd never seen a man before, and he was hers. A shiver of satisfaction shot down her spine at the thought.

She scooted over in the booth to make room, and Alex slid in next to her, settling Jillian on his lap, who turned in his arms and ran a little hand across his scruffy cheek. "You gots whiskies! Pops gots whiskies, too."

"I do! Because I ran out of the apartment in a hurry." He shot a hard glance in Angel's direction, so she slid a hand onto his inside of his thigh and squeezed. He huffed, the corner of his mouth quirked, as she smiled at him sweetly, silently bribing him to lighten-up.

"I'm fine," Angel murmured under her breath.

"It's pokey!" Jillian stated, still touching Alex's face.

"It is!" Angel agreed.

Becca decided she needed to give Alex and Angel some time alone. "Come on, sweets! Let's go play some games."

"Zander, can you p'yay with me?"

He kissed her cheek. "I'd love to, and I will in just a minute, sweetheart."

"Kay. Are you hungy? We have pizza!"

"I see that!" Alex said indulgently. "Okay, I'll have a piece then come play games with you."

Angel's forehead came down to touch Alex's broad shoulder, and she squeezed his thigh again. Becca rose and lifted Jillian off of Alex's lap, turning away with her toward the arcade portion of the restaurant.

Angel lifted her head and looked into Alex's profile. His jaw was set, and she could see him fighting with himself as he reached for the disgusting pizza. She knew he wanted to yell and scream at her, but her hand on his thigh and the way she leaned into him softened him as she knew it would.

"Zander will you play with me?" Angel teased sweetly, echoing Jillian's innocent question.

"Hmmph!" He grunted and tried to keep a straight face. There was nothing he wanted to do more than play with her and she knew it.

"Don't be mad."

He closed his eyes briefly then glanced in her direction. Steady, his eyes held hers. "We agreed no secrets."

"What secret? I left a note."

"You know I don't want you out without—"

Angel interrupted with a sigh. "Yes! I *know*! But I'm so tired of it. Babe, come on. I can't stand having someone follow me around all the time. I can't pee! I can't buy tampons! It's out of hand, not to mention annoying."

The muscle in his jaw worked as his teeth clenched. "It hasn't been that long, and Swanson did make bail. He has to have some sort of resources. I don't trust that he'll leave you alone."

"I know," she answered gently.

"So don't ask me to take risks with you!" His voice was low but with an undercurrent of anger.

"You're very sweet to worry about me, but I'm perfectly safe. Can we compromise?"

"Why does everything have to be a fucking negotiation?" He grunted and lifted the pizza to his mouth. It was soggy and floppy. After one bite he grimaced and he threw it back on the plate.

"You aren't the one under constant supervision! How about this? We go to the gym and I'll show you I can take care of myself! I've been working on self-defense and fighting with Becs. If I kick your ass, you let me have some freedom. Deal?"

"Even if you can kick the shit out of someone one-on-one, it might be a group of them. Have you forgotten the last time?"

"No. I got away from two of them," Angel pointed out. "So compromise?"

"Sure. When I'm not with you, Cole or one of the others is with you at all times. End of compromise."

Angel cocked her head, an exasperated expression flashing on her features. "Ugh! You're impossible. Okay, how about this? I'll stay with you at the estate if you lighten up a little."

"Angel. Enough. I want you to stay with me at the estate but not enough to take risks with you. You'll stay with me because we can't be away from each other, and that's it."

Angel huffed and pulled her hand off of his leg, but he moved quickly and grabbed it in his.

"Are you going to dispute it? It's a fact."

"No. It's just—"

His fingers threaded through hers, and his eyes softened. "It's *just* the way it is. Besides, Max misses you, and if you don't mind, I'd like to fucking breathe."

Her breath left, and she understood his frustration. He loved her. And, she loved him more than she loved total independence.

Alex continued as Angel paused. "I have to go out of town, and I know you won't go with me, so I want you at the house. I may even have Cole stay there with you."

"Even with the new security system?"

"Yes. Why take risks?"

"At some point, we have to have a normal life."

"I agree. But it's too soon. That bastard is out there."

"Cole mentioned you're having Swanson tailed, too."

"I am. So?"

"So, in that case, I'll ask Becca to stay with me. It would give me some time with Jillian, and she'd love Max."

"She can stay, but I still want Cole there. The house is big enough. He won't bother you."

"He doesn't bother me. In fact, he should get to know Becca. Don't you think?"

"I don't know. He's more responsible, but she has the baby, and I wouldn't want her to get involved with him until I'm certain he wouldn't fuck her over. Jillian doesn't need to get attached to someone who won't stick around for the long haul. She already has one loser dad."

"Bean will be okay. If not, I'll kick Cole's ass." His thumb started rubbing the top of her hand and he was joking around. She knew he wasn't angry any longer. He was so good. Her heart swelled with love for him. She could deal with his controlling, over-bearing ways. She knew it was only because he cared. He was so concerned for her, and for those she loved.

"Okay." One thing was certain. Alexander Avery would make one stellar dad to some lucky kid someday. The knowledge flowed over Angel like a warm blanket of honey.

His hand was still laced with hers, and he used his other to touch her chin and nudge it up. "Okay," he repeated her words then settled his mouth on hers for a warm, gentle kiss. He lifted his head then kissed her once more before pulling back. "My mother and father invited us out to dinner on Friday night. Will you come with me?"

"Will Ally and Cole be there?" Angel had to ask. Obviously, Cole and Ally knew the two of them were dating, so she assumed his parents would be curious.

"No. It's just us." He didn't elaborate, but he wanted her to meet his parents, and it was important they have an opportunity to talk to her and get to know her. He knew they'd love her as much as he did. He wanted to meet her father, too, but wasn't sure how to finagle that without sounding pushy or giving her clues about his intended proposal. He knew he wanted to do it right, though, and that meant meeting her father and getting his permission before he asked her to marry him.

"Wow. That sounds kind of official."

"It kind of is."

His finger traced the line of her face, both of them staring at each other. Angel's sweet mouth split into a bright smile, and he was pleased the prospect made her happy and not reticent. "I can do official. Before the show, then?"

Alex grinned, happiness exploding inside his heart. "Right."

"Okay."

"Zander!" Jillian's blonde head appeared at table level. "Come pway!"

"Okay!" Alex was sorry the moment with Angel was interrupted, but he adored Jillian. "I'm all yours."

"Yay!" Jillian clapped as Alex stood.

He was about to let go of Angel's hand and go off with Jillian but he stopped. "Why don't you come play, too, Anga." He smirked at her. "You're so good at *playing*," he insinuated with a wink. Angel laughed lightly, and blushed despite herself. Alex was always surprised at how often she left him stunned. She was so beautiful, and he loved her more than anything.

"Yeah, Anga! You come!" Jillian insisted.

Becca slid back into the booth, laughing. "Go practice, you two."

Angel shot her a warning look.

"Yes, let's practice," Alex agreed, bending to lift Jillian with one arm while still holding Angel's hand. "What should we play?" he asked the little girl.

4

Under Wraps

ALEX WAS ANXIOUS about the coming evening. He'd spoken to his father about Angel more than his mother, but that was to be expected. He spent more time alone with his father over business lunches and at the office, and since his mom was constantly nagging him to settle down, he'd always done his best to avoid the subject with her. Alex had no doubt his father would be taken with Angel, as she was accomplished and beautiful, even though Charles would be decidedly pickier about his son's choice than his mother would. And he might be shocked that Alex had gotten so serious so fast, given his past aversion to commitment. His mother, Cora, had never worked outside the home, but she was heavily into the charity scene, which would give her and Angel quite a lot to talk about. This was going to be good. Finally, his mother would get what she'd been after since he'd graduated college.

His father made reservations for 7 PM at Chicago Cut, which was an elegant steak house complete with white linen, candlelight, and crystal. It was one of Charles' favorite places to take Cora; the food was delicious and consisted mostly of succulent steak and fresh seafood. There were private dining rooms, and Alex had no doubt one of those had been reserved. This was an important evening, and noise and distractions of others dining nearby would not be allowed to intrude.

He was anxious, but Alex sensed Angel was nervous. She'd taken the afternoon off to shop and had Cole deliver her to his apartment without protest, allowing the couple to get ready together. Alex could see her distorted image through the steamy glass on the shower door in his large bathroom, water rushing over him as he rinsed his hair. She was still wrapped in a towel, her hair in some obnoxiously large rollers the size of beer cans, and rubbing lotion scented like her perfume all over her legs. He loved that scent, mixed in with the smell of her body, which was already ingrained in his subconscious. He loved how, when she was excited and the pulse at the base of her throat throbbed, the heat released it all around him when he made love to her. His cock twitched at the direction of his thoughts, and he chuckled.

"What's so funny?"

"Nothing. I just like having you here. I never thought I'd want to share a bathroom with all this girly shit, but it's nice." He smiled and turned to rinse off his body, away from her so maybe she wouldn't see the reaction of his body at her mere presence. Not that he needed or wanted to hide it, necessarily, but they had reservations, and tonight was important. He didn't want to be late by starting something he would need to finish. "Are you feeling okay about tonight?"

By now, Angel had placed an overnight bag on the vanity, flipped it open, withdrew a small, pale pink bag filled with her makeup, and was putting some sort of moisturizer on her face. She was beautiful, without a stitch of makeup on, but when she made herself up, she was stunning. He couldn't wait for the first seconds of his father's reaction.

Alex's thoughts raced back to their first night together; the near backless dress that had given him a perpetual boner the entire evening and later. He groaned inwardly as his erection bloomed full and hard, throbbing and bobbing as if it had a mind of its own. *Fuck*, he mused. He shut off the water and grabbed the towel he'd hung over the top of the shower, waiting for his use.

"I'm a little bit on edge. I can't decide if I'm anxious or excited."

Alex stepped out of the shower, his hair dripping, water cascading down his muscled arms, broad shoulders and chest, and the towel hanging on and supported only by his dick. He grinned at her, and Angel's brown eyes slid down his body. The corner of her mouth lifted, and her eyebrow cocked simultaneously.

"Looks like you're the excited one."

"Yeah, but we can't," he said regretfully, running the flat of his hand down her back, over the curve of her butt, stopping to squeeze playfully. "I was remembering our first night together. After Tru." He bent to kiss her shoulder, lingering over the soft, scented skin; he ran the tip of his nose along its line. "Mmmm… you smell amazing."

Angel watched them both in the mirror that was half-fogged over with steam; a shiver running through her and making goose bumps pop out on her arms. She couldn't tear her eyes from the reflection.

He was so beautiful. Physically perfect with that gorgeous face, but also so loving and protective. She heard it in his voice, could see it in his green eyes as they smoldered over her, and felt it in his briefest touch. His lips moved up the curve of her shoulder to the cord of her neck, his hot breath mixing with the soft sucking of his open mouth, and a shiver skittered over the entire surface of her skin. She leaned into him slightly and closed her eyes. It felt right, being here with Alex. Her heart overflowed, and she wanted nothing more than to melt into him and disappear. "I love you," she stated softly.

Alex's gentle nuzzling stopped suddenly as he lifted his head to look at her, but the hand at her hip pulled her tightly against him. God, were more absolute words ever spoken? Angel was still facing the mirror, and Alex watched her profile. Her hand came up to cover his in a gentle squeeze.

"Yeah. This is it. Us, I mean." There was no hesitation or question in his voice. He commanded this as he did everything else, except it didn't sound or feel like it to Angel. It was a simple statement of the inevitability that was Alexander Avery. If she didn't have a choice; it was because of God or fate or the revolving of the planets as much as it was Alex's subtle demands.

This is it. Thud. Angel's heart banged against her chest with the strength of an atomic bomb. It was true. She knew it, too. She was going to grow old with this man. Her eyes burned and her throat ached. Alex's hand wrapped around the back of her neck, his thumb rubbing beneath her ear as he used the hand at her hip to turn her fully into his embrace. His eyes burned, into hers, his hard cock pressing into her stomach; she couldn't help herself, her body leaned into his, pushing against his erection as her arms slid up his arms and over his shoulders to hold him back.

His breath rushed over her lips, and his forehead touched hers as he waited for her response.

"Yes, it is."

Alex's heart swelled to the point of pain as a brilliant smile lit up his handsome face. He didn't realize how much he needed to hear her admit she was his, would be his... always. It hurt, yet it was a relief; one he craved.

"Right, so don't be anxious about tonight." He smiled gently, pulling her into a tight hug, his hands sliding down, both hands moving up beneath the edge of her towel to cup her naked ass and squeeze. They were so close, his towel now discarded, and he wanted nothing more than to throw hers to the floor and take her right there. He wouldn't, but he couldn't resist a passionate kiss, his mouth claiming hers in hungry ardor.

"Oh, babe," he groaned, finally pulling his mouth away. Angel sucked on his lower lip and nipped at it with her teeth, her breathing heavy. "I wish we had time. I'd lay you out and lick every inch of you."

She let out a breathy sigh, her fingers digging into his back, her forehead coming to rest against the smooth skin of his neck. "I know. I wish I didn't have to go to the station later, either."

"I can call Darian," Alex said softly, his voice a low, hungry growl. "We could go to the estate and stay the whole weekend alone together." She was still wrapped in the arms of this glorious, naked man, and she never wanted to leave.

Angel wanted to kick herself for being so fucking *Angel.* "It's too last minute to bail on him. I can't. Dammit!"

"That's another job you should re-think." Alex reluctantly released her and retrieved his towel from the dark brown marble floor. Soon, it was covering his head and he was briskly rubbing his hair dry as he moved from the bathroom into the bedroom.

Angel frowned. "So, do you intend to lock me in the basement as your sex slave, then? Is that to be the only thing I'm good for?"

"No." It came as a low rumble from the other room. "But it sounds good in theory, and I'd make it worth your while."

Angel's lips curved into a soft smile. *No doubt.* She resumed her makeup application and could hear Alex moving around, opening dresser drawers as he began to dress. It wasn't long before he reappeared in dark dress slacks and a light yellow, Egyptian cotton button-down. The fabric had a soft, but very expensive sheen to it, and it was still unbuttoned over his magnificent chest. Angel couldn't help letting her eyes soak him in while he went about shaving and putting a small amount of hair gel through his dark strands. He wasn't wearing a belt, and the top button to his slacks was also open, leaving the thin trail of hair that moved south from his navel visible. He was so hot. She licked her lips then reached for a dark burgundy lip gloss and began to apply it to her full lips, trying to ignore the way her body was reacting, the scent of his cologne wafting around her in a delicious dance.

Alex was watching her in the mirror beside him as she applied it. Her face was perfectly made up, her hair now piled on top of her head in soft curls, some falling out in a deliberate mess that was absolutely irresistible. Her brown eyes were glowing out of a lush blanket of black lashes and smoky shadow. "You're so gorgeous; you should be illegal."

"Funny, I was thinking how completely fuckable you are."

He glared at her with mock admonishment. "Don't start with me."

She smiled and turned into the bedroom to retrieve the dress bag hanging on the back of Alex's closet door. "Who would you have me start with then?" she teased softly.

He chuckled and finished getting ready, letting Angel do the same. Never in his life would he have considered sharing his space, his home, his life, with anyone. Ever. But, damn, if this wasn't fucking perfect.

*****

Alex was a lot of things as he stepped out of the car at the valet station at the restaurant, but the most prominent was proud. It was a classy, high-end establishment, and he exited his Audi, leaving the keys in the ignition, discretely handing a folded twenty-dollar bill to the uniformed attendant.

"Thank you, Mr. Avery," was the quiet response as the man waited to enter the car while another attendant opened the door on Angel's side. Alex watched how the young man's eyes widened, a small smile and a look of awed admiration settled on his face. He was little more than a boy, but he was male; and Angel was too beautiful for words.

Alex was bathed in satisfaction when she shook her head silently and waited until he was able to move around the back of the vehicle; extending his own hand to help her out of the car. Something about the gesture made him feel like a fucking god. This woman, probably the most independent he'd ever known, chose him, not just to help her from the car, but as her partner, and it made him feel invincible.

The world moved in slow motion as her manicured hand came out and found its way into his; her long legs, sheathed in sheer black silk stockings, swung around; and those amazing black pumps, which sparkled softly in the low lights of the entrance, found their way onto the pavement as he helped her from the car. Electricity passed between them as their hands touched, his warmly closing around her more delicate one.

Angel was wrapped in an elegant black shawl that completely covered her wool cocktail dress to protect her from the cool fall air, but he'd seen the breathtaking dress that lay beneath. Those incredible legs and stunning face with her classic, delicate features, red lips, and sultry eyes as she looked at him; stopped his heart. She was elegant and perfect. And, she was his. Possessiveness reverberated through every cell of his body and filled the air around them.

Everyone knew it. Restaurant employees and other guests stopped and stared at the stunning couple as they made their way inside, though they barely noticed anyone other than each other. Alex, imposing in his perfectly tailored, black Hugo Boss suit, light yellow shirt, and patterned tie in shades of pale yellow, charcoal, and black, curved an arm around his ravishing model-esque date as he led her through the heavy cherry doors, held open by yet another uniformed attendant. The couple was elegant and perfectly groomed, as if they were stepping out of the pages of a magazine. Even with Angel in five-inch stiletto pumps and her hair piled up,

Alex was half a head taller. They were a perfect match and looked magnificent together.

"Good evening, sir. Madame." The attendant nodded.

Angel smiled at the man as Alex answered, "Good evening."

In the entry, Alex removed Angel's shawl and handed it to the coat check girl with another generous tip before turning her toward the hostess stand with a hand gently guiding on the small of her back. Angel's dress had a modest neckline in front and neat cap sleeves, but the fitted style echoed her curvy figure and stopped two inches above her knees. The back had a keyhole opening that was again modest but subtly sexy. She wore a single long strand of pearls and small matching earrings. Alex thought she couldn't have picked anything better for meeting his parents. She looked the part of a socialite who would easily fit in with his family and their obligations. He shook his head in astonishment. Angel was so many and varied things. She could be easy and carefree, angry with eyes blazing, the accomplished psychologist, the soft, sexy and sometimes demanding lover, the gentle nurturer she turned into with Jillian, or the wild cat with the potty mouth who argued with him at every turn. He fucking loved every exquisite side of her.

As they waited for the hostess to end a phone call, his lingering grin was telling.

"What is it?" she questioned. Gazing up into his face with a smile.

"Nothing. I just think you're pretty unbelievable."

"Birds of a feather."

Alex laughed out loud, his eyes alight with amusement. "Right. So, let's nest."

Angel rolled her eyes playfully, unable to hold back a small giggle. "Well, I walked right into that one."

"This way, please." When the hostess asked them to follow her in, Angel took in the opulence of the restaurant as they were ushered through the main dining room toward the back of the restaurant. She noticed the clinking of the fine china and crystal, the tuxedo-clad servers, the candles twinkling, and the dark wood lining the ceiling and up the walls in sections against the rich cream wallpaper. It was nothing less than she expected, but it paled in comparison to the elation she felt being at Alex's side. Some discrete and other not so inhibited glances told her that other women found him attractive and were envious of the possessive hand at the small of her back which guided her between the tables. The smile tugging gently at her lips would not be denied. She knew the position she was in, and she was euphoric.

They reached a small room and the woman stopped, using her arm to indicate they continue on without her. "Here you are. Your parents are already inside, sir. Enjoy your evening," she said pleasantly.

"Thank you, Sandra." Alex noticed the almost imperceptible lifting of Angel's brows at his familiarity with the hostess, and his devilish grin spoke volumes. "We always came here for my mother's birthday. It's her favorite restaurant in Chicago," he murmured in her ear. "Relax. They're going to love you."

Inside the small room, one table sat in the center, and a man rose from his seat next to a very elegant woman. The man was an older version of Alex, with graying at his temples and a few deeper lines to his face, but still breathtakingly handsome. His mother was elegant and beautiful, appearing much younger than her age. She had deep green eyes that matched her son's.

"Mom, Dad, may I present, Dr. Angeline Hemming."

His father reached for Angel's hand and covered it warmly with his other one. "It's very nice to meet you, my dear. I'm Charles Avery, and this is my wife, Cora."

"Very nice to meet you."

Alex pulled out the chair next to his mother for Angel, and once she was settled, took the one to her left.

"Perfect, son." Charles' eyes twinkled. "I have a very good view from here."

"Don't get any ideas, Dad," Alex chided, amused. He winked at Angel.

Cora reached out and covered Angel's hand with hers. "Don't pay any attention to them, darling. I've been dying to meet you ever since Allison mentioned Alex was seeing someone."

Angel smiled. "We've only been dating a short while." She sat back as the waiter appeared and laid the linen napkin in her lap. "We're not... um, it's not—"

"Nonsense!" Cora scoffed. She leaned closer, happiness shining from her face. "This is a quite a big deal. My son hasn't brought anyone to a family dinner since his senior year in high school. I was beginning to wonder if he'd ever find a nice girl and settle down. That last one..."

"Mother," Alex warned gently. "No embarrassing childhood memories or unneeded rehashing. Angel is more than aware of my past aversion to close relationships."

Alex's father smiled at Angel and reached for the wine list, his expression telling her this topic was not one Alex embraced.

Angel couldn't help a short laugh as she glanced from Alex to both of his parents. "Yes, thank goodness. If it weren't for that, I doubt we would have met."

Alex's eyes met hers and held. "Yes, we would have. At the concert. Allison would have still been after you for that."

"Mmm... probably." Maybe it wasn't Whitney's phone call but the inevitability of fate that brought the two of them together after all. Alex's look said she shouldn't doubt it.

"So it was fate!" Cora remarked happily.

"You're quite an accomplished musician and singer, Dr. Hemming," Charles remarked. "The crowd that night loved you."

"Call me Angel, please, and thank you."

"Alex is also quite talented."

Angel nodded, her gaze sliding in her lover's direction, a smile gently tugging at her lips. She gave Charles her full attention before she answered with a nod. "He is."

The evening progressed with questions about how they met, Angel's family, and her work, and most of the time, Alex's hand was on her leg or rubbing her fingers. None of it went unnoticed by his parents.

Alex felt Angel's discomfort just once, when discussing the way her mother left her father when she was only a baby, and felt unease of his own when the details of her work came up. It was still a sore subject with him, and Angel's exuberance as she told them what she could only solidified how much she loved it. She explained how she worked to profile sex offenders and other criminals, her role with the district attorney's office, and vaguely explained portions of her cases that wouldn't reveal too much. Alex's parents seemed enthralled with her.

His father ordered wine, and the wait staff delivered everything without disrupting the conversation once. The food was delicious, the company engaging, and the evening flew by. During one particularly in-depth discussion about his mother's involvement in the American Cancer Society's upcoming fundraiser the coming February, Charles nudged his son.

His lips thinned in a smile, and he nodded. "She's a keeper. Don't fuck it up, or I'll kick your ass."

Alex laughed softly and leaned closer to his father. "I don't plan on it. I'm buying a ring this week."

"*What?*" Charles Avery was beyond stunned. "I had no idea you were that serious so quickly."

Alex huffed under his breath and smiled. "Aren't you listening? And you see her, right?" His green eyes slid from his father to the woman he was speaking about. "It's not like it was a decision I made. Obviously, that's never been my M.O. It just happened."

Charles' hand came down on his son's shoulder. He had been concerned Alex would never find anyone to spend his life with but knew it would take someone special to shift his focus. He'd given up so much when he dropped out of Juilliard to take the helm at Avery, and Charles was happy to see his son find fulfillment, both in the business and, now, in his personal life. "Oh, yes. I definitely get it. I'm proud of you, son. You always do what needs to be done without complaint and without compromise. I expect that tenacity from you in marriage. It's not always a bed of roses."

Alex reached for his wine glass, still studying Angel as she talked with his mother. Both women seemed enthralled with the other, using their hands in animated ways and laughing together. "Believe me; we fight like cats and dogs. But, funny thing is, it's a huge turn on. It doesn't last long, and making up is reaaaaalllly good," he joked.

Charles laughed and Cora paused to look in the direction of her husband and son, briefly, but then waved a hand at them and turned back to Angel.

"Your mother obviously adores her."

"I'm glad. Maybe now, she won't be shoving her friends' insipid daughters down my throat constantly. I'll be glad to see an end to the nagging."

"They're not all *insipid*, but she obviously approves of your choice. She'll be over-the-moon, and I'm sure she'll want to host a big engagement to-do with half of Chicago in attendance." Alex inwardly cringed, his eyes never leaving Angel. The big parties wouldn't be important to her. He felt certain she'd rather they donate the money to some cause. "When are you planning to propose? Have you met her father?"

"Not yet. But, I definitely will. I want to start off on the right foot with him. She's been his whole world for years, and I can't just waltz in there and announce she's mine. I'd like to get to know him and ask his permission."

An expression of quiet satisfaction settled on Charles' face. "I'd expect nothing less from you. From either of my sons."

"Huh!" he huffed. "Cole is getting better, but I'm not sure he's quite *there*, yet."

"He's doing well at Avery. When do you plan to have him take over security? Are you sure he's ready?"

"It's a huge undertaking, but he's surprised me. I'm not quite ready for him to switch over, but not because he isn't up to it. He needs to get licensed, which requires a lot more work experience. Besides, I still need him where he is. That cocksucker, Mark Swanson, is still on the loose. I'm not satisfied Angel is completely safe yet."

"It's been a few weeks, and you did bankrupt him."

"Yes." Alex's chest expanded in a deep sigh as the conversation turned serious. "But he still managed to make bail, so someone is funding him. Not enough to save his company, but enough to put his slimy ass out on the street."

"I'm sure it will be okay, son. He has fewer resources than before, so maybe he'll let it be."

"I hope so."

"When is the trial?"

"It's set to start in two months. I don't know why the fuck they wait so long. It's not like it's disputed. All of us are testifying."

"What does the district attorney say?"

"That the defense will stall as long as possible, even though they have no case. *Because* they are scrambling to come up with something."

"Well, it will come to an end eventually, and I'm sure your mother and Allison would love to help Angel plan the wedding."

"*If* she agrees."

Charles was incredulous. "What? You think she might refuse?"

"She loves me. But, marriage might take a little persuasion," he said softly, making sure the women weren't privy to the content of his conversation with his father.

His father smirked and waved the waiter over. "Well, that's good. It's about time you moved on from beautiful dingbats who just wanted your money. You've never been weak on the persuasion front."

Alex laughed, and both women looked their direction, just as the waiter approached.

"Yes, sir?"

"We'd like to see the dessert tray. Should we order aperitifs or coffee?" he asked the women.

"Oh, nothing for me, thank you. Unfortunately, I have to get to the station in about an hour," Angel said.

"Yes, unfortunately," Alex grumbled.

The server waited patiently for a response. "Um, coffee all around, please, Nathan. And, the check."

"I wish I could continue the evening longer, but I'm afraid I even have to skip the coffee. I'm so sorry."

Alex removed the napkin from his lap and set it beside his plate. He knew better than to fight his father for the check, so he made a move to rise and help Angel out of her seat, but her hand covered his to stop him.

"Why don't you stay with your parents? I've monopolized your mother all evening, and I'm sure she'd like some time with you. I can get a cab."

She smiled at Alex and he smiled back. "No." It was one word that held a wealth of meaning.

It was late evening in Chicago and Swanson was out there somewhere. Cole and Bancroft's gang had been given the night off, and Alex couldn't help but be slightly annoyed she'd even suggest such a thing.

"But—"

"But, nothing. I'm taking you. Mom, Dad, please stay and enjoy dessert."

Both men stood with Angel, and Cora reached for her hand. "It's been so nice to meet you. Alexander, bring this young woman to brunch on Sunday," she commanded gently. "We aren't finished visiting. I'm so looking forward to planning some events with you, and I know Allison adores you, too."

Angel's smile was brilliant, and her cheeks held a faint pink blush that was a striking combination with the frame of her dark hair and alabaster skin. "It was so wonderful meeting you both." Still holding Cora's hand, she turned to Charles. "I'm so sorry we didn't have much time to talk." She had enjoyed the evening immensely, and her anxious worry dissipated mere minutes after meeting them; maybe even seconds.

Cora seemed the perfect, doting mother, one like Angel had never had. Despite protests from Alex, she'd spent half of the evening regaling her with tales of him as a young boy; sitting on his grandfather's knee the first time he plunked on the piano before his third birthday, and how he'd been able to play almost anything by ear after only a couple years of lessons. *"Of course, his interpretations of the songs got better as he grew up, but Charles and I were so amazed at his natural talent."*

Alex's face softened, and he'd tolerated the conversation when Cora told how he'd been accepted to Juilliard, and his grandfather had the rare piano made just for him. Angel had seen how lovingly his fingers caressed the ivory keys the night they'd made their plan to catch Mark Swanson. It was obvious how much it meant to him, and Angel's heart sank a little at the thought he'd given up that dream, given how gifted he was.

It was also obvious how proud both of his parents were of him, she thought as they moved toward the foyer of the restaurant, Alex's fingers threading through her own as they walked side by side. Cole had said it; Alex never failed, but he worked his ass off in everything he did. Angel admired him even more after an evening spent with his parents. She glanced up at him lovingly and bit her lip when his gaze slid to meet hers.

"What are you thinking?"

"Just about how gushy you make me."

A sly smile curved Alex's mouth, and he glanced at his Rolex. "I happen to like you all gushy."

A small giggle escaped Angel as they reached the coat check-room, and Alex dug out his money clip and peeled a hundred from it, handing it to the woman inside. Her eyes got wide at the generosity as she peered at the couple through the opening of the pass-through to the room.

"Do you have your claim check, sir?"

Angel doubted the woman even noticed she existed, standing next to him, or that his arm was possessively around her waist. The girl stared at Alex adoringly, leaning forward through the opening toward him, and Angel huffed in amusement. *Fucking magnet*, she thought and almost rolled her eyes. *Hi, Moth. Meet Flame. You'll be toast in two seconds.* It took effort to smile sweetly and not glare at her.

"I'd like it very much if you'd allow me to find the lady's shawl myself and for you to make yourself scarce for, say, about twenty minutes?"

Angel leaned into Alex's arm, his hand again firmly wrapped around hers. The coat check girl gasped but quickly regained herself.

"Um, well, sir, we will have other—"

"Oh, come on," he coaxed, glancing down at her nameplate, "Sally." Alex let go of Angel's waist to unfurl another bill and pushed them both into Sally's hand. His voice took on that tone; the smooth-as-silk, yet demanding tone that exacted acquiescence without a word of protest. "Just take the money, let us in, and shut the door behind you. And don't let anyone in."

The girl's cheeks flushed bright red, but she numbly took the money and opened the door, stepping back out of the way.

"Perfect" he practically purred, his voice like butter. Angel could visibly see the girl melt into a puddle as Alex's hand returned to her lower back, guiding her past and into the small room lined with rows of racks, only half of them full. "Twenty minutes, Sally."

Once the door was closed, Angel laughed softly. "I guess your dick is feeling better."

In one swift move, Alex had his jacket unbuttoned and pushed Angel against the far wall, coats pushed aside to cuddle them like a cocoon. Her breath left her chest in a huff as her back came in contact with the white painted blocks behind her. The contrast between the cold concrete and the heat of Alex pressing into her front was striking. "You tell me," he growled softly. "I've been insane to touch you all night."

"Wow, Mr. Avery. I didn't expect this from you. You're always so in control."

His lips quirked devilishly, and he bent his head. "Just because I want you, doesn't mean I'm out of control. Twenty minutes, remember, babe?"

Angel nodded, the move almost imperceptible as Alex's head swooped and he took her mouth hungrily, sucking her tongue into his mouth, followed by teasing tugs on her lower lip with his teeth. He was so fucking hot, and Angel's insides began to quiver and flood with fire. Her heart thumped wildly in her chest to the point it might thunder free of the confines of her ribs. She slid her hands up the fine linen of his shirt to tug on his tie.

"No time to undress... much," he murmured, shoving his hands over the curves of her ass and down the side of her legs to grasp the hem of her dress and pull it up to her hips. He bent and lifted her, pushing between her legs as her fingers fumbled with his belt and zipper, yanking his shirt out and pushing the top of his silk boxers down. He was hard as steel, and hot, like molten silk in her hand. "I only intended to kiss you. All I've been doing all night is staring at that mouth."

"Uhhh..." she breathed, freeing his erection at the same time he reached between them to pull her panties aside but found none. When his fingers touched her slick heat, he stopped and looked into her face.

"Had plans for me tonight, did you?" He smiled softly, loving that naughty side of her. "That is so fucking hot." She wasn't able to reply as he pushed inside her body and took her mouth again.

She'd didn't know when, but she'd known Alex's hand would find its way beneath her dress at some point in the evening, and he'd find it extremely arousing to find her without panties. Garters and stockings yes, but no panties.

One of Alex's arms was bent at the elbow and flat against the wall, under her shoulder, and the other held on to her hip as he moved in her, the hungry kisses never breaking, except for breath. Angel clung to him as he drove into her, pulling at his shoulders and clutching at his hair wildly. They were hungry, but love made them hungrier; the few days since they'd made love felt like years.

It wasn't long until Angel's breath was rushing out in wild pants, and Alex was turning his head into the curve between her shoulder and neck as he came hard, muffling his groans by sucking on her skin. He heaved against her, her wet heat and muscles grasping in spasms around him as she came.

"Christ!" Alex growled. "I'm calling Darian. I want to take you home. Now."

He was still holding her but moved away from the wall.

She rested her head on his shoulder and shook her head. "Babe, I can't. I want to. But I can't. Maybe you can come with me to the station?" Her finger ran down his cheek, teasing, and she kissed him with an open mouth, softly tempting. "I can let Christina leave early. Then, you can take me home after the show."

"Okay, but what do I have to do to get you to forget about other shit and just concentrate on me?" Alex let her legs slide to the floor and began doing up his pants. Angel pulled her skirt into place and looked around on the floor under the row of coats in search of the purse that had dropped to the floor when he'd grabbed her.

"I do concentrate on you. You distract me from my work all day." She moved to him after she'd found her purse and straightened his tie. "I need to use the bathroom before we go." Her eyebrow shot up. Alex took her hand and brought the back of it to his lips. He loved her more than he could stand. More than he thought he was capable of.

"I'm running down your leg, hmm?" His gaze held hers steadily, daring her to deny it. "I find that very sexy. It screams you belong to me."

"Okay, Tarzan, but it's going to get on my dress, and I don't want it ruined. Plus, I can just see it when I take it into the cleaners. 'Um, can you please make sure to get the industrial strength jizz out of the skirt? Thanks,'" she mocked wryly and jabbed him gently in the ribs with her elbow.

Alex burst out laughing and scanned the coats for Angel's shawl before wrapping it around her. They were both still laughing softly when they walked out the door of the coatroom under the glance of the embarrassed attendant.

"Thank you," Alex murmured with a sexy smirk, unconcerned with her opinion of what they'd just done; unconcerned that his parents were still on the premises, and if they saw them emerge, they would know what just went down. He didn't make excuses for his decisions; he owned every fucking one.

5

Scare

ALEX SAT IN the chair across the desk that Darian usually occupied when he was in the station during Angel's show. She smiled at him, and Christina hovered in the other room, looking into the studio through the window divider much more than usual. She normally sat at the desk and only stood to give Angel cues about her callers. Tonight, she was definitely enjoying the view, and it was more than obvious in the way her head kept popping up.

Angel couldn't help the grin tugging at her mouth, but Alex seemed oblivious to Christina's attention, concentrating as he was on her. He looked like James Bond, leaning back in the chair, his tie hanging undone, and the top two buttons of his shirt open, but still in his suit. He was plucking at his lower lip with his thumb and index fingers as his eyes studied Angel intently. His dark hair was shiny, even in the dim light of the room, and Angel was astounded how it could look so mussed but still perfectly gorgeous. His impatience was evident by the way his hand kept raking through it. He was so beautiful it should be fucking illegal. Who could blame Chris for staring? And it was even harder for Angel. She knew what he was thinking... she had carnal knowledge of what was underneath his clothes. *Damn.* He looked as good clothed as he did completely nude. His suit was perfectly tailored to his muscled frame, but it wasn't even that or the fact he was so built. He was commanding and oozed confidence without even trying.

Her call ended and a three-minute commercial break started. "Stop it," Angel said softly.

Alex's brows shot up. "What am I doing?" He mocked innocence for four whole seconds before he grinned devilishly.

"You *know.* Quit it. I'm working." Angel tried to put a stern look on her face, but she really wanted to go over and crawl onto his lap, and Alex could see right through her and huffed in amusement.

"Hey, you invited me. I can't help it if you want to jump my bones."

"Correction," she murmured wryly before a small chuckle escaped her chest, "*bone.* Jump your *bone.*"

Alex laughed, amusement radiating through him like the sun on a summer day. Fuck, she was gorgeous and funny as hell. "Yeah. Well, it wants jumping." His tone was teasing. "Since we can't give Christina a show, it will have to wait. I'm glad I came. I like listening to you work. It's interesting. I never miss your show," he admitted. She knew he listened the few weeks after they met, but not that he continued to do so.

She took off her headphones and got up from the chair to sit on the edge of the desk closer to Alex. He reached out and ran a hand up her thigh, toying with the clip of the garter on her silk stocking. "Hmmm. I didn't know you listened every week."

"I like hearing your voice. And, it might give me insight into how you're mind works; how you process relationships. I don't want to fuck this up."

"Please. You're going to do what you're going to do. Period."

"I said, I don't want to fuck it up," he said seriously, meeting her eyes. "I meant it."

His hand was working its magic; his slightest touch sent shivers and love washing through her entire body. "I know you do." She reached down and grabbed his hand, stopping the gentle caresses and holding it. "I trust you."

"Good. Because I don't want to hurt you, and I care about how you feel." Alex tugged on her hand until she was leaning down, close enough for his open mouth to take hers gently. The kiss was soft, teasing, and it did all sorts of delicious things to her. Her hand rested lightly on the soft cotton of his shirt, exploring the hard muscles underneath.

"Is that a first for you?" Angel asked when the kiss ended.

"You are all kinds of firsts for me, and you don't need me to tell you that."

She was being seduced by the intensity in his deep green eyes, the love in his expression, and the steady caress of his rubbing fingers. Her breath left her in a huff. "Mmm… I'm glad."

Christina cleared her throat over the speaker. "Sorry to interrupt, um, Angel, but twenty seconds. The call is on line one."

Angel pulled from Alex, moved around the desk, and carefully replaced her headphones, adjusting the mouthpiece, while he groaned aloud in annoyance. "*Fuck.*" Angel sent him an apologetic look that said she was just as sorry as he was that their contact was cut short.

Christina counted down from five with her fingers, mouthing the words: *five, four, three, two, one…*

"We're back. I'm Dr. Angeline Hemming and this is After Dark. Who am I speaking with, please?"

"Hi, I'm Lizzie." The caller's voice was tentative and timid.

"What can I help you with, Lizzie?"

"My marriage is in shambles, and I don't know how to save it."

"How long have you been married?"

"Ten years."

"Did something traumatic happen, or has it just been gradual distancing from your husband?"

"Both, I guess. He works long hours, and I've been lonely for a long time. When I'm home, he goes to see his family, and other stuff, usually without me. His mother hates me. I feel lost." The callers' voice was soft, but she wasn't crying.

"Wow, that's tough. He needs to grow some balls and stand up to his mother. Have you told him how you feel?"

"Yes. It only made it worse. We have two kids, so I tried to make it work, but I don't feel that he loves me at all."

Alex listened to Angel and watched her features, wanting to see her reaction. Shit like this was sure to color her view of marriage. That and the fact her mother split when she was a baby. She got a little crinkle above her nose that he found adorable, but she was looking down at the desk and messing with a pen lying next to the stack of paper in front of her.

"Are you sure it's work keeping him away? Is there a chance he could be cheating?"

Lizzie hesitated for a beat. "No, but I—met someone online and we… well, we… I had an affair, and now my husband doesn't trust me."

Alex could see Angel visibly deflate as the caller continued. Her expression told it all.

"I did it because I was lonely, and the other man made me feel like I mattered when my husband has forgotten about me. It was last year, and he's still holding it over my head."

"I see. Well, two wrongs don't make a right, obviously. Unfortunately, I see this quite often. It sounds like no one in that situation is happy. I'm not condoning cheating, Lizzie. You should have left him before it got to that point, but I can understand your motivation. Please don't compound the situation. There is no excuse for cheating or abandoning a spouse. It sounds like you should both go to marriage counseling, if you love him and you're willing to work very hard to rebuild the trust. If the feelings are gone, it's probably best for everyone involved to move on. No sense in prolonging the inevitable."

Lizzie sighed, the sound heavy, even through the phone lines. "I know. I've been telling myself that. I just wanted to talk to someone about it. Thank you, Angel."

"You're welcome. Do your best to help the children maintain a relationship with their dad."

"I will. Thank you."

"I wish you the best, Lizzie. I hope you'll find happiness."

Alex wanted to talk to her, to ask her about her feelings on marriage, but as the call ended and Angel moved on to the next one, his phone buzzed in his pocket. It wasn't a number programed into his phone, nor was it one he recognized or called before. He stood and walked through the glass door and into the hallway before answering so his conversation wouldn't disturb Angel's show. It was one in the goddamned morning, so who in the hell had the audacity to call at that hour? It wasn't a family emergency. It wasn't Bancroft or Cole's number. So, who in the hell was it?

"Alexander Avery," he said into the phone.

"Come outside." The hair at the back of his neck stood on end as he recognized the raspy voice.

"You must have me confused with the idiot you thought you called. You can go straight to hell." Alex glanced through the window at Angel, who was watching him and taking in his expression. He didn't want to scare her, so he shot her a small smile, but it was forced and didn't reach his eyes. She could probably see right through him. He turned his back to her to finish the call. "What the fuck? Angel has a restraining order, so what are you doing here? I should call the cops and have your moronic ass arrested." Alex's mind raced as his words grated out. Where in the fuck was Bancroft or his guys? They should be trailing Swanson and letting him know if that bastard was anywhere near either them or his family.

"I'm not here to hurt her. I just want to talk, to make a deal. With *you*."

Alex debated whether to go or not. There were cameras, but Swanson might have a weapon, and he was not an idiot. Alex's voice lowered but it was harsh. "You're either deaf or ignorant. I've already told you I don't negotiate with slimy fuckers like you. It's my advice that you get out of here and stay the hell away from Angel."

"Or, what?" Swanson snarled sarcastically.

"Or, you'll be sorry."

"We'll see which one of us will be sorry. I want my money back. Give me the five million I lost, and you'll never hear from me again."

"I'm not giving you shit. You don't need money where you're going. Those boys will fuck you up the ass for free," Alex growled into his phone, his knuckles turning white as he clenched it tighter.

He could almost hear Swanson's fury through the line, and it pleased him more than it should have. Pricks like Swanson were a waste of oxygen. Logic demanded Alex keep his composure, but his fury told a different story.

"I plan to leave the country. Disappear. Just give me my god-damned money!"

"You pathetic fuck. You're in no position to make demands of me."

"If that's the way you want to play it, fine. But remember, I'm losing my patience, and desperate men do desperate things."

The phone went dead, and Alex realized how much the skin of his face was burning. His whole body felt on fire; his heart pounded like a bass drum as his fingers closed over the phone and squeezed with all the force he could muster. He was furious, frustrated, and he wanted to throw the phone against the wall with all his strength. He was going to explode, but he needed to call Bancroft and Cole immediately.

What the fuck?

His fingers were frantic as he dialed Bancroft and stormed off down the hall to the lobby. Bancroft's phone rang five times then went to voice mail. "Where are you guys? Swanson came to the radio station, and you guys should be all over him. Call me back. Immediately."

It occurred to Alex something might have happened to his security team. They knew he accepted no excuses, nothing less than perfect performance, and should have been at their post. Alex became even more disturbed at the thought.

Cole's phone rang in his ear. "Come on. Pick up, goddamn it!"

When his brother answered there was loud music pounding in the background. "Yeah?" he practically yelled into the phone.

"Cole, have you heard from Jason?"

"What?" Cole yelled again.

"Has Bancroft been in touch with you?" Alex's voice was louder in response, and he glanced down the hall in the direction of the studio hoping his voice didn't carry that far. He didn't know how long it would be until Angel had another break, but he didn't want her coming out and overhearing any of this.

"No? Should he be?"

"Was he on Swanson tonight or was it one of the others?"

"He was."

"Goddamn it!" Alex exploded as a creepy coldness slithered through him. It did not sit well. Bancroft had been with Avery for several years longer than Alex had been at the helm, and he didn't make mistakes.

"Jesus, Alex! What happened?" The din behind his brother died down as he apparently left the club.

"Swanson showed up at the station making threats. He asked me to come outside, but I refused. He wants money, and it can't be good if Bancroft hasn't been in touch to let you or me know Swanson was here."

"Shit! You're right. He would have called for backup. I'll call Wayne and the rest of the team. We'll find him. Is Angel okay?"

"Yes. She's here with me. Start with Jason's last known location and keep me posted."

"I'm on it."

"If something bad happened to him, text me. Text me either way. I can't take a phone call Angel might overhear."

"She's going to find out, Alex. You can't keep anything from her." The sound of a car door slamming and an engine starting came through the phone.

"I know. I just—she's working, and she's already scared. She doesn't need to be even more terrified."

"Right. That's smart."

"Send Wayne over. Angel's assistant is here with us, and I don't want to walk out into an ambush. Tell him to check the lot out to make sure it's clear and hang back. I don't want Angel privy to anything. I'll tell her after I have her safely home."

"Okay, later, man. I'm out."

When Alex walked back down the hall toward the studio, trying to calm the frantic thudding of his heart and get his demeanor under control, he could feel a bead of sweat rolling down from his temple over the side of his cheek to his jaw. Reaching up, he brushed it away. He took a deep calming breath and shoved his phone back into the clip on his belt. Glancing at his watch, it glowed 1:15 in the low light in the hallway. It was getting close to the end of the show, and he wanted nothing more than the light of day. He was getting sicker by the minute of Mark Swanson and the bullshit hanging over their heads. He had plans for Angel and the beginning of their lives together, but it would all have to wait until they put this son of a bitch away. Until he could be sure they were safe from further threats.

*****

Later, lying in the big bed in his room at his estate, his mind worked overtime. Angel was asleep in his arms as the sun came up with Max lying on the other side of her. She sighed and snuggled closer to his side, her naked thigh sliding between his, the curves of her breasts and hips against his harder contours like two perfect puzzle pieces. Alex closed his eyes, tenderness flowing through him, and his arms tightened around her of their own volition.

The phone on the bedside table was eerily silent and dread began to creep over him. Something was horribly wrong, and he knew it. Cole should have been in touch by now, and Alex would be damned if he'd sit around waiting for the phone ring. He eased away from Angel, carefully un-entangling her body from his and moving out of bed. She sighed and rolled over, pulling the covers up around her shoulder to bunch it up in front of her. She looked so small in the middle of the king-sized bed with its high headboard.

Alex quickly put on a pair of white lounge pants he pulled from a drawer in his large dresser. It was huge, as was all the furniture in his room—a dark mahogany, it blended with the darkness in the room. He grabbed his phone and waited for Max to follow out of the room before he closed the door behind him. Alex's fingers were already dialing Cole's phone by the time he'd made it three feet down the hall. The ringing seemed obnoxiously loud in the silence of the big house, and he turned the volume down and went downstairs. He'd barely turned on a lamp when Cole answered.

"Hi, Alex." His tone was grim. "We're still looking, but we haven't found Bancroft. His car was where we thought it would be." Cole hesitated a beat, and Alex's blood turned to ice. "Alex, it was torched. Completely gutted."

Alex sucked in his breath until his chest expanded to full capacity then let it out in a rush. "Any sign of him?"

"No body inside. Wayne's team went to his apartment to double check, but we didn't expect him to be there. It doesn't look good."

"Son of a bitch! Did you call the police?"

Cole sighed. "Yes. They have a forensic team going over the car, but that shit can take days. I do know that they found his phone in the car."

Alex's heart began to pound the minute Cole answered his phone, and his voice was louder than it should have been. Max whined from his spot on the floor next to the couch as his master paced back and forth. The animal had no trouble sensing Alex's agitation. "Can you trace the call that came in on my phone? Find out where that bastard is!"

"Already thought of that. It's one of those disposable, pay-as-you-go phones. Impossible to trace those things."

"Arrrghhhhhh!" Frustration burst from Alex's chest. "The timing couldn't be worse, Cole! I have to go to Sydney on Monday!"

"I'll take care of her, Alex. I won't leave her side."

"I appreciate that Cole, but you aren't licensed to have a firearm yet. The way this is going, muscle may not be enough. I don't want either one of you at risk."

"I know I'm not licensed for Christ's sake!" Cole's voice was laced with impatience. "But, so what? I don't give a shit; I can still carry one to be safe."

Alex was torn. As much as he wanted Angel safe, if something happened and Cole used a gun on Swanson, his career could be over, or worse. He could be charged with a crime. "You know that's not smart." He ran an impatient hand through his hair and sighed heavily. "Just double up with Wayne or one of the others.

The house is big enough, so you stay with her 24/7, and the others can rotate and just be here on their shift."

"What about her work? You'll have to tell her about Jason if you want her to stay home the entire time you're gone. Besides, when you get back in town, if he isn't caught, nothing will have changed. Will you expect her to stay on lockdown?"

"Hell, I don't know what I expect. Let's just deal with what is in front of us."

He walked to the bar and pulled out the scotch and a glass, splashing two fingers into it and quickly lifted it to his lips. The earliness of the hour hadn't occurred to him, but its pungent odor assaulted his nostrils, and his hand paused mid-air. He couldn't afford to have his senses dulled in any way. The glass clinked on the marble surface, and the liquid swished on the sides as he set the tumbler down hard, resisting the urge to fling it across the room.

"I just know I'm going to be going out of my fucking mind. There is no way I can reschedule the trip because this deal is on the chopping block, and we may lose it."

If it wasn't a billion dollar deal, he might have been able to blow it off, but it had been in the works a long time and was just about done. The hotel chain was family owned, a high-end conglomerate that had been built from the ground up by the retiring patriarch. The man was worried about keeping the legacy alive, refusing to close the deal without meeting Alex in person. He was dying, and Avery was taking control, allowing 49 percent to stay in the hands of his only daughter, who was young and without a head for business. It was a way to ensure he didn't need to worry about the child after he was gone. Alex had been approached by the man, personally, and was the one to proffer the deal; it would be impossible to send someone in his stead. It was an honor to be trusted that much, and he couldn't screw it up.

"Maybe it's best to just go and get it over with. Then you can get back as soon as you can," Cole suggested. "Besides, we don't want Swanson to think he's rattled us, and we're off our game. This thing with Bancroft is bad enough."

Alex sighed, and his chest expanding was almost painful. "Yeah, maybe."

"I'll move into the house with her and never leave her side the entire time you're gone."

"I don't know."

"It'll be okay. We'll get the cops involved to help so I can concentrate on Angel. It's no different than if you were with her on the estate, Alex."

Alex looked at the smooth surface of the bar in front of him, leaning on it with his hip, and shook his head, though his brother couldn't see it. "Wrong. At night, she'd be in my bed."

"Concede that, but it will be fine. I'll have back-up."

"Okay. I'll plan on leaving Monday and getting back as soon as possible. Are you going to Mom and Dad's for brunch Sunday?"

Angel would keep her workout appointment with Becca no doubt, but maybe he'd be able to convince her to come to the house later so he'd be able to put a plan together with Cole in person.

"I can." Cole sounded uncertain. "Doesn't it depend on what Angel is doing?"

"Yes. Let's plan on meeting up at Becca's gym on Sunday, then it will be a natural transition to the folks."

"Sounds good. Will you tell Angel what's going on?"

Alex sighed again. "Fuck, I don't know. We agreed no secrets, but I think knowing Bancroft is missing will freak her out. She knows I want her at the house when I'm in Sydney and that you'll be there." His mind cranked to work out a feasible solution that would keep Angel out of harm's way and still accomplish what he needed to be done for work and finding Bancroft and Swanson. "I feel like an asshole leaving when we don't know where Bancroft is."

"What can you do here? Not a damn thing. It's up to the investigators and our team. You have to trust us. Trust me, Alex. But, honestly, my gut tells me what we find isn't going to be good."

Alex's chest tightened. Cole only reiterated what he was thinking himself. It wasn't going to be pretty. Swanson was trying to make a point, and he was more dangerous than they even realized. "You're right, Cole." His next words sounded foreign, like someone else was speaking. "I'm afraid Swanson is going to be a problem as long as he's breathing. If I give him money, he'll just blackmail me forever. If they lock him up, he'll get out at some point, and it will all start again."

"Alex!" Cole's voice was harsh. "What the hell are you thinking?"

"Nothing." His face burned, and his skin crawled. He wanted to kill Swanson. He'd never hated someone so much in his life. "I'm not going to chase the fucker down, if that's what you mean, but if he threatens me or Angel and he gets in front of me, that's another story."

"Don't forget who you are and what you are responsible for, Alex."

Alex's lip curled in snarl. "*Exactly.*"

Cole hesitated. Alex's tone was stone cold, still as death, and Cole understood his brother's meaning clearly. "Okay, bro. Will you be with Angel all weekend."

"Yes, but keep a team on us, from a distance. Get someone to watch Mom, Dad, Josh, and Allison, again too."

"I'm on it."

"Good. Keep me updated on Bancroft. I'll text you tomorrow morning about meeting at the gym."

"Okay. Later."

*****

It was a beautiful Saturday morning, but Alex had spent a sleepless night. After he'd returned to the bed with Angel, she'd immediately snuggled up against him again, but sleep continued to elude him. He should have dropped off the minute he'd crawled back under the covers, but he hadn't fallen asleep until the early morning hours, and now, he woke with a start.

It was dark in the room, even though the clock said 11 AM. Angel must have closed the electronic shades he'd installed because of his travel schedule; jet lag required sleep during daylight hours on occasion. The fact she'd done so should have assured him nothing was amiss, but his heart seized at her absence.

"Shit!" he muttered and scrambled from the bed, frantic at not knowing where she was. In light of the past evening's events, he was on edge and agitated. He was naked and quickly found the lounge pants by the side of the bed on the floor and pulled them on in a rush.

He was already calling for her before he hit the bedroom door. "Angel? Angel!"

He ran through the house, briefly glancing in each of the spare rooms, the bathroom, then sprinted down the hall, jumping down the stairs three at a time. The dark hardwood floor was cool beneath his feet as they slapped on his way past the great room and into the kitchen. He glanced around quickly, but there was no sign of her or Max. His heart started to pound even more erratically, and his hand landed on his bare chest in protest of the pain.

"Angel!" he shouted again. Nothing. No response, no sound. His hand ran through his hair as he turned around in a circle, searching for what, he didn't know. "Angel!"

His feet rushed to the windows near the kitchen table and the door leading to the deck, his eyes scanning out and down the multiple layers. Max's distant bark drew his gaze down to the lowest level where there were chaise lounges around the large and ornate in-ground pool. Angel was with him, and he was prancing around as she picked up a ball and threw it across the lawn so the dog could chase after it. For the first time, he hated the vastness of his property.

Alex burst through the back door, and it banged loudly as it slammed against the railing of the top level of the deck. His eyes never left Angel as she turned, startled by the sound. She was dressed only in his midnight blue bathrobe, her hair flowing down her back. He sucked in a breath in relief as he went down the stairs in a rush, yet still panicked. Her eyes were wide as he reached her at the same time Max returned and dropped the ball at her feet. The golden retriever barked and pranced at her feet, begging her to throw the ball again.

"Max! Enough!" Alex yelled at the dog and he cowered, dropping to lie down at the couple's feet.

Angel scowled at Alex then bent to her knees to rub Max's head and ears with both hands. "It's okay, Max. It's okay, baby," she cooed before glancing over her shoulder and up at Alex. "What's your problem?" she demanded angrily. "He didn't do anything to you! We were playing!"

Alex had the grace to pause, his face heating as it flushed. Alex's chest was still rising and falling from his frenzied search, and he turned away to scan the edge of the property, lacing both hands together on top of his head. Breathing hard, he realized how vulnerable they both were, out here in the open, even with the security cameras and the privacy fences. Someone could easily take them out with a rifle.

Angel stood up and moved around him, her posture communicating her irritation with him. "Well?"

Alex's eyes met hers, and his jaw tightened, the muscle working back and forth as his teeth clenched. "Get in the house," he commanded.

"Why? We were having a nice time until you showed up."

His patience was gone. "Angel, get in the house!"

She was startled and jumped at his loud demand but didn't have a chance to walk toward the stairs, let alone protest. Alex bent and hoisted her over his shoulder, her hair dangled around her face as he hauled her up the stairs. "I don't know why you have to make everything so goddamned difficult." He muttered, then hissed out a whistle for Max to follow. The dog ended up beating them, weaving up many levels of stairs and deck platforms in front of Alex and his unwilling burden. "Can you consider that I have a reason for what I tell you?"

"Oh, you mean you aren't just being a Neanderthal prick?" Angel sounded off in disgust; her position pushed on her stomach and made her words more of a squeak.

Alex ignored her and kicked the back door open, then unloaded her a little too hard. She stumbled and fell back hard on her ass with a painful grunt. Angel glared up at him, her eyes shooting fire and her chin jutting out.

"Yeah, sure!" He turned and threw the deadbolt then keyed in the combination to arm the alarm. "Maybe I care about your little ass!" Alex turned and threw his hands up. "Maybe I know something you don't! Jesus Christ!"

Max whined and lay on the gleaming marble floor, plastered up against Angel's leg. Automatically, her hand went to stroke his silky head. She wanted to be pissed at Alex, but her anger cooled as she realized the implications.

Alex walked around her and went through the motions of making coffee. He was furious, and she could actually feel his fury in the air around her. She sighed. "What is it?" Her voice was quiet now, and Alex's breathing slowed and the heaving of his chest lessened.

"As long as Mark Swanson is loose, we can't act like our situation is normal, Angel. You can't go outside like that."

"But Max had to go out, and I—"

"I don't give *a fuck* if the world is ending! You don't go outside without me, Cole, or one of the other men. Even that might not be safe! Do I make myself clear?"

"Don't talk to me like one of your peons, Alex."

Alex threw the scoop, still full of coffee across the counter, his careless movement knocking over the steel canister with a clatter and a scatter of grounds. He turned. "No, I'm talking to you like the woman I'm in love with who I don't want to get killed! Do you always have to argue with me? Stop being so careless and use your head for Christ's sake!"

Angel climbed up off the floor and stomped off toward the stairs. Her eyes burned. Obviously, something had happened. She got Alex's point, but he was being a dick, and he'd hurt her feelings, talking to her like she was a moron. It was an easy mistake. "*Okay!* Stop shouting at me like I'm an idiot! It was a mistake. I'm sorry!"

They'd had a great night, and she was happy when she woke with Alex draped over her. When the dog whined to go out, licking her fingers to wake her up, she'd automatically risen to take care of him. When she'd gotten up, she'd thought about attempting to make breakfast for the two or them. Now she was frustrated, and angry tears threatened to tumble unabashed. She angrily brushed an errant one away as she stormed upstairs to get dressed, willing herself not to burst out crying. She never cried before she'd met Alex. Now, her emotions were close to the surface, and she hated it.

Alex braced his hands on the edge of the counter and hung his head as Angel fled. *Fuck.* He sighed heavily. He hadn't had a chance to tell her the gravity of the situation, and he realized his fear had made him harsher toward her than he should have been.

He left the mess and walked slowly through the house and up the stairs to his room. He knew he'd find her there. She'd be either getting ready to leave him or maybe breaking something valuable.

When he pushed the door open, he was surprised to find her with both elbows at shoulder level, leaning on his big mahogany dresser with something in her hands and pressed to her nose. His eyes roamed over her, searching for shaking shoulders or other clues that she was crying. She inhaled then rested her chin on her hands. If she'd heard him enter, she gave no indication.

His big hands closed over her shoulders and pulled her gently back against him, her arms dropping to her sides. He pressed a kiss to the top of her head. "I'm sorry," he said softly as his eyes closed, rubbing his lips and chin across the silk of her hair then kissing her head again. "Something happened."

"I figured."

He turned her in his arms and pulled her close to his chest, his strong arms wrapping around her and lifting her up so she was more level with him. Angel's arms slid around his shoulders, and he bent to kiss the line of her neck then nuzzle into the collar of the robe to plant one on the curve where it met her shoulder.

Angel's feet were dangling a good foot off the floor, and she buried her face into his neck, resting her forehead on his chin. He walked to the bed and maneuvered so he could lie down with her still in his embrace. He half sat on the bed's edge, pulling Angel up with him so he could lean on the headboard, his hands stroking down her hair and body over the robe.

"He showed up at the station last night."

Angel gasped, but Alex continued. "When I left the studio for those few minutes, it was because Swanson called me."

A chill ran through Angel and she snuggled down further into Alex's arms.

"He wants me to give him five million dollars so he can leave the country before the trial."

"That won't make him go away."

Alex shook his head. "No. We all know he'd only milk me for more if I acquiesce to his demands. You'd never be safe, and I'd always be at the end of his leash. Besides, the reason we took that cocksucker down still exists. He doesn't have dick now, so he's desperate and even more dangerous."

"What happens now?"

Alex closed his eyes, hating he had to say the next words. "We'll figure it out, but there's more. Bancroft is missing. His car was found burnt up. He wasn't inside."

Angel pulled away and quickly sat up so she could look in Alex's eyes. His expression was grim. "Do you think we'll find him?"

He responded with a slow nod. "We will. But it's not certain what his condition will be." Alex's thumb moved up to touch her chin, which had begun to tremble, and her dark eyes filled. "So, you see why I freaked when I couldn't find you. He or his thugs could be anywhere. As big as this estate is, you would have been an easy target for a rifle hit."

"Couldn't you have just said so?"

"I didn't have time to argue, and I was freaked out. I wanted you in the house. And while you're here, I'd try to stay away from the windows."

"This is ridiculous, Alex. I can't stop living." Her face fell, and she leaned back into him. "I was looking forward to today. I wanted to go to the gym then maybe meet you for lunch and a movie. I suppose the entire day will be spent with me on lockdown, and you and Cole working on this crap."

Alex's fingers threaded through her hair, and she closed her eyes at the sensation. When she was in his arms like this, it was hard for Angel to feel anything but safe and even harder to reconcile the danger they were both in. "Yes, we have to figure it out."

Her head was on his chest and her arm around his waist. "At least this means you won't be going to Australia?" she asked hopefully.

"I have to go, but maybe you can go with me."

"No. I can stay here and work with the police and Kenneth. Besides, Bean's birthday is next week. I can't miss it."

"Angel," Alex began, but she interrupted.

"No, Alex. I'll leave after the party, but she's just three, and her heart would be broken."

"I knew you'd say that." Alex's heart screamed. The last thing he wanted was to disappoint Jillian, but it wasn't worth risking Angel. The problem was, she'd never agree to leave Chicago before the party. He'd have to figure it out with Cole before he left. He smacked Angel playfully on the curve of her rear end. "As I said, we'll figure it out. Get in the shower, and let's go to the gym."

"I'll just have to shower again later—wait, you're coming too?"

"Yeah, you're stuck with me. Becca is waiting, right?"

Angel nodded and pushed off Alex to rise, and he followed her. For the first time, he saw what was in her hand.

"Is that my business card? You were sniffing it?" His eyebrow raised and a quizzical look crossed his handsome face.

"Uh huh."

"That's weird. Why?"

"No, it isn't weird. I sprayed some of your cologne on it. Now it smells like you."

His lips twitched in diversion. The thought that even when they were fighting she'd do that filled him with delight. "I thought you were pissed at me."

She shrugged, not sure what to say. It was a small thing of him she could have with her at all times. "I wanted to be able to smell you, even when you're not with me. Even when I hate you, I love you."

The back of his knuckles traced her cheek. "I know. Me, too."

6

What to Do

WHEN ANGEL AND Alex arrived at the gym, Cole was waiting in the parking lot for them. He'd been there often, when he'd followed Angel before she knew who he was, and had gotten a membership so he could keep an eye on her without interruption. He'd found it amusing to watch her and her friend Becca workout. It wasn't the actual work out that was funny, they were both in great shape and gorgeous, and their exercise routine had a practiced flow no matter how they chose to mix it up. It was their discussions about life and the way they brushed off men who dared approach them, which was so amusing.

In the beginning, he'd had to quell the urge to laugh out loud on more than one occasion so he wouldn't blow his cover. He'd always hung back, several machines away, close enough to watch, but not so close they'd notice him. Too bad today's mood was clouded with Bancroft's disappearance and the rest of the shitstorm surrounding Swanson and his threats. He was definitely preoccupied because he wanted to be helping with the search.

He was leaning against his dark blue SUV, with arms crossed and sunglasses on, the cap on his head backward, as Alex pulled into the parking lot and stopped three spaces away. Cole nodded at him, giving him the all clear to exit the car, then went to open Angel's door for her. All three were dressed in exercise gear, and Angel gave Cole a small smile. He was looking more like Alex every day. His muscles were slightly beefier, where Alex's were long, lean, and defined, except the jaw—sometimes scruffy with two days' worth of beard growth, and the way he'd taken to having his hair-cut was shorter and closer to the way Alex styled his.

"Looking good." She punched him in the stomach playfully, and the smile he gave her in return was genuine, his white teeth almost blinding in the sun. He truly liked Angel and was apprecia-tive of the changes he'd observed in Alex since he'd met her. His brother seemed happier, at least, when he wasn't preoccupied and consumed with worry.

Alex pulled two duffel bags and a garment bag from the backseat of his Audi, silently watching Cole and Angel. He was pleased with Cole's dedication to Angel, and it was obvious Angel was at ease with Cole and the situation. Jealousy tightened his gut at the thought of how much time Cole could spend with Angel, but he was thankful for his brother's protection of her. Moving around the rear of the car, Angel took one bag from him, and he placed it gently over her shoulder.

Alex glanced at Cole, but both of them in sunglasses pre-vented him from being able to read his eyes. He didn't want to ask about Bancroft in front of Angel. He was confident Cole wouldn't say anything specific until they were both in the locker room and out of earshot, and it could be very bad news. "Any sign of any-thing here?"

"Nope. I've already been inside and did a sweep. Nothing at all suspicious."

"But you didn't go into the women's locker room, obviously," Alex's tone was cautious.

"No, the place is pretty busy and so I wasn't able to. I'm not sure how to handle that, Alex. We can ask one of the employees to go in, but I figure it's clear if the women in there aren't running out screaming. Honestly, I don't expect Swanson to make a move in a crowded place like this. It's too active for him to go unnoticed and too huge for him to get away if there was a commotion."

"He could be hiding somewhere. In one of the shower stalls, maybe."

"Becca knows practically everyone who comes to this club and there are cameras everywhere. She'd know if the creeper was here," Angel interjected, her free hand reaching out to wrap around Alex's bicep as they walked through the parking lot, her fingers gently squeezing the muscle in reassurance. "Plus, she knows what he looks like now," she continued. Angel being an actual victim removed her professional obligation and the gag order. And, it's been all over the news, so it was just about certain Swanson had lost any support system that remained after his stepdaughter's rape when this latest attack was reported.

"It might not be him. He could still have help," Alex interjected.

"Even though he's broke?" Angel asked.

"Who knows. Blood is thicker than water. The mob might still be helping him. We can't take chances."

The sky was a pristine blue, cloudless, and the sun bright, the temperature slightly cool. Alex felt Angel shiver but wondered if it were the weather or fear that shuddered through her. He hated it. Fucking hated it.

"There aren't cameras in the locker rooms, Angel," Cole murmured. By now, they were to the doors, and he was holding it open so Angel and Alex could precede him inside.

Alex's mouth was pressed into a thin line. "Maybe we should have skipped this today."

"It'll be fine. Besides, I need to work out and I'm pretty sure you need to punch something." Angel took his hand and threaded her fingers through his, trying to ease a little of his anxiety. "Right?" She smiled and took off her sunglasses. The club was well lit, but not nearly as bright as outside. Alex couldn't argue. He was filled with tension.

"Hi! Welcome to Bally Fitness!" A perky young woman, braids bobbing, dressed in a tight, hot pink sports bra and black spandex shorts, smiled at them, her eyes bouncing off Angel and toward the two men, her gaze appreciative. Angel smirked. She knew a lot of the trainers and instructors, but this one was new. Her skin was dark, with a slight orange tint. Angel speculated there were a lot more fake things about her besides her tan. Angel and Cole showed their membership cards and signed in. "What about you, sir?" She eyed Alex and bit her lip.

Please, Angel thought. *A little more obvious, maybe?*

"He's my guest," she said a little too sweetly. She widened her eyes and flashed a saccharine smile. "How much for a visitor pass?"

Alex's lips twitched at the sticky tone, and he couldn't help a chuckle. She was jealous. If it weren't for the other shit going on, he'd be downright giddy at Angel's possessive tone.

"Oh! Well, it's free to try for a week. All you have to do is fill out this form." She turned then placed a piece of paper and a pen on the desk and pushed it toward Alex.

"Is that really necessary?" He glanced at her nametag that was sitting on her low cut shirt making sure her cleavage was overly exaggerated. "Alicia?"

"I'm afraid so, Mr.?" The woman waited for him to fill in the blank, smiling brightly at him. "How am I going to get in touch to follow up if you don't?"

"Avery. Alex Avery." He let go of Angel's hand so he could pick up the pen, handing her the garment bag and setting the duffel on the floor.

"I'm going to find Becca, okay, babe?" Angel tugged Alex's arm to bring him lower so she could speak into his ear. He leaned down to hear her words, not quite a whisper, and got a whiff of her perfume. "Don't let her bite off your dick. It's mine."

Alex laughed softly, delighted by her boldness and sure she intended the counter girl to hear. In light of what was weighing them all down, he was pleased Angel was able to tease. It made him relax a little. He wrapped the fingers of his left hand around her forearm, gently jerking her closer, for both Angel's benefit but also to reassure her by making a point in front of the other woman. His mouth pressed to hers briefly, but still taking her by surprise. "I'll see you in a minute." He released Angel and pulled the form forward to begin filling it in. "Cole." Alex's head nodded in Angel's direction, silently telling him to go with Angel.

"On it." Cole reached for the bag she was holding then picked up her duffel bag and flung it over his shoulder with his.

"I can carry something." Angel glanced up at him as they walked further into the club.

"I've got it. Where's your friend?" His eyes scanned the club in front of them and left to right as they walked. He let Angel walk slightly in front of him so he would be at her back yet have a clear visual of what was in front of her.

It was an impressive, upscale club, with a huge Olympic size pool, racquetball courts, basketball courts, a track that ran around the outside of the second level, several classrooms for spinning, Zumba, aerobics, and yoga, as well as a hundred machines for cardio, two weight rooms, machines and free weights. There were mats laid out, with the six bags hanging from the ceiling in the free weight room, with a ring off to one side. Off to the left, beyond the indoor pool, were tall windows with a clear view of the outside pool, complete with waterslides and what looked like an area for kids with more water toys, including a huge bucket that, when full, would tip over onto the children squealing below.

"She should be getting out of a class and said she'd meet me at the locker rooms. They're over here." She pointed to a set of doors on the far wall, both together, one marked women and the other men. "You like her, don't you?" She goaded knowingly as she poked him in the arm with a pointed finger. When he didn't answer, Angel's eyebrows shot up as she stared him down.

There was a bench between the two doors they would be able to wait on. Cole set the bags down and waved Angel toward it, bristling. "I don't have time to be interested in women right now. Have a seat."

Angel didn't have time to sit, though, because Becca appeared on the stairs in front of them. "Hi!" she called as she rounded the corner and made her way down the last of the stairs.

Cole and Angel turned toward her.

"Is something up?" Becca's blonde hair was pulled up in a messy bun, and a sheen of sweat glistened on her face. She dabbed at her forehead with a towel that hung around her neck. She was fit, the muscles on her stomach defined and visible between her Capri yoga pants and lavender sports bra. "You don't usually bring the muscle. At least, they don't usually tag along inside the building." Her blue eyes met Cole's then flashed back to Angel's. "What's going on?"

"Hey, Becca," Cole said. "Nice to see you, again."

"You, too. Well?" she questioned Angel.

"Maybe I just wanted to work out." Cole picked up Angel's bag and handed it to her, unwilling to share.

"What? Am I mentally challenged?" Becca looked at him pointedly with a slight shake of her head, but then spoke to her friend.

"I don't know? Are you?" he retorted.

Becca huffed and turned to Angel. "Where's your man?"

"He's getting drooled on by the babe at the counter."

Becca rolled her eyes and pushed open the door to the locker room. "You mean Tropicana Barbie? Bitch is practically radio-active. Every time she walks past me, I get third degree sunburn," she said wryly. Angel chuckled, and Cole snorted sarcastically. "Come on, let's put your stuff away."

Angel smirked then glanced back at Cole. "Becca usually starts me out on cardio for warm-up, so we'll be upstairs first."

"Wait." Cole commanded. "Becca, would you mind going in there and looking around?"

Her eyebrows shot up. "What am I looking for?"

"Cole, you said it yourself, this place is busy. He won't be in there."

"Oh, that freak? In the girls' locker room?" Becca questioned. "There's a camera on these doors and security would be here in two seconds if a dude went in. Someone is always watching. Plus, the women in there would have a conniption fit, but sure, I'll take a pass."

"Not just him. Anything that looks suspicious. Thanks." Cole's eyes roamed over Becca's firm ass encased in black lycra as she turned away. Angel caught it.

When her friend disappeared behind the door, Angel turned back to Cole. "No time, huh?" she teased. "Is it safe for her, if it's not for me?"

"He's not targeting her. She's an employee here, so no big deal for her to check things out without drawing attention to what she's doing."

Just then, the door burst open and Becca's blonde head popped out. "Nothing in here but the Red Hat Society. Twelve sets of flat-tire boobies and saddlebags. Interested?" Becca said wryly, but lowering her tone to close to a whisper. She smirked wickedly at Cole.

He smiled back against his will, and their eyes met briefly as he waved Angel in through the door. Becca was spunky, in a similar way to Angel, and he liked it. She was beautiful, too; more girl-next-door, fresh-faced than Angel, but beautiful.

Angel laughed and shoved Becca back through the door. "Tell Alex he owes me a fight."

"What?" Cole asked.

"He doesn't believe I can defend myself. So, I'm going to show him." Amusement danced over her features, and Cole thought she was in an awfully good mood considering all that was going on. He wondered if Alex had told her about Bancroft's disappearance, but in case he hadn't, Cole wasn't going to give her the perspective he thought she needed and risk pissing off his brother. "We have a bet."

"Sweet!" Becca exclaimed with a laugh bubbling up inside and spilling out. "Let's get the warm-ups out of the way! Can't wait to see my girl kick your brother's perfect ass."

When the women disappeared into the locker room, Cole went to find Alex, glancing up at the ceiling and sweeping the room. There were many security cameras in the club, and it wasn't likely anything would go down here. He found Alex walking toward him, alongside the glass wall and doors that surrounded the indoor pool and separated it from the rest of the facility. "Are you still alive? That chick looked ravenous." Cole said. He tried to smile, but despite the jokes from before, he could tell Alex's mood was surly.

"Yeah," Alex said abruptly. Cole realized that his brother didn't even have to try with women, yet sometimes he barely noticed. Women couldn't seem to help themselves falling all over him, though some were worse and more obvious than others. Becca's description of the girl had echoed his own opinion of her. "How do things look?"

"I don't expect a disturbance. The place is pretty locked down," Cole murmured as he and Alex entered the men's locker room, already peeling off his shirt, to find an empty locker and throw it inside.

"Agreed. I would've asked Alicia to check the membership register, but it's unlikely Swanson or any of his goons would join using their real names."

"True. Don't let Angel know you remember that girl's name. She might be missing a brick or two, but she was hot."

Alex had his shirt mid-way off and paused, pulling his arms down so he could look at Cole. His shirt wrapped around his strong arms and his solid back bare. The reluctant smile that crossed his face indicated he might have noticed but was done thinking about it. Without answering, he finished removing his shirt and tossed it to join Cole's in the same locker. He rummaged through the bottom of his bag for a combination padlock hiding there, before shoving it into the locker, pushing it shut with a clang, and locking it. He ran a hand through his hair as they exited the locker room. "Where are they?"

"Cardio tier."

"Okay, let's head up there."

"So what's the plan? Did you tell Angel about Bancroft being missing?"

"Yes." Alex's chest rose in a deep sigh. "Not in the way I wanted, but there was no easy way to tell her. I want to keep things as normal as possible and not give Swanson any clue that I'm the least bit spooked. So, I guess the plan is to work out, stop back at the house, get Max, and go to the folks for brunch."

"Have Mom and Dad met her already?"

"Yeah. You should have seen Mom go all gooey over Angel the other night." They climbed the stairs to the upper level together, both shirtless and the focus of several admiring stares as they passed. "Allison and Josh will be there, too. Angel can hang out with them while you and I figure things out and follow up with the team."

"But you're still going to Sydney?"

Alex shrugged. "I don't want the folks agitated by any of this, so as long as you're with Angel 24/7, I will. She wants to invite Becca and her little girl, Jillian, to be at the house, but I'll leave Max with Mom and Dad."

"What the fuck? I don't have enough to worry about?" Cole's voice grew hard. "I need to be looking for Bancroft."

Alex knew Cole was right. He also knew he could try to convince Angel to go with him, but he did promise her and was certain, no matter what the degree of danger was or how much he protested, there was no way Angel would miss Jillian's birthday.

"The others can do that. I need you to be with Angel, Cole. I'll be worried sick every second I'm gone."

Cole nodded. "I know."

"You know how stubborn Angel is. To get her to stay at my place, I had to make a deal. It was before this latest shit with Swanson and Bancroft or no way in hell it would be in play. Believe me, if I had my way, it would just be you two. Or better yet, she would be on the plane with me."

"Why isn't she?"

"She has a birthday party to attend."

"Since when did you make deals that weren't work-related?"

"Yeah, I know. A lot of things have changed."

"Obviously. Whose birthday is important enough to risk her safety?"

"Becca's little girl is turning three. That's part of the reason why I agreed to allow them to stay at the house."

Cole sighed heavily and rubbed the back of his neck. "I get it, but try to convince her anyway."

Alex's eyes scanned the huge room lined with one cardio machine after another. Rows upon rows of treadmills, elliptical machines, and bikes stretched in front of them at the top of the stairs, and Alex searched for the two women. They were on two treadmills along one wall, both of them running at a good pace. "I'd try, but it would just end in a fight. I have to pick my battles. I'd convince her if it were anyone other than that little girl. Angel adores her like she was her own child, and Bean would be heartbroken."

"Bean? Her name is Bean?"

"Jillian. Bean is a nickname."

Soon both men were running on treadmills at a good vantage point from the women. Close enough to keep an eye on them, but in a corner of the room so they could watch the entire scene easily as they worked out. Alex's shoulders and neck were tight, and getting his blood pumping was helpful. Twenty minutes later, Angel zipped past his machine, followed by Becca.

"Meet you in the ring, sexy," she panted out between breaths and the heavy rise and fall of her chest.

"You shouldn't have left it all on the treadmill if you wanted a shot at the title," Alex teased back. He didn't want her to worry or be afraid and did his best to squash his anxiety and keep his apprehension about Bancroft from showing on his face. The team was on it, as well as the police, and there wasn't a damn thing he could do about it, so it was best just to try to take her focus off of it. "You can't take me, little girl. You'll just end up on the mat."

"Pfft!" Angel scoffed over her shoulder. "Hurry up!"

He moved one foot then the other to the frame beside the moving belt, shut the machine off, and followed. "Are you sure you want to do this? I'll have you under me in short order." A sly grin slid across his mouth, flashing his white teeth as his eyes followed every move she made.

Angel smiled back, her dark eyes sparkling, warmth spreading through her. No matter what was happening, there was no getting around how sexy Alex was or how he made her feel with his gentle teasing or his scorching glances. "Or, you might be the one who ends up on the bottom."

"There are worse places to be." Alex winked with a cock of his head when she looked over her shoulder at him, just before she climbed in the ring. She began an exaggerated boxer's dance around the ring, punching the air and waggling her eyebrows at Alex flirtatiously. He only chuckled. She looked amazing. Sexy and strong, with her hair tied up in a knot on top of her head. Her sports bra and tight spandex capris left little to his imagination, especially since his imagination had firsthand knowledge of what lay underneath. "You look gorgeous."

"Hey, now, let's keep focus," Becca admonished with a grin.

Cole took up his position, leaning against the wall on the north side of the ring opposite the door to the room. It was clear to both Alex and Angel why he would pick that vantage point, and Becca moved to one of the corners of the ring to encourage her friend. "Come on, Angel. Give it to him good!"

Alex was torn about his match with Angel. There was more riding on it than the bet. He could let her win to give her confidence, or he could prove her vulnerability so she'd be more careful. It wasn't an easy decision, and Angel was independent and proud. The outcome could scare her into being more careful, but he also needed her to have confidence in her ability. It was a tough call.

Alex shot Becca a look. "She gives it as good as she gets it, Becca, trust me."

"If you weren't so beautiful, I'd have to punch you myself, Alex," Becca warned.

"Enough flirting and bullshit. Get on with it." Cole complained in irritation. "I've got other stuff I should be doing, Alex."

"Just when I was starting to think you were an improvement on all the other meatheads around here," Becca said pointedly. "Cranky much?"

"Yeah, and referring to me as a 'meathead' isn't helping," he said flatly, his eyes never leaving the ring.

Becca's lips pursed mockingly. "I could have said mouth breather or bottom feeder. Or how about meat*ball?* Do you like that better?"

Cole frowned; his mouth pressing into an irritated line. "Alex, I'm outta here in thirty minutes," he warned and watched Alex climb into the ring behind Angel. "Finished or not."

"Okay. Come on, babe. Show me what you've got," Angel goaded, using both hands to signal Alex to bring it on, while she bounced from one foot to the other. "Come at me."

Alex did as she asked; rushing forward, he grabbed both of her forearms and tried to twist her around. Angel pulled her right elbow toward her body and twisted her arm up and over Alex's, breaking his hold, but Alex recovered quickly, grabbing her by the shoulder. Angel needed her left hand so she repeated the twist move to free it from Alex's grasp then quickly placed her left hand over his, the other on his elbow, and twisted.

Before Alex knew what hit him, Angel had him in an arm-bar hold by twisting his thumb back painfully. It had him facing away from her and bent at the waist, his wrist bent back and his arm straight in a painful position behind him. Angel was free to bring her knee up to his abdomen and solar plexus in several blows. "Huh, huh," she grunted, and Alex's breath left as she knocked it out of him. Her moves were practiced perfection, and though she didn't hit him with enough force to hurt him, he felt it, and she made her point.

Angel moved away as quickly as she took hold of him, and Alex straightened. "Once I get an assailant's face below waist level, I'm the winner," she said. She showed little signs of exertion, her breathing only slightly heavier than normal.

"That's good, babe. I'm proud of you, but it's more likely he'll try to take you down from behind when you don't see him coming."

"Okay." Angel turned her back to Alex. "Go."

Alex sighed and ran a hand through his hair. He didn't want to hurt her, and he wasn't using all his strength. He cast a glance at Cole, who nodded in Angel's direction, silently telling his brother to put more into it.

When he pounced on Angel, he pulled her into a bear hug, effectively pinning her arms, bent across her chest, and locking one hand around his other wrist to hold her tight.

Angel promptly stepped to the outside and hooked a leg behind Alex's, using her knee to push against the back of his, knocking him off balance and twisting to clock him with an uppercut to his jaw. It had the effect she was looking for, and he had no choice but to release her.

"See, babe?" Angel said as he recovered from his stumble. "Years of classes. Satisfied?" Her question was accompanied by cheeky grin.

Alex had to admire her skill, though it still wasn't enough for him to feel at ease. She was good, no doubt, and she would be able to take care of herself in many situations, but Swanson was desperate, and he wanted revenge. Nothing could be taken for granted. Nothing.

He decided to prove his point later in the evening.

*****

The Avery estate was secure. Iron gates, brick walls, and cameras lined the perimeter, and the acreage was big enough that the house was a good distance from any of the entrances. Lush foliage and large trees prevented a clear eye line into the windows, but Swanson's phone call still tortured Alex's composure. The bastard was determined, and he felt certain it would only be a matter of time.

The fall weather had turned the leaves all shades of gold, brown, and red, and the coolness of the air prevented the family from taking their meal outside on the patio as was his mother's preference when possible.

Angel was in the kitchen with Allison and his mother, and the men were in his father's den having drinks with a college football game on the television in the background. Cole was playing pool with Josh, giving Alex a chance to talk to his father.

"Have you gotten the engagement ring yet? Your mother is driving me nuts about it." Charles Avery, elegant as always, was in dress slacks and a cream, Irish wool sweater Cora had given him the previous Christmas. It was beautiful, but he found it itchy and had only worn it twice because of that. His fingers pulled at the collar, reaching in to scratch. Cora's rules made sure that everyone was dressed for dinner, and Alex, Cole, and Angel had showered and changed at the club after their workout.

Alex stared at the amber liquid in his glass, concentrating on how the glass and ice reflected the fire and turned the scotch a darker color. "No." He shook his head and met his father's eyes. "I think Mrs. Dane set it up for tomorrow."

Charles' eyebrows raised and the intense green eyes that mirrored his son's were intent. "Given our last conversation, I thought you'd have done so already."

"Tomorrow." Alex's attention was still honed in on his glass, and he took a swallow of the burning liquid and felt it all the way down. "I'm leaving for Sydney afterward, so I'll leave it in the safe at the office. I don't know when I'll ask her. Other shit is in the way right now. This trip, being one."

"Obviously, you're preoccupied. Do you want to postpone it? Is that what you're thinking?"

"No. I just want to wrap up this deal. After that, I might take Angel away for a while."

"Where are you thinking? Somewhere warm? Hawaii?"

"I'm thinking to Joplin. I still need to talk to her father, and we've never met face to face. I know Angel misses him." His lips twitched. "Honestly, it might be the only destination she'd consider taking off for. She's always got cases she's working on, and she's dedicated. I'm not even sure if there is a window, but I'll be working on that."

"How? You can't change the court dates."

"I'll call Kenneth Gant, the district attorney, to see what can be done. I don't expect he can move much, but maybe there is a small window. I'd talk to Angel about taking a break, but she's a workaholic, and if I'm going to propose, I want it to be a surprise."

"I think it will be, Alex. You haven't been together all that long. It will be unexpected from you, given your history."

"Yeah, well, that's the operative word. *History*."

"Hey, Dad," Cole called from the other end of the richly paneled room. It was masculine, all warm caramel leather and heavy wood. "I lost. Josh needs a worthy opponent."

When their father went to join his son-in-law, Cole deposited himself next to Alex and reached for his father's abandoned glass, refilling it with three fingers worth of the 18-year-old scotch.

"What do you want me to do?" Cole lowered his voice so only Alex could hear the question. "Besides stay next to her?"

Alex inhaled, his chest visibly rising as he shook his head grimly. "Kill the fucker."

"I know you're not serious, Alex. I meant what's the plan."

"I'm not so sure anymore, Cole. Just get her out of here. Take her on a trip to see her father. I'll leave the jet."

Cole leaned forward, his elbows resting on his knees and head raised to look at Alex. "You have to take the jet so you can get back more quickly."

Alex considered his options. Cole was probably right, though his instincts told him that access to the jet allowed Cole better security than a commercial jet, but he knew he'd go crazy if something happened and he wasn't able to leave immediately. He didn't need delays or airline schedules getting in his way.

Alex pulled out his phone. "I'll call Mrs. Dane and have her arrange the plane for very early morning. I'd like you to stay at the house tonight so you're there with her when I leave."

"So you're not going to try to convince Angel to go with you again, huh?"

"I know her well enough to know it would be a waste of time. Better to concentrate on getting the deal done and getting back as fast as I can."

Alex's face was full of tension. The last thing he wanted was to leave, but if he stayed, not only would the business suffer by losing a huge deal, but also, Angel would be scared. He had to keep everything under control. It couldn't appear he was rattled. Hiding it from Swanson was one thing, but keeping Angel in the dark was harder. Deep down in his gut, he didn't want to. It felt like a lie, but he didn't want her to worry any more than she already was. There was nothing worse than being consumed by worry, and he was consumed enough for both of them.

7

Sparkle and Pain

ALEX WISHED HE could just get on a plane and be done with the Sydney trip. The deal was too big to send someone in his place, or he wouldn't hesitate. It was a huge hotel chain in Australia, and it would be Avery's first real foothold there. He couldn't trust it to someone else, and he couldn't blow it off. He'd been working on it too long.

He'd tried to relax when they visited his parents, but desire to enjoy the day with Angel and watch her easy interaction with his family was clouded with his thoughts. He'd snuck away whenever he could to keep in touch with the police, Bancroft's own team, and to call Kenneth Gant. It felt strange to call Angel's ex-lover even though this wasn't the first time. It didn't get any easier.

So, it was late, and he was pensive, silent in the car on the drive back to his own estate with Angel at his side. He could feel her eyes on him, studying, and wondering if she should ask the questions he knew she wanted to ask. Angel watched the lights that periodically lined the interstates and side streets pass over his features, the tension clearly visible on his handsome face. She reached for his hand as it rested on his leg, her fingers entwining with his as she drew it toward her and up so she could run a soft kiss over his knuckles, then softly moved her lips back and forth over his skin until he glanced at her.

"What?"

"I was going to ask you the same thing," she murmured, her eyes locked on him as she placed another series of kisses. "Except, I already know."

Alex's mouth opened a bit as he drew in a ragged breath, nodding twice. "This isn't the best time for me to leave."

Angel smiled gently, finally resting their hands in her lap as she twisted slightly in her seat. She leaned her head back on the supple leather headrest of the expensive car. "It never is. I always miss you."

Her eyes were soft when he tore his eyes from the road for another look in her direction; this one more lingering. He squeezed her hand with his as his heart swelled within his chest then tightened. "Me, too." He shook his head in a series of short moves. "But, I think we both know, this time, it's not about missing you. I'll be crazy with worry. I wish you'd just come with me."

Angel looked out the front windshield and bit her lip. "You know the answer. I have to work."

"Fuck work."

"Okay, then you fuck work."

The fingers of Alex's left hand tightened around the steering wheel, and he pulled his right hand free of her grasp to join it. "If this was just about me, I would, but I have stockholders and my family to think about. I think you should just stop working on criminal cases."

"Right. I just tiptoe through the tulips and twirl," Angel spat sarcastically. "I have patients and victims to worry about. Plus, did you forget what I went through? How can you ask me to give that up? I thought you understood, Alex."

"What I understand is I don't want to lose you because of a job!" he growled. "You'd still have the radio show. I can syndicate it."

"Great. My boyfriend buys me a career." She huffed. "No thanks."

"That's not what I meant, Angel, but it's a hell of a lot safer! Those people who call the station might be silly sometimes, but they aren't stalking or threatening you!"

Angel ignored him, sitting in her seat seething. This wasn't how she wanted the evening to turn out. They'd had such a fun day, and she'd felt so strong when she'd taken him to the mat in the gym. But maybe he let her. She'd felt more resistance from those muscles in one of their lovemaking sessions.

"Fine. I don't want to get into it."

Angel shrugged, her feelings still stinging. "Then don't."

"Do we have to fight tonight?" Alex's tone was pissed, and his firm line of his jaw shot out.

"You know it's not just work for me. I'm in a position to really help people. And, I can't go anyway. I can't miss Bean's party."

"Kids are resilient. She'll get over it. That bastard is out there, Angel. You'd think you wouldn't want to put her in danger."

Angel gasped. She hadn't really considered she was putting Becca and Jillian at risk along with herself.

"Never thought of that, did you?"

"Even Mark Swanson has to have some compassion for a three-year old."

Alex shook his head solemnly. "You never know. I don't trust him to care about anything or anyone other than himself."

"I can't run from that fucker forever. At some point, it's got to be about real life. Doesn't it? I want us to be able to breathe and concentrate on each other."

By now, Alex had pulled through the iron gates of his property with Cole's SUV close behind. If there was anything Alex wanted, it was a normal life. The type of life that used to make him cringe; that included intimate dinners the two of them cooked together after work, a wedding, kids, family vacations, and in-laws.

Alex pulled the car into the garage and shut off the engine, turning to look at her as the doors closed behind them. "Nothing I want more, but that doesn't change the fact that until he's behind bars or—" He looked at her intensely.

"Don't say it." Angel tensed. She knew what Alex was thinking, and it was dangerous for him for him to consider.

"Well? It's the truth. I'm tired of this shit. And now—" He stopped before he mentioned Bancroft's disappearance.

"You're better than him."

"Maybe. But I'm protecting something that means everything to me." His green eyes were made darker by the dim light in the garage and emotion.

Angel's throat tightened, making it almost painful to speak. She reached out a hand to cup his cheek. "I know."

"Do you?"

"I do. I get it, baby."

His hand came up to cover hers, and he turned to kiss her palm. "Let's get inside. I'll draw you a bath while I pack."

Angel's eyes became liquid with unshed tears. "I'll help you pack."

Cole pulled into the fourth stall, at the edge of the garage, and climbed out just as Angel and Alex exited the Audi. He went behind them to check all the doors to the garage in an effort to make certain everything was secure. He could sense the tension that vibrated around the couple, and it was even clearer when they met at the front of the car.

Alex pulled Angel close to his side and placed a kiss on the top of her head, his eyes meeting Cole's in a desperate, yet silent, plea to keep her safe while he was away. Cole's solemn expression said he understood, and he gave a short nod.

Max had been left at their parents' property at Cole's request. If he had to watch over two women and a kid, he didn't need the dog to worry about as well.

Angel preceded Alex through the entrance that led from the garage into the laundry room off the kitchen. The two rooms were separated by a large door, which was built-in to look like part of the wall.

"Night, Cole," Angel said on her way out of the room and toward the stairs, hovering, waiting for Alex.

"Night, Angel. Do you need anything else from me tonight, Alex?" Cole asked. The dim light of the moon shone in from the hall, casting long shadows across the room.

Alex threw his keys on the marble countertop, slid the already loosened tie from his collar, and tossed it to join the keys. He shook his head and went to arm the security system. "We're good. I'm leaving straight from the office tomorrow, so I'd just like you up when I head out in the morning."

"Sure, no problem. What room should I take?"

"The one off the den tonight, then please move upstairs to the one next to mine tomorrow."

"Will do. Did we get that other thing resolved?" Cole's eyebrow shot up.

"Not yet. I'll call you, and you keep me informed about Bancroft's whereabouts."

"It doesn't look like it will be happy news in any case. It's been almost forty-eight—" Cole stopped when Alex held up his hand abruptly and threw a hard look in his direction. "Um, goodnight."

Alex rubbed the back of his neck and walked slowly toward the woman waiting at the foot of the stairs for him as Cole disappeared down the opposite hall and the other set of stairs. Alex was grateful he didn't have to tell her to wait or argue any further. Arguing with Angel wasn't how he wanted to spend the evening.

His arms enfolded her small frame at the same time as her arms wound around his broad shoulders. "Come on, you." He lifted her off the floor and pushed her against the wall of the stairwell, burying his face in the soft curtain of hair, to nuzzle softly at her neck and across her cheek. Alex was assaulted by the sweetness of her warm breath at the same time as the headiness of her perfume engulfed him. He inhaled deeply, just savoring her nearness.

When he pulled back to stare into her face, her beautiful eyes were languid and full of desire.

"Ugggg…" He groaned and dropped his forehead to lean on hers. "I have to pack."

Angel wanted to bring her knees up to pull Alex more fully into the saddle of her open legs, but the pencil skirt she was wearing impeded her progress. Still, her chin tilted and her mouth opened, silently begging him to kiss her. Her lower lip brushed his top one, and when the tip of her tongue peeked out to rub softly against it, Alex was beyond resisting.

He pushed her more fully into the wall, using both hands to pull her skirt up as his mouth took hers in a passionate kiss. Over and over, he ravaged her mouth with his, their tongues fighting in the same way their words did earlier. He pressed his hardness into her soft heat, and they both moaned and panted in want.

Alex wasn't gentle, but then, he didn't feel gentle. He was hungry and angry and worried sick. Angel was equally desperate to have him inside her, his hands on her flesh, his mouth taking what it wanted from hers.

Once he had her legs around his waist and Angel was pinned to the wall, held in place by the soft digging thrusts of his hips, Alex's fingers ripped at her blouse and white lace bra. He was always so turned on by her lingerie. There wasn't a time when he'd peeled her clothes away that he'd been disappointed. Always sexy, beautiful, alluring; he'd suffered many uncomfortable moments in his office or meetings just imagining or remembering images from the previous night.

Her buttons clattered on the hardwood floor at the foot of the stairs, and his hands made short work of the front closing of her bra. Something about this woman made him wild in so many ways. He wanted, and wanted, and fucking wanted, and she gave and gave. But still, it was never enough. Would it *ever* be enough?

Alex's forearms and hands flattened against the wall behind Angel, and though his hips continued their onslaught, he pulled his mouth away, dragging it down her jaw to kiss his way down the cord of her neck. Her soft pants drove him crazy, and the answering movements of her pelvis against his told him she wanted him as much as he wanted her. Still, he fought for control. His brother was in the house, and he already had her breasts bared and her skirt around her waist. A few more seconds and her matching lace panties would have been in tatters.

"This reminds me of that night in the station," he ground out.

"Alex, don't stop," Angel begged in a whisper. "Don't stop."

One strong arm curled around her waist and the other went beneath her bottom to lift her off the wall and against him. Alex turned and carried her up the stairs and into his room, which was commanded by the massive bed. He bypassed it and went into the master bathroom, to set her down on the long marble vanity between the double sinks. Her arms tightened around his shoulders. "Don't stop."

"Just for a while, baby. Once we get started, I won't want to stop until we're both exhausted, so I have to pack my goddamned suitcase. Let me run you a bath; I'll get that out of the way then we'll pick up where we left off."

He ran two fingers down her cheek, using one to lift her chin. He meant to leave her with a soft, open-mouthed kiss, but Angel demanded more. Her fingers slid into his hair at both sides of his head, and she kissed him hard, thrusting her tongue into his mouth and sucking on his, tugging on his hair at the same time. His erec-tion throbbed and demanded attention as Alex pulled her against him and kissed her back roughly, but slowing gradually to a gentle nipping and mutual sucking as his mouth ghosted around hers. "Uh... Babe, you're killing me. I have to stop. Now," he got out, between heavy breaths.

Finally, he moved away to light a candle and flip off the bright light. He turned the water on in the huge whirlpool bath. It was oval and crafted out of marble in a cream mosaic; the pattern subtle, but rich. Angel watched the fitted, fine linen shirt stretch over the hard muscles of his back, and her eyes wandered down to his perfect ass wrapped in black wool dress slacks. Everything Alex owned was well tailored and fit him perfectly. He was gorgeous—a shock of almost ebony hair falling over his forehead as he bent over the bath, the brilliant green eyes a striking contrast. He was perfect: strong, romantic, beautiful, confident... everything. She bit her lip, wanting him to turn around so she could see the tangible evidence of his desire. The heat between her legs was almost debilitating, manifesting in a deep throb. It was all she could do not to press the heel of her hand against the offending flesh.

Angel was rendered speechless, sitting on the marble, leaning back on her straight arms, watching Alex. Her blouse and bra hung open, her skirt pushed up around her thighs, which were still spread as Alex had left her. One of her high-heeled black pumps landed with a thump on the plush rug resting on a big expanse of black marble floor, causing him to glance over his shoulder as he adjusted the water temperature.

He grinned, catching full sight of her as he straightened, then added some of Angel's bath gel to the water. Instantly, the air was filled with the scent of her perfume, and Alex went to light another candle. Angel watched him, and their eyes never wavered as he started to slowly undress her.

"Get your sweet little ass in there. If you're a good girl, maybe I'll join you."

Angel's mouth lifted in a wry grin. "Humph! If you're a good boy, maybe I'll let you."

"It's one and the same, so it works." Alex chuckled. "Come on, sweets. I'm tired and I have to get packed." He lifted her gently down until her now bare feet touched the comfortably heated floor. His fingers lingered, gliding over her flesh, and his eyes closed as they leaned into each other. Alex kissed her temple, his warm breath preceding his mouth as it slid to her cheek and then a shoulder he'd just bared. It didn't take him long to have her skirt undone and pushed to the floor with her blouse, leaving Angel in the skimpy patches of expensive white lace.

"Fuck," he muttered.

"Okay," Angel answered, a smile curving her luscious mouth. "If you insist." Her hand went for the sizable bulge in the front of his boxers. His slacks were undone and hanging open from their play in the hallway, so she had easy access.

Alex's head fell forward as pleasure rippled through him. Instinct told him to lift her, rip away her panties, and give them both what they needed, but it might be a week before he saw her again, and he didn't want to rush. Reluctantly, his hands closed around her wrists, halting their movement as he kissed her mouth with unabashed hunger.

"Babe." Alex drew in a calming breath and put space between their bodies. Angel's head fell back, and she looked up into his face. He could see the love and the longing in her eyes. The candlelight cast a golden glow across her skin and turned the lace to a soft peach. "I'll be back. I promise. This will be the fastest packing job in the history of time."

Angel sighed when Alex disappeared through the door of the bathroom and removed her bra and thong. She stood, totally nude and grabbed some bobby pins to put her hair in a massive mess of rumpled curls atop her head, her full breasts lifting. She was disappointed he was able to leave her when she wanted him so much, but he had business to attend to, and if anything, Angel would be the last one to interfere with his work.

The mirror gave Alex a good view from the front, and he could clearly appreciate the womanly curves of her hips and ass, the gentle lines of her waist and back. She was like a porcelain statue but alive, and the candle cast a golden glow to her smooth skin.

"You're so beautiful."

Angel's eyes widened as they met Alex's burning gaze in the mirror. He was peaking around the doorframe, watching her, his look like a physical caress that burned her skin.

"No fair. Go."

His eyes wandered slowly over her breasts in the mirror taking in their firm, round shape, the nipples—erect and telling, then over the fine curve of her back and gentle slope of her butt and supple thighs. "I can't help it. I could look at you forever."

Angel's eyes softened, and she wanted to go to him. "If you want to pack, you need to do it, Alex." Her voice was soft, not trying to be seductive, but it was, nevertheless. "I want those hands on me."

His lips lifted in a soft smile, but he left without another word.

*****

While Angel was in the bath, Alex meticulously packed five of his designer suits, five crisp dress shirts, matching ties, pocket squares, along with two pair of Italian leather dress shoes, his leather dopp kit, socks, boxers, Nikes, shorts, and T-shirts in two pieces of the Louis Vuitton luggage set Allison had given him after graduation from graduate school. He wished he didn't need to use it quite so much.

There were two messages on his cell phone: one from Mrs. Dane, and one from Sid Walters. Alex sat down on the edge of his bed and listened to both of them.

Hello, Mr. Avery. I have looked into flights. Most of them don't leave until Monday evening and, due to time change and date lines, won't get you to Sydney until Wednesday morning. It's quite cost-prohibitive, as well. I almost fell over at the price. It's almost $13,000 for round trip, business class. I was positive that wouldn't be acceptable to you, so I've taken the liberty to arrange the company jet. It will cost less overall, and you'll have it at your disposal. The pilots will be ready to leave at 7 AM and I will have a car pick you up at six. Have a good trip, sir.

Leave it to Mrs. Dane. Alex could always count on her efficiency and sharp decision-making ability. The money was relative when working on a deal this size, however, he felt easier having the plane on call. The next message was from Sid, another of the men hired to protect Angel, and who helped intercede the night of Angel's flat tire. His voice was devoid of emotion, and his message was long.

No news, Mr. Avery. We haven't found anything, and the car holds little clues, but has been impounded by Chicago PD, and their forensics team is working on it. Other than residue from the gasoline used to torch it, the chemists haven't found anything. Most likely, that will be a dead end, too. Wayne and I believe they've killed Mr. Bancroft, despite no blood evidence at the scene. We've been partners for 30 years, and we've worked on similar cases. If we don't find a missing person in forty-eight hours, it's probably a homicide. It doesn't bode well that neither his family or Avery Enterprises has been contacted for a ransom, which means it's probably not a kidnapping. I don't hold out much hope we'll find him alive. Cole will be on duty with one of the others to watch Dr. Hemming, and we, as well as the police, have been in touch with Jason's wife. Cole advised us you are going out of town. Rest assured, at least two of us will be with Dr. Hemming around the clock.

Alex sighed heavily as he set the alarm on his phone and laid it on the dark mahogany nightstand next to his bed. He shook his head and ran his hand wearily through his dark hair. Dread and acceptance slowly crept over him, making the hair on his arms, legs, and the back of his neck stand up eerily. His mind went to work devising a way to get Angel to lay low. She wouldn't go with him, but maybe there was another way.

Angel padded out of the bathroom wrapped in an oversized white towel. It was plush and soft and a contrast against her skin, now flushed pink by the hot bath. Her hair was still up, but wet tendrils clung to the sides of her face and back of her neck.

The room was cast in low light, lit only by the lamp sitting next to the bed and another by the chaise in the corner where his two suitcases sat, but Alex could see it reflecting off water droplets still clinging to her bare arms and shoulders. His heart was gripped with fear after Sid's call, but he quickly masked his trepidation so as not to upset Angel and ruin this night with her. She came to stand in front of him, and his hands reached out, running down both of her arms.

"I was waiting in there, but I had to get out. I'm all prune-y." One of her hands rose, and she pushed her fingers into Alex's hair, sending shivers through him. He closed his eyes.

"Mmmm. I'm sorry. I had some work. That feels great."

"I figured," she answered softly, still threading her fingers through his short, but thick, hair over and over again. "It's okay. I know you're tired. How early is your plane?"

"Mrs. Dane arranged for me to me leave at 7 AM, but I have something to do at the office first. I'll call the pilot in the morning and back him up a few hours."

Alex's hands wrapped around both of Angel's hips, he pulled her closer—in between his knees, and the scent of the perfume that laced the bath water assaulted his senses. He longed to touch her bare skin, though his fingers massaged her lower back through the damp towel.

"Private plane, hmm?"

"Apparently, Mrs. Dane didn't like the rates of commercial flights. It was really nuts."

"More than the company jet?"

"Maybe not, but close. This way is better anyway. I can get back much more quickly if I have to."

"I'm not sure how." Angel leaned down and kissed the side of his mouth. Alex's hands slid up her back, bringing her breasts closer as his hands pulled the towel free and let it drop. She gasped softly when he bent to take a nipple into his mouth. "It's a fifteen hour flight."

"Mmmm," he answered, but his tongue and lips played with her nipple with a series of flicks, sucking, and soft nips with his teeth. Angel moaned, and it only excited him more. His cock swelled and thickened, the head now visible above the low waistline of his boxer briefs; his slacks still open from their play in the hallway, and had removed his shoes and socks. He dragged his mouth up her chest to kiss and suckle at the base of her neck. "Counting the hours already? I know you've never been to Australia, so…" Alex teased, his voice filled with sex.

Angel's arms tightened around Alex's shoulders, and she kissed wherever she could reach: his shoulder, the side of his face, and finally, his mouth. Alex sat up straighter, sucking in his breath at the same time his hands come up to hold both sides of Angel's head so his mouth could latch on to hers.

The kiss became wild and intense as Alex angled her mouth so his tongue could plunder deep inside the recesses of hers. She tasted amazing, and he was hungry. Desire pounded between them like a pulse; his actions commanded the same intense response from Angel. Her body quickened and opened, heat pooling, in anticipation of the delicious pleasure to come. It was like liquid fire between them, as if they were connected by it, flowing and ardent.

Angel climbed onto Alex's lap, her knees finding purchase on the bed's edge on either side of his legs. She pushed him back to fall upon the bed and followed him down, never breaking the kiss. His hands roamed her naked body, and she ground her hips into his, moaning as his full erection rubbed against her sensitive and fevered flesh.

Alex took control, rolling over, and soon, Angel was the one on her back with Alex between her thighs. It was more than clear they were feeling carnal, but Alex had a point to prove. He rose up on his knees and caged Angel in with his arms, pulling his mouth from hers. Her breath was coming in shallow pants, and it pained him what he was about to do. He looked down at her while her hips rose toward his, now obviously distanced, and her fingers pulled at his back and shoulders until finally, sensing his resistance, Angel opened her eyes.

Alex stared into her eyes. "Today at the gym, you were good. Strong."

Angel sighed, her brow knitting, perplexed that he would stop their lovemaking to discuss the time at the gym. "But you let me win?"

He shrugged a little. "Let's just say, I wasn't as strong as I could have been. You did great, though. Swanson is no match for me, so you'd probably be okay, if you were on your feet. But this is the position you need to get out of." She frowned harder, anger welling inside her chest. "So get out of it, Angel," he said evenly.

"You're ruining this to fight with me?"

"I don't want to fight, and I want to pick up where we left off in a minute. I just have to know you can take care of yourself in the most vulnerable of positions."

"Way to douse a fire, Alex. You're such a dick." She pulled back both arms and shoved him hard in the shoulders. It jolted him, but he was quick to come right back. She hit him again harder, her eyes beginning to burn. She felt the force of her blow ricochet through her wrists and down her arms, and still Alex was unmoved. Why in the fuck was he ruining their night? It started out so spectacular.

"See how vulnerable you are?" His hips settled back into the cradle of her hips. "Now it's worse." His hands grabbed her wrists and hoisted them above her head. "Now you are helpless. Remember how that asshole had you face down before? You couldn't defend yourself like that, but it can happen this way, too."

Angel turned her face away from him and went limp, tears falling softly from her eyes. He made her painfully aware she couldn't defend herself like this. She was pissed at him for pointing that out, and for reminding her of Swanson, when all she wanted was to make love to him all night. She wasn't sobbing, she was too strong to do that, but she felt like her heart was breaking. "You asshole," she cried harshly.

"Honey," Alex began, remorse filling him. "I'm leaving and I just have to know you can fight in all positions."

Angel was still reluctant to turn her face to his.

"Look at me," he commanded. He rose up on his knees again, releasing her hands. "Now—" he began, but as soon as she had space to move, Angel's feet took purchase against his hips, and she pushed with all her might, able to straighten her legs and hoist him completely off of her body. Part of her wanted to punch him in his face, but instead, she twisted and pushed again until she was completely free of his body weight as he stumbled away from the bed.

"Satisfied?" she yelled, scrambling naked off the bed and storming into the bathroom, shutting the door with a resounding slam.

Angel had removed him with enough force to almost knock him on his ass. Good thing he recovered or he would have crashed ass first into the big dresser on the opposite wall. Maybe his methods weren't the best, but the result was what he wanted. Now, they could both be certain Angel had the skills to displace Mark Swanson if he got her on her back. He sighed as relief washed through him. He could go to Sydney with a little less anxiety with that knowledge.

It didn't solve the immediate problem of her anger, however. As soon as he straightened, he went to the closed door of the en suite bathroom and leaned against the frame. "Angel."

When she didn't answer, he continued, "Babe, I'm sorry. I just needed to be sure you could protect yourself. How you fought at the gym was impressive, but I needed to know you could defend yourself if taken by surprise. I only did it because I love you." She still didn't answer, and he waited a full thirty seconds before he added, "I love you. I can barely leave as it is."

The door opened abruptly, and Angel, now wrapped in a new towel, glared up at him with red, swollen eyes. She was scared. More scared than she wanted Alex to know, and she'd just wanted to get lost in Alex's arms. One more perfect night left together because a week apart would feel like a year.

He reached out and pushed her hair back gently then brushed the knuckles of that same hand against her cheek, not moving out of her way.

Angel's eyes fell and she nodded. "You should go to sleep. It's a long day tomorrow."

His arms slid around her, and he tugged her gently into the room. Angel was forced to put her arms on his to steady her balance. "I wouldn't be sleeping right now if we hadn't stopped. We'd be making love all night. That doesn't have to change." He bent his head and brushed his mouth against hers. "Kiss me."

"You'll be so tired," she said softly, still a little resistant and hurt, but didn't pull her mouth away or stop him when he opened her robe.

"I have fifteen hours to sleep on the plane, if I want to. Kiss me," Alex insisted in a guttural whisper.

He pulled her tight against his body, his mouth returned for another kiss, this time more demanding, and it wasn't long until they were both breathless. Alex's warm hands roamed Angel's curves before turning her and laying her down on the bed.

She marveled at his strength and her own lack of resistance. He handled her with ease, his movements so smooth she barely registered how she ended up on the bed, or how the covers pulled back. She sighed, watching him stand to shed the rest of his clothes. His body was magnificent and she was aroused just looking at him. The pleasure he was capable of giving her was only multiplied by her love for him.

Her arms and legs wrapped around him when he came back to her after turning out the lights. The candle still burned in the dark bathroom and cast a romantic glow over the two entwined in the bed.

Hands roamed and teased anxious flesh; kiss after passionate kiss communicated their desperateness at the pending separation. When Alex moved lower, kissing across Angel's shoulder, down her chest, and over her breasts, his fingers played and teased her until she was writhing beneath him. He tried to move lower, intent on pleasuring her with his mouth, but she held onto him.

"Alex." His name was like a moan that tore from deep inside her, making his dick ache and swell, becoming even more impatient. "I want you. Inside."

"There's time," His voice was muffled as he continued to worship her skin. "Let me take care of you."

"You will," she breathed. "Just, please." She needed his mouth on hers, to feel his heartbeat against hers as his body claimed hers. The need to be close was stronger than the sexual desire, which, with this man, was unimaginable. "Please. I want to hold you. I'll miss you."

Alex raised his head and looked into her dark, liquid eyes. He could see her want, but also fear. He didn't hesitate to move up into the cradle of her body, leaning forward to torture her lips with teasing licks and nibbles. He held himself at the base of his cock and found her slippery entrance. She was so hot he thought her tight flesh might burn his. It was utter heaven when he pushed inside.

She arched her back to take him in, at the same time reaching up for his hungry kiss. Kiss after passionate kiss, his mouth never left hers while their bodies pushed and pulled against each other. Each time he filled her was better than the last, and she clenched her muscles tight every time. Alex moaned. "Oh, Angel. Fuck, it's so good," he ground out before taking her mouth in another penetrating kiss, their tongues fought lasciviously, the kisses ardent and all consuming.

Her fingers in his hair pulled his mouth tighter against hers, and he dug deeper and harder into her body, but with slow, measured precision. She could barely take it, it felt so good, but fought the orgasm building inside her. She never wanted it to end.

But, as each endless second passed, it was more impossible for both of them to resist. Alex gritted his teeth to hold back as long as he possibly could, but when he felt Angel lose her battle and moan into his mouth, he gave in, falling over the abyss of ecstasy with her.

8
Departure

THE NEXT MORNING Alex was anxious and apprehensive. His bags were packed, and Cole was awake and sitting in his kitchen with a strong cup of black coffee in front of him. He'd been on the phone with the Chicago police and other members of Alex's private security team since 6 AM, but still no signs of Bancroft. Not one new clue. It was unnerving. At least if Swanson made a new threat or something happened, they'd know what to do next.

The case wasn't broadcast on the local television stations because, to do so, would mean giving the criminal information about the investigation. Only the car, found torched and empty, hit the news. It might seem like a dead end to most of the officials and agencies involved, but the lack of evidence didn't mean a damn thing. Alex, Cole, and most of the officials involved were convinced who was responsible. Kenneth Gant had no doubt, either, and because his office was prosecuting Mark Swanson, he had to be kept abreast of every new development.

"Are you ready to go?" Cole asked, observing his brother shrug into his expensive charcoal suit jacket. To an outside observer, Alex looked perfect. No sign of the turmoil he was dealing with inside his head. Cole admired Alex's strength. The more he got to know the professional side of his brother, the more he admired the dedication to the family that required he toss over his own dream to do what was best for everyone. And, the obvious love he had for Angel showed just another complex layer. At one time, Cole would have found Alex's steadfast perfection annoying, but now, it was something he himself aspired to. "I figured you'd dress more casually for this trip. Won't it be at least a day and a half before you get to Australia?"

"I have business first, but yes, you're correct. We cross the international date line so I'm already behind by a day," he answered absently. He was clearly preoccupied as he reached for his own cup of coffee setting on the edge of the marble island. He took a drink and grimaced. It was cold. "With downtime in Los Angeles to re-fuel included, it will be close to eighteen hours. Ideally, I should have left yesterday."

"The business this morning must be important." Alex glanced up as he smoothed down the collar of the fine light wool of the jacket.

"Yes, it is." Alex frowned, but his voice was soft.

"That's a long way. Too bad you can't just Skype with the owners of the property."

It wasn't as if it hadn't occurred to Alex. He'd turned it over and over in his head to find a way out of going. "This guy is old school. The handshake means more than the actual contract. Believe me, if I could skip it, I would."

"So…" Cole began.

"Just keep her out of trouble and don't leave her side. I'm trusting you, Cole."

Two pairs of serious green eyes met. "I know."

"If you need to sleep, make sure two of the others are here to relieve you. But please, stay with her the entire time. I mean it; don't leave her side. Not for a minute."

"Alex, I got it. You don't need to keep hammering me about it."

Alex swallowed. It was true. He was belaboring the obvious. "Okay." Angel was still sleeping, but he'd need to go say goodbye.

"I'm surprised you aren't already halfway to L.A. by now."

Alex pulled at the cuffs of his shirtsleeves to straighten them from under his jacket. "Yeah, I should go. But I just want to let Angel know I'm leaving." His hand smoothed down his silk tie, in patterns of dark mauve, smoke grey and black, as he turned to leave the kitchen. His shiny Italian leather briefcase waited on the hallway table as he whisked past it and up the stairs toward the bedroom. His mood was somber, the coming trip and business dealings held none of their usual excitement. His heart was heavy, and it showed on his face.

Angel was still sleeping soundly, and Alex wasn't surprised. They made love until almost dawn, both of them feeling desperate and sad, though he was getting used to his displeasure at leaving her. That was normal, but now he was also feeling a heightened sense of fear. The timing for this trip couldn't be worse.

Alex lifted the blinds a few inches and soft light filtered in, rays falling across the bed. The sheet and blankets were wrapped around her, but her womanly form was still visible beneath as they hugged her curves like a cocoon. She was lying on her side, facing him as he sat gently down next to her, her lush lashes creating dark crescents on her cheeks; her mahogany hair a wild mess on the pillow around her head. He couldn't help but touch her.

"Babe?" Alex's voice coaxed her lashes to flutter then lift, as his hand rubbed down her arm to her back in a gently kneading caress through the covers. Her warmth seeped through and into his fingers. "Honey, it's time for me to go," he almost whispered. He bent to place a soft kiss on the corner of her mouth. "Don't wake up. I didn't want to leave without saying goodbye. Cole is here, but I have to go in a few minutes."

Angel's sleepy eyes rose to meet Alex's, and she got that little crinkle between her brows he loved. At the same time, her mouth dropped into a small pout.

Angel moved closer, curling her body around his sitting form, one arm curving around his back. She lifted her head to rest it on his thigh, looking up into his face. He was beautiful and strong, perfectly groomed, his hair combed and held in place with a small amount of gel.

She was cuddling up like a small child, but she was ruffled; the hours of making love leaving an indelible stamp on her. Alex's heart tightened. He was in awe of how stunning she was, even in this unobtrusive state, and still shocked at the protective instinct that filled him so full he thought he'd explode with the force of it. His chest felt tight and full at the same time. He loved her beyond words.

Alex struggled with leaving, but he knew the sooner he did, the sooner he'd get back to her. "Yes. Go back to sleep, sweetheart."

"What time it is?"

"7:45."

"You're late for Mrs. Dane's schedule. My first appointment is at nine, I think." She rolled onto her back and stretched.

"You don't know for sure? That isn't like you."

"I guess I'm a little preoccupied, Alex."

He nodded, running his hand through the long, silky strands of her hair. "I know you like to be so strong, but it's understandable to be scared. I hesitate to even talk about this because I don't want to make it worse, but I promised no more secrets between us."

Her soft eyes sharpened, and she sat up enough to prop up with one bent arm. "What? Did they find Jason?"

Alex shook his head as his hand threaded into one side of her hair, pushing it away from her face gently. "No, but that's just the problem. It's been more than two days, and I'm sure we can expect something from Swanson or to find Bancroft very soon."

Angel sat up all the way, her hip still touching his thigh, and pressed both hands to her forehead. When her dark eyes met his, they were full of tears. "Find him? Dead?"

"Either that, or that prick wants money. He's desperate."

"Killing Jason won't make you pay." Her eyes were liquid with unshed tears.

"No." Fear gripped Alex's heart at the implications of what they both knew; Bancroft was just to show Alex he was serious, and Angel was the real target to drop Alex to his knees. "He doesn't get a reward for hurting people, but he's trying to get my attention." Alex's usual bravado was shaken, and Angel could see it. "And, he has it."

"Don't let him shake you, Alex. That's what sick bastards like him live for." She tried to make her expression wry, but Alex could see the fear in her eyes.

"I know. Just keep Cole and the others close." He took her in his arms and pulled her close. "Don't go out at night. Follow their instructions exactly."

"Jillian's birthday party is Friday night at Becca's parents'. Jillian will be heartbroken if I don't go."

"I know. Cole will have several guys on the perimeter of the house and on both ends of the street." When Angel started to protest, Alex stopped her, his voice low and insistent. "You can't talk me out of it. Not now."

Angel didn't want to. Her presence was putting everyone in danger, and she decided maybe she should try to get out of it and make it up to Jillian another way. She rolled her teary eyes at Alex, trying to lighten the mood. "Not ever. I love that caveman part of you. Surprising, I know."

She was rewarded with a sad smile from him.

"See? You're learning." He used a bent index finger to nudge her chin.

"I'm trying," she said, her voice betraying the sadness she didn't want to expose. She didn't want him to go. The way he was lingering by her side, and the loving caresses were telling—Alex was also hesitant.

"And I'm just trying to keep you safe."

"I know. Maybe I shouldn't go, but how do you explain it to a three-year-old? I've turned it over in my head ten times, and every scenario ends up with Jillian crying her eyes out. She won't understand if her Auntie Angel isn't at her party."

"I know. You two might as well be joined at the hip. But, safety comes first. If anything happens—" He stopped for a few seconds to stare into her eyes. "*Anything*, Angel. You stay in familiar surroundings where the guys are better prepared to protect you. Promise me."

"Okay," Angel sighed. Normally, she would have been annoyed at being told what to do, but Alex was just being protective. It made her all warm and fuzzy with love swelling up inside until it had nowhere to go but out. "I promise."

Her hand curled around the back of his neck, tugging his head toward her, and when his forehead touched hers, their breaths mingled. Angel closed her eyes, inhaling the delicious scent of his skin and cologne. She sighed. "You have to go."

He nodded against her, his mouth reaching and taking hers in a soft series of kisses. "I do," he whispered against her mouth. "But, I don't want to." His voice was muffled by a low groan, his reluctance tangible.

She breathed deeply, enjoying the way his mouth was ghosting over hers, followed by soft sucking kisses. She pushed down the sadness welling up inside her and tried to enjoy his kisses and the way they were always so perfect together. Weakness was unlike her, and she didn't want Alex to know how fragile she was feeling.

"I don't want you to, either. Screw billion dollar deals," she said, the amusement curving her lips mid-kiss was forced, but she wanted to put Alex at ease about leaving town.

Alex sensed her desperation by the way the fingers of one hand clutched at the hair at his nape and the other pulled on his shoulder. He pulled back and reached for both her hands with his, holding them between their bodies as his intent green eyes searched hers. He knew his expression showed his anxiousness, his brow furrowed with worry. "I'll get back as quickly as I can."

Angel nodded. "I'll be fine."

Alex raised her hands and kissed the inside of one wrist then the other before meeting her eyes again. "You *will*." His low words were like a hopeful command to the universe.

The truth was, he was terrified of leaving. He felt sick inside, and it was unsettling. If it were up to him, he'd flush the whole goddamned deal and be done with it, but the board of directors would probably fire him in that case. "I'd say fuck it if I could. Even though my father started the business, we're publicly traded now, so I'm still accountable to the board." The corner of his mouth lifted slightly. If he was going to ask this woman to be his wife, he'd be damned if he'd be unemployed, no matter his savings account.

"Even the great Alexander Avery has to kiss ass sometimes, eh?" Angel's fingers traced his jaw, her face serious.

"Want me to kiss yours?"

Angel had to laugh. "Now, there's an offer I can't refuse!"

Alex smiled, his breath rushing over her face one final time. "I'll call you from the air." He kissed her once more soundly on the mouth then got up and buttoned the one button on his sleek suit jacket.

"You look hot. Don't bring back any Sheilas!" she teased.

Alex took a step forward, cupping the side of Angel's face with his hand. "I love you." And before she could repeat his words, he was gone.

*****

When Alex walked onto the floor that housed his office, Mrs. Dane looked up from her desk, which stood in the large room lined in glass windows. The solid door between his private suite containing his luxurious office and her space was closed. This fact wasn't unusual, but she stopped him as he passed with a raised hand.

"Sir, Samuel Fackler is waiting in your office. From Exquisite Jewelers?" It was a question, since she thought he ought to remember an appointment he requested in the first place.

"I thought he wasn't coming until nine." His expression hardened, the tension he was feeling on a personal level making him more stern than usual. "You know no one goes into my office when I'm not in it." Alex's sour mood made his patience short.

"I took the liberty of calling to request he arrive early because I knew you'd want to go to the airport as soon as possible. And, if I may be so bold, Mr. Avery, he *is* toting a couple million dollars' worth of diamonds. I assumed it would be acceptable in this case."

Alex was duly chastised and cleared his throat. "Only two million?"

"I didn't ask."

"Well done, as usual, Mrs. Dane. Thank you."

"Good luck, sir." Her rosy cheeks plumped when she smiled wryly. She knew her young boss well and usually enjoyed the rare occasion she could get the better of him, though today, she sensed his unease.

"Hold my calls," Alex paused, making a half turn back to her. "Unless it's Cole, Ken Gant, or the police."

The older woman's eyebrows lifted in surprise, though she knew better than to verbalize her questions, so all she said was, "The police?"

"Yes. That's correct."

After Alex walked through the door, the man seated at the conference table on the far end of the room stood and smoothed down the front of his jacket. The younger man had a commanding presence that demanded respect. "Good morning, Mr. Avery. It's nice to finally meet you."

This wasn't the first time Alex had purchased from the man's store, but it was the first time he'd done so himself. Alex proffered his hand to shake the other man's firmly. The elder gentleman's advanced age and professionalism suggested he was indeed the shop owner here to work with him directly.

"Good to meet you. And, please, call me Alex. I see you're set up already. Thank you."

There were two black leather briefcases, one deeper than the other, and six fine, wooden trays fully lined in suede that were already laid out on the surface of the table. The morning sun shone in from all directions, and the rings radiated gloriously, spraying spectrums of color in all directions. Next to them was a black box full of what looked like clear plastic envelopes the size of a recipe card.

"Oh, my pleasure, Alex. I have a beautiful selection of flawless stones, and beautiful settings for you to choose from. Your secretary explained your requirements for size and quality for the gems over the phone, but was vaguer on setting style, so I brought many different types."

"Something simple and stunning. Angel wouldn't want anything ostentatious. She wouldn't want anything gaudy or screaming money."

Alex indicated that Sam should take his seat and Alex took his at the head of the long table. It was a long rectangle with curved sides and had two-dozen burgundy, plush leather armchairs around it.

"But… your assistant said you wanted something very expensive. She said, '*even for you.*'" Mr. Fackler stopped what he was doing, looking for acceptance of what he was laying out before continuing.

Alex smiled wryly, releasing the button on his suit jacket as he sat down. "What I want and what I get may be two different things in this case."

The older man frowned. "I don't understand. Most young ladies would adore a large diamond."

"Angel isn't like other women." He grinned again. "That said, I want the ring to be beautiful and unique, like the woman receiving it. But, I want anyone in contact with her left in no doubt that she is off the market."

The old man smiled at the younger one's conviction. It was obvious he was in love and not just going through the motions because he'd been given an ultimatum. "I see. Shall we start with the diamond then move on to the setting? Depending on the gem you chose, it may narrow the setting choices."

An hour and a half later, Alex had settled on a 2.2 carat round diamond and a simple setting that would not detract from the stunning gem. He was pleasantly surprised by the price tag of only $140,000.

"Is that all? I was prepared to spend ten times that."

The older man smiled. "We can do that, Alex, but the young lady will need to accept a much larger diamond. The quality is already top of the line, so size is the only way to increase value."

Alex grinned. "I'll be lucky if she accepts this one. She's up to her armpits in philanthropy, like my sister, and will already see this as excessive."

"Well, in any case, it's going to be magnificent. I'd be shocked if any woman would refuse a ring like this."

"When will it be ready? I'm leaving town, but I'd like to have it right away when I return."

"I could have it done this afternoon, if needed."

"Not necessary. A week should be fine. I'll have my best friend, Darian Keith, pick it up if I'm not in town." Alex was pleased with his choice; confident that though it was probably larger than Angel would want, he trusted the simple setting would suit her elegant style. "I really appreciate that you came by."

After the jeweler left, Alex tied up some loose ends with Mrs. Dane, signed some contracts, checks, and purchase orders that would be due the coming week, leaving a detailed schedule with her, and made a brief call to his father, telling him he was on his way out.

Sitting in the back of the company limousine on the way to the airport, he dialed Darian.

"Hi, man. I thought you fell off the face of the earth!" Darian's pleasant voice came over his phone.

"Yeah, sorry. I've been busy. I'm on the way out of town. Cole will be with Angel at the station and everywhere else. I'd really rather she cancel this Friday's show."

"What's going on?"

"That fucker who attacked her is out on bail, and one of my security guys disappeared. His car was found incinerated."

"Holy shit. Really? Was he killed?"

"We don't know yet. He was abducted, but there hasn't been a ransom demand."

"I see why you'd be concerned."

"She won't want to take the week off, and as much as I'd like to ask you to make some excuse to change the programing, I promised to be upfront with her about everything."

Darian paused. "She'd see right through anything I'd come up with anyway. But reporting in must be cramping your style." Darian was more than aware of his best friend's need for control.

Alex's elbow rested on the window, his thumb and forefinger slowly tugging at his lip as he looked out the window. "Yes and no. This whole situation really has Angel rattled. She's scared, even though she tries to hide it from me."

"Yes, I saw part of that when the two of you were on the outs."

"There was more to it, but that was different. I love her strength, and the way we tease each other is sexier than hell, but I have to admit, that little part of her that needs me, sort of rocks my world."

"Jesus. You've turned into a sap!" his best friend teased.

Alex's expression was sober despite the humor in Darian's voice. Another call came in, forcing him to pause with Darian. "Could be." He pulled the phone away and looked to see who it was. "Hey, Darian, I have to go. Can you pick something up for me on Friday?"

"Sure. Where?"

"Exquisite Jewelers."

"Wouldn't be a ring, would it?"

"Yes."

"Holy fuck," Darian's voice was incredulous. "I mean, I'm surprised and I'm not surprised. When?"

"After 6 PM next Monday. Keep it in your safe, and keep your mouth shut with Angel, please."

"Dude, you wound me," Darian said in mock consternation.

"Gotta run." He pushed the button to take him to the new call from Cole. "Hello?"

The limousine pulled up to the gated yard for the Field Base Operation on the west side of O'Hare. The plane would be waiting for Alex's arrival; the pilots would have retrieved the plane from its domicile at Chicago's other airport, Midway, earlier that morning. Midway was a good distance from any of the Avery residences, and it was standard for the plane to be brought to O'Hare for passenger pick-up.

"Angel is at her office, in a session with her first client. It's quiet. I just wanted to give you a call before you left."

"Any word on Bancroft?"

"No. I really thought Swanson would have made another move by now."

"I did, too."

"I feel responsible. I shouldn't have taken the night off on Friday."

"They would have just taken you instead, Cole. I feel pretty shitty myself, but I'm glad it wasn't you. Every time my phone rings, I expect bad news. Makes me sick."

The car parked directly next to the sleek, white Gulfstream jet waiting on the tarmac. The driver unloaded Alex's suitcase and garment bag from the trunk before opening his door and waiting as he got out. Alex shoved his Tom Ford sunglasses on as he moved from the car and into the plane, still talking to his brother.

Cole sighed heavily. "Yeah, it's coming, I guess."

Alex nodded, taking his seat in the fine, ivory leather seats. The twelve-passenger plane was luxurious and laid out for working and sleeping when needed.

Alex set his briefcase on the seat opposite his. "Yes. On the off chance Angel has a lag in her client load, I don't want her taking on any new clients without a thorough background check." He stopped, rethinking. "Scratch that. No new ones. None."

"I'll mention it to her. If she cuts me off at the balls, I'm blaming you."

"Yes, mine are safer. She needs them." Alex smiled when Cole chuckled at his brother's joke. "Sorry, I should have told her, but I've had a lot going on. Tell her I'll call her. If anything happens, no matter how slight, let me know." Alex removed his laptop from his briefcase and fired it up. He had one more call to make before his plane took off.

"Will do. See ya."

"Bye."

Alex typed out a name into Google, not really expecting to find a direct contact. The main business number showed up on Wikipedia. He shrugged out of his suit jacket and laid it, neatly folded, next to his briefcase, and picked up his phone again.

"Mr. Avery, the flight plans are filed, and we will be taking off as soon as we get clearance," the co-pilot leaned into the passenger compartment after the outer door was closed and secured.

Alex looked up from his phone just long enough to nod as he dialed. "Good. The sooner, the better," he said just as the ringing on the line was answered.

"Standish Capital Ventures," a professional female voice said upon answering.

"Good morning. Marvin Standish, please."

"May I tell Mr. Standish who is calling, sir?"

"Alexander Avery, CFO of Avery Enterprises."

"One moment, please. I'll see if he's free."

Some generic music filtered through the phone as the plane began to make its way onto the taxiway. Alex pulled the window shade down so he could remove his sunglasses. Taking off in planes was becoming so tedious he tuned it out completely. His hand raked down his face and over his jaw before yanking on his tie to loosen it. He was tired and feeling drained, if he was honest. It would be nice to sleep on the plane, but it was unlikely.

The call went to voicemail, another female voice delivering the message.

You've reached the office of Marvin Standish. Mr. Standish is unavailable at the moment. Please leave your name and a detailed message, and he will return your call. Thank you, and have a nice day.

"Mr. Standish, my name is Alexander Avery. I'm not sure if you are familiar with me, but my family operates Avery Enterprises, which is headquartered in Chicago. I have a matter of utmost importance to discuss with you and would like to set up a meeting. I'm traveling now but should be back by the 17th. Please call my assistant, Martha Dane, to let her know when you are available. She has instructions to clear my schedule for your convenience. I look forward to meeting you." He left his office number then hung up.

He hoped he didn't need the meeting—that Bancroft would be found by then, and he hoped, above all, what Cole and Bancroft had said about the Standish family kissing off Mark Swanson was true. Standish's sister was divorcing Swanson, and it was his niece who had been raped, so hopefully, there would be no love lost between them, and he wouldn't be squeamish about helping Alex locate Swanson. The Standish family wasn't known for being squeamish, and it was testament to how desperate Alex was feeling that he would engage them in any way.

Alex sighed deeply, stress weighing on him heavily. He couldn't believe he was trying to set up a meeting with one of the biggest mafia bosses in Chicago, but taking it up the ass never was his forte, and the helplessness he felt at waiting didn't sit well. He'd be damned if he'd let Swanson keep control. He'd rather take the offensive and handle the situation as quickly as possible. If he had to work with less than honest people and bend the law himself, so be it.

He shut his phone down when the pilot's voice came over the speaker telling him they were cleared for takeoff. His eyes closed as the plane lifted from the ground, praying his exhaustion would allow a few hours sleep. The small jet was fairly sound proof and was stocked with cold bottled water, sodas and an assortment of small

liquor bottles and snacks, and the seats were luxuriously comfortable. The only thing missing was Angel. Fear gripped his chest.

Maybe if she were with me, I could fucking breathe.

9

Cat and Mouse

ALEX WAS IN Sydney. He'd called Angel four times a day, like clockwork, on the two days since he left. He was hoping to wrap it up and be on his way home by Saturday morning, though that was almost Friday in Chicago.

The big house was lonely without Max, even though Cole, Sid, and Wayne were there most of the time.

It must cost Alex a fortune, Angel thought.

Waiting for Swanson to make his move and to hear news of Jason Bancroft felt like a ticking bomb attached to her chest. The first night Alex was gone, Angel made them all Hot Naked pasta, and they'd played board games for hours as a distraction. It helped to get her mind off her anxiety, but the shit hit the fan when Alex called and found out the men weren't on strict guard duty. He'd read all three of them the riot act, especially Cole, which effectively put an end to the pleasant evening. Angel had retreated to Alex's room with her caseload and laptop, pissed off just enough not to speak to him. Everyone's nerves had been raw.

The time was dragging. Every time she went anywhere, she was under escort, and when she had court on Tuesday, Sid and

Cole went with her, never letting her leave their sight. She felt the security at the courthouse should have been enough, given everyone was subjected to search and X-ray, but Alex left no doubt there would be hell to pay if they didn't stay in close proximity.

Later the same day, Cole was driving her to Toys "R" Us to pick out some gifts for Jillian's party, though she wished she could go by herself. She wanted to get a few things at different stores and felt guilty making Cole follow her around all day. Angel glanced at her watch. It was almost 10 AM, which would make it one in the morning in Sydney.

Cole noticed. "When's the last time you've heard from my brother?"

"Last night. He called earlier, but I was in session, then I got voice mail when I tried to call him back. He's probably sleeping. I hope, anyway."

Angel was pensive, and it showed in her tone. She felt uneasy, constantly waiting for the other shoe to drop, when Swanson would make his move. Since the call to Alex at the station last Friday, they hadn't heard a peep from him; unless, you counted the disappearance of Jason Bancroft. Chills ran through her, causing goosebumps to race up her arms, over her back, and down her legs, and she shuddered.

"Are you cold?" Cole leaned forward and flipped on the heat. It was late September, and though the temperature was still fairly moderate, it was getting colder at night, so the mornings were brisk, but Cole had a feeling that wasn't the reason Angel was shivering.

She nodded and rubbed her hands over her arms, under her blazer. Her hair was pulled back into a chignon, and she was wearing her glasses; still perfect in appearance, but more somber than Cole had become accustomed. "Just a little." Her face turned away as she looked out the window. She was preoccupied. "Will this fucker ever leave us alone?"

Cole turned a brief glance in her direction, his eyebrow rose at the abruptness of her question. When his eyes were firmly back on the road, he answered, his hand tightening on the wheel until his knuckles were white. "Honestly? I doubt it, Angel. Even if Alex were to acquiesce and hand over the cash, it would just give him bravado to extort from Alex for the rest of his life."

"Yes," Angel said softly as Cole said her thoughts out loud. "I've thought of that."

"I'm sure Alex has, too. Swanson has proven he'll stop at nothing. We don't expect to find Bancroft alive."

She nodded sadly, still looking out the window, the street and buildings blurring, because both the car was moving and her eyes weren't focused. Bancroft's face flashed in her mind, and her heart sank. "What is he going to do?"

Cole shot her another quick glance. She was looking out the window as if mesmerized, her words coming as if she were in a trance. He knew Angel was asking what Alex's plans were, not what they expected out of Swanson.

Cole ran a hand down his face to the clean-shaven skin of his jaw. "Um, we're still figuring it out, Angel. He hasn't told me exactly what he wants to do, but knowing Alex, it's not like him to wait around like a sitting duck. My guess would be that we'd try to find Swanson, using every resource at our disposal. Not sure what happens after that."

"Kenneth will prosecute if we make it to court. He has a strong case with my testimony and the forensics. He'll win. We finally have enough evidence... if it makes it to court."

"Big *if*. The cops haven't found a goddamned thing."

More chills ran down her arms, and her eyes filled with frustrated tears. "After everything we did to get that bastard, he is still as slippery as a snake. Alex said he should have killed him when he had the chance."

"Yes." Cole's voice was stoic. "He's mentioned it to me, too. More than once."

Angel's head snapped to her left, to look at Cole's profile. "Do you think that's what he's planning? I don't want Alex to stoop to that, Cole. He's too good for something like that."

Cole shook his head. "I didn't think he'd ever go that far, Angel. That night in your apartment?" His shoulders lifted in a visible sigh. "Well, I saw a side of my brother I'd never seen before. But overall, Alex is rational. From the start, everything he's done to take Swanson down has been legal, very calculated and methodical. He would have spent less than the millions he used to ruin that fucker financially just to order a hit on him and be finished with it. If he were going to do that, he would have done it months ago. He doesn't go off half-cocked, so I don't expect him to start now."

Angel's own logic echoed Cole's reasoning, and she was relieved. "I know. The last thing I want is anything bad to happen to Alex, or any of you, because of me."

Cole wasn't ready to let the subject drop. "I expect when Alex gets back all the stops will be pulled out and the coffers opened to find Swanson and haul him back behind bars."

"Why isn't he just doing that now? Why wait until he comes back?"

"Our directive while Alex is gone is pretty singular: to keep you safe around the clock. If we divide our ranks to track Swanson, someone isn't watching you. Besides, he'll try again as long as Alex doesn't pay, and we can't risk something happening to you."

"I wonder if it really is the money he wants, or if he's out for blood. Revenge is a dirty thing. He may even lose sight of the reason he's angry and just focus on the goal. That's when perpetrators get extremely dangerous."

Cole pulled into the parking lot of the toy store and shut the car off. Without making a move to get out, he looked at Angel. "Yeah, but we got this." One corner of his mouth lifted in a half-smile. "What are you getting Jillian for her birthday?"

"I'm thinking a doll and an iPod shuffle, but I've also enrolled her in dance classes. I know she loves it, and Becca can't really afford them on her salary. She wouldn't let me do it just because, so this is a good way for me to get around her pride."

"You're a good friend, Angel."

"I love that little girl to pieces, and dancing is kind of our thing."

Angel had picked out a doll and clothes, a stroller, and accessories to go with it, and a pink iPod Shuffle. It wasn't long and they were back at Alex's estate. Cole ordered pizza for dinner, and Wayne and Sid were waiting at the gate for the delivery boy. Alex's house was filled with half a dozen agents, and it felt invasive and safe at the same time. She felt claustrophobic despite the huge size of the house. All of them milling around constantly forced her to retreat to Alex's room more often than not.

After grabbing a piece of pizza and a diet Coke and taking them to the bedroom, she'd flipped on the news and absently munched on the pizza, in between peeling off her clothes. She threw the half-eaten slice back on the plate and padded naked into the bathroom. She showered, changed into a pair of sweat pants and T-shirt, then unpacked all of her packages and laid them out on Alex's bed. She'd purchased wrapping paper and beautiful organza ribbon to wrap the gifts.

She planned on spending the evening making pretty packages and phone calls to Becca, Ally, and her father. She hadn't spoken to her father in over two weeks, which was unusual. She'd been reluctant to tell him about the specifics of the Swanson trial and how badly she'd been hurt or that she'd been attacked at all. It was early morning in Australia; too early to call Alex.

Angel flopped down and dialed her father's number.

"Hey, honey," he answered. "I've been meaning to call you, but I've been under the weather." She could hear the cold in his voice and the stuffiness in his nose.

"Oh, Daddy, I'm sorry."

He coughed on the other end, but the sound became muffled as he held the phone away from his mouth. It took a good thirty seconds for him to get it under control, and despite the distance, she could hear how deep it was. "Yeah, it's been pretty crappy."

"Have you been to the doctor?"

"Nah. I'm a tough old bastard. I'll get over it."

Angel shook her head wryly. "You're not old!"

"Last time I looked, I was sixty."

"That isn't old, Dad. When you're better, do you want to come to visit? Maybe come to Chicago for Christmas? I'd love for you to meet Alex."

Angel had mentioned Alex once or twice, but things were getting more serious between them. Though Angel was a grown woman, her father had been her whole world for most of her life, and her heart still needed his approval.

"I'd love to meet him, baby, but you know I hate to travel. Why don't you two come down here?" He coughed again. The raspy, nasty kind of cough that sounded, and felt like it ripped the lungs out of the person's chest.

Angel went back to visit at least once a year, but the only reason was because her father was there. There was absolutely nothing there to bring her home besides him. She still had hope he would move closer. She had an idea.

"Maybe. Dad, would you consider moving here? Alex and I are getting closer, and like you, he is overprotective. He hates my job."

"I'm sure hate is a strong word, Angel."

"No, he worries about me, the same as you. He understands how much it means to me, though."

"He sounds smart. I think I'll like him."

Angel leaned back against the pillows near the headboard. "He's really amazing. You'll love him. I hope."

Her father chuckled, but it brought about another cough. "He better be if he's with my little girl. I'm glad you found someone to take care of you, honey."

"He tries." Angel smiled.

"I'm sure you don't make it easy," her father teased.

"No. You know me well. It's just... I've never let anyone but you take care of me before. This is different, but it's getting easier." She smiled, love for both men overwhelming her.

"It really would mean a lot to me to have the two of you meet. I've met his family and they're great. His little sister has become a good friend, and his older brother is like a brother to me, too."

"I'm glad, honey. I always regretted I couldn't give you more. You deserved siblings."

"Hey, you did great by me! I had Uncle Will, and Ben was like the brother I never had."

"I think maybe Ben harbored a crush all those years."

Angel loved Ben, but they were more like brother and sister. "No, Ben and I were cool as friends. I wouldn't change my life, Dad. Except, I'd like you closer. Alex wants me to move in with him, and I'll still have my apartment. I'd love it if you'd come and move into it."

"Sweetheart, you know where I stand. My life is here. Besides, I don't retire for a few years, and I have to stay with the school system to get my pension."

"I have enough money, Dad. I want you to enjoy life."

"I am enjoying life. Will, Ben, and I go fishing every weekend in the summer and hunting in the winter. I like it here. It's all I know. I wouldn't know what to do with myself stuck inside a little apartment in the city."

Angel sighed. She was never able to change his mind. "Okay. Alex is very busy, but I will discuss Christmas with him. Are you sure you're up to having company? I can have someone come in and clean the house if you want. You need someone to take care of you."

"Save your money." He started coughing again.

"Get some soup and go back to bed. I'll call and check on you tomorrow. If you're not better, I'll expect you to go to the doctor."

"Yes, ma'am."

"I love you."

"Love you, too, kiddo."

Angel had just started to cut the pretty white and pink paper to wrap the baby doll when her other phone began playing Alex's ringtone, and her heart leapt in her chest. She dropped the scissors and grabbed the phone.

"Hi!"

"Hey, babe. How was your day?"

"It was good. Cole and I went shopping for Bean's birthday presents."

"I wish I could have gone with you. What'd you get her?" His voice sounded tired. It would be early morning in Australia but Angel was sure the time change was hard on him.

"A doll and an iPod."

"A *doll?*" he asked sardonically. "I want to get her a tent."

Angel smiled. "Alex, she's a little girl. What is she going to do with a tent?"

He huffed. "What do you mean? She likes tents."

Angel grinned at his teasing. "Yes, she likes tents made out of blankets."

"Mmmmm. Me, too." His voice was warm, despite his exhaustion.

"I remember."

"Yes, that was fun."

"It was the first time you made me give in." Angel settled onto the floor and leaned up against the bed.

"It didn't hurt so much, did it?" Sex oozed from his voice in a deliberately sexy taunt.

"No. It felt amazing."

"I miss you."

"I do, too. Let's both get new careers." Angel smiled softly, and while she was joking, part of her was serious. She hated the time he spent traveling as much as Alex hated that she worked with all sorts of unstable people.

Alex chuckled. "Okay. I'll be a concert pianist, and you have your choice of rock and roll goddess or my personal sex slave."

Angel laughed out loud. "Hmmm. How will I choose?" she asked playfully.

"You don't have to. You can do both. You're *verrrry* talented."

"Maybe I want you to be *my* sex slave."

"No problem."

The tight bands of fear around Angel's chest loosened for the first time since Alex left, and he was all she could think about. How sexy he was, how much she loved him, how she missed him. She honestly couldn't imagine life without him.

"You better not be practicing your skills while you're away."

"Who needs practice? I'm gifted."

They both laughed together. He *was* gifted and they both knew it.

"I talked to my dad and invited him for Christmas, but he doesn't like to travel. Maybe we can go to Missouri?"

Satisfaction settled around Alex. Considering they'd only been together a few months, he shouldn't be impatient about meeting her father, but he was happy it was finally coming up because it solved his problem of asking permission to marry her. "Yes, I'd like that. I was hoping we'd take a couple of weeks away together. Maybe we can spend some time there then go to Greece for New Year's."

Angel paused, her hand tugging thoughtfully on a strand of her hair. Hearing Alex speak of the future was exciting, overwhelming, and comforting all at the same time. She drew in a deep breath. "Yes. That sounds nice."

"Yes, it does. What's Cole up to?"

"I don't know. I'm in the bedroom by myself. I think eating pizza with the others."

"Pepperoni and cream cheese?"

"No!" Angel pouted.

"Stupid bastard," Alex laughed. "In the bedroom all alone? Sorry, I'm not there to remedy that."

"Me, too. We should switch to Skype." She chuckled devilishly.

"I would if I weren't at the office."

Her thoughts about how to get naughty and lure Alex into a live chat session despite his location was interrupted when her other phone rang, and she gave a frustrated groan. She picked it up, glancing at the screen. *Unknown number* flashed as it continued to ring, and the smile fell from her face. Alex heard the ringing, and it put him on alert.

"Who is it?"

"It's blocked."

"Answer it, but keep this line open," Alex's voice instantly hardened, and Angel could almost hear his muscles coil.

"Okay. Hold on." Angel answered the ringing phone while still holding Alex's phone in the other hand. "Hello?" She could hear nothing but wheezy breathing. "Hello?" she said again, more forcefully. He still didn't answer, and the silence was terrifying. "Listen, you crazy motherfucker, say something!"

"Tsk, tsk, gorgeous, you don't want to piss me off or that little girl might get a very special present for her birthday." Mark

Swanson's voice rasped in her ear. Angel's heart began to pound like a hummingbird's. It was painful, and she struggled to keep her voice even.

"What do you want?"

"To tell you I'm watching you, Angel. Tell Avery to pay up, or else he won't like the consequences. He thinks he's crippled me, but all he's done is piss me off."

Angel's breath caught in her throat. Her mind raced, she should tell him to fuck off, but the fact he knew about Jillian's party was terrifying, and worse, Bancroft was missing. If there was the slightest chance he was still alive, she couldn't antagonize him. Angel held the other phone up so Alex could hear the conversation. Maybe she could keep him on the phone longer so the police might be able to track the call. "He won't pay you."

"We'll see. I'm through dicking around. If he doesn't think I'm serious, I'm about to show him."

"Where is Bancroft? We know you have him."

Swanson laughed, the sound wicked, like he'd lost his mind. "Congratulations," he sneered. "I tried to reason with Avery, but he wouldn't listen," he said, as if to himself. "Now he'll understand."

"You have Alex's attention, Mark. And… I—I'll drop the charges. Just let Jason go!" Angel's blood pressure rose, and the pulse in her neck and wrists throbbed in time with the painful thudding of her heart.

"Do you think I'm stupid? The DA won't go for that."

It had been worth a shot. Criminal matters went to court, regardless of what the victim wanted. "They'll have no choice if I refuse to testify." She stammered, trying to find words that would help but knew it was a lie. There was enough physical evidence from the attack to convict Swanson without her testimony.

He ignored her. "Get a piece of paper," he commanded. "Now!"

"Okay." She had to set Alex's phone down, but Angel grabbed a pen from the bedside table and tore a piece of the wrapping paper off to write on.

"Go ahead. I'm ready." She could hear Alex's voice coming from the other phone telling her to pick it up, but she threw a pillow over it so Swanson wouldn't be able to hear it.

"Tell Avery to wire ten million dollars to this account." He proceeded to rattle off a routing number and account number. Ten million was twice what he'd asked for before. Angel swallowed hard. Her hand trembled so much, she hardly recognized her own writing, but she managed to get it down.

"Alex is—" She stopped, not allowing herself to tell Swanson Alex was traveling, and scrambled to think of another reason to stall him. "Um, it might take time to get that kind of cash. That's a lot of money. I don't even know if he has that much."

"He can get it. Every time he fucks me over, the price goes up, understand? If I don't have the money in that account by 6 PM tomorrow, all bets are off. Gotta say, I'm sort of disappointed, Angel. I expected more of a fight from you."

"I don't want anyone to get hurt."

"Too late. You're next unless Avery gives me everything I want," he sneered, and the line went dead.

Her whole body started to shake violently as she dropped the phone. She removed the pillow from the other one. "Shit!" she said into the room as she reached for it.

Angel mentally kicked herself. She shouldn't let him see her fear, but she didn't feel she should bait him. He wanted to scare her, and he did.

Alex exploded. "Goddamn it! I should never have left!"

"What would you do? Listen to that psycho's heavy breathing with me?"

Alex's frustration was palpable.

"Angel!" Alex's voice was loud enough for her to hear it without picking up the phone. She reached for it.

"He killed Bancroft, Alex." Angel's voice wavered for the first time. "I know he's dead for sure. I'd hoped..." her eyes filled with tears. "Swanson is such a sick, evil fucker."

"I know, baby." Alex tried to calm down. His rational mind told him he needed more facts before he could formulate a plan. "What did he say? Tell me exactly what he said."

"He wants ten million dollars by tomorrow night at six, wired to a specific bank account. He gave me the numbers."

"That's more than he originally asked for. What is the account number?" Alex's voice was deadly calm. Too calm: it was cold as ice.

"Alex, you can't pay him!"

"Just tell me what the numbers are, honey. I'll use them to find out where the bank is located."

"Oh." Angel nodded and gave Alex the numbers.

"What else did he say, Angel?" His voice was coaxing. "Tell me everything."

"He said you will have no doubt he's serious."

Alex was silent for a good minute, and Angel's heart felt as if it would fly from her body.

"Alex?"

"Jesus Christ. It's okay, honey. I need to speak with Cole and the police. It'll take care of it." Alex being Alex, his voice alone should have reassured her, but she sensed his fury. "I'll get this contract signed today then I'm on a plane. I don't want you going to the party. In fact, get Becca to cancel it altogether. We can't trust anything he said. He is probably lying in wait, and we can't risk any of you."

She knew he was right, but she was sad for Jillian. "Or, it might be a way to trap him. Why don't we just let him think it's happening?"

"Maybe. Assuming he knows about it, that is? You're the psychologist. Do you think he'll fall for it?"

"He doesn't really need to risk showing himself... unless he doesn't get his money."

"Right. Exactly what I'm thinking, too. We'll have to flush him out. Please put Cole on."

"Alex, please let the police handle it." Fear seized her heart. This was about revenge as much as money, and Angel knew it.

"*Fuck* the police, Angel. They aren't doing a goddamned thing! Do you want to keep living like this? Give the phone to Cole!" he demanded harshly. She was startled at his barking tone. She could hear him moving around his office, and his briefcase snapping shut; his voice was as cold as steel.

Angel opened the door to the bedroom, rushing down the hall and down the stairs into the great room. Cole was on the floor, using the coffee table to hold his plate, and Sid and Wayne were both sitting on the leather furniture around it. They all glanced up at Angel as she rushed into the room, their faces concerned.

"Cole, it's Alex," she said, holding out the phone to him. "He wants to talk to you. Swanson just called me on my other phone."

"Shit!" he muttered, shoving away from the coffee table and getting to his feet before reaching for the phone. He took it. "Hey, Alex." He disappeared into the kitchen, listening to Alex on the other end of the phone. She stood fidgeting, and Wayne threw down his pizza.

"What did he say? Anything about Bancroft?" he asked. They were both stoic, their expressions contrite.

"He's dead." Angel was in shock, like she was out of body. Her heart hammered, but she was numb otherwise and sank to the couch. "I mean, Swanson didn't mention he killed him exactly, but he said it was 'too late.'"

"Anything else?" Wayne asked.

She shrugged, not because it meant nothing, but because she felt helpless, and what she was about to say was known among them. "He said he wants money, but I don't think that's his goal."

"No, we've seen his type. He wants blood," Sid remarked.

Cole hurried back into the room and began bellowing orders at the others. "Wayne, ask two of the guys outside to come into the house on your way out, but don't tell them where you're going." He was carrying a handgun, and he shoved it into the front of his belt. "Take Sid, go to the airport, and rent an SUV. Use your personal credit card. Make sure it has tinted windows and a GPS. Then meet us back here."

The two men left their meals unfinished and left without asking questions.

Cole turned toward her. "Angel, call Becca. Tell her to pack a bag and have it ready. Then pack one yourself. Take things that don't require much space and enough for at least two weeks. Take sensible shoes and warm clothes you can move in."

"What is Alex planning?" Angel asked. Based on the weak way the police were handling things, Angel was sure it was something.

"I'm calling the police to see if they can track the call. Give me the phone the call came in on." Cole dialed a number on his phone. Angel guessed he didn't get Alex's *fuck-the-police* directive. "Detective Samuels, please." He looked up at Angel. "We may not be able to place it exactly, because he was using one of those disposable phones when he called Alex at the station. No doubt this is no different, but maybe we can find out what cell tower it was transmitted from."

Angel went to Alex's room, retrieved her other phone, and handed it to Cole, who was in the middle of the call. He rattled off Angel's phone number to the police officer he was speaking to. "No. Yes, she's here. Okay. How long?"

Angel sat, still as stone, as Cole spoke to the detective and gathered they would arrive shortly to take her statement. When he hung up the phone, Cole stood in front of her, and she looked up into his face. His whole body was tight and filled with tension.

"I'm surprised Alex had you call the police. They'll just fuck things up, won't they?"

"Probably." He nodded. "But we have to cooperate with them or we'll be accused of obstructing justice." He put both hands on her upper arms and squeezed. "Call Becca, Angel. Then let Darian know you won't be there on Friday night. Alex wants us to plant your car there, along with your assistant's, but we don't want either of you there, and have Darian run a file tape from a past airing so it appears you're live. Unless Swanson listens to every show, he won't pick up on it. It's a shot to buy us some time. We're all going on a little trip."

"What?"

"Alex will meet us with the jet."

"Where?"

"Location to be determined."

"How does Mark Swanson know what we're doing?" Angel was anxious and wringing her hands. "How does he know about Jillian's party?"

"I don't know, but Alex is freaking the fuck out."

Angel's head snapped up. "*I'm* freaking the fuck out, Cole! I don't wig out, but I've never had a perpetrator I'm working with murder anyone before."

"Do you blame Alex? If he hadn't destroyed his business—"

"No!" She shook her head adamantly. "It's my fault. If I would have let the tests stand, he would have gotten away with raping that young girl, but that's it. Now you, Alex, Becca, and Jillian… everyone I care about, is at risk. Your family. Becca's family. All because I couldn't let it go."

"Alex didn't let it go, either, Angel. He has been like a man possessed."

"But, because of me."

"You and Alex are so alike, and you both are stubborn as hell. You both do what's right. Angel. You couldn't have seen this coming."

"It's my job to see sick creeps like Swanson for what they are." She ran a weary hand through her long hair. "I suck." She stood and began pacing.

Cole's lips pressed into a thin line. "You did see him for what he was. Isn't that why you didn't let it go?"

Angel's head snapped around to look at him. He was right. She nodded.

"Can you please call Becca now? Just tell her you want to start your sleepover early, in case the phone is bugged. And pack your bag?"

"Okay." She nodded and walked back up the stairs to do his bidding.

10

Fright & Flight

BECCA ANSWERED HER phone on the third ring.

"Hello?"

"Hey, Becs. It's me." Angel could hear Jillian jabbering in the background, though it was getting late and she should be heading to bed soon. Angel wasn't looking forward to this conversation.

"Hey. No more, Jillian. You've had enough banana. Sorry. The last thing I need is her crapping in her pants at her party."

Angel couldn't help but smile, amused at her friend's lack of tact. Of course, they were like sisters, so it wasn't the first or, Angel suspected, the last time. "Yes, that would be bad." It would be equally bad to have that happen on the road. "Becca..." Angel paused, unsure how to say what she needed to say. "Cole is sending someone over to pick you and Bean up. I want to start our sleepover early. Can you pack some clothes, and I'll have one of the guys pick you up?"

"Um... now?"

"Yes." Angel closed her eyes, hoping she wouldn't ask questions. She couldn't tell Becca anything over the phone, per Cole's instructions. "I'm just really excited, and I can't decide how to wrap my gifts. I thought you could help."

"I have so much to do before tomorrow night."

"I *know*." Angel's voice took on a more desperate tone. It was so hard trying to get Becca to agree without spilling her guts. "Um, I'll help, but I'm stuck out here in this big house alone. I just thought it would be fun."

"How horrible. Hanging out at your rich boyfriend's mansion. You poor thing," she joked.

"Yes, I know, right? You can suffer with me. Just pack a bag. I don't know how long Alex will be gone so bring a lot of stuff."

"Okay, I guess, if you promise to help me tomorrow. But, I can drive out. I don't want to have to move the car seat. It's a pain in the ass."

Angel saw the logic, and even more importantly, Cole could move the car seat to the rental behind the locked gates of Alex's estate. It would be safer. "Okay, sure. I'll text you the address. Then text me when you get close. Someone will meet you at the gate."

"Fort Knox, much?" Becca asked incredulously. "I can't wait to see his pad. I bet it reeks of money."

"Anga! Anga!" Jillian's voice cried out happily in the background. "Talk to Anga!"

"Angel, Jillian wants to talk to you, okay?"

"Yes. Start packing, then."

"Okay." Questions laced her voice. It was clear she knew this shit was weird, and thankfully, she didn't require an immediate explanation. "Here she is."

"Anga!" Jillian's exuberant voice exploded over the phone. "You comin' over?"

"Not tonight, sweetheart, but you and Mommy are going to have a few sleepovers with me, okay?"

"Reedy? Yay! Can we make a tent with Zander?"

Angel smiled, even as her heart constricted. "Zander is away on business, baby. But I know he loves to camp with you, so maybe when he gets back, okay?"

"Tay."

"We'll talk about it. Go help your mommy pack, okay? Bring some toys, some coloring books, and your crayons."

"Will you color?"

"Of course, I'll color. Go find Mommy and give her the phone, Bean."

Jillian didn't reply into the phone, but Angel gathered she was running in search of Becca. "Mama! Anga want to color at her house! I want bing dat preencess book, kay?" Her little voice was excited.

The sound of the phone apparently being fumbled around and dropped was followed by a dull thud when it landed on the carpet of Becca's apartment. "Sorry. I'm getting stuff together. I'll see you in a bit?"

"Yes, and thanks for doing this on short notice. I'll text the address as soon as I hang up."

"Sure. See you in a bit."

When Angel hung up, she went to find Cole. He was still in the living room, but alone, and pacing, back on the phone with Alex, from what she could gather.

"I'll have to get the locals involved to pull that off, Alex." As Cole listened, he sensed her reentry into the room and met her eyes. "No, I get it. It makes sense. Don't worry, Alex."

Her suspicions regarding the caller were confirmed.

"Yeah, yeah, I will. Angel just came in. See ya."

Angel wanted to ask to speak to him, but Cole ended the call before she was able to ask.

Time was moving slower than hell. Every minute felt like it passed in slow motion. Angel felt short of oxygen, as if she'd forgotten to breathe, and she gasped in a deep breath. "What did he say?"

"He said to make arrangements for the 'party' to continue as usual—" he used two fingers to emphasize the word, "—and to get you the hell out of here."

Cole moved toward the kitchen. "I have to look something up online, so can you come in here so we can keep talking?" he asked, motioning for Angel to follow. "We have to paint the illusion that it's all going on as planned tomorrow at the James'." He sat down at the table near the patio door where his laptop was waiting. "There is a lot of logistical bullshit I have to arrange before we can leave. Wayne and Sid are getting a car, and we'll leave sometime in the middle of the night. Hopefully, we'll get you, Becca, and the kid out of town and out of danger. Alex said, and I agree, that we shouldn't tell anyone other than Wayne and Sid what's going down."

Angel pulled out one of the chairs and slowly sat down next to Cole, who started searching the Internet for something. "But, I thought background checks were done on all of the guys."

He glanced up through a frown, still hunched in front of the computer. "We did, but we can't be too careful. Someone is feeding that prick information, and we don't know who."

A chill skittered over Angel from head to toe, causing her skin to itch. She reached up and scratched her scalp with vigorous fingers. She tapped the surface of her thumbnail on her lip, her mind racing. If Swanson had a plant in Alex's security team, any one of them could have been killed at any time. A deadly calm settled over her.

"Can I help?"

"Just get your stuff together for now. If you have any cash, bring it. Credit cards leave trails."

"We can stop at an ATM. I can get more."

"What's your daily withdrawal limit?"

"Five hundred, I think. I don't ever push it, so I forget if it's three or five." Cole nodded silently, intent on the screen in front of him. "What are you doing now?"

"Scouting locations."

"Ah. So something within 20-ish hours of here."

"Very good."

It would take Alex no less than fifteen hours to get back, if he left immediately. That was impossible, and Cole's to-do list would delay their departure as well.

"When you decide, how will you tell Alex where to meet us? He'll be over the ocean for hours."

"He has something to do in Chicago before he catches up with us."

"Why?"

"I didn't ask. Neither of us had time; he just told me what he needed from the team and me. We have to get moving, Angel. When Sid and Wayne get back I'll brief them, but the others will be stationed to cover Becca's folks and our parents."

"But..." She shook her head slowly. "If you don't know if you can trust them, I don't get it?" She wanted to know what was going on with Alex. It would drive her crazy wondering.

"Wayne will be with one team and Sid with the other. That's the only way we can keep an eye on them."

"You can't do that. If they can bump off Bancroft, they can do the same to Sid or Wayne. It's not safe."

Cole stopped what he was doing and looked Angel straight in the face. "Angel, let me worry about it. Don't take this wrong, but seriously, I do not have time for twenty questions. They are both highly trained. When will Becca get here?"

This prompt dismissal of Angel was indication he had a lot to do and not much time to do it. The walkie-talkie sitting next to Cole's laptop came to life, and Cole put a finger to his mouth to shush any conversation between himself and Angel. "This is Avery. Over?"

"The grounds are quiet."

Cole raised the device to his mouth and pressed a button with the same hand. "Good. You two can call it a night."

"Are you sure, sir? Wayne and Sid have not returned from their break. Should we wait for them?"

It wasn't a break, but obviously, that was what they'd been told. Angel's brain tried to piece together Cole and Alex's plan without much to go on.

"No. They'll be back soon, and the security systems are secure. I'll see you back in the morning."

"Roger, that. Night."

Cole pulled up the security monitors that were tied in through his computer monitor and he watched the two of them clear the gates. "Angel, please go pack." He'd asked her to do it three times, and this time his tone was stronger. Finally, she got up and left the room without the answers she needed.

*****

Angel left the door to Alex's room open as she quickly wrapped Jillian's gifts. If they were going to skip the party, then the least she could do was have some pretty presents for the little girl to open. She heard Becca and Jillian arrive when the front doorbell rang and then some talking filtered through the house. She couldn't hear exactly what was said, just muted voices from the floor below as she opened one of Alex's drawers. She didn't have many clothes with her that weren't suits and dresses, and she was sure he wouldn't mind if she borrowed a couple pair of sweat pants and T-shirts.

Really, she was packing them for him. She had little doubt he'd be so focused he'd have forgotten to stop home for appropriate clothing for wherever they were going, and he'd have nothing with him but suits and ties. She found a big duffel bag in his closet and wondered if she should take that or leave it for him, just in case. She found a pair of Alex's Adidas on the closet floor and picked them up to shove them, unceremoniously, in the bottom of her own gym bag. The other things followed, as well as the two pair of yoga pants, her workout jacket, a T-shirt from the fitness center, and her cross trainers.

"Anga! Anga!" Jillian called happily before bursting into the room in front of Becca and tumbling into Angel's arms when she stooped down to scoop her up.

"Bean! I'm so happy to see you!" Jillian's chubby arms encircled Angel's neck tightly, and Angel hugged her as hard as she could without hurting her. "Mmmm! I missed you so much!"

Jillian sat back in Angel's arms. "Me, too. Mama said wez gonna have a sweepover!"

Angel kissed the rosy cheek closest to her, reluctant to put the little girl down. She smelled of soap and baby shampoo, the ends of her curly hair still damp from her bath. She was dressed in fluffy pink-footed pajamas. "Yes, and what pretty pjs! I love pink!"

Jillian's eyes got big as she spied the two boxes with the beautiful organza bows. "Are those for my birfday?"

"They are! How'd you get so smart?" Angel tickled Jillian's ribs, and she let out a squeal.

"I don't know." She shrugged her little shoulders. "Is this Zander's room? It smells nice yike him."

Becca rolled her eyes and plopped down on the bed. "His whole house reeks of sexy mancave. I bet he didn't have to beat you over your head to get you here, did he?" she asked sardonically, eyeing the open duffel bag that was now right next to her. "Looks like Angel is busy, sweets. Come sit by Mommy on this gigantic bed." She held up her arms, and Jillian went easily from one woman to the other. "What's going on? You didn't invite us over here just to leave, did you? I mean, if you're trying to set me up with Cole, that's a bit extreme."

"Yes, I'm trying to set you up with Cole." Becca's head snapped up at her friend's words.

"Really?" Becca cocked her head to one side and smiled, lowering her voice. "Because he is completely doable."

"Yes, I will, but not tonight. I didn't want to tell you on the phone, but something's come up."

Jillian was lying next to Becca, and Angel cast a glance her way wondering if she'd be able to convey the seriousness of the situation in a way that wasn't scary.

"What is it?" Becca asked seriously, concern washing over her features. "Has something happened?"

"Uh huh. I'm really sorry about this. You don't know how sorry, but Mark Swanson made bail and has become a problem." That was the understatement of the century, but Angel could not explain fully as long as Jillian was within earshot.

"That guy is a major creeper. Why the hell did they let him out, anyway?"

"Good question. But, we, um, need to go on a little adventure. All of us." Angel nodded at Jillian. "All of us. Now. Tonight."

"But—" Becca began.

Angel sat next to her and started to rub Jillian's back. It was late and she should be exhausted. "The adventure is more important than the other... *thing*." Becca started to protest but Angel shook her head. "Um... I'll explain, but it's late. Bean, are you tired?" Angel directed her attention to the toddler. "Birthdays don't come if you're tired. Did you know that?"

"Okay, but can I sleep here?" She opened her mouth in a big yawn.

"Sure, baby." Angel pulled back the covers and helped her climb beneath, then reached over and turned on the bedside lamp. "Bec, would you mind switching off the overhead light?" She smoothed the silky curls on Jillian's head over and over.

"Do you want to watch one of your princess videos? I bet Mommy brought one?"

"No." She shook her little head and snuggled down into Alex's oversized bed. Angel pulled the dark wine and black comforter up and pushed it around her little body. "But can you sing to me, Anga?"

"What would you like to hear, sweet pea?"

"Yittle Mermaid." She yawned again, this time even bigger. Lowering the lights had the desired effect, and her eyes seemed to droop. Angel marveled at the long, long lashes that framed Jillian's bright blue eyes and how dark they were considering her blonde hair. She was a beautiful child.

Angel smiled. "Okay." They'd watched Little Mermaid hundreds of times, and Angel particularly liked it; one, because it was her all-time favorite Disney movie, and two, because it was about a young girl standing up for what she wanted. She knew Jillian was asking for "Part of Your World".

Becca stood and moved to the leather chair in one corner. It was plush and luxurious, and she sank down in it as Angel began to sing to her little girl.

Before Angel was half way through the song, Jillian was fast asleep, and Angel was able to stop and move to the end of the bed across from where Becca waited.

"What's the deal? You want me to cancel the party?"

"No. At least, I don't think so, but we can't be at it." Angel's expression was apologetic, and she kept her voice just barely above a whisper. "I'm sorry, but that fucker kidnapped, and most likely murdered, one of the bodyguards. It's too dangerous."

"Maybe for you, but I can't cancel my kid's party, Angel. My parents have gone to so much trouble."

"I understand." Angel had as well, but it was of little consequence. "But, Swanson called me tonight and demanded an unthinkable amount of money. He thinks I can get Alex to do it, and he said he knew about Jill's party. We can always re-do the party, but it's too dangerous to be there when Swanson or his goon troop might show up. We can't risk it."

"Oh, my God! Should I have my parents leave, too?"

"Maybe. Cole and Alex are making the plan. Only Cole and two others will be privy to the details, and all I know at this point is Cole is taking you, me, and Jillian away from Chicago."

"This is really scary, Angel. Maybe you should have just let it go. Before, I mean."

Angel's mouth tightened. Yes, she should have. She'd already gone over it in her head twenty times, and she felt terrible that her friends were in danger because of her.

"Yes, I realize that, but what's done is done. All we can do is deal with this shit now. I'm sorry! If there were another way, I promise, I wouldn't ask this, Becca. I wish it didn't involve you or Bean, but Alex isn't taking any chances. I know him, and he'll protect everyone involved, but that means following his plan, whatever it is." She sucked in her breath and stood up, rushing back to her task of gathering a few toiletries and shoving them in her bag. "I trust him."

"I can see that or you'd be kicking him in the balls for ordering you around." Seeing Angel's distress, Becca tried to lighten the mood; though she also felt anxious and frightened.

"He's involved because of me. Everyone is involved because of me." Angel picked up the last couple of things from the bathroom counter and walked briskly back, shoving them with more force than was needed into her bag. Her heart was racing, and she felt sick to her stomach; the back of her eyes began to burn with unshed tears. "Do you know how hard it was for me to sing to Jillian when I blame myself for everything? I feel like I'm going to throw up."

Becca watched Angel zip up the bag and dump it on the floor next to the bedroom door. From what Angel had said, Mark

Swanson was a weasel-y little man, so she wondered how serious a threat he could really be in the face of Cole and the other bodyguards. "You said he probably murdered someone?"

"Yes. Last Friday night at the radio station, the man who was assigned to tail Swanson was abducted and his car burned... after Swanson called Alex and tried to extort money."

"I take it your boy told him what he could do with his threats."

Angel ran an agitated hand through her hair and sat back down on the bed to finish the conversation. She nodded. "Yes. But, when Swanson called me, I could hear the evil in his voice, Becca. He won't stop even if he gets the money. That's what scares me."

"How much money?"

"Ten million."

Becca's eyes widened, and she swallowed.

"My nature wants to tell him to go fuck himself, but he's crazed. He's capable of anything, and to goad him would be sheer stupidity."

"Will Alex give him the money?"

Angel's dark eyes met hers. "Not likely. We think it would only make him more relentless, but he may have changed his mind. Cole will know."

"Should we go downstairs and try to find out?"

"Yes." Both women stood and walked across the large room toward the door. Jillian was still fast asleep on the bed. "But, I'm fairly sure we'll be leaving tonight."

Becca sucked in her breath and followed Angel silently down the stairs and into the great room. Cole was talking to Wayne and Sid, all of them concentrating on what the others had to say and didn't hear them come in.

"So, what about the party?" Sid asked.

"It goes on as planned. I've called the detectives on the case, and they've agreed to assign more operatives. You're to go downtown and pick up two detectives they are assigning to the case. One is a woman. Bring them back here and give them access to the house."

Angel and Becca walked in, and Angel cleared her throat. "Alex is letting someone else in here?"

Cole's head turned at the sound of Angel's voice, and he nodded before he even registered he was doing so. "Yeah. Go," he said to Wayne and Sid. "I'll be in close touch with you and the police. Alex demands we keep to the plan one-hundred-percent unless something unforeseen happens."

Wayne put a hand on Cole's shoulder. "Good luck, young man." In his words, Angel was reminded how much of a rookie Cole was. Cole nodded and shook Sid's hand.

"It's been great working with you guys. Hope you find Bancroft."

Wayne nodded grimly, and both men turned and walked out.

After they left, Cole faced the girls, directing them toward the couch with his hand. "Have a seat."

Becca sat down but Angel hesitated. Cole's stoic demeanor was to be expected, but she wanted to know the plan and what was happening with Alex.

"What's happening?" she asked, finally sinking slowly to sit next to Becca.

Cole tented the fingers of both hands but didn't take a seat.

"We're leaving. The local police will protect your parents, Becca, and the party will take place as planned. It will appear that way from the outside."

"But, the guests?" Becca asked, her face twisting in disbelief.

"Will be decoys and all cops. Hopefully, none of the real guests are in Swanson's pocket, but it's a risk we have to take. Sid and Wayne will each have a team on stakeout outside, and a policewoman and her partner, disguised as you and I, Angel, will attend in our stead. She'll use your car, etcetera."

Angel nodded. "Okay."

"What about the rest of us?"

"We're leaving in the SUV that's parked outside."

"I have to get more clothes. I didn't have much here."

Cole sighed. He didn't want to waste time, and Alex wouldn't be pleased at the delay, but they'd need all the cash he and Angel could get out of a twenty-four hour ATM before they left the city. After that, there was to be no use of cards.

"Shit. I don't really want the vehicle seen at your condo, Angel. The whole point is to slip away without anyone knowing. We don't know who knows what or who may be watching. Alex doesn't want us to take any chances."

"I get it, but, I don't have anything, and we can't buy anything, right?" She looked at him without flinching, her mind already working through each scenario.

"Right."

She stopped as she had a thought. "Kenneth might have a key. Maybe he can go get a bag for me. Or send someone."

"Sending someone is preferable. Swanson's crew knows Ken."

"Yeah." Angel nodded and got up to get her phone.

"I won't tell my little brother that Ken still has a key."

Angel was rummaging through her purse from the entryway and answered Cole from there. "I'm sure he'd rather that than us going, given the situation."

Cole shook his head, skeptically. "I think we both know, he'd prefer neither one."

*****

Becca was upstairs sleeping with Jillian, and Angel was lying down on the sofa, wrapped up in a blanket Cole had found in an upstairs closet, with her laptop open in front of her on the coffee table. Time slogged by while they waited for Carrie, Ken's assistant, to arrive.

Angel kept her computer on, hoping Alex would buzz her on Skype, but her eyes were getting heavy. It was close to 1 AM, which would make it late afternoon in Sydney. Was he still there? Even if he was on his way back, the chances of him being over the US were slim. He'd have to land on the West Coast for fuel.

Cole was stretched out on the second sofa, an exact mirror of the one Angel was curled up on and across the coffee table on the other side. His arm was flung over his eyes, even though the only light was coming from the property lights outside the house and filtering in through the window blinds. Cole insisted they be kept closed so it was only what could leak in around the edges.

"Where do you think Alex is?" she asked softly. She wasn't sure if Cole was awake, but if not, he wouldn't answer. She was surprised when he did.

"Not sure. I'm unclear on the rest time required for the pilots. I think it's been enough time between flights, and if so, he will be on his way. He said there is some FAA regulation that requires pilots a certain amount of downtime for their hours in the air. He was pissed when he realized it could cause a delay. Alex is like a caged animal when he can't do what he wants, when he wants to."

"I'm sure he's more anxious than usual, but I assume he'd be in touch." She sighed softly, and turned onto her side. Her eyes closed. He'd been in Sydney less than 24 hours. But shouldn't 24 hours be enough rest for the pilots?

"He is always engaged, Angel. Believe me; something is happening on his end."

Yes, she knew if there were anything Alex could do from where he was, he'd do it. "I know."

"He'll call when he gets to LA. My guess is will be early morning when they land at LAX. Try to get a few hours of sleep, Angel. As soon as Carrie gets here, we're out of here."

"Where?"

"South."

"Just South?"

"Yep."

"I'd suggest my dad's, but that's probably the first place Swanson would look."

"If he chooses to tail us. Alex hopes he'll find that bastard before he knows we're gone."

"That's why he's coming to Chicago first?" Angel sat up and put her feet on the floor to face him. "Did the cops find something?"

"Not that I'm aware of." Cole got up off the sofa and walked into the kitchen. Angel listened to him clanging around and sat, stoic in the silence. She wanted to scream, her chest felt compressed, her frustration bottled up without an outlet.

"This sucks, Cole," she said when he came back with a plate of sandwiches and two bottles of water. He handed her one of the waters and set the plate down, only to grab one of the sandwiches, taking a big bite. "I wish I could do something."

"Yeah," he said with his mouth full. "The waiting is the worst. I just want to get the hell out of here." He took another bite and devoured it, glancing at his watch at the same time. Angel picked up one of the sandwiches and sniffed it. Peanut butter. "You should eat."

Angel ate the sandwich then decided to go pack some food for them to take on the road trip, making a mental note to call Liz after 8 AM and tell her to cancel all of her appointments indefinitely.

Indefinitely... Fuck! she thought. *That bastard has made chaos of so many lives.* Jason Bancroft and his family had paid so dearly. Her heart pounded and skipped a beat. She felt sick and helpless. Guilt, anger, and frustration permeated every cell in her body. That bastard had to pay. No matter what, he had to pay.

Cole's walkie-talkie beeped and static loudly filled the silent house. *"The young lady has arrived with Dr. Hemming's things."*

He picked it up and responded shortly. Angel was putting some fruit, crackers, chips, and some turkey and cheese sandwiches in a small cooler she'd found under the sink. As she listened to Cole crisply bark out orders, it was clear this job suited him, and he was assuming control in Bancroft's absence. Cole was professional and in control; his demeanor all business.

"Have Sid follow her home, and you meet me in the garage with the stuff." He came into the kitchen still speaking into the walkie-talkie and when he was done, he nodded toward the stairs. "Get Becca and the kid. We're out of here."

11

Deadly Resolve

ALEX WAS ON his way to the airport. He'd called the current owner of the Australian hotel chain they were acquiring and explained he had a family emergency in the States and was unable to sign the contract at the same time. Fortunately, they'd discussed the terms of sale over dinner the prior evening and the details had been typed up by a secretary at the office earlier that morning while Alex was speaking to Angel. What started as a nice morning call turned into a nightmare with that bastard, Swanson, tormenting Angel, while he strained to hear what was being said from her other phone. It had spurred him into instant action.

Alex was so furious; it was all he could do to contain his anger. He was helpless in Australia, so he had to finish his business and get the fuck on a plane. The head of the Australian office sat across from him in the limousine on the way to the Sydney airport as Alex gave the contract a quick once-over, signed it, and left it with her for the other party to sign. He didn't like to leave his deals open-ended, but in this case, there was no choice. Anxiety made him nauseous and his skin burn, his thoughts taunting that he shouldn't have left Chicago with this shit up in the air. He'd known it when he'd boarded the goddamned plane at O'Hare, and now, he felt like a caged animal.

His demeanor was pensive, and he didn't talk to the woman other than brief responses to her questions. He yanked at his tie to loosen it. "Please, send someone to the hotel to get my things and ship them to the office in Chicago," Alex instructed, reaching into his suit jacket for the key card to his room and handed it to the woman. "Room 1215."

"Thank you for coming, Mr. Avery. I learned a lot from listening to you negotiate the contract last night." She knew better than to question something so important that Alexander Avery would leave his belongings at the hotel and fly off before a deal was done.

"My pleasure, Susan." Alex tried to be pleasant, though his face showed strain. "Keep me informed, and good luck with the takeover." He shook her hand.

"Yes, sir."

The car arrived at the airport, barely stopping, when Alex bolted out the door and up the steps to the waiting plane. He had his laptop and that was it, but he didn't care. Material things meant little in lieu of what was going on with Angel and Bancroft's disappearance. Though all of the new security agents had thorough background checks, Alex was unsure whom he could trust beyond Cole, Sid, and Wayne, and told his brother the three of them were the only ones to know the details of the plan. The issue was, he needed to protect his parents, Allison and Josh, and also Becca's family, so the others would have to be stationed with them. Keeping Becca and Jillian with Angel would help, but Allison and Josh would have to stay with the folks so that Wayne could be present there, leaving Sid to stay with the operatives at Becca's parents' home. Jesus, it was a logistical nightmare, and one he didn't want to deal with. It was dangerous splitting Wayne, Sid, and Cole up, but with everything that needed to be watched, he had to have one person he knew for certain he could trust in each place.

When his seatbelt was buckled, Alex nodded to the pilot that he was free to request clearance from ground control so they could begin the taxi to the runway.

This was going to be a long fucking flight. It would take him as long to get to Chicago as it would for Cole to drive the girls to Joplin, and he was still jet lagged. He couldn't have his ass dragging, but he acknowledged that sleep on the flight would be impossible. He was wound tighter than a drum. Joplin might not be the ideal place to send them. What if Mark Swanson knew Angel's background? He might look there first, but at least Angel's father, his good friend, and the friend's son were there to help Cole protect them. It was a trade-off he'd have to live with.

Hopefully, the women could lay low at Angel's childhood home with Jillian, while Cole and he hunted Swanson down. The cops in Chicago sure as hell weren't going to get the job done, but that was the logical place to begin. Thank God for electronics. He was counting on the bank routing number and the cell tower used to transmit Swanson's call to Angel to help pinpoint Swanson's location. If that didn't work, he'd have to call Swanson and arrange a meeting. The chances of that bastard falling for the bait were questionable, given his request for an electronic transfer. But it might be all he had. His hands curled into fists and Alex closed his eyes. This fucker was going down if it was the last thing he did.

The money would be a problem. Alex wasn't able to send ten million even if he wanted to. He had it, but not all in cash, and it would take time to liquidate that much. Besides, he wasn't going to pay off a fucking murderer. Swanson deserved a lot of things, but money wasn't one of them.

Alex's phone rang, and he removed it from the clip on his belt. It was his office in Chicago. The plane was moving, but not yet into position to take off, and though the plane had onboard cellular capability, his phone would need to be turned off during takeoff and landing. "Yes, Mrs. Dane?"

"Marvin Standish called. He said he is available to meet next Monday. Will that work, sir?"

Alex ran a hand over his face as the plane came to a stop, and the pilots did their run-up and system check. "No. I have an emergency. I'm on my way back to the US, now. I'll call him myself."

"I hope everything is all right, Mr. Avery."

"Me, too. I'll be in touch, Mrs. Dane." Alex hung up and scrolled through his recent calls, finding the Standish Venture number.

"Sir, we've been cleared," the pilot's voice came over the cabin intercom. Alex shut down his phone. He had no choice but to wait until they cleared ten thousand feet, and the pilot gave him the okay to use his phone. He inhaled, his chest expanding, but resistant as the air filling his lungs. Tension had every muscle in his body aching and his chest felt like tight metal bands were constricting it.

Alex's hand yanked at the dark rose and black silk tie he wore, loosening it and pulling it free. He freed two buttons on his dress shirt and sat back in his seat. He closed his eyes and mentally went over the plan as the plane accelerated and took to the air. He could only hope they could pull off the fake birthday party and Swanson would never know it wasn't real. That, at least, would give Cole time to get Angel and the girls out of Chicago and give Alex enough time to get back.

Marvin Standish was the first stop. Hopefully, he'd get some of the answers he needed.

*****

Alex was exhausted and it showed on his face. He hadn't slept much in the past two days, and he struggled to re-tie his tie and smooth down his hair. There was a good amount of stubble on his chin but there was nothing to be done about it. It was early afternoon on Friday, the day of Jillian's party. He'd spoken to Cole only briefly, but knew he and the women were driving south and were now on the other side of St. Louis.

Alex hadn't spoken to Angel because Cole said she was asleep in the backseat with Jillian. He felt a little more at ease now that they were out of Chicago with some distance separating Angel and Mark Swanson. They'd been on the road for about six hours now, and they would travel more at night, and sleep during the day.

Cole's plan was to find a hotel on the outskirts of one of the suburbs where they were large enough to get lost in but still inexpensive enough to pay cash without too much notice. Alex and Cole thought a suite was best. The one bedroom and a sofa bed in an attached sitting room allowed Cole to stay in the main room with Angel and the others at all times. Cole positioned himself on the sofa bed by the door, which was the only way in, or out, of the room. That was the smartest and safest decision.

Alex passed his hand wearily over his jaw, then used his index finger and thumb to rub both eyes at the same time. They felt gritty, as if they were full of sand. Alex was sure they were red and irritated. He probably looked like he was just coming down from a drug binge, he thought. He didn't care about his image; however, the man he was seeing would be at the top of his game, so it would behoove Alex to be as professional as possible. Alex himself was used to being the one at the top of the corporate food chain, but this was not his usual playing field. Here, he didn't hold all the cards; of which, he was painfully aware. It was unsettling when the stakes were this high.

Alex shrugged into his black Hugo Boss jacket, smoothing down the collar and tugging the cuffs of his sleeves down so the linen, now less than crisp after the fifteen hour trip, just showed beyond the fine, expensive wool. The white gold cufflinks that peeked out, engraved with two entwined As, now had a double meaning. He was conscious that his clothes, at least, were polished perfection, his expensive black dress shoes shone like the lacquered baby grand in his study, and his nails were trimmed—manicured to perfection. He pushed on his sunglasses, hoping to hide the effects of his sleepless nights. He'd present confidence, even if a little less fresh than was his norm, and his gut was a mire of fucking knots.

As the limo stopped in front of the high-rise just a few blocks from Avery Enterprises, Alex pulled a small comb from his breast pocket and ran it quickly through his hair. When he walked into the lobby, heads turned. Alex was a formidable presence, and he was well known in the Chicago world of business. It was unlikely he'd go anywhere, in Chicago especially, that someone wouldn't recognize him from the local news or some article in Forbes or Business Weekly. He walked to the reception desk that sat in the center of the lobby, just before the elevators.

"May I help you, sir?" A middle-aged woman with short, mousy brown hair looked up from her work and met his eyes. She smiled pleasantly.

"Yes, thank you. I'm Alexander Avery. I'd like to see Marvin Standish, please."

"Of Avery Enterprises?" she asked. "Is Mr. Standish expecting you?"

Alex shook his head. "Yes, and not exactly, Miss..." he waited for her to tell him her name.

"Mrs. Towner."

"Well, Mrs. Towner, I've been traveling, and my secretary had arranged a meeting for Monday, but I'm afraid the matter is somewhat urgent and can't wait that long. I was hoping he might have a few minutes now."

"I don't make his schedule, sir, but I will contact his office to inquire. One moment."

The woman was extremely professional, Alex mused, *given that she worked for the mob.* Alex doubted most of the people employed at Standish Ventures were aware of his illegal activities. Alex didn't want to know at this point, but Standish had information he needed, and surely, given the outward appearance, not all of his businesses were shady. Maybe there was a modicum of decency lurking somewhere beneath the man's murderous surface and he would be willing to help Alex locate Mark Swanson.

The lobby gleamed with slate grey marble on the floors and halfway up the walls. It had been polished to a high sheen and was adorned with a lot of silver-colored sconces and other fixtures. The elevator shafts were shining metal and glass; the doors covered in glimmering mirrors. The large windows that made up the entire outside wall were tinted blue-grey, dark enough to keep the sun out, but still, the street filled with people walking and heavy traffic were clearly visible. It was elegant and impressive. Obviously, if all of his businesses were shady, the IRS and the Chicago police department would be so far up Standish's ass, his eyes would be pushed out of his skull. There was no way he could maintain a building like this, in the middle of Chicago's financial district, if all his income was hidden. It sure as hell made for a good front to keep them off the scent of his more nefarious dealings. Alex couldn't help but acknowledge the man's aptitude.

But, Alex didn't like shady. He didn't like money exchanged under the table, and he didn't like sleazy bastards getting ahead with deception, theft, and murder. His thinking nagged at him while he waited for the receptionist's call to end. He pushed his thoughts down and told himself if this shit were going to wring millions from him, he'd rather 'invest' in Standish's help than Mark Swanson's treachery.

Mrs. Towner hung up the phone and spoke to Alex in a calm, even tone. "Mr. Avery, you may go up. Mr. Standish has a few minutes before his next meeting. His office suite is on the 23rd

floor." She handed Alex a plastic key card. "Give this to the elevator attendant, and he will take you up."

Accepting it, he wondered how to many unfortunate bastards,
this was a one-way elevator ride. "Thank you. I appreciate your
help."

Alex waited as the floors passed. The ride up was fairly swift,
and after the last of the others alighted on the nineteenth floor, it
went straight up without further stops. The attendant handed the
key card back to Alex. "Here you are, sir. Please give this to the
gentleman just to your left."

It must have been some security measure, and it appeared the
elevator attendant was not allowed outside its confines.

When the doors opened, Alex saw the wall was floor to ceiling
dark wood. It had an unusual grain to it. The carpet on the floor
was plush, and Alex's shoes sank a good two inches as he proceeded out and turned to find the man who would take the key. It
didn't take him long. A huge, dark-skinned man, impeccably
dressed, was standing, waiting for Alex. His hand was outstretched,
and Alex put the key into it.

"Hello, I'm Alexander Avery. I'm here to see Mr. Standish."

The hall outside the elevators was short, and a set of ceiling-
high wooden doors was at one end and a solid wall on the other,
suggesting the office took up the entire floor of the building. The
man positioned there didn't speak, just indicated that Alex should
proceed toward the doors. He was more than huge, very tall with
wide girth, and had to weigh at least four hundred pounds. Alex
wondered what type of firearms he was hiding, but it was certain,
he was packing something deadly.

The other men, similarly dressed, and bigger than average,
opened the two doors and waited for Alex to enter. Inside, there was
a young woman seated at a desk quietly working on a computer. She
seemed to keep her head down and not pay attention to his arrival or
the others in the room. The set-up was similar to Mrs. Dane's space

outside his office with another set of doors, which Alex could only assume would lead inside Marvin Standish's private office.

When Alex walked through, the first man remained outside and went back to take his position near the elevators.

"Mr. Standish is through those doors. He's expecting you, Mr. Avery," the smaller of the two men said. Still, he had to be six-two, two-fifty. He and the other man followed close behind Alex, one at each shoulder.

"Before we go in, sir, I'm sorry we have to make sure you aren't armed or wired."

These were polite criminals, Alex scoffed mentally as he nodded. "Fine." He unbuttoned his jacket and held it open so the men had a clear view inside.

"I'm afraid that's not good enough, sir."

Alex's mouth quirked on one side. *These "wise guys" were so polite.* He supposed they needed to appear above reproach to get away with the shit they did. If it were only theft, money laundering, and extortion, he would be surprised. Only serious criminals would care about outward appearances.

The larger of the two patted Alex down: under his arms, the waist and legs of his pants, his inseam up to his balls, and even around his ankles. The experience was slightly rough, designed to give the message that they were serious about protecting their boss and it wouldn't be in Alex's best interest to fuck with any of them. Like anyone would try to take out Standish in his own building. That would be incredibly stupid. It was funny how his mind had started to work on some criminal level, but it was somehow comforting. If Alex lacked anything, it wasn't intelligence, and thinking like them might help his negotiations and maybe keep him from getting killed.

"Do you do this before all business meetings?" Alex asked cryptically. He couldn't help himself. His demeanor scoffing and incredulous, like he dealt with bad shit like this on a daily basis.

One of them eyed Alex warningly but did not offer a reply. Instead, he spoke to his partner. "He's clean."

After that, Alex was allowed inside. There was an older man, with dark, thinning hair in a light grey suit, sitting behind a massive desk in front of the window. The room was large with two sofas, a large screen TV, and a wet bar on one side, while the office was on the other. Again, similar to the set-up he had at Avery, only his was more suited for business.

Marvin Standish stood when Alex entered; the two men, who Alex was beginning to think of as goons, took position on either side of the door, standing stone still with their hands crossed in front of them. Alex glanced back at them then at the small man in front of him.

"Mr. Standish, I'm Alex Avery. Thank you for seeing me on such short notice." He walked forward and reached out to shake the other man's hand.

"Call me Marvin." He indicated two large chairs in front of his desk, and Alex moved to take the one on the right. "I've been interested in doing business with Avery for a while."

Alex settled into the chair at the same time Marvin sat back down behind the desk.

"I'm afraid this isn't about business. I'm aware Mark Swanson was married to your sister."

"Yes. I sat back and watched you flush that piss-ant down the drain. It must have cost millions; decidedly more than he is worth."

"Depends on your perspective, I guess," Alex responded, his voice devoid of all emotion.

The man behind the desk smiled. "I have to admit, it was amusing. Brilliantly played, though I'm dumbfounded why you bothered. Perhaps you can shed some light on your reasoning?"

"My motives were purely personal. Avery lost a shitload of money in the process, but I'd do it again. I'm sorry about what he did to your niece."

Marvin Standish's eyes widened, and his hand came up to his mouth and hovered there.

"You see; I'm dating Angeline Hemming. She was the clinical psychologist assigned to test Mark Swanson for the DA's office, for your niece's case. I'm well aware of the accusations."

"You mean the rape."

"Yes. Angel believed your niece and wanted desperately to find conclusive evidence through her testing procedures, but Swanson was able to cheat the tests. Angel, being Angel, couldn't live with that, so she taunted the bastard over and over trying to crack his resolve. She even lied to him to get the prick to come after her. She risked her own life so the D.A.'s office would be able to convict him on new charges where the key witness wasn't afraid to speak up."

A slow smile spread over Standish's face. "She sounds like a firecracker. And, very dedicated to her work."

"She is, but she's reckless. She took a huge personal risk. She's stubborn and headstrong. At times to her detriment."

"Well, I'm grateful for her diligence. I'm just glad Swanson was her target." He smiled wider.

Alex was annoyed. This was no laughing matter, and though he himself was proud of her convictions, in his opinion, her methods needed work.

"When I figured it all out, I put my plan into action, and it worked but only served to make the bastard even more vengeful. He's stalked and tormented Angel. He broke into her home and brutally attacked her. Currently, he's trying to blackmail me for an exorbitant amount of money."

Alex was still holding his sunglasses and slowly replaced them in the breast pocket of his jacket.

"You don't seem like the type of man to go along with something like that." Standish's eyes narrowed, clearly sizing Alex up.

"No," he answered without a second's hesitation.

"It's nice to know someone wanted to stand up for the poor girl. Your business acumen is legendary in Chicago and beyond, so I'm going to assume you know what's up with my company."

"To an extent. I haven't had the success I've had by being ignorant of what I'm up against before going into any situation. I use knowledge, rather than lies or bullshit illusions, to conduct business; I put the truth on the table and let the cards fall where they may." It was a risk to admit to a man ensconced in the mob, as this one was, that he knew about his illegal dealings. "And this is the truth; I'm in love with Angel, and I will do anything to ensure her safety. I don't know the details of your situation, and I don't need to. I have no ill will or intentions toward you or your businesses. I'm here for no other reason than our mutual problem."

"I see."

"Good."

Standish studied Alex, trying to determine just how far he would go to accomplish his goal. "I wanted to have him permanently put to sleep, but unfortunately, my sister's stomach is not as strong as mine. I don't understand her squeamishness, considering what he did to Sherry."

This was the first time Alex heard a name associated with the girl Angel felt so bad for. "I thought if I ruined him financially, he would be contained due to a lack of resources, but it only made him more dangerous. Angel is professional, and she is careful about professional ethics, but in the case of this dirty fucker, she pushed and pushed. He could have killed her. I believe he would have, if my brother and I hadn't been close by."

"How'd you keep this out of the news?"

"The DA is a personal friend of Angel's, and exposing her name or address might be dangerous to her and detrimental to her future work with their office."

"Ahhhh. And why didn't you just end him then and there?"

"I've asked myself that many times since. I certainly had the opportunity."

"So what do you want from me? To take him out?"

Alex put his hand up and shook his head. "As much as I have wished that fucker dead and buried, no. One of my security operatives assigned to keep Angel safe disappeared a week ago, and we believe Swanson has him. Alive or dead, he has him."

"I did hear of a disappearance on the news, didn't I?"

"Yes. But the police have no leads. What I need from you is just probable places to look. Where he could be hiding or where he would take a hostage to hold or kill them."

Marvin Standish studied Alex for a minute, and Alex held his stance. To appear uneasy at all would not help get what he wanted. Standish was wondering if Alex could be trusted, and what the consequences would be for sharing locations where some of his own dealings had taken place in the past, and would again.

Part of Alex didn't believe Standish would help him, and though he wanted to plead his case, his acute business mind stopped him. *After you close the deal, shut the fuck up and wait for the other guy to crack.* Those were his rules. Good thing Marvin Standish wasn't as practiced with that technique. It didn't take more than thirty seconds for the response to come.

"You and I have similar goals, Avery. Mark Swanson is particularly slimy, even by my standards. The family is what it is, but we do not condone the beating and raping of women, blood relations or not. If I hated him before, I despise him after what he's done to my niece."

Alex sat silently still waiting. This was what he had hoped for, but still Standish was a criminal, surely far worse than Swanson could ever be, due to the power and money he wielded.

"How do I know I can trust you?"

Alex was outwardly calm. The stakes were higher, but this was business, and he'd treat it as such. "You don't," he said simply.

"You aren't stupid, and frankly, I have nothing to offer other than my word. I can tell you this; nothing means more to me than putting that heinous bastard away. I don't care how much money I have to spend, or what I have to resort to, to do it."

"Yes, you do have money. My boys can take care of it, for a price."

Standish had just said he hadn't already killed Swanson due to his sister's sensibilities, but his new offer to do so gave Alex pause, and shook him out of his momentary forgetfulness that this was indeed a killer sitting in front of him.

"Tempting as that sounds, the police are involved in the search for my employee, and that would be too suspicious and not in your best interest. I just want to find Swanson, and, hopefully save the life of my man."

"The police involvement is a problem. Let's just say, I don't need my secrets exposed and rifled through."

"I get it. I don't plan to involve them. I'll hunt him down myself."

"Alone?"

"I'm at my wall. The bulk of my resources are engaged elsewhere, but I'm done toying with this asshole. I tried to do it on the straight and narrow, but you can't reason with the unreasonable. If things have to get a little messy, so be it. You have my word, I will not disclose anything we discuss, now or at any time in the future."

Marvin Standish smiled a wicked grin. "Good, because you know, I'm very comfortable with messes." It was a barely veiled threat. "Understood?"

"Understood. I knew my risks when I walked in here, but Angel is worth it to me."

"If Swanson was to have an accident, my problem would be solved and I'd be able to look my sister in the eye and tell her honestly it is not on my hands."

Alex should have been shocked or shaken, but he wasn't in the least. His first and only priority was putting Swanson down. In jail or in hell, it mattered little at this point.

Marvin nodded at the two guys still stationed at the door. "Tell Millie to print out the addresses for the house in Northbrook and the one in Rockford."

"Northbrook?" Alex asked. He expected Englewood, maybe. It was notoriously crime-ridden and dangerous. Northbrook was one of the nicest suburbs in Chicago. Marvin nodded, and Alex tried to think more like a criminal. Northbrook's police would be less concentrated, and Standish certainly had the money to set up shop where he'd have more freedom with fewer eyes on his illegal activities. It made sense, in a twisted way. Rockford was west of the city by sixty or so miles, and Alex could also see the logic behind that choice.

"Should I expect anyone else to be in occupancy at either of these locations? Beyond Swanson and his entourage?"

"No. Mark wouldn't show his face anywhere we would be. Although, I'm not sure he'd risk these places, regardless."

Soon the piece of paper was folded and shoved into his pocket, and Alex was rising to leave. "Thank you, Marvin. More than anything, I'm trying to keep Angel safe."

The older man reached out to shake his hand. "I understand, and because she tried to help my niece at the risk of her own life, I am willing to help. Maybe we can do business sometime."

Alex smiled. Here it was. The tricky place he'd have to wiggle out of. "I'm afraid this will be my only foray into side-stepping the law, but if it's legal, I'd be happy to partner up on a deal or two." Happy wasn't the exact emotion he felt, but he owed him now, and as long as it was something legal and wouldn't drag Avery Enterprises down by association, it should be fine. In any case, he'd cross that bridge when he came to it. For now, it wasn't a concern.

"Maybe you could broker some property for me, since I may need a new one after this. Or advise me on some wise stock investments."

"I can advise on a few investment opportunities, certainly. I do well, but I'm not always right. Only most of the time." He offered a sly smirk.

The other man laughed. "No worries, Alex. I understand the risk."

"Well, I can promise you I won't advise you to buy anything that I wouldn't be buying myself."

Marvin Standish gave a solid nod. "Good. I think that's a risk we can both live with."

"Counting on it."

Alex exited the offices then the building quickly, pleased with the results of the meeting. He sighed deeply, tension leaving his chest. Obviously, the man was used to getting his meaning across with few incriminating words. He was good at it. That was scary as fuck, if he was honest. He had two armed killers at his back, and now, he had just promised to help Marvin Standish in the stock market.

"At least it'll be legal," he muttered softly, pulling out his phone. Calling his driver, Alex asked he be picked up, but he was anxious to speak to Angel. He hadn't talked to her since before he left Australia, but he'd do that once he was in the car. He needed to stop by his apartment to get some things, keeping the façade of Jillian's party, then to his parents' estate. With any luck, Swanson would show his ugly mug and do something stupid so the police could take him back into custody, though he doubted that would result in obtaining Bancroft's location. Alex would rather bash his fucking head in and needed little provocation anymore. Mark Swanson deserved a quick trip to hell. The thought should have made him shudder. *Should have.*

12

Party On

THE BLINDS WERE drawn so they could try to get some sleep despite the daytime hour. However, Jillian had slept most of the night on the road and didn't hold the same interest in a nap as Angel, Cole, and Becca. The adults were tired, and she was on full-throttle.

There was a desk along the wall in the sitting room to the right of the sofa bed Cole had pulled out and camped on. He had ESPN on the television, and Becca sat at the desk helping Jillian color a picture in her Little Mermaid coloring book.

Angel was more than wiped out since she hadn't been sleeping well since Alex left. She'd showered, hoping the hot water would work some of the kinks out of her neck and shoulders. She needed a workout, but it was out of the question because Cole insisted they all remain in the suite together. He couldn't let Angel go without him, and he couldn't leave Becca and Jillian alone in the room. Angel understood, but she was restless and wanted to defuse some of the pent-up energy.

What little luggage they had was still in the back of the rented vehicle, and Cole had brought in the one bag Becca had packed

most of Jillian's things in, so Angel was left to put on the same
clothes she'd worn all night. She couldn't quite convince herself to
reuse her panties, so they were now zippered into an inside pocket
of her Coach purse, and she was going commando. No doubt, Alex
would approve if he were in any kind of close proximity. *If he were
aware of it, period,* Angel mused. A sad smile settled on her face as
she looked in the mirror above the single sink in the bedroom part
of the suite, towel drying her long hair. She sighed deeply at the
turn of events.

Since she and Alex met, this was the longest they'd gone
without being in touch. She longed to be in his arms, held close
to him, but she missed just talking to him; his sexy teasing and the
snarky banter they engaged in had become a big part of her
world. Alex had, in a short time, become the center of her
universe. How amazing it was that such utter happiness could
turn to constant worry. That was the worst part of loving
someone, and for the first time since forever, she questioned her
career choice. It was one thing to put oneself in danger to follow
your convictions and completely another to risk those you cared
about.

She hated Mark Swanson for turning her world upside down.
Fucking hated him.

After she'd combed through her damp hair and decided
against blowing it dry, Angel wandered into the other room and
crawled onto the open sofa sleeper with Cole. He was staring at the
TV, the remote firmly within his grasp, his phone perched on his
stomach lying in wait.

"Have you heard from anyone?" she asked.

"Not yet."

"Mmm… What time will we leave?"

"Maybe nine? You should try to sleep."

"I can't sleep, and you're one to talk."

"I know, but I can sleep when we get to Joplin."

"I can ask Will and Uncle Ben if we can spend part of the time at their place. They have a small farm on the outskirts of town, and it will be fun for Jillian."

"Remote is fine if they and your father are there as well. And they're armed."

"What the hell? This is bullshit!" Angel's frustration burst through her words. "Everyone's life is turned upside down because of this one asshole."

"That's putting it mildly," Cole muttered. "Alex is holing up at Mr. and Mrs. James' and setting up all this fake shit, which, my gut says will be for nothing."

Angel turned on her side toward Cole so she could continue in softer tone. "If he doesn't kill anyone else, it won't be for nothing."

"Yes. But Alex is hoping he'll make a move so the police can catch him."

Angel's heart tightened. So Alex would be right in the middle of it.

"Why does Alex need to be there?"

"He doesn't have to be. He's Alex, Angel. He orchestrated this stakeout. Do you really expect him to wait around off-site?"

Angel knew Cole was right. "No. How can you stand all of this waiting?"

He changed the channel and glanced over at her. "I'm used to it. It's my job."

"You're good at it."

"Mama, is it time to go to my birfday party yet?" Jillian put down her crayon and looked up at her mother expectatnly. Becca hugged Jillian and let out a big sigh. Angel's heart fell. It was so unfair to Jillian. "Will we have cake, and clowns, and games?"

"Honey, you know how we're on this trip?" When Jillian nodded, Becca's sad eyes met Angel's over the toddler's head. "We might have to go to your party on another day."

Jillian's face fell and crumpled as she started to cry. "But it's today!" she wailed loudly. Becca gathered her up in her arms, but Jillian struggled. "I'm tree today!"

"Ugh," Cole groaned. "Poor little squirt."

Angel nodded.

"I know you're three today. I'm sorry, baby. Angel had something important to do, and she really needed our help. We can't go to the party today."

Jillian cried harder and harder, the tears rolling down her face as she wailed loudly. Angel's heart broke for the little girl. At barely three years old, all she knew was something she'd looked forward to wasn't going to happen, and it wasn't fair. Angel doubted anything would console her, but she'd do her best.

She got up and went to kneel in front of Jillian, who was still on Becca's lap.

"Honey, we'll still have your party, I promise. Zander was so disappointed to miss it, and he didn't have time to shop for your present. Since he couldn't come today, we thought we'd have a little adventure. When he gets back from his big business trip, we'll have an even bigger party, I promise. Would that be okay?" Angel coaxed gently. She reached out and ran a comforting hand through the toddler's blonde curls.

The little girl sniffed and looked at Angel, her chin still trembling and big crocodile tears tumbling down her cheeks. Jillian nodded weakly and went into Angel's arms when she held them out. "Why don't we get the presents I have for you, and you can open them today, okay? Maybe we can get some cupcakes, and we can play some games with you, sweetheart." Angel kissed her temple. "I love you so much, Bean. I'll make it up to you. I promise. We're going to have a great time on this trip. And when we get where we're going, I'm going to take you horseback riding. One of my daddy's friends has horses, and I'll take you there. Won't that be fun?"

Cole watched Angel try to comfort the little girl. There were so many sides to her, and it was easy to see why she'd gotten to Alex. Becca, to give her credit, had dealt with the situation like a trooper. She could have pissed and moaned, complaining about her plans being ruined and refuse to cooperate with what Angel needed. Instead, she was understanding and supportive. The two of them were like sisters, and a strong support system for each other. From what he could tell, Becca's baby daddy left her high and dry with the kid to raise alone. It was clear the threesome was tight. He was curious about Becca and how she and Angel came to be so close.

"Can I pet them and give them kisses?"

Angel smiled brightly. "Of course! We'll feed them, too! They love apples and carrots, but their favorite of all is pears."

"I yike pears, too." Jillian began to liven up, and Becca looked relieved.

"So do I." Angel looked up at Cole hopefully. "Can we get her gifts out of the car? Please?"

"Uh…"

"And some cupcakes and candles?"

"Angel, getting the gifts from the car is doable, but going to the store—"

"I can lock the door behind you, and you can make up some dumb secret knock," she said wryly. Her eyebrow shot up, and she pursed her lips. "Okay?" She had a sparkle in her eye that reminded him of the real Angel who faced things head-on, not the resigned one who packed up her shit and hauled ass to avoid a bad situation. When he stopped to consider it, it was more like Angel to stand up.

"I can go with you, and we can pick up some food, too," Becca said. "Angel, can you give Jillian a bath and get her into some clean pajamas in the meantime?"

Cole looked uneasy. "I don't know if it's a good idea to leave Angel here alone."

"The door will be locked, Cole, and you have a key. I won't open it for anyone."

Her response settled him, and he finally agreed. After putting on his worn white sneakers and grabbing his coat, he pulled his keys out of his pocket.

"Need any money?" Angel asked, secretly pleased that Becca was going with Cole. The last guy she dated was a loser, and nothing would please her more than a spark igniting between those two. She'd already seen interest on both sides. This was good.

"Nah, I got it. Ready?" Cole asked Becca. She was already putting on her jacket and shoes.

Angel scooted Jillian off toward the bathroom.

"Hey, Becs?" Angel called and motioned for her to follow.

"Yeah?"

"Can you bring my bag in? I need panties."

"Yeah, no problem." She turned and followed Cole out. "Do the safety thing. Whatever the hell you call it."

"Anga!" Jillian bellowed. Angel was amazed how resilient children were. After crying her eyes out mere minutes ago, the little one was laughing and happy at the prospect of her bath. "C'mon!"

"Coming!" Angel called. "See you two in a bit."

By the time Angel had the bath water adjusted and running, Jillian had her clothes off and in a pile on the floor in front of the tub. The hotel provided toiletries, and thankfully, there was one more bottle of the shampoo and conditioner on the counter next to the sink. Angel grabbed two of them and picked up Jillian to put her into the tub.

"Bubbles! Bubbles!" Jillian demanded, and Angel proceeded to dump half of the shampoo under the water streaming into the tub. She swooshed it around in the water to make it bubble more. and Jillian squealed. "More!"

"We have to save a little to wash your hair, Bean."

The phone in the other room started playing the Nickleback song that signaled a call from Alex. Angel hopped up anxiously to get it. Her purse was thrown on the bed, only a few feet away. The water had only filled a couple of inches, and Angel had returned to the bathroom to keep an eye on Jillian before she answered.

"Hello?"

"Hey, babe. It's good to hear your voice." His voice was weary.

"Yeah, I've been going crazy." She sat down next to the tub so she could keep a close eye on Jillian. "You sound tired."

"I'm okay. Did I catch you in the bathtub?" His voice held a teasing lilt despite his exhaustion.

Angel smiled and reached her free hand into the tub to hand Jillian a washcloth. "Nope, but Jillybean is!"

"Aw, you're on baby duty."

"Mmm. Bean is being a very big girl about rescheduling her party. I told her you wanted to be there." Angel said it so that Jillian could understand it was Alex on the phone.

"Iz dat Zander?" she asked, her little voice, though echoing in the small ceramic-clad room, was muted due to the rushing water. Angel decided it was full enough and shut it off.

"Yes, honey." She nodded. There were a couple of plastic cups on the counter near the mirror, and Angel took one and un-wrapped it so Jillian could play with it in the bathtub. The little girl busied herself filling it and dumping it over herself then the sides of the tub.

"Sorry about that," Angel said, settling in so she could keep an eye on Jillian and still speak to Alex. "Are you okay?"

"Yeah. I'm holed up at the James' with the cops and Sid's team. I'm suspicious of everyone and trying to figure out which of them informs that prick what we're doing."

Angel leaned one shoulder on the tub. "I know. I bet you wish you'd never made that call into the radio station. Everything is so fu—um, messed up." She caught her word choice given the child within hearing.

"Yes, but no. This is a pain in my ass, and I am not happy about any of it, but I am glad I made that call."

"I really miss you."

"That's cuz I'm so lovable." The smile in his voice radiated through the phone.

She laughed. "Yeah, okay. You're a lot of things, but lovable? Are you Fozzie Bear, now?" At the name of the Sesame Street character, Jillian looked up at Angel, dropping the cup then picking it up again to resume the endless cycle of filling and dumping it out.

"He died, I think." Alex joked. "I think I heard Miss Piggy fucked him to death."

"What a way to die."

"Yes. You can try to kill me when you see me next." They both laughed softly, and Angel's heart leapt.

"Surprised you're still breathing, as it is," Angel shot back dryly, followed by another giggle.

"We spend so much time on the phone, we may have to re-sort to phone sex," Alex teased. "Or Skype. That would be even better."

"Mmmmm." Her eyes widened and she smiled. "That would be great, except I'm far from alone here."

"I know, but it's a nice thought." He huffed out a small laugh.

"I wish." As much as Angel wanted to joke and tease with him, the seriousness of the situation intruded. "Can you tell me the plan? Cole told me only bits and pieces."

"I'll stay here and hope something happens. There hasn't been any contact at all, so we're expecting something to happen soon. It goes without saying that the money doesn't move." It was hard trying to explain what was going on so Angel would know what was happening but not give details that might foil the plan.

"Alex, I have some money saved..." she began.

"You don't have ten million." His voice took on an impatient tone that she would even suggest it. "Even if you did, I wouldn't let you give him ten cents, Angel. I'm not paying that fucker for hurting people. I'm done dicking around with this."

"What does that mean?"

"If we pay him off once, it will never end, and we're not going to live like that." His voice was low and determined. "I have an idea where to take this, so it stops now."

"Did they track the tower the call came from?"

"Yeah. Ken requested that, but the call originated in Chicago, so it's like looking for a needle in a haystack. But don't worry; I've got this, babe. You have to trust me."

"Then how do you know anything? What's next?"

"It's a trade secret."

"Ugh! Really?" She groaned and soaped up the cloth to begin washing Jillian's arms and hands, then her legs, feet, and back. Alex could hear the water sloshing over the phone. He laughed at her predicament.

"How do you like it? Hmm?" Amusement laced his voice. "It's a bitch, isn't it?"

"Fine." Angel was exasperated, but his point hit home. "Then tell the police what you know and meet us."

"The police stood around for a full week with their dicks in their hands waiting for shit to fall in their laps. It's pathetic. I've spent all day on this, and I'm certain the only reason it's in play at all is because I'm bankrolling it. That said, they're here now, and everything is set up. Now we wait."

"I can't stand the waiting."

"I agree. So, I have other plans. I'd tell you more, but the phones aren't secure."

"Is it okay if I call anyone? Ally called and I haven't called her back. Also, I haven't told *anyone we're coming.*" At Cole's instruction, Angel was careful to keep names and locations out of conversations, so she emphasized the words so Alex would understand. She wondered if calling in general was a bad idea.

"Not unless absolutely necessary. We probably shouldn't even be talking now."

"I'm glad you called, though."

"I needed to hear your voice, but I probably won't call again. We can be in touch on Skype or chat, but no more phones, okay? Email Allison if you need to, but be conscious of what you say. Can you just show up at your destination without calling ahead of time?" Alex was careful not to give any specifics over the phone in case the call was being monitored.

"Yes."

"Just get where you're going, babe."

The water was getting tepid and Angel needed to warm it up before she finished the little one's bath. "Jillian's getting cold, and I need to shampoo her hair and get her out of the tub."

"Okay. I'll be in touch somehow. Be careful. Is Cole around?"

"Um…" Her hesitation gave her away. Given the worry about the vulnerability of the phone, she didn't want to say Cole and Becca weren't there.

"*Angel.* Is he around?" Alex demanded.

Shit. Angel cringed inwardly, knowing Alex wasn't going to tolerate the fact she was alone in the hotel room with the baby.

"He's making dinner." She hoped that would be sufficient to tell Alex he was out getting food.

"It might be his last meal."

"Oh, Jeesh." Angel rolled her eyes. "I'm fine, Alex. I can fight better than him anyway." She laughed, but Alex was far from amused.

Being so far away, he felt helpless to protect her, and although Swanson was most likely still in Chicago, he didn't want her unprotected. She could fight well, but still, where the fuck was Cole? If anything happened to Angel or Jillian, there would be more than hell to pay. Brother or no.

*****

Alex sat in the living room of Mr. and Mrs. James' home. The police had relocated them to his own parents' estate, and Wayne was there with them, the rest of the team was surrounding the house and ground, save Sid and two others, who were with Alex. His stomach ached and his head throbbed. He felt strange and out-of-body; his hands were tingling, and he was all hopped up. It had to be a combination of lack of sleep and the many cups of coffee he'd been downing which had him feeling so fucked up.

Most of his security team was positioned at his parents' property, and the bulk of what was here at the James' home, were police and the two detectives assigned to Bancroft's missing person's case. There were police vans outside disguised as catering trucks and a children's entertainment company, but the bounce house that was scheduled to be set up was cancelled because it would have blocked the view of the backyard. The illusion was in place, but there was no guarantee Mark Swanson had plans to hit the party, despite the hints he'd dropped to Angel. It was all they had, though, and at least they were prepared. The time spent at police headquarters after his meeting with Marvin Standish only had Alex more pissed and convinced that if he wanted something done, he'd have to do it himself. The police didn't have a single new lead on Jason's disappearance and, from what Alex could see, were doing little to dig for any.

He was also agonizing because he'd forgotten to ask Marvin Standish who might be helping Swanson. Alex was certain someone on his security team was a plant. Anger tightened his gut. They had run background checks on all of them. They'd been sent to Alex via email so he could look them over again, but he hadn't had the time.

Ken Gant had been at the station earlier that day, and he was also worried about Angel. Jealousy wheedled underneath Alex's skin, but he had to ignore it and concentrate on the task at hand. Ken had wanted to be on location tonight also, but it was a conflict of interest for the prosecuting attorney to be on scene. And, it was dangerous. Alex was allowed only because his own security team was present and consisted of licensed PIs. He had paid for the illusion and made a hellish scene when they tried to dissuade him from being there. Leaning his head back on the sofa, he closed his burning eyes as his exhaustion finally caught up with him.

The blinds were drawn so no one could see the party inside was an illusion, but there was audio of children's voices, along with Barney the dinosaur and Disney songs playing for illusion. He lifted his head to glance around. Sid was talking to someone by the closed front door, and others were stationed at the windows, in the garage, and both of the other entrances to the house. It was a modest, middle-class home, but it was clean and the furnishings were well taken care of. Alex regretted that this family was involved. But, the obvious threat on Swanson's call to Angel had predisposed everything that was happening now.

How long had they been here? He glanced at his watch. It was 7 PM, and the party should be ending soon and nothing. Fucking nothing!

Alex motioned Sid over, and he excused himself from the detective he was speaking to and came over. "Yes, Alex?"

"In half an hour, the party is supposed to end. What happens with the trucks?"

"We were just discussing that. I suggest that the trucks leave at the allotted time and our team hang out here for a while afterward. The other 'guest's' cars will have to go, too."

Alex ran a hand through his hair and nodded. It made sense, but there was no use wasting more time here. "I think I'll get out of here, then."

"We suggest you stay. Swanson thinks you're out of town, but if I and the others have to stay here, you won't be protected at your home."

"Sid, this asshole has to go down, and maybe we can catch him if we give him a little bait."

"You sound like Dr. Hemming, and she was a huge pain in my ass. If you don't mind my honesty, it just makes things more difficult for us."

Alex's mouth quirked slightly on one side. He understood the frustration. He'd shared it even, but he was exhausted, and the sooner he got going, the sooner he could start his search. If this stakeout didn't yield an arrest, then he'd wasted the whole goddamned day when he could have been getting ready to start tracking Swanson. He understood, but he was itching to get started. He was so tired, but the dark of night would be the best time to poke around the addresses that Standish provided.

He considered telling Sid about his meeting earlier that morning, and he wished he could take him along, but doing so could leave Wayne a sitting duck. Alex's phone vibrated from the clip on his belt and he pulled it out. "Restricted number" flashed on the screen, and his breath stopped. It had taken longer than Alex suspected for Swanson to call, considering the money hadn't been transferred and the deadline had passed an hour earlier.

There was a set-up for a wireless phone trace that had been connected to Alex's phone then through a piece of equipment being monitored in one of the bedrooms. "This is it. I'm sure this is the call."

Two of the detectives scrambled, one alerting the man with the tracing equipment and another coming closer and sitting down next to Alex so he could listen in.

He nodded, indicating they were ready and Alex could answer.

"Alex Avery," he said into the phone, trying to remain calm. Every nerve in his body was at attention.

"Where is the money?"

Alex considered his words carefully. "That's too much to get together that fast. Most of it is tied up and has to be liquidated."

"I'm not fucking around, Avery. Sorry, I wasn't in the mood for birthday cake. You people are stupid as fuck. You think I'd tell that bitch I knew about it and then show up? I'm not anywhere near where you think I am, and you'd better start cooperating."

Alex's hand tightened around the phone until his knuckles turned white, his heart and mind began to race, and a hot flush rushed underneath his skin. If he wasn't here; then where? If he knew about the stakeout, what else did he know? "I told you before; I don't negotiate with sick fuckers like you, Swanson."

"Yeah, you did. But, I think you're gonna change your mind." Swanson sounded amused, and it made Alex's blood boil. "The package you're after has been returned to the place of procurement. My advice is to hurry, or you might be too late." His laugh was obnoxious and eerie. Alex had a slight moment's pause that maybe he was completely mad.

One of the detectives jumped up and went into the other room to get on his com and order officers to the radio station. They would find Bancroft there. Alex felt like the floor had just dropped from underneath him.

"We knew he was dead already. If you think killing one of my guys will motivate me to pay you off, you are fucking delusional or completely insane." His voice was low and deadly calm. "Either way, fuck off."

Mark Swanson's breath sucked in with a hiss. "Careful. You don't want to piss me off more than you already have. You'll understand I'm serious. If you don't want something similar to befall the lovely doctor, or maybe worse, I'd suggest you reconsider. I think I'd enjoy making her beg."

"You cowardly fuck. Why don't you be a man and come out in the open? Come and get me, you sorry bastard!"

Swanson laughed at Alex's obvious fury, his hideousness making Alex all the more livid.

"That's an interesting thought, but I like my plan better. I'm gonna take your little girl, and do all kinds of unspeakable things to her if you don't pay up." Swanson's tone became insidious. "Do you hear me? You have one more day."

The phone went dead in his hand, and Alex wanted to fling it against the wall with all of his might. "Motherfucker!" he yelled.

"Mr. Avery, why didn't you just tell him you'd meet him with the money? At least give us a chance to set him up?"

Alex stood up angrily and got in the man's space, his face mottled with rage. "He's not going to meet me for the money! He wants it wired to that account I've already given you people. Are you brain dead?" Alex was incensed with rage. "With Bancroft dead, he has nothing to bargain with. We just have to find him before he gets to Angel. Do your fucking job, for Christ's sake! Stop waiting for me to land this bastard in your lap!"

"First, we should get a detail over to protect Dr. Hemming."

"You're too late; behind the fucking eight ball again." Alex moved away and grabbed his jacket. "Sid, you're with me."

"Mr. Avery, you have to tell us what you know."

Alex shook his head. "No. I don't have time to waste answering your questions. You heard what that crazy bastard said."

Wayne stood by Alex waiting, and soon, both of them were moving toward the door. "Mr. Avery!" the detective called again. "How can we help if you don't talk to us?"

"I've been talking to you for a goddamned week, and you've done nothing!" Alex yelled. "You sit around with your heads up your asses, and one of my guys gets murdered! That isn't the kind of help I need."

"Calm down, Mr. Avery," the man began. The three others emerged from the adjoining rooms at Alex's outburst. "This isn't helping anyone."

Alex huffed and shook his head wryly. These idiots didn't seem in the business of helping anyone. "I'm out. Let's go, Sid."

In less than sixty seconds, Alex and Sid were buckled into Alex's Audi and speeding away from Becca's parents' house, toward downtown. Alex was tense, his shoulders rigid and his hands gripped tightly around the leather-wrapped steering wheel. Merging on to I-90, they headed in the direction of KKIS.

"I wonder if I should call Darian," Alex muttered, as if to himself.

"If you want my opinion, Alex, I'd say let the police crime scene people handle it. It will probably be pretty gruesome."

"No doubt." Alex didn't feel secure calling Cole on his cell, so he asked Sid to contact him on the walkie-talkie.

"Come in, over?" Sid said, speaking into his device. The police band type like they had was equipped to block monitoring. Alex made a mental note to call the home security people who set up the wireless system at his house to inquire about a way to block monitoring on his personal phones.

"Yeah, I'm here." Cole's voice was muffled and filled with static as it came through. "Anything?"

"We're going to the radio station now, but Alex had a call from the suspect."

Alex cringed. They would be traveling, and Angel would hear the exchange on the walkie-talkies.

"Yeah?" Cole waited.

"He said we'd find Bancroft there."

"Shit." Cole paused. "We knew this was coming. Should we maintain our course or return to the city?"

"Maintain your course."

"We should arrive in a few hours then."

"Ten-four," Sid answered. Alex motioned for him to hand over the walkie-talkie so he could speak to his brother. "Hold on, Cole. Alex wants to talk to you."

He took the walkie-talkie from Sid, pushing the button that would allow him to speak to Cole. "Is the kid asleep?"

There was a slight hesitation before Cole answered, perplexed. "Uh, yeah, why?"

"I don't have time to ream your ass right now but don't fucking leave her again. Is that clear?"

"Yes. Sorry, we were—"

Alex cut Cole off. "Good. Put Angel on."

The next voice was softer and sad but still distorted. "Hey. I'm really sorry about Jason."

"I won't be able to get online tonight, so I wanted to let you know."

"What are you going to do, Alex?"

"Whatever I have to do. Whatever it takes."

"That scares me."

"I know, babe. I'm sorry."

"What did he say?"

Alex swallowed at the tightness in his throat. He was steering with one hand and holding the heavy device with the other. "He was pissed that the money wasn't wired. It's what we expected. I don't want you to worry about it. Just get where you're going and hole up there. Remember what I asked about Will and Ben?"

"Yes."

"Okay, do that. Tell Cole."

"Alex, don't tell me not to worry about it! I'm going nuts over it. Just please come down here. We can stay with them until it's over."

"I'm not going to run from this prick, Angel. You have to trust me. I will keep all of you safe, if it's the last thing I do."

Angel's voice broke. "Don't say things like that. You made me need you so you better not do anything reckless! You better not leave me, Alex! He's not worth it."

"No, but I will, okay?"

He could hear her heavy sigh, even with the interference. "Nothing is worth losing you. I love you."

"Me, too. It's going to be okay, babe. I promise. I'll be in touch when I can."

"Be careful."

"I will. Bye."

He let go of the button and handed it back to Sid, glancing in his direction.

"I'm going to set you up at my folks with Wayne. I don't trust anyone else. It's not safe to leave either of you alone with the others. Make up some fake assignment for them. Be creative but keep them busy. I don't care what it is."

"Shouldn't one of us go with you? It's not safe for you to be alone."

"I realize that. I have someone in mind to help me, but this fucker is going down."

13

Unlikely Allies

THEY FOUND JASON Bancroft in a bloody heap, slumped against the door of the radio station. His jugular had been cut, and he was lying in a sticky pool of his own blood that stretched a good six feet around him.

When Alex and Sid arrived, the police were already there, and the station owners had been called to the scene. The ambulance on scene turned its flashing lights off as it began to pull away.

The police were blocking off the parking lot with yellow "crime scene" tape, and they prevented Alex and Sid from walking in, but it was close enough to see how gruesome the scene was. Alex cringed.

"I'm sorry; we need to keep a perimeter around the scene clear."

Alex nodded his understanding. Even though he was involved, he knew they wouldn't let him through, and really, he didn't need to see that gruesome, bloody mess up close.

"Fuck!" Jason had been alive until this evening. Alex turned from the scene and yelled again. "I should have just paid the bastard off!"

He felt sick to his stomach, and it wasn't due to the salty stench of blood that permeated the air. His mind was torturing him. *This is all my fault*, he thought.

"Do you think paying would have stopped him? This guy is a sociopath. He gets off on torturing people, and he has no remorse," Sid said.

Alex put both hands on top of his head. His gut started to ache. Bancroft's kids were now fatherless. and his wife was a widow. "Goddamn it!" he swore under his breath. His throat tightened, and his eyes burned.

"Two of the detectives who were at the party tonight arrived; I'm going to talk to them," Sid said.

Alex nodded. He'd removed his jacket and tie at the James' house, and his sleeves were rolled up. It was getting cold. The late fall air was crisp, and the lake always made it breezy. Alex was immune to the biting burn as it whipped across his face.

He leaned up against his car and watched Sid walk away. He rubbed the back of his neck. How the fuck was this going to end? He went over the possibilities in his head. After this, it was even more repugnant to pay Swanson off, but he was openly threatening Angel, and the last thing she'd want would be to keep running and hiding from that cocksucker. The cops seemed content to do the barest minimum, but to be fair, Marvin Standish wouldn't tell the cops what he'd told Alex. The position Alex was in was dangerous; precarious, at best. His whole world could come crashing down and destroy his entire family.

His gut was burning with the knowledge of what needed to be done, and it went against everything he was, but Mark Swanson had to be stopped. At any cost.

Sid returned to where Alex waited. "The coroner is on his way. There isn't much we can do here. They'll do an autopsy, but the cause of death is pretty clear. Poor bastard."

"So who tells his wife?"

"The police will handle it."

"I feel like a pussy if I don't go talk to her. Offer my condolences. *Something*."

"I'm guessing, she won't be consolable at the moment."

"Yeah." Alex sighed. He was tired and tormented. His right hand kneaded his neck wearily.

"There will be time to talk to her. Maybe at the funeral."

"If this shit is over by then," Alex responded soberly. His expression turned from sadness to determination. "Let's get out of here."

His phone began to ring, and Alex pulled it out. It was Darian. He answered at the same time as the two men got into Alex's Audi.

"Hello?"

"I just got a call from the station owners. Apparently, there's a dead guy in front of the station? Is it related to last week's car fire? Your security guard?"

"Yes."

"I'm sorry. Is there anything I can do?"

"Not really, D. Just let them clean this shit up. The coroner and crime scene detectives are here. Has Angel's show been arranged?"

"Yes, the production team set up a pre-recorded show, and it's on a timer. Thank God."

"It's best to keep everyone away then. Is that possible?"

"For now. There is always a syndicated show via satellite after Angel's gig, and that runs all night, until about 5 AM, when the morning jocks take over. Will it be clear by then?"

"I'm not the one to ask." Alex started the car and pulled away from the curb.

"I picked up the ring tonight. It's stunning."

"Just hold on to it. I have shit I have to do for a few days, so I may be a little out of pocket."

"Okay. Alex? Be careful."

"I will. Thanks."

Alex threw his phone in the console between the seats.

"What's the plan, boss?" Sid asked.

"We're going to my parents' place, and we'll release all the guards except you and Wayne. I want you heavily armed, so if you don't have all of your shit, you need to get it."

"Most of it is in the trunk of Wayne's car. He has it with him."

"Good. My dad is a collector, so he has a couple of rifles and some handguns in the house, too. I hope he has ammunition, but I'm not sure."

"Does he hunt?"

"No. We never hunted. My mother would have freaked if we actually killed anything, but Cole and I learned to shoot as kids. Dad likes the history surrounding old guns, and even if they never really get used, he'll leave them to Cole and me."

"Alex, I really don't think Swanson will come after your parents or your sister. He knows Angel is your real Achilles heel."

Alex knew this but couldn't fill Sid in on his plans. It was no use implicating Sid or Wayne if he did have to kill Mark Swanson. The less they knew about it, the better. But, Alex would be an idiot to go after him alone. "Obviously, I've had Cole take Angel away from Chicago for exactly that reason, but everyone I care about is at risk."

"Do your parents know what's going on?"

"Cole had to tell them some of it to get them to hole up in the house."

"I understand."

"I'll tell them more when we get there."

The car was speeding north of the city, the Chicago skyline and the full moon brilliant against the gleam of Lake Michigan.

Sid knew the way to Alex's parents' estate, and the two of them remained silent the rest of the forty-minute drive.

Alex's brain was turning the events of the evening over in his head; his instincts to do the right thing colliding with his need to see Mark Swanson stopped. He considered that maybe the deeds of other men might sometimes dictate whether other, good men's lives took a less than savory turn. Love, fury, and desperation just to survive might make a man do things he might not otherwise do. Alex was at that precipice, and he knew it. He'd been pushed as far as he could tolerate.

When Alex punched in the security code that would grant entry to his parents' estate, his eyes strained toward the floodlights positioned all around the house. The glare blinded him, keeping any vehicles in front from being visible. The house was surrounded by trees, and the road leading in had only one or two other properties on it. It was very isolated, more than his home, but both were on security lockdown. With the window down, the engine was still quiet enough to hear the crickets chirping. The rustic, nature smell should have reminded Alex of his youth and all the times that Cole and he would build forts in the woods surrounding the house, but not tonight.

The house itself was only twenty years old but had a classic craftsman styling with stone chimneys and foundation. The outside was painted a light slate gray with bluish tints, but the brightness of the outdoor lights made the color appear more whitish yellow. The lights were motion sensitive and were usually off, but at Alex's instruction, his father had left them on continuously. To be fair, his family had done what Cole had instructed without many questions, but Alex knew he'd have to explain once inside.

The car sidled up to the house via the curved driveway. The garage entry was around the side of the house, but Alex decided it best to leave his car in front so the security team could leave. Sid and Alex got out of the car and walked up the stone steps to the porch.

"You and Wayne stay here, but excuse the others for the night. Tell them you'll be in touch with their assignments." Alex's

voice was low as his hand went to his phone. He texted Allison to
alert her they arrived and were at the front entrance. In less than
thirty seconds the door was opened by his brother-in-law, Josh. He
was tall, thin, and gangly, maybe two inches taller than any of the
Avery men, though they all stood at six-foot-two. His hair was
combed, and he was wearing jeans and a sweater.

"Hey, man." Josh stood aside so the two men could enter,
closing the door and resetting the security behind them. "It's good
to see you." He reached out and shook Alex's hand.

Max barked and came bounding in from the kitchen to jump
up on Alex. "Down, Max." Alex commanded but bent to ruffle his
fur. "I missed you, too, buddy."

Alex's sister and mother appeared in the entryway, coming
from the family room and both came forward to greet him.

"I'll go find the others," Sid murmured.

"They're in the kitchen," Allison answered, pointing toward
the back of the house.

"Thank you. Excuse me." With that, he disappeared in the direction of the kitchen.

This was the first time Sid had been here, but Alex would
make introductions later. He wrapped his arms around his sister,
her eyes questioning. She smelled nice, the way she always did. He
doubted she'd changed her perfume since elementary school, but it
suited her.

"Honey, is everything all right?" his mother asked.

"Yes. Is Dad around? I'd like to speak to everyone together.
Including Mr. and Mrs. James."

"Dad is entertaining them in the den. I think they're playing
pool," Allison said.

"They are," Josh added.

Alex hugged his mother and kissed her on the cheek before
ushering them into the den where his father and the other couple

were leisurely talking. Becca's dad bent over to take a shot but stopped when he saw the others enter the room.

"Alex!" Charles said. "Son, I'm so glad to see you. What's going on?" He didn't waste time but got straight to the point. "The women have been worried sick."

"Hi, Dad. Can you all have a seat, please? I don't have a lot of time, but I'll tell you what I can."

"We know there was some stakeout at the James' tonight. They told us that much."

Alex nodded. He wanted a drink, but his exhaustion and everything still in front of him made that a bad idea. "Allison, will you get me some water, please?"

"Certainly." She went to the far side of the room and grabbed a cold water bottle from the refrigerator behind the bar.

The others were seated, looking up at Alex with a mixture of concern, confusion, and curiosity in their expressions. Ally handed the water to her brother then went to sit down.

"First, where are the girls and Cole?" Cora asked.

Alex walked to the door of the den and closed it. If any of the security team were still in the house, he didn't want them to hear the discussion and, most especially, any details of his plan.

"They're on their way to Angel's father's house in Missouri." He could see a question about to come from his mother, and he put up a hand to stop her. "Last week, after our dinner, I went with Angel to the radio station during her show. One of the perpetrators from a case she is working on has been threatening her."

His father's expression became enlightened. He was putting two and two together about Alex's intervention on the business end with Mark Swanson's dry cleaning business. "I see," he said.

"Yes." The others didn't know what Charles understood, but Alex would leave him to explain later. "He raped his stepdaughter, and Angel has been trying to put him away, but the slimy bastard cheated her testing methods, and she didn't have the evidence. I stepped in, thinking if I could ruin him financially, I could accomplish what Angel couldn't. I thought if he was penniless, he couldn't evade the law, pay for lawyers... but it only pissed him off." Alex shook his head. "You get the picture. I can't tell you all of the details because I don't have time, but he's still threatening to hurt Angel, and he abducted one of our security guys and killed him."

Cora gasped, and Emily, Becca's mother, put a hand to her mouth.

"Holy shit," Josh said. "We heard about the man disappearing from that area of town last week. Is that related?"

"Yes. Angel wanted to be here for Jillian's birthday, but I couldn't risk it. She got a call from that bastard, and he knew about the event. I sent them out of town to keep them safe, and we have all of you together here so we can do the same for you. The police haven't done a lot so far, but maybe they'll find a clue on Jason's body. He was found tonight at the radio station."

"I had no idea Angel's job was so dangerous," Charles muttered. "Why would she involve herself in something like this?"

"She's got something in her past that drives her." Becca's mother spoke up for the first time, and the others looked at her. "Not many people know, but someone hurt her in college. Angel is a wonderful person, and she thinks more of others than herself. She's been amazing to Becca and Jillian."

Alex swallowed, his heart swelled with both pride and fear. "Yes, she loves them both very much." He glanced around at the six pairs of eyes on him, all waiting to hear the rest of his explanation. "Anyway, his name is Mark Swanson. He's trying to extort money from me by threatening to hurt Angel. He wants the money he lost when his businesses got flushed."

"The man with all of those drycleaners?" Cora's expression was astonished.

"Because of you?" Allison asked.

Alex nodded. He felt agitated by his sister's question. It sounded like an accusation, and he already felt guilty as hell. There was no way a few words from her could make him feel any worse. At this point, he didn't even remember how much Allison knew, how much Angel had told her, or even how much he had shared. His heart was heavy, and he was more afraid than he'd ever been; his mind was racing, trying to figure out how to bring it to an end.

"I took out his business. But, he was threatening her already, Allison. He attacked her in her apartment and almost raped her. Cole and I stopped him, but the bastard was let out on bail and he skipped, and since, it's gotten worse."

"Oh, my God." Ally sat down by her mother.

"This is the security job you have Cole on." His father assumed correctly.

"Him, Wayne, Sid, and Bancroft, yes."

"How much money is he asking for?" Charles asked quietly.

"Ten million at last request, but it keeps increasing each time I refuse."

"Alex, your mother and I will help with the money."

He shook his head. "No, Dad. I won't pay off a rapist and murderer. I can't do it. Even if I did, he'd be extorting me for life."

"Yes, I can see that."

"Sid knows the plan. He and Wayne will be stationed here with all of you. The security on the houses has been increased. Keep the lights on outside. The rest of the team are being dismissed because there is a leak, and we don't know who it is. Wayne and Sid are the only two I trust completely. This is a dangerous man, and I'm convinced he's insane."

"Where are you going, Alex?"

"I'm going to try to find Swanson and deal with him."

Cora gasped again. She stood up to walk quickly toward her son. "Alex, why can't you leave this to the police?"

"Because, Mom. We've lived like this for months. Angel and I made a plan to crack him and it worked, but then they let Swanson out of jail. I can't expect a different result with the same actions."

"Alex—" Cora's eyes flooded and her voice cracked.

"I can't waste time discussing this right now. I'm getting a shower and a change of clothes, then I have to leave. Allison, please pack some food, a thermos of coffee if we have one, and some water."

His sister nodded, and the rest of them sat there stunned.

"Are the girls safe?" Emily asked.

"As safe as we can make them, but the sooner we find this guy, the safer we'll all be. Believe me, my entire life is somewhere out there with Cole. I'll do everything in my power to keep them safe, but I don't have time to waste. I can't tell any of you what I'm planning to do. If anyone asks, you don't know, and that's the way it has to be."

Emily started to cry raggedly. Her husband put his arm around her shoulders, trying to offer some comfort.

"Maybe we should go with you," Josh said. "You shouldn't go alone."

"I'm not going alone." Alex ran a hand through his hair and stood up. "I'm going to take a shower, then I need to speak to Allison alone."

He walked briskly from the room, leaving the others agape behind him. He took the stairs to his old room two at a time. Hopefully, his mother hadn't trashed his old hockey bag and some of his clothes. He needed boots, jeans, and sweatshirts, and he had no time to go back to his place to pack a bag.

Alex rummaged through his closet and was just pulling out some old boots he had from when the family vacationed in Colorado his senior year when Ally knocked on the door. "Come in," he murmured. Next, he found socks, some T-shirts and a black zippered hoodie in his dresser, with a couple pair of jeans and some of his college sweats. He'd need to try them on to see if the shirts fit, but the sweatpants would work. He hauled his bag out and started quickly shoving everything into it.

"Allison, I need you to call Kyle. I don't have his number. Tell him I need to meet him somewhere. Preferably on the west side or central."

"The warehouse where the band practices is on the south side, but they might be playing somewhere. It's Friday night, Alex, and it's almost midnight."

"I know the fucking time, Allison!" The tension inside his chest felt like a pressure cooker ready to explode. "Jesus Christ! I don't have time to dick around with explanations! Can you just do as I ask? Please?" He was on his haunches on the floor next to the bed and glanced up at Allison, who was standing in the open doorway.

"Okay, but what if he doesn't answer?"

"Text him my phone number. Tell him I need to speak to him about Angel and follow it with 911. He'll call me. And don't mention this to Mom, Dad, or Josh. Or the James'."

"All right, Alex. I'm really sorry about your security guy."

Alex stood and kicked off his shoes, and began pulling the tails of his shirt out of his dress slacks. "Thanks. Can you excuse me?"

"Yes. Should I just meet you downstairs then?"

"Yeah, and can you ask Dad if I can borrow some boxers and a couple sweatshirts?" Alex was decidedly broader, the hours in the gym making a significant difference since his first years at college. "I'll try these, but I don't think they'll fit me."

"What if they are the grandpa boxer kind?"

"He's not that old, Allison," Alex spat.

"Yes, but older than you."

"I don't have the luxury of being picky right now. Just do it! Throw them on the bed while I'm in the shower."

Alex's temper was on a short lease, but goddamn it, didn't he just tell Allison what the fuck was going on? Wasn't Jason Bancroft just slit like a fish and left in an oozing puddle of his own blood? The whole thing was so incredibly surreal. He felt strange, as if he was watching a movie rather than living through it.

Worry that he might be getting into a situation that could get him killed, didn't seem to matter. That he may have to resort to all matter of despicable acts to end this didn't faze him, either. He was numb—on autopilot. Getting this over was his singular purpose. Determination consumed him. Failure was not an option.

After he showered, Alex quickly toweled off and ran a quick comb through his hair. He changed into old jeans and one of his old football T-shirts. It was tighter in the shoulders and sleeves, and it seemed a little shorter than he remembered, confirming that the sweatshirts in the same size wouldn't be comfortable. He didn't take the time to shave.

When he went back into his room, there was a stack of his father's clothes waiting for him on the bed. He pulled on a Chicago Bears long sleeve T-shirt over his other one, shoved the underwear, sweatshirts, and other things into the hockey bag, and zipped it closed. He sat down on his bed and put on his socks and boots, lacing them up in a hurry.

He knew he should take a gun, even if using it was a big risk. There were laws against carrying concealed weapons, and he wasn't registered to carry. *Fuck it.* Alex didn't care.

Alex threw the black hoodie on top of the huge bag and slung it over his shoulder, leaving his room to walk down the stairs and back into the den. Everyone, including both Wayne and Sid, were there, though they were sitting down, talking things through. They all watched him re-enter the room. The mood was somber.

When Alex walked in with the big black bag, he dropped it on the floor just inside the room. Cora stood up, her demeanor anxious. "Are you leaving right away?"

He pulled out his phone. The screen had a text from an un-known number. "Yeah, Mom. Did you or Allison pack any food?"

She nodded and began to walk out of the room. "Yes, I'll go get it."

"Thanks." Alex flipped open the message, and it was from Kyle. There were two messages because Alex had been in the shower and hadn't answered right away.

What's going on with Angel?

WHAT IS GOING ON?????

He quickly typed in a response.

I need your help. I'll tell you when I see you. Where can we meet?

This is freaking me out. Is she okay?

Yes. I'll explain. Can you meet me at O'Hare? Park your car in the garage, and I'll pick you up at American Departures on the top level.

When?

"Alex what's going on?" Charles asked.

"Just give me a minute, Dad."

One hour.

Do I need to bring anything?

Alex sighed, contemplating what to say, and if it was smart to say what he needed to say.

This is very serious shit, so interpret that.

Okay, I get it.

Good. See you in an hour.

When Alex looked up from his phone, his mother had re-turned with a small cooler and one of those fabric grocery bags with the Whole Foods logo stamped on the side. Everyone was staring at him expectantly.

"Dad, can I speak to you? Sid? Wayne? You, too." Alex nod-ded his head indicating they should follow him back into the great room by the front door. He picked up the big hockey bag. The size made it awkward, but it was big enough to shove a rifle into it without being conspicuous. He lined up the handles of the grocery bag and the cooler, picked them both up with his other hand, and headed out of the room. The three other men followed.

"Dad, I need weapons. Can I take some of yours?" Alex spoke in hushed tones so his voice wouldn't carry into the room they'd just left.

Charles' face instantly changed. Concern flooded his features. "Jesus Christ, Alex! Is that necessary?"

"It's a precaution."

Wayne and Sid were both in the hallway. "Yes, you can't be too careful, Alex, but, I think one of us should accompany you. We can carry legally."

He shook his head adamantly. "No. I need you here to protect my family." He addressed his father next. "I won't be alone. But I do have to get going."

"Which one do you want?"

"A hunting rifle with a scope, and a couple of small hand-guns." He knew his dad had one semi-automatic in his collection because he had taken Alex and Cole to the shooting range to prac-tice with it on more than one occasion and named it. "The Herstal?"

"Christ, Alex—" Charles didn't believe in violence, but his own father had taught him to shoot when he was young, and he'd put Cole and Alex both into gun safety classes when they were boys. He felt knowledge and being open with his children was a valuable part of keeping them from getting involved in dangerous activities. Still, that was a serious weapon, and if Alex was asking for it specifically, he expected to need it.

"Dad!" He raised his voice then glanced in the direction of the room where the others remained. He was frustrated, exasperated, and in a hurry. He lowered his volume but the urgency remained. "I don't have time to debate this! I said it's a precaution." His gut told him the likelihood of using it was higher than he wanted to disclose to his father. "I'm going to find this ruthless motherfucker since the cops can't do their job. I'll get them involved, if and when, I locate him."

"If it's that dangerous, then I don't want you—"

"It's not up for discussion. Please, just get them."

"Are you sure you know what you're doing? What about possible repercussions for the company?" Charles was getting angry himself. "It will be all over the news."

"Fuck the company! I'm trying to keep people from dying! Regardless if you help me or not, I'm still doing this." The muscle in Alex's lean jaw was working back and forth as he clenched his teeth. "Yes or no?" he demanded.

Charles nodded. He could see the determination and the fury behind his son's eyes. He'd seen it before, but this was more.

"Sid, help my father, please."

Alex was left with Wayne in the tiled entryway of the big house. "Did you let the others go for the night? I don't want any of them to see me leave."

"Yes. But, you still need to be cautious. If one of them is feeding Swanson information, they may be lurking anywhere. I'll try to determine who it is. We haven't added anyone since Sid was shot."

"Yes, I'm aware." Alex was still holding the bags and the cooler but he didn't register the weight. "Find out where Swanson's nephew is. I'm sure he's out, too."

"Yes. He was just an accomplice. His bail was as much as Mark Swanson's. Just expect him to be around. It's probable Swanson will have at least one or two guys with him."

"I agree."

"He's still using that pre-pay phone, so we haven't been able to track it."

Charles and Sid returned with the rifle case and two smaller cases. Alex recognized them, and his father had given him the Herstal as requested.

"Is there ammunition?"

"Inside the cases. I put more bullets for the handguns in the rifle case."

Alex set everything on the floor and took the two smaller cases, unzipped his bag, and stashed them inside. "Thanks, Dad."

He stood and picked everything up again.

"Alex, I know you're a grown man, and I have to trust you know what you're doing, but don't get these out unless absolutely necessary. If you're not prepared to fire it, don't expose it. Someone as dangerous as you say this person is will take it and use it against you."

"Yes, I know. I remember the lessons, Dad."

The first time Alex had seen a gun up close, he was twelve years old. Charles had taken Cole, Allison, and himself out into a field and showed them how to turn the safeties on and off and how to remove the magazine from the gun to disarm it. Charles talked about how dangerous guns were then proceeded to show them. He shot a full gallon of milk from a hundred yards away using the Herstal he had just entrusted to Alex. Alex remembered that day as if it were yesterday. The container exploded with such force it spewed pieces of plastic and milk twenty or more feet in all directions.

That's what happens to a person when they get shot. It's not cool. It's not fun. Knowing about guns is about safety, and disarming them, not violence. Got it? They'd gotten the message, loud and clear.

Sid, still carrying the rifle case, Wayne, and Charles accompanied Alex out. They all waited while Alex loaded everything into the trunk of his Audi, but Wayne and Sid were scanning the scene. They were practiced; one of them looking north and west, the other south and east.

"Isn't your car a little fancy for a manhunt?" Charles asked. Normally, Alex would agree, but one of the neighborhoods Standish provided was decidedly upscale and that was where his search would start, and the Audi would be inconspicuous there.

"It's a search." He shut the trunk. "Hopefully, a short one."

Charles' arms were outstretched, and Alex went in to hug his father. Hugs between them were rare. "Be careful, son," Charles said as he patted Alex on the back.

"I will, Dad. Can you tell Mrs. Dane to clear my schedule on Monday and Tuesday, just in case I'm not back? I'll be in touch if it needs to be longer. Take Sid with you when you go into the office."

Charles nodded. "I'll be glad when this is over."

Alex turned to Wayne, who handed Alex his walkie-talkie. "Take this. You'll need it to talk to us and to Cole."

Dressed as he was, Alex looked younger and less imposing. Devoid of the designer suits that were his usual armor, Alex seemed much more vulnerable. Charles knew it was an illusion, that underneath, Alex was still immovable, but his fatherly instincts kicked in.

Alex was a good man, responsible, and prepared to get his hands dirty to protect people he loved. Wayne's law enforcement background might nag at him that he should convince Alex to leave it to the police, but knowing what he knew Mark Swanson was capable of, and seeing how little the police department had done, he understood Alex's decisions.

"Be careful." Charles put a hand on his son's shoulder.

"I will, thanks. Keep me updated if the police find anything, and I'll do the same." Alex shook their hands, and within seconds, he was in the car and heading away. It was two in the morning. He hadn't slept, really slept, in almost thirty-six hours. It wasn't ideal, but he had no other recourse.

He merged back onto I-90 and raced west toward O'Hare. Traffic was still busy given it was Friday night in Chicago, but not so much that it slowed him down, though. He was calm as he maneuvered around slower traffic, his mind filled with Bancroft and the gruesome scene at the station, the mess Swanson left everywhere he went. He was like a fucking flash fire in a drought, leaving a wide swath of destruction in his wake. Alex forgot to breathe for a few seconds and he sucked in a deep, abrupt breath. His life had definitely changed. Six months ago, he'd be out with Darian or fucking Whitney senseless at 2 AM on a Friday night, and now this mess.

He thought about Angel and the love that now devoured his heart and dictated his every move. It was hard to believe he could love someone that much. But he did. He'd do anything for her. Do anything to be with her and build a life with her. He was still absorbed in his thoughts as he raced through the tolls in the I-Pass lane, but then he realized, that I-Pass was a way he could be tracked. He'd have to pay cash at the tolls from now on.

He took the exit to O'Hare and followed the signs to the departing flights and for American Airlines. American was at the west end of terminal three, and Kyle was leaning up against one of the metal pillars waiting with a blue duffel bag at his feet. He was wearing an old army camouflage jacket, jeans, and black boots.

Alex hadn't seen or talked to him since the night at Angel's apartment after the benefit. He still looked similar. His hair had grown out, no longer shaved, but controlled with gel. Kyle wouldn't know what car to look for, so Alex pulled up to the curb and rolled down the window.

"Hey, Kyle," he called out.

Kyle's head snapped in Alex's direction, and he pushed away from the pole and bent to pick up the bag. Alex popped the trunk and the lid lifted. Kyle deposited his bag in the trunk alongside Alex's things. He took note of the rifle case but just closed the trunk lid before sliding in next to Alex.

Alex pulled out the paper with the list of addresses he'd gotten from Marvin Standish and punched the first address into his GPS.

Kyle buckled his seatbelt. He pulled out a pack of gum and shoved a piece into his mouth before holding the pack out for Alex to take some.

"Wanna tell me what the hell this is about?"

The GPS started its guidance as the car left O'Hare. The GPS girl's voice was loud and annoying.

Alex gave Kyle the rundown of Angel's case and the problems with Swanson, ending with the ransom demands and Bancroft's body being found at the radio station a few hours earlier. He may have left out some of the finer details out of respect for time, but in general, Kyle understood.

He leaned back in the passenger seat. "Holy shit! Fuck, I wish she'd never gone to grad school. This wouldn't be happening."

Alex's lips pressed together. He couldn't help feeling jealous. "Forgive me if I'm happy about her choice, though I agree, I wish she'd use her degree in a less dangerous way."

Kyle studied Alex as he drove. Though it was early morning and the sun wasn't up yet, the lights along the interstate and in the suburban neighborhood that was their destination were well lit.

Kyle shook his head. "Knowing her, she'll tell us both to fuck off."

"Pretty much, though she has acquiesced to some of my requests during all of this. My brother took Angel, Becca, and Jillian out of town until we find this abhorrent asshole. She wasn't happy about it. Jillian's birthday party was tonight. Or should have been."

"Yeah. She loves that kid. Becca had her a few months before Angel and I split. So what are we doing?"

"I have to find this prick. The police are worthless, and I want it over."

"Judging by your text, you think it might get messy."

"It's pretty much a given at this point."

"Awesome," Kyle said flatly. Maybe he should have asked more questions before signing up for shit like this. He was so close

to getting a record deal with a major label, and while dying to help
a friend was noble, it wasn't his idea of wise. It would've been different if it were something necessary to take care of Angel, but this
wasn't a rescue mission, it was a wild goose chase as far as he was
concerned. "Why me? Don't you have any friends?" He shot Alex
a disgusted glance. His gut still burned because this rich dickhead
was fucking his ex-girlfriend.

"I asked you to help because I know you care about Angel.
Your vested interest made you the most likely to agree. Swanson
has proved he will not stop, and I'm at the end of my rope. He's
forcing my hand."

"You're richer than God. Why don't you just pay someone to
bash the fucker's head in?"

"You're the second person in twenty-four hours to ask me
that." Alex shook his head, incredulous that the solution seemed as
easy to Kyle as it had been to Marvin Standish. He huffed. "It's not
that easy. He won't be waiting for us like a sitting duck. He won't
go down without a fight."

GPS girl was talking. *In point two miles, take the next left onto
Addison Street.*

"The address is up here." Alex turned off the GPS and headlights off as he navigated slowly down the street. "I'm going to
drive past, then we'll go a couple blocks over and park."

"I thought he wasn't a sitting duck? If that's true, how do you
have an address?"

"You don't want or need to know."

"I think if I'm going to risk my life, I need to know."

Alex shot him a dirty look. "Whatever. Swanson is connected to
the mob. I met with them and asked them to tell me where I could
find him. Happy now?" Alex asked caustically. He leaned down to
look out Kyle's window at the house as they drove past slowly.

The house was all dark, but that didn't mean there wasn't
anyone inside. The hour would dictate that at least some of the

occupants would be sleeping. The hair on the back of Alex's neck stood up.

"Shit." Kyle would have made some mocking remark under other circumstances, but this was serious.

"As you said, I'm richer than God."

"Yeah, you're an idiot for getting involved with them. This is heavy shit."

Alex drove around the corner and over two streets, pulling up and parking in front of another house. He shut the engine off and turned to Kyle.

"A few months ago, I may have agreed, but with Angel involved, my perspective has changed." He met Kyle's eyes unflinchingly. "If you're going to pussy-out on me, do it now."

Kyle didn't hesitate. "I must be crazy for agreeing. Let's go."

Alex nodded and popped the trunk. "Do you have any weapons?"

"I have a knife and a gun."

"Good."

It was as if they were part of a SWAT team, both of them stood at the back of Alex's car, shoving guns in their waistbands and pulling their shirts down to hide them. Kyle reached into his duffel and pulled out two black stocking caps, the kind that covered the face. He handed one to Alex.

"You're sort of scaring me, Kyle." Alex joked. He wasn't quite whispering, but his tone was noticeably lowered.

"You said it was serious shit, didn't you? I figured you for an amateur." Kyle chuckled softly to himself.

"Why? Because you're on parole?" Alex shot back, smiling. A big part of him wanted to dislike Kyle, but the truth was, he was a good guy. They both shoved the caps in their back pockets and began the three-block walk back to the house in question.

"Do you expect any other members of the organization to be here?"

"No. Just Swanson and maybe one or two others."

Kyle nodded.

When they got about half a block from the house, they both put on the stocking caps, and Alex pulled up the hood of the sweatshirt he was now wearing over both shirts. The layers kept out the cold, though his adrenaline should have been sufficient except for the unusual deadly calm that he'd felt since this decision was made.

All of the windows were dark and difficult to see in, despite putting his nose to glass and his hands around his eyes. It was still pitch black outside, but the streetlight at the front of the house would make it too easy for neighbors to see what they were doing.

Alex motioned for Kyle to check out the south side while he would do the north.

"Meet in the back," Kyle whispered.

Alex nodded. "Be careful not to shoot me," he whispered back.

Kyle shook his head, flashed his knife, and headed off.

Alex crept across the front lawn and around the house. There were three windows. One was small and obviously a bathroom. Still, Alex checked them all. They were all locked, and blinds prevented seeing inside. He wasn't surprised to find the gate on the six-foot privacy fence locked. He reached up and curled his fingers around the top of the fence, using the strength in his biceps to pull him up and over in one smooth motion. He landed on the ground, in a crouch, thinking too late there might have been a guard dog on premises.

Looking around him, Alex saw Kyle propel over the fence into the yard on the other side. The backyard was large, and there was a pool, now drained for the season. No dog in sight. He was sure he could shoot the criminals but was thankful he didn't have to shoot an animal.

Kyle hunched down and rushed up to the side of the house toward the walk out on the lower level. Alex pointed up the stairs connecting two levels of the deck and went up to check the doors and windows on the upper floor of the house. All locked, with no sign of anyone, and every window was covered by blinds.

Alex was disappointed they came up empty. When he went back down to the yard, Kyle was waiting, crouched low by the fence on the side closest to the stairs.

Kyle shook his head, an indication that he, too, had found nothing.

It took the men literally half a minute to get over the fence and back to the street. A minute more to jog to Alex's car, and soon, they were inside. Both had already removed the ski masks on the run back, and Alex now unloaded the gun from his belt and flipped open the glove compartment to stash it inside.

"That was fun. Thanks for the invite," Kyle joked, resting his gun next to Alex's before shutting it.

"Fuck!" Alex ran his hands through his hair. He was frustrated.

"What now?"

Alex started the engine and drove to a position across from the house but almost a block away. He pulled up and parked. It was close enough to see if anyone came or went without being so close that anyone could see inside the car.

"We wait to see if anyone comes out when the sun comes up."

"If they don't?"

"If not, then it's not likely we'll find Swanson here. I have a one other address to check out, but I need to get some sleep first. I've been traveling, and it's been almost two days since I've slept."

"Sleep now."

Alex ran a hand over his face and scratched at his jaw. He was so tired, he almost couldn't feel his hands, and he'd be no good at all if he didn't sleep soon, but the last thing he wanted was to miss something. "Are you sure?"

"Yeah, man. No sense both of us staying awake."

"*Will* you stay awake?" Kyle had to be getting tired, as well.

"No problem. I don't want this asshole to hurt Angel, either. As long as I can catch a few hours before the performance, I'm good."

Alex studied the other man. "Listen, Kyle, I really appreciate your help with this, and I owe you an apology. I have no excuse for how I acted the last time I saw you, other than I was jealous as hell." He held out his hand.

Kyle took his hand and shook it. "Angel has that effect on men."

"It was new for me, and I didn't handle it well, but it's still no excuse. I'm sorry."

Kyle met Alex's gaze. "Yeah. I remember how that feels."

While Alex couldn't feel sorry that Angel had left Kyle and they were now together, he could empathize with the other man's pain. He'd fucking kill something if she left him. What could he say that didn't sound boastful or arrogant? He decided it was best not to say anything at all. Instead, he nodded then reclined his seat by pushing the lever on the side. He pulled the stocking hat back out of his pocket and plopped it over his eyes.

"Thanks for keeping watch. Wake me up if you see anything move."

14

Stolen

IT WAS DARK and the gentle hum of the wheels speeding across the pavement was soothing. Angel hadn't slept much during the day, so the feeling of relaxation was a welcome change to the tension that had been coiled inside her for the past week. When Becca and Cole returned with burgers and Jillian's gifts, she'd spent two hours playing with the little girl after dinner. Angel logged on to iTunes and loaded up the Shuffle with kid songs and some of the favorites they liked to dance to.

Jillian loved the babydoll, too, and she was holding it, while fast asleep in the car seat, next to Angel in the back seat of the SUV. Jillian's head lolled to one side, and Angel adjusted the doll to help prop her head up. She had a pillow, but it wasn't enough.

Cole and Becca were chatting away in the front seat, their soft voices carried, and Angel could hear her friend telling Cole about the asshole she'd met just after college who knocked her up and left her high and dry. She had her seatbelt on but turned slightly toward Jillian so she could rest her own head on the back of the seat and closed her eyes.

She'd heard so many asshole stories. Hers and Becca's experiences had certainly structured her stringent opinion on the opposite sex, and the calls from weepy, weak women on the radio show week after week hadn't helped. She sighed and pulled out her phone. *Their phone*, she mused. After what happened to her in college then Kyle's betrayal with Crystal, Angel didn't think she'd ever trust a man again, other than her father. Now, she trusted a few of them. She trusted Cole and Kenneth, Sid and Wayne, and Alex above all of them. They'd all proven themselves many times over the past months. Alex was unwavering—solid as a rock.

It had been seven hours since she'd spoken to him. They'd been driving for two and a half hours, and she wished her mind would shut off so she could get some sleep. She sighed. She wished Alex would call, or at least text. What was he doing?

Cole told her Jason Bancroft had been found with his throat slashed. After that, she'd been unable to eat anything. They expected Mark Swanson to kill Bancroft... but to find out he was alive until today, that there was no doubt now he had been murdered because Alex had refused the ransom, made her sick enough to throw up in the bathroom of the hotel suite.

Angel's elbow was resting on the ledge under the window, and she propped up her head with her hand. Mark *fucking* Swanson. He was the epitome of evil; the worst, most ruthless criminal she'd ever had to deal with. Never had she hated someone as much. She seethed with it. If only she could have put him away on the tests alone, then none of this would have happened, and two little boys wouldn't be fatherless. A woman wouldn't be a widow. Her stomach tightened painfully, and she swallowed. Angel wasn't one to cry easily, but this frustration filled her up so much she wanted to scream with it, and tears burned at her eyes. *If only... If only...* Her mind kept screaming as the miles fell away. But "what ifs" didn't do shit to solve the current situation, and that's all any of them could concentrate on now.

Cole was taking some back road that wound around left then right. She guessed they were in the Ozark Mountains, judging by the trees, hills, and sporadic small towns. She'd spent a lot of time here camping and boating with her father, Will, and Ben during her adolescence.

There were small gas stations here or there, out in the middle of nowhere, almost tiny in comparison to those in Chicago; many were only distinguished by the lighted signs out front that touted "live bait." It was late fall, so most of the tourist resorts would be closed. It was very dark, and the roads were only two-lane and not lined with lights, most of the businesses closed because of the season and not just the lateness of the hour. The trees, mountains, and scattered clouds blocked much of the moonlight, making everything outside dark and covered in midnight blue shadows just dusted with slivers of silvery light. The trees covering the mountains looked like an inky black abyss only distinguishable by the jagged shapes of their tops.

The soft green glow from the console in front of Cole and Becca was the only light inside, and the only light outside were the headlights of a car behind them that would disappear and reappear as the road curved around the mountains.

"You all right back there?" Cole called softly, glancing over his shoulder for a second then back at the road. "Are you sleeping, Angel?"

"No, but if I were, I wouldn't be now," Angel retorted. "I'm just thinking about everything."

Becca turned sideways in the front passenger seat so she could look back at her friend. "Are you doing okay?"

"Not great. I'm sad about Jason. It makes me sick inside."

Becca nodded. Her face was all in shadow, but Angel could see her head move. She didn't know him that well, but she had met him and spoken to him briefly the few times he was trailing Angel when she was with her. Her heart felt for the obvious sorrow and guilt she knew Angel was feeling. "I'm sorry, Angel."

"No, I'm the one who's sorry." Her stomach twisted again. She could belabor the fact that if it wasn't for meeting her, Alex wouldn't have spent millions, Jason Bancroft would be alive, Jillian's birthday would have gone off without a hitch. Now everything was fucked up. The worst was thinking about how terrified Jason must have been and now the loss felt by his family, made worse by the fact she didn't really know him that well. After Cole had come clean about the security detail, she'd spent a decent amount of time with Jason and should have taken a more personal interest in him. Now, he was dead because of her. She couldn't imagine what it would be like to lose Alex, and they weren't even married. In comparison, they had just begun. "This whole fucked up mess is my fault."

Cole was listening. "Alex would disagree. He thinks it's his fault."

"Because he didn't pay Mark Swanson off." It was a statement rather than a question. Angel knew Alex would shoulder all of the responsibility. It's what he did best.

"Yeah."

"He's wrong."

"You didn't make him do what he did, Angel. He knows that."

Angel was irritated. Why wouldn't he just let her take the fucking blame? Maybe it would make her feel better, at least. "Cole, please stop. If he'd never met me, he wouldn't have been involved. Those are the facts. Sunshine and my ass are not a good combination. Don't you know that by now?"

A short laugh burst from Cole, and though Angel wasn't trying to be funny, his amusement did cause a much-needed smile to curve her mouth.

Becca reached out and grabbed Angel's hand. "Don't be so hard on yourself, girl. Life happens... shit happens, and who knows if it could have been different? This guy is off his rocker, and you had the case before you met Alex. Working with Darian, you would have met him at some point. Don't wish away something that has been so good for you."

"I could never wish Alex away."

"That's my girl." Becca squeezed her hand before letting it go. "Don't worry about the party. Jillian is fine. As soon as she sees those horses, she'll be over the moon. She's so excited about it."

Angel was looking forward to getting home to Joplin and spending time without the pressure of her job; to get away from the reality of everything connected to Mark Swanson. It would be a great little retreat, but she wished Alex were with them.

"Yes, she'll love them. I'll call them when we get there. Cole, will you turn on the music? I need something to occupy my head so I can fall asleep."

"Sure, Angel. Should I stop before you fall asleep? You didn't eat anything. Are you hungry?"

She shook her head even though he wasn't looking at her. "No. I'm sick to my stomach. I'll eat in the morning. But if you want to stop, go ahead."

"I'm good. Becca, what about you?"

"I'm fine. Jillian will probably have to go to the bathroom, but I'd rather not wake her before she wakes up on her own."

"Sounds good." Cole leaned forward and turned on the stereo, and two minutes later, her iPhone buzzed. Alex must be sending a text.

Hey, babe. I wanted to say goodnight. Don't forget to call me when you arrive.

Angel's fingers flew over the keys. *Are you okay? What's going on?*

We're watching a house where we think Swanson might show up. Nothing so far.

We?

Yes. When he didn't volunteer who was with him, Angel's curiosity wouldn't be denied.

Who's with you?

Kyle.

Angel's eyebrows shot up in astonishment. Kyle was the last person she would have guessed.

Kyle?

He was the obvious choice.

Angel could see the logic behind it, but she was still surprised.

Haven't you slept yet? It's not healthy, Alex. Nothing you can do for JB now. Pls. take care of yourself.

I'll get a couple of hours. Kyle's taking first watch.

Be careful. Both of you.

We will. I'll call later. Love you.

Me, too. XOXO

She pulled her purse from the seat beside her and shoved her phone back in. She pulled her black hoodie over her body, pulling her knees up on the seat under it. She was leaning against the door with her head resting against the seat when she closed her eyes. The soft music filled her mind, and soon, she fell into the welcome bliss of a dreamless sleep.

*****

Bright lights flashed behind Angel's closed eyelids as they fluttered open when the engine shut off, and she heard the door of the car open. She blinked a few times at the unwelcome glare. They were stopped at a gas station, and Cole was disappearing inside the convenience store across from the gas pumps where he'd parked the

SUV. The door opposite her opened, and Becca was reaching in to unbuckle Jillian from the car seat.

"Come on, baby. Let's go." Jillian was half-asleep still, but Becca still pulled her out of the car seat. Jillian put her head down on Becca's shoulder, and closed her eyes again. "Are you coming, Angel."

"I don't think so. You go ahead." Her voice was groggy. She was sleeping well and didn't want to wake up. "I'm so tired."

"Okay. Jillian didn't wake up, but Cole said we needed gas. I don't think we'll stop again, so I'm going to wake her up. She'll go right back to sleep."

Angel nodded, her eyes already closed again. Sometime later, her mind barely registered when Becca returned the little girl to the car. Her subconscious could hear Becca and Cole talking, though the words weren't clear. She pulled the sweatshirt closer around her. It was almost Thanksgiving, and though there was no snow on the ground, it was still cold with the engine off. All the heat had escaped when the doors had been opened.

She was startled when the door slammed and the engine roared to life, though she felt like her eyes were glued shut. The heat was soon filling the space, and she'd just stopped shivering when Jillian began to wail.

"Fuck!" a strange voice cursed. Angel's eyes snapped open, and she sat up, her hand flying to Jillian in the car seat. Her eyes flew to the front seat. Becca wasn't in the passenger seat, and it wasn't Cole driving. Her heart stopped and plummeted to the pit of her stomach.

The man was big and burly, and Angel recognized him as someone who lived in her building. Her skin started to burn. This was bad. He didn't have a mask on which meant he didn't care that she could ID him. She wasn't going to live through this. And here was Jillian beside here. Somehow, she'd have to save the baby. Her heart had resumed its beating, but it was racing and threatening to fly from her body.

"Anga!" the little girl cried. "Anga! Where's iz Mama? We yeft Mama!"

The man glanced back over his shoulder and menacing eyes met Angel's. "Shut that kid up if you know what's good for you."

Angel swallowed and caressed Jillian's head. "Baby, it will be okay. Angel is with you."

The SUV was racing and took a right turn down a dirt road lined with evergreen trees. The man was reckless, and the vehicle swerving. Surely, Cole would alert the police, and they'd put out an APB on the vehicle.

"Why are you doing this?"

The man laughed harshly. "Don't play dumb."

"I'm not an idiot, but why take her, too?"

"Shut up!" He mumbled something under his breath and made another turn, this time to the left. Angel was scared, but she had to keep her wits about her. Their best chance meant she'd have to remember as much of the route as possible, though she didn't know how she was going to manage it. Her mind was racing. She reached down and slid her Vans back on. Not the ideal shoes for walking in this weather, but it was all she had. She pulled on the hoodie and zipped it up, reaching behind the seat for her coat and Jillian's.

The rocking and jumping of the vehicle as it took bumps too quickly and made careless turns dictated she couldn't take Jillian out of the seat. Though, it would be easier to jump out of the vehicle with Jillian in her arms, on the off chance it slowed or stopped, she couldn't risk her safety.

"Bean, Angel will take care of you, okay?" She said softly. "Can you stop crying for me, sweetheart?" she asked softly. She stroked her head over and over, wiping at the tears on Jillian's cheeks with gentle fingers.

She drew in a shaky breath, her mind racing. She bent and picked up Jillian's shoes from the floorboard behind the driver's seat. They had Velcro closures so Angel had them on in less than thirty seconds.

Jillian was still crying, despite Angel's efforts.

"I said, shut that brat up!" the man yelled.

"She's three years old, asshole," Angel retorted. She sized him up. He was easily twice her size, but he was overweight and probably clumsy as fuck. It wouldn't be easy, maybe it would be impossible, given Jillian would be involved. Angel wanted to distract him. "Swanson isn't man enough to do the dirty work, huh? You're an idiot to take the fall for him."

"Shut up, bitch! You don't know what the fuck you're talking about."

He turned again, this time right, and off the road onto a worn dirt path. Two tire tracks were worn into the grass between close groves of trees on both sides. Angel's eyes flashed around. Thankfully, the sun was just starting to come up and turn the sky a light purple, so it wasn't pitch black. She'd have no chance of finding her way out of the maze of trees and back to the main road if she could see nothing.

"When Swanson lets you take the fall for him, you'll go to prison for the rest of your life, you know. That will be fun," she goaded. She'd have a better chance if he were distracted.

He raised his arm and slammed it down on the console. Angel and Jillian both jumped at the loud bang; Jillian's face crumpled, and she started to sob. "I said, shut up, you stupid whore! Do you think you'll get out of this?"

The car was slowing down, so Angel decided she needed to make a plan. She had to try to fight him right when they got out. She couldn't run because she couldn't get Jillian out and carry her at a run. He would quickly overtake her. Her mind raced. The guy was a moron. He hadn't tied her hands, and if it weren't for Jillian in the car, she would have gouged his eyes out by now. So what could she do short of that?

The solution came to her, and she was pissed at herself for not thinking about it minutes earlier. *I'll text Alex.* She'd turn the sound to silent and then the man driving wouldn't hear when he responded. She reached for her purse but it wasn't on the seat next to her. Panic began to well-up inside her chest. Her eyes darted down to the floor, but it wasn't there. She quickly unbuckled her seatbelt and turned around begin rummaging behind her.

"Looking for this?" The man held her purse up from the front seat. "Yeah, I'm not brain dead."

"Could have fooled me." She was pissed, but she wasn't stupid. She was terrified, and it wasn't likely she'd be getting out of this alive, but if she were going to die, she'd go down fighting. After she made sure Jillian was safe. Maybe they were unaware of Jillian's presence in the car. Maybe she was a complication they didn't plan on.

"You and I are going to have some fun. I'm going to enjoy making you suffer."

"Do you really want the blood of a three year old on your hands?"

"Shut up."

"Seriously, do you?" Angel's voice took on a dead tone. "She's just a baby."

"Who cares? Not my problem."

She closed her eyes. She could play calm, but she wasn't calm; adrenaline shot through her veins and made her blood thunder in her head. She had to get him off-guard.

"Okay. We can have fun, if you'll make sure she gets safely back to her mother."

"We aren't in negotiations, lady," he spat. He was grotesque. Fat, slimy, and nasty. She could smell the sour stench of his sweat from where she sat. Angel scooted closer to Jillian and put her arm around the back of the car seat. "Hush, honey." Angel took Jillian's hand and kissed her on the head. This time, it was shampoo and baby powder in her nostrils. "It's going to be okay, Bean. I promise, okay?" she said softly in as soothing a tone as she could manage. "We have to hush so the man is nicer. Okay?"

Jillian's wide blue eyes locked with Angel's. She nodded and sucked in a hiccupping breath. "Kay."

"Good girl." Angel stroked her cheek and kissed her head again.

They were going over some decidedly bumpier terrain, and the SUV was rocking back and forth as they took the bumps, albeit at a crawl. This would have been her best chance of jumping out and making a run for it, if she didn't have Jillian.

The car slowed, and Angel craned her neck around the front bucket seat that was blocking her view, to see out of the front window. An old, light blue Cadillac was waiting in a small clearing off to one side of the path. Mark Swanson and one other younger man, who was maybe twenty, were dressed in hunting garb and leaning against it nonchalantly, but they stood away from it as the SUV came to a stop.

Angel drew in a shaky breath. This wasn't good. It was as bad as it could be. There would be no way she could run and no way she could fight all three of them at once. She'd have to try to reason with them. Swanson wasn't after Jillian; he was after her.

The man driving hopped out, and came around to open her door, and yanked Angel out roughly. Her coat and Jillian's fell on the ground by the car as Jillian began to scream again.

"What the fuck is that kid doing here?" Swanson demanded. "Are you a fucking moron?"

The man stammered, trying to make excuses. "I didn't see her in the car, boss."

"You didn't see her? You ignorant motherfucker! Get her in the car! Leave the kid here."

He nodded to the Cadillac, and the big man, who still had a firm grip on her upper arm, began to shove her toward the car. Pain shot through her arm, but the panic closing her lungs down hurt more.

"Please, you can't! It's cold and she won't be found!" Tears burned in Angel's eyes as she pleaded. "Please! She's just a baby."

Mark Swanson paused a brief moment. "I said, get her in the car!" he barked, and the man resumed shoving Angel into the open door. She started to struggle, trying to pull away, swinging her fist and landing a blow to the side of his face. Her hand exploded in pain. She was released instantly, only to be backhanded with such force she went sprawling on the ground.

"I'm going to enjoy this, gorgeous. More than I thought," Swanson sneered.

"Please don't hurt her." She was panting and out of breath, silent tears tumbled down her face as she realized the futility of the situation as she crawled up to her hands and knees. "I'll do whatever you want, and Alex will pay more for her. I'll talk to him." Her heart was aching. She wouldn't give up on the hope that Alex or Cole would find her, but she needed to talk to him. To hear his voice one more time, in case she didn't make it through this ordeal alive.

Mark Swanson's eyes narrowed momentarily as he regarded Angel's defeated posture. He wasn't sure if this would be as fun if she wasn't fighting, but the idea of more cash was intriguing him more than her suffering, though they were running neck and neck.

"Get the kid."

Angel was filled relief. "Thank you."

"Doesn't mean she's free and clear. Depends how nice to me you are."

Hate welled-up, and saturated every single cell in her body. She vowed she would kill him or die trying, after she made sure Jillian was safe.

The younger man went to the car and roughly unbuckled Jillian and pulled her out. The sound of the toddler screaming at the top of her lungs filled the silence and felt like an echo. Angel got to her feet. Jillian was reaching for her as the boy walked forward with her in his arms. Angel stepped forward, and instantly, Jillian was clinging; legs wrapped around her waist, her little arms tight around her neck. She was sobbing into Angel. Angel hugged Jillian tight.

"It's okay, baby. I've got you. Angel's got you." She kissed her temple, her eyes glaring at Mark Swanson over the top of her head.

"Careful, sweet pea. Be nice." He nodded to the car, and Angel got in, still holding Jillian. "Blindfold her."

"Can I have her coat?" Angel asked, and the big, goony man who kidnapped them picked it up and flung it inside the car before slamming the door. Jillian wouldn't let go of Angel long enough to put the coat on, so Angel wrapped it around her as best she could.

Angel let out her breath, as Jillian's little body shook in terror, when the younger kid got in the back seat next to them.

"Should I tie her hands, too?"

"Angel will be good, won't you, gorgeous?"

Angel nodded and let the kid put a blue bandana around her head, covering her eyes and tying it in the back. Jillian didn't stop crying.

"Anga!"

Angel's arm tightened. "It's okay, Bean. Shhhh. Just shhh. Okay?"

*****

The trip in the car was maybe two hours. Jillian had cried herself to sleep in Angel's arms. She was getting stiff, her rear end falling asleep. The men in the car were silent except for taunting jibes about how they were going to make Alex pay in multiple ways.

When they started talking nasty to Angel, Mark Swanson berated them.

"No one touches her until I say. Until I'm done with her, understand?"

Angel's panic began again. Death would be better than being gang raped by these dirty bastards. Even if it meant never seeing Alex again, she'd rather that, than have to live with seeing pity in his eyes when he looked at her.

Her education told her that women learned to live with rape and domestic violence through counseling and went on to live fulfilling lives, but she was quickly learning that while it sounded practical in theory, it might not be that easy in practice. She had never been so grateful that the first time, in college, she was blissfully unconscious. She was certain Mark Swanson would be merciless and extract his revenge slowly and thoroughly.

And what would Alex do? He'd go crazy. Whether he found her before she was killed, or if she was hurt, even a little, he'd literally lose his mind. She was certain someone would die. She couldn't bear it if it were Alex. No matter the cost to herself, Mark Swanson's death would be a welcome consequence, but there were three of these sons of bitches, and she didn't want to buy her life with his.

When the car stopped, the men got out, and Angel waited inside. She was still as a stone, numb. Maybe she was resigned or maybe she was determined, but either way, she was stoic. Mark Swanson might try to humiliate her, he might rape and abuse her, but she'd never give that sadistic fucker the satisfaction of groveling or begging for mercy. He could go fuck himself. She knew even if she were to do that, it wouldn't matter anyway, so there was no way was she would beg. Her jaw jutted out and her teeth clenched, and suddenly, the door was yanked open.

Jillian was startled in her arms and jerked. Soon, her arm was taken in a vice-like grip, and she was pulled, stumbling from the car. Her arms were firmly around Jillian, but her legs were asleep from so long without moving, and the blindfold was still in place.

"This way," Mark Swanson's slimy voice rasped in her ear, and a shiver ran through her when she realized he was the one who had her in his grasp. "You smell sexy."

"Fuck off."

"Careful. I still have the kid. I think she might come in handy after all."

He was guiding her, and she willed her legs to move forward without being able to see. Her steps were hesitant, and her resolve growing more and more with each one. This bastard wasn't going to break her.

"You really are a slimy fucker. Don't you have any bit of remorse for the shit you do to people?"

He chuckled.

"Kill me if you want, but leave her alone. She's innocent."

"Don't tempt me, Angel. But then again, tempting me is something you're quite good at."

Angel's stomach lurched.

A door opened. She heard the squeak of the door and the creak of the wood beneath her feet. The house smelled musty, so it would be old. The time it took to walk from the car to the house and the stench of manure would indicate it was a farm. They must be close to the western edge of the Ozarks, or there wouldn't be this much land used for pasture. The degree of stench lent to the theory that a feedlot was very close, if not on site. The mooing from cattle was distant but not miles away. She catalogued all of these little facts so, if she had a chance, she could give Alex clues to her location.

Inside, she was taken to a staircase. "Stairs, going down."

"How many? I don't want to stumble and drop Jillian."

He pulled off her blindfold so she could see then pushed her in front of him. It was dark, the stairs rotting wood, and the basement looked to be unfinished. There was one light bulb hanging from the ceiling in a loose socket and a cot sitting in the middle of the room. There was a drain in the middle of the floor, and from what she could see, there was a leak of some sort near the far wall. The mold in the air was unhealthy, she could smell it. There was an unenclosed toilet near the water trail that ran from the leak in the ceiling and trailed off toward the drain. It was probably from the bathroom upstairs and rampant with bacteria. The entire place was a cesspool. The small half-windows near the top of the walls on all four sides were painted over with black paint. Obviously, this place served a similar purpose in the past.

Jillian was awake and looking around, but still clutching to Angel for dear life. Angel quelled the sarcastic retort she wanted to make. She had to think of Jillian.

"What happens now?" Angel asked. Her arms were starting to shake, having held Jillian for more than two hours, but she wouldn't attempt to set the little one down until the men left the room.

The young man handed Angel's purse to Swanson. They'd been careful not to call each other by name, so Angel had no clue who they were. She felt agitated and threatened when he began rummaging through her purse, pulling out both of her phones.

"Should I call Alex?" Angel was desperate to get her hands on her phone, not even knowing what she'd be able to do with it when they all watched.

"Why two phones?" Swanson inquired.

Angel sighed. She didn't want to tell him. She didn't want him to call Alex, on that phone, she didn't want him to take it from her.

"The iPhone." She had no choice. She needed Alex to know where she was.

"Put the girl down and take off your clothes to your underwear." Mark Swanson leered at her, his top lip curling slightly as he reveled in her discomfort.

"I can't." Angel frantically tried to finagle a way to keep her clothes on. Fear of Swanson's true intentions aside, she'd be worthless getting Jillian out if she didn't have her clothes. "I mean, it's not a good time for me. I'm on my period, and I haven't been able to clean up in hours. Please, not in front of Jillian." Her voice became pleading. "If you're trying to torture him, trust me… he'll be tortured, clothes or not." Angel felt a sadness that went beyond fear. Alex would be so devastated. "Just knowing you have me will kill him."

Swanson considered for a moment. Angel set Jillian on the cot then sat next to her, putting her arm around her as Jillian huddled close.

Mark held up the iPhone. "What's the password?"

"Twelve Ten." It was Alex's birthday, though she didn't let that out.

Swanson opened the phone. He nodded toward the bed. "Get the kid."

The bigger man came forward and snatched Jillian off the cot amidst a new set of cries.

"Take her upstairs," Swanson barked at the man, who was staring at Angel, waiting with wide eyes to see if she would be made to strip. "Take off your clothes." He stood there, almost licking his lips. "Take them off!" he hollered sharply, causing Angel to balk.

The big man made it halfway up the stairs then turned back to watch, Jillian was struggling in his arms. "Anga! No, Anga!" she cried over and over.

"If you push me, I'll make you strip all the way. Do it or I'll strip you myself and take great pleasure doing so."

What did he think? That she'd just stand there meekly and let him? Angel's mouth set, and she pulled off her shirt and sweats, exposing a purple lace bra and panties. For the first time in her life, she cursed her penchant for matching lingerie. What she wouldn't give for a white cotton bra and granny pants.

"Wait," Swanson said, glaring at her grotesquely. "I think I have a new appreciation for purple. Mmmmm."

Angel sat huddled, her arms in front of her on the cot, trying to shield as much of her body as she could. She was shivering in the cold basement, and the blanket on the cot was an old, wool army blanket. It would rub the skin right off her body if she had to use that. Though her body was beautiful, her eyes were red-rimmed and bloodshot, and her hair was a mess.

Swanson took a couple pictures with the iPhone and sent a text to Alex after opening her old messages and hitting reply. Avery would soon get the picture, Swanson thought. He was getting desperate, unsure if he wanted the money, to fuck Angel until she begged for death, or to kill Alexander Avery. They were all equally palatable prospects.

"You better hope he's tortured. You better hope. I'll be back for fun and games later after I read through all of your messages. Get that kid to shut up."

"Um, can I please keep my purse? It has my tampons in it."

They had already searched it, and Swanson nodded to the kid, who then threw it on the floor.

With that, Jillian was returned to Angel by the apish man, then all three men went upstairs, shutting the door at the top. The scraping noise it made was followed by the metal upon metal sound of a padlock being put in place.

She wasn't free, but for the moment, they were okay. Angel sighed in relief, trying to comfort Jillian, and hoping for a miracle.

15

Unimaginable

ALEX'S PHONE RINGING woke him up from his uncomfortable position slumped against the car door, his neck bent
crookedly against the window. The edge of the steering wheel was
digging into his thigh, despite that he'd moved the seat way back.
He was stiff, and his muscles protested, but he'd been so exhausted, he'd basically passed out. When he sat up, he glanced at
Kyle, who shook his head, mouthing, "Nada" and waving his hand
in front of him.

It was Cole's name flashing on the screen of his phone. Alex
quickly answered. "I thought I said no phones?" he snarled. "I
wasn't kidding, Cole!"

"A-ah-lex?" A woman cried on the other end of the phone. It
wasn't Angel, so it had to be Becca.

"Becca? What's the matter?" He sat up straighter, reaching
down to press the electric lever that would take his seat out of
recline.

She broke down, sobbing hard into the phone. Alex's heart
seized up in his chest, and his blood ran cold. "Becca, calm down.
What happened?"

Kyle was listening intently, his eyes trained on Alex's face. Alex pointed to the house they were watching, silently telling him to get his eyes back where they needed to be despite the hysterical woman on the phone.

"Oh, muh, my God, Alex! We st-stopped to get gas and wh-when—" she stopped and sobbed some more. She was clearly hysterical.

"Becca, please try to calm down. I can't do anything until I know what's going on."

"Wuh—When I was in the bathroom, someone sh-shot Cole and drove off with with Jill and Angel."

Alex's skin turned to ice, and despite the almost cold temperature in the car, he broke out in a sweat, his heart starting to race. "Where are you, Becca? Did you see anything?"

"We were the only ones there. Me and the store clerk. We didn't hear a gunshot or anything. When I came out, Cole was on the pavement bl-bleeding, and the SUV was gone!" She snuffled and continued to sob. "Oh, God!"

"Is Cole dead?" he had to ask, even though he dreaded the answer. His chest closed down. He couldn't breathe, he couldn't move, and his mind kept hearing her words repeat over and over: *they drove off with Jillian and Angel.* Kyle's head snapped around at Alex's words.

"No, but it's bad, Alex. The clerk called 911, and the volunteer fire people came—paramedics. They took him on life flight to a hospital in Springfield. There was blood everywhere. So much blood."

Alex put the phone on speaker and started the engine. The tires screeched when he began speeding out of the neighborhood toward the interstate. He was probably going sixty-five in a thirty-five, but the speed limits weren't a consideration.

"Okay, Becca, I have to go." Alex's mind was racing faster than his Audi in order to determine what needed to be done and what was the fastest way to do it. "Keep Cole's phone ,and I'll call you back. Can you get to the hospital? Take a cab if you have to."

"The sheriff's deputy is taking me right now. I'm calling from the squad car. Alex, will you find them?" Her frantic voice was broken and thick.

"I'm going to do everything I can, but I have to go now. Bye."

Alex merged onto I-94, turned on his caution lights, and floored it.

"What happened?" Kyle was clearly dismayed.

"They've got her." His breath rushed out in anguish. "And Bean. Fuuuuuccccckkkkk!" Alex yelled at the top of his lungs and pounded hard on the steering wheel three times. "Goddamn it! I'm going to kill that motherfucker with my bare hands. I swear to God, Kyle, I'm going to kill him! Jesus Christ! I can't even fucking breathe."

"Alex, don't hyperventilate." Kyle pulled his seatbelt on then held out his hand. "Give me the phone and tell me who I should call. You just drive. Are we going to the airport?" Kyle was panicking, but Alex lost it; his jaw set, his expression glazed over. Livid was an understatement.

"No. It takes hours to get out of Chicago even on a private jet." His voice was hard and impatient that he had to explain. "They'll be able to track us. I'm just going to drive like a bat out of hell." If he were going to get away with murder, he'd have to think about every detail. And right now, he felt murderous. He tried to inhale deeply, but his lungs felt like they would crack with the effort.

"Even if we head down there, what can we do? How will we find her? Where are they?"

Alex ran a hand through his hair and spoke quickly. "Somewhere in the Ozark mountains based on what Becca said. Get the radar detector out of the glove compartment and turn it on."

Alex was going almost ninety, but he planned to go faster as soon as the radar detector was operational.

"Okay, it's on," Kyle confirmed, and Alex responded by flooring it. The car shot past everyone else on the highway. "Alex, put your belt on."

"The tolls will slow us down," Alex muttered, not registering Kyle's words.

"Alex?" Kyle tried again but was interrupted when Alex's phone pinged. He glanced at the screen. "It's an incoming text. It says it's from Angel."

Alex's muscles coiled, becoming rigid and hard. His nostrils flared. That bastard had her phone. "It's not her. If he has hurt her, I will kill him. I'll rip his heart out of his living chest, I swear to fucking God." His voice was low and ferocious, and he felt physically sick, a giant hole in his chest, his stomach lurching. "Open it."

Kyle's hand began to tremble as he tried to do Alex's bidding. "Fucking hell. It's a video text. Fuck. I don't want to see this."

Alex felt like he'd been punched in the gut. "Just open the fucking thing up, Kyle!" Alex commanded. "If you're too much of a pussy to do it, give me the phone," Alex snarled. The muscles of his shoulders and neck began to burn as if acid was eating at them.

"Take it easy, Alex. I'll open it." Kyle opened it and looked at the image. He sighed in relief. "Okay."

"What is it?"

Sounds of talking and crying came across the screen. Alex could hear Jillian screaming and Swanson talking to Angel. *I'm gonna fuck you long and hard, gorgeous. Mmm… I've been waiting for this.*

With what? A strap on? Angel spat sarcastically. I doubt I'll even be able to feel your puny little dick.

Fear gripped Alex's heart. Angel's bravado would only make matters worse. Though he admired her strength, for once, he wished she'd back down.

Swanson laughed loudly. He was enjoying her pushback. *I was hoping you'd be nice, but it's just fine if you want to fight. I like it better that way.*

One of them hauled off and slapped her hard across the face. Alex could hear the scuffle, Angel's grunt, and then the sound as she was knocked to the floor. *Why wasn't she fighting back?* His mind screamed. The thought of her helpless at the hands of Mark Swanson made him sick. He was so upset he could barely see the road in front of him. His foot pressed the accelerator to the floor. "That's enough. Shut it off," he demanded. *"Motherfucker!"*

"There's a cot in what looks like a basement; they have her stripped down to her panties and bra. There was a large man behind her, but his head wasn't in the shot. They've hit her a few times because her cheek was already bruised, and she has a black eye," Kyle said sullenly. "I can't believe this is really happening."

Alex's jaw set like a stone, his hands clenched and unclenched around the steering wheel a few times. He felt like he would vomit. His mind filled with many painful ways he would make Mark Swanson suffer a slow death. He'd take pleasure in spilling that fucker's blood. "Is there a message?"

"It says *'I've got your little girl. If you want her back, it's still $10 million. And the kid, so another five will do.'* Greedy fucker, isn't he? No one's got that kind of money."

"Whether I do or not, he gets nothing but a slow death." Alex inhaled a ragged breath. He didn't even care that saying the words out loud to anyone could implicate him if Swanson did have an accident. Right now, all he cared about was getting to Angel.

"At least we know she's alive," Kyle breathed out. He'd seen a lot of fucked up shit in his life, but this was way too close to home. "This guy... *Fuck!* I don't even know what to say. Angel's going to get herself killed!"

Yes, at least they were alive, and that was something, but his soul was on fire, and he knew it would burn until that bastard took his very last breath. He wanted to call Angel's phone and tell Mark Swanson he was a dead man, but he needed to buy time to find their location and get down there.

Alex nodded. "Yes. She needs to back the fuck off. Call him back and hand me the phone, Kyle."

Swanson answered with a laugh. "Alex! How nice of you to call. Seems I've got something you want. Are you ready to make a deal?"

Alex took a deep breath and steadied his voice. "Yes, you have something I want."

"I know. I find it so satisfying. I may even keep her and play a little, just to teach you a lesson."

"You've got my attention, Swanson. Okay, I'll give you the money, but only if she isn't harmed further." It took all Alex had to remain calm and tell Swanson what he wanted to hear, but he had no choice.

"Wire the money, then I'll tell you where to find her."

"No."

"No? You should reconsider." Angel screamed shrilly in the background, and Jillian's cries intensified. "My boys are getting restless. They don't like to wait, and I'm not sure how long I can hold them off."

Alex's teeth clenched. "You listen to me, you sadistic fuck; I'll give you the goddamned money, but on my terms. If either Angel or Jillian is harmed, I'll hunt you down like a dog." His voice was deadly calm. "Do I make myself clear?"

"You're not in a position to make demands, Avery. I'll gut her like a fish."

"You need the money or you are fucked. The cops will find you eventually, or the mob will take you out for what you did to your wife's daughter. We both know it, so I think it's in both of our best interests to make a deal. Killing Angel gains you nothing but my wrath. So this is how it goes down. It will take 24 hours to get the cash together then I have to get to you."

"Wire the funds, Avery!" Swanson was getting agitated. Gone was his sarcastic amusement, and frustration filled his voice. "Or else!"

"Or else what? You'll suck my dick?" Alex asked sarcastically. "Fuck off. You want the money or not? You don't get a dime until I lay eyes on Angel and Jillian. Until I walk out with them."

"You're in no position to make demands!" Swanson's anger was rising.

"Oh, I think I am." He kept his voice hard and unemotional. He had to make the lie about to come out convincing. "I was intrigued because she was a big challenge; one I've clearly won. I'm not in love. If you kill her, it will sting, but it's not going to end my life. But I promise, it *will end yours*." Alex shut up and waited, his pause designed to drive home his point. He wouldn't speak again until the other man did.

Seconds passed, with Kyle listening and watching Alex's face intently. He admired his resolve.

Alex could hear Swanson's sigh on the other end of the line. "Call me when you get the money together."

"When I do, you will give me an address or the deal is off."

"How do I know you won't ambush me."

"Hmmnph!" Alex huffed out a sarcastic laugh. "Guess you'll just have to trust me."

He hung up the phone without giving Swanson a chance to answer.

"You have huge balls," Kyle said incredulously. "Huge—motherfucking—balls."

"I've earned them."

"Now what?"

Waiting on anyone or anything wasn't Alex's forte, and he now had 24 hours to get Angel and Jillian out. "There's an app on my phone. It looks like a little green radar screen. Bring it up."

Kyle looked at Alex seriously. "You do know he plans to kill Angel, the kid, and you, if he gets his hands on you. You know this, right?"

Alex nodded. "Without question." His voice was deadly calm and resolute. Kyle wondered what he was thinking.

"How can you be so calm?"

"I'm not calm. I'm fucking flying out of my skin, but I've held out up 'til now. He won't expect me to just give in. I think he'd even be disappointed if I did. He loves the game; that's the sort of prick he is."

"But, pushing his buttons? You're putting Angel at risk."

"He has to be agitated or he has an advantage."

Kyle did as he was asked, though he questioned Alex's reasoning.

"Okay, now bring up the green radar app. Open it; there are two numbers, click on the second one."

"Is this what I think it is?"

"Yes. It's going to locate my phone; *Angel's phone.*"

"Even at this distance?"

"We don't know the distance, do we?" Alex wasn't used to having his actions questioned, but he owed Kyle for coming along. "If they aren't in the middle of bum-fuck, and there's service, it should locate her."

Kyle grinned. "This is awesome! We're gonna sneak up on him."

"Yeah. But we don't know how many others he has with him. I don't expect this to be a walk in the park."

"We know he has that big burly fuck we saw on the video."

"Yeah, and at least one more. You up for it?"

"I never thought I'd be grateful for the bullshit I went through as a kid, but it might come in handy now." Kyle grew up on the south side of Chicago and saw a bunch of gang activity growing up. By some miracle, his family moved to a modest suburb when he was fourteen, which he knew changed the course of his life.

"What do you mean?"

"When I was younger, we lived in a shit neighborhood. I got in with some bad kids: drugs, fighting, stealing shit. When I was fourteen, my friends and I boosted a car and got busted. It was my first offense so I got probation, but my dad got a second job and moved us to one of the western suburbs. My dad is a factory worker. He's sixty, and he literally worked eighty hours a week. We never saw him, and my mom worked at a fast food joint around the corner from our house because they could only afford one car. My world was night and day different. The schools, the people, the expectations; everything changed. And, seeing my old man work his ass off so he could give my brother and me a better life gave me a new respect for him. He taught me that life is earned, not taken."

"He sounds like a great man," Alex said. After this was over, Alex decided he would put his father to work at Avery, doing some fluff job, overpay him to do it, and set up some investments in his name. It was the least he could do to repay this debt.

"Would you really kill him?" Kyle asked seriously.

"If he touched or hurt her," Alex murmured in explanation as if it were enough. His heart was slamming against his ribs; his face was infused with heat.

"Wow," Kyle murmured.

Alex glanced to his right, meeting Kyle's eyes then back at the road in front of him. "This is going to get bloody. We have to get there and take them out before he knows what hit him, and I'm sure we're outnumbered. I understand if you don't want to be part of it."

Alex slowed down for a tollgate and chose the cash lane. He dug in his pocket, pulled out a roll of bills, and peeled one off. "That will be $2.25 sir," the woman attendant said.

He handed her a twenty but didn't wait for change. "Keep it."
By the time the words were out, he was already accelerated to 60
miles per hour and speeding away.

"Of course, I'm in all the way. You warned me this was serious shit, and you weren't kidding. But, it's Angel, so I'm in."

"It keeps getting worse and worse, and unfortunately, I see
only that one solution. I've tried to convince Angel she needs a
new career path." He sighed heavily and raked his hand through his
hair again. "She won't budge."

"I never had any luck in that department, either," Kyle mused,
a woeful grin twitched at the corners of his mouth. "Do her eyes
still sparkle when she's pissed? I remember how beautiful she was
when she's challenged."

"Very much." Alex agreed. Jealousy stirred in his gut. Kyle
was still in love with Angel but he understood. "Now, please get
that radar app up, Kyle."

Alex's anxious energy was palpable, and Kyle sensed it.
Whatever Mark Swanson said on the phone, Alex was hopped-up
as hell. Who wouldn't be, given the situation? If he hadn't had
proof of Alex's true feelings for Angel the last time he'd seen them
together, it was crystal clear now. Angel wasn't the kind of woman
anyone had superficial feelings for. He'd loved her, too. He
doubted he'd ever get over her, and even though it was apparent
he'd never have a chance of getting her back, there wasn't a day
that went by that he didn't think of Angel and how he'd fucked
things up. Retreating into his thoughts, he booted up the app and
got it going. "Don't you want to check on your brother? Tell your
folks?"

Alex nodded. "Yeah. That's the next on the list. After the app
locates Angel's phone, I'll call my parents and get them on a
plane."

"Will this give us an exact location?"

"It works similar to GPS tracking, so it will give a town or area it's close to on the map but give us driving instruction when we get closer."

"Cool."

"Yes. I'd be fucked right now if I didn't have it. I wouldn't know what the fuck to do with myself."

"*We'd* be fucked," Kyle pointed out. There was a double meaning behind it and Alex caught it. He nodded.

"Yes." Alex inhaled and flexed the fingers holding the steering wheel. "I'd be going crazy if I wasn't going after her."

"It's searching."

"You're a much better sport than I would have been. I was never jealous before I met Angel, but now, even the thought of her with you in the past fucks me up."

Kyle shook his head and shrugged. "Yeah, well, I screwed up. I can't blame you or Angel for any of it. It's my own fault she left me."

Alex paused. "She's under my skin and in my head; she's all I think about. If you loved her like that, I imagine it rips your guts out."

Kyle nodded. "I'm not going to lie, Alex. There will probably always be a part of me that loves Angel. There isn't anyone like her, but I want her to be happy." He looked back down at the phone in his hand.

"I don't get how you could choose that—" Alex paused briefly to choose his words carefully. Crystal was an idiot and she was trashy. Alex couldn't fathom how Kyle could risk losing Angel over someone like her, "—other woman over her."

"I was an idiot. Angel wanted to leave the band, and I was sore at her. I was selfish, and I guess I wanted to show her I didn't need her. It just made it easier for her."

Alex shook his head. He knew Angel would protect herself and not take bullshit from anyone. Even if she were hurting, she would have straightened her shoulders and told Kyle to his face to go fuck himself. That was Angel, and he loved that about her.

"Forgive me for asking, Alex, since I probably have no right, but what are your intentions with Angel?"

"Easy. I'm going to marry her as soon as she'll agree."

"Are you sure she'll agree?"

Alex knew whatever he said would hurt the other man, and he had no desire to do so. He answered as simply as he could. "I am."

Kyle nodded. Avery was a commanding asshole; he'd give him that. He wore confidence like an expensive suit. "The app is pointing to a location just south of Houston, Missouri. When you come to Rolla, take Highway 28 South."

"Thanks. Can you hand me the phone, please?"

Alex's fingers worked with practiced precision. He didn't need to look down as he dialed Mrs. Dane first.

"Alexander Avery's office." Her voice was cool and professional as always.

"Mrs. Dane, please have the jet ready at O'Hare immediately. Have the pilots file the flight plan for Springfield, Missouri. My parents will be taking it. This is an emergency, so it has to be done right away."

His voice was contrite, and she'd learned that tone evoked no argument, no questions.

"Yes, sir. Will there be anything else?"

"No, thank you." Alex ended the call and dialed Cole's number. He needed an update on Cole's condition before he called his parents. It wouldn't do to be ignorant of the situation in the face of their questions.

"Hello?" Becca answered. "Alex, have you found them?"

"I'm working on it. I'm on my way. Any updates on Cole?"

"They won't tell me anything since we aren't related." She started to cry. "The sheriff and the police keep questioning me about it, but I didn't see any of it happen. I'm so scared for all of them. I'll just die if something happens to my baby. They keep saying they'll find them, but I don't think they will."

Alex shifted in the leather seat and ran a hand over his face in impatient agitation. He didn't think they would either. In the week the Chicago police had worked the Bancroft case, they hadn't found anything, but Alex was beginning to think he'd been too hard on them. Maybe it wasn't lack of effort but more that Swanson was a slippery son of a bitch. Alex was seeing the situation with new eyes, but he had no idea how to comfort her. "Let me speak to someone, please. A doctor or nurse who knows what's going on."

The city had long been left behind, and Alex was speeding down the interstate, passing cars as if they were standing still.

"Okay." Alex listened to Becca's tearful plea for someone familiar with Cole's condition to take the phone. "His brother is on the phone and would like some information."

"Mr. Avery?" A deep male voice came on the line. "This is Dr. Peters. I was in the ER when they brought your brother in."

"How's he doing?"

"He's in surgery. He had a gunshot wound to the chest, and he was bleeding badly, so they took him in right away. We were sure one of his lungs was punctured, but it wasn't clear if there was arterial damage or if it was just a vein that had been severed. I haven't had an update from the surgery team yet, but it was imperative they get in there and find the source of the bleeding. He was in very serious condition, but we're doing everything we can."

Alex swallowed. "Thank you. Please update me as soon as you know anything new. Becca James is a close personal friend of the family, so she can be updated as well. My parents are on their way."

"I'll let the staff know to expect them. I'm very sorry about your brother."

"Thank you, doctor. Please put Ms. James back on."

"Hello?"

"Becca, I'm going to get Jillian and Angel back. I'll do everything in my power." Alex's throat tightened and started to throb. He swallowed twice, but it wouldn't ease at all. "Angel is my whole life now, and I adore Bean. I'm going to find them if it's the last thing I do." Anguish created physical pain. He'd let his adrenaline run him, and his brain kicked in, methodically planning and carrying out what needed to be done, but his emotions were boiling inside, his heart aching, and memories of Angel played over and over inside his mind.

She sucked in her breath on a sob. "I know, Alex. I'm praying. I'll keep praying."

"Me, too. I'm calling my parents now, and they'll be down there in a couple hours. Just hang on."

"Oh-okay." She sniffled. "Thanks, Alex."

"I'll be in touch."

"Bye."

"Cole is bad." Alex muttered to let Kyle know what he'd learned in the briefest way possible. He decided to dial his father's number. His mother would be a hysterical mess he didn't have the nerves to deal with. His father could fill in Allison, Josh, and his mother.

"Alex?" his father answered quickly, his voice laced with concern.

"Hi Dad." There was no easy way to break the news, so he blurted it out. "I'm having the plane meet you at O'Hare. You and Mom, maybe Allison and Josh, need to get to Springfield, Missouri right away."

"What's happened?" Charles' voice was panicked.

"Please remain calm, Dad. This isn't good, but for Mom's sake, don't freak out. Angel and Jillian are missing. Someone hijacked the vehicle while they were getting gas. Becca is fine, she was inside at the time, but Cole was shot." He inhaled through his nose, waiting for his father to explode.

Surprisingly, he didn't. "Oh, my God," he breathed out.

"Yes. It was in some Podunk town in southern Missouri, but they took him by life flight to Springfield. He's in surgery now, and Mrs. Dane is having the plane readied. Becca is there. I'm going to get Angel and the baby."

"What the fuck, Alex?" His father's voice was frantic. "Call the police."

"Dad, Becca talked to the sheriff's department, so they know. I have to do something. I can't wait around for Swanson to kill Angel and Jillian like he did Bancroft."

"I understand, son." Charles' voice was solemn.

"Will you tell Allison and Josh? They may want to come with you."

"Okay. We'll come right away."

Alex heard his mother in the background. "Charles, what is happening?"

"Call me after you get to the hospital."

"Do you need me to wire any money? Do you need anything?"

Alex shook his head even though his father couldn't see. "I told you before; I'm not going to pay this fucker off. That hasn't changed."

"Then what's your plan?"

"To take them back. Just—take them back."

"You make it sound so simple."

"It's not at all, but it is what it is. I've had enough."

16

All or Nothing

IT WAS COLD in the basement which had become her prison. Angel's stomach was rumbling, and Jillian was finally sleeping on the cot and covered up with Angel's coat. After they'd beaten her on video for Alex's benefit, they all left her alone. The minute they'd gone, she scrambled back into her clothes.

There was no telling how much time had passed, but it felt like forever. She didn't have on a watch, and those bastards had taken both her phones. She'd curled up with Jillian, trying to comfort the little one, playing games of itsy-bitsy spider and telling her stories until she fell asleep. Angel assured her Zander would find them, though she herself was frantic with worry. This place was in the middle of fucking nowhere, and she had no clue where "nowhere" was. Alex would try everything possible to find them and spare no expense; she was certain. He might even pay Swanson off, but she knew he would come after her. She was lying on the cot with Jillian and closed her eyes. Her face and body hurt where she'd been hit and where she'd landed when they knocked her to the floor. She forced herself to sit up. She was exhausted, and she wanted nothing more than the blissfulness of sleep, but that would do nothing to get them out of trouble. The time spent contemplating hurt either way. What if she never saw Alex again? Her heart couldn't bear it.

The light from the one bulb was dim, but she wandered around looking for something she could use as a weapon. There were metal fittings on the cot, but they were small, and she'd find it hard to get a good grip on them. She'd have to be too close in order to wield any real damage to her attackers, which wouldn't do. She paced around the room, both hands threading together on the top of her head.

If she were alone, it would have been easier to escape, but most likely, she would have been raped by now. She shuddered at the thought. She'd counseled at least a hundred rape victims during her career. Women who had been brutalized and beaten, raped and sodomized, three who had been gang raped. They'd lived through it; damaged forever, but they lived. She knew she would, too.

It was horrible enough to consider the possibility of such an unspeakable act, but more than having to endure it, she couldn't bear the thought of it coming between her and Alex. He was a real man, one of integrity and purpose, and in her heart, she knew he wouldn't look at her differently or turn away from her. But... it would rip his heart out. Even if he said he didn't think about it whenever he touched her, how could he help it? It would torment him because he had been unable to save her from it. And Alex suffering like that would kill her.

She flushed. What was she even thinking about that for? If that happened, she'd be killed. She'd never make it back to Alex. She mentally shook herself. She'd be better off using her energy to figure out a way to escape.

Angel glanced back at Jillian. If Jillian weren't here, she would fight to the death, but she had to stay alive to get Jillian back to Becca, no matter the consequences to herself. She looked around again. Was there anything in here that might help her get out? The basement was completely empty, save a water heater and furnace. She might be able to pull some of the copper pipe along the ceiling loose, but it would be hollow on both ends, and if she used it to try to stab someone, she would run the risk of it pushing back into her own body. The cot had wooden legs and frame. She considered breaking them, but if one of the creepers came down before she was ready for them, they'd see what she was up to and most likely beat her more, or worse.

The foundation of the house was cinder block and some of the mortar was coming loose. Angel ran her fingers along it and tried to pry a few large pieces loose, but the stuff was so old and rotten, it crumbled into small chunks and dust.

"Damn it!" she breathed out. She stood and ran a hand through her hair again. The door to the basement creaked then opened with another scraping sound. The house was filled with humidity and the door was swollen beyond the confines of its original dimensions, causing it to scrape against the floor every time it opened.

She quickly resumed her position on the cot next to Jillian, sitting close and placing a hand on the sleeping child. The last thing she needed was to have her captors get suspicious about what she was up to. Boots on the stairs appeared, and Angel breathed a silent sigh of relief that it was the young kid. He was carrying a plate and a glass filled with some sort of liquid.

She tried to get a better look at him. He had a missing front tooth, and his brown hair was overly long and greasy. His clothes hung off his thin frame, and though she wasn't near him, he just looked like he smelled bad. Angel wondered if he was some sort of addict. He leered at her and licked his lips. She was revolted and couldn't help her grimace.

"Where are the others?" Angel asked. *Was he the only one here?* she wondered.

"Don't know. Gone to town for supplies, I guess."

This kid is an idiot, she thought. He saw her as a small, helpless woman. She was small, but not helpless, especially now that she knew the other two were gone. Angel sized him up, all the while trying not to give him any indication of her intentions. *So there was a town; how far away was it? Did needing supplies mean they were planning on staying a while? Had they contacted Alex?* Her mind flooded with questions.

"How long have I been here?" Her stomach growled painfully.

He walked to her and handed her the plate. It had a peanut butter sandwich and a banana on it. Her nostrils picked up the scent of the peanut butter, and her instincts were to grab the sandwich and eat it right away, but it could be laced with something, and she couldn't take that chance. The banana was a safer bet.

The young man's eyes narrowed. "Eat," he commanded.

"What's your name?"

He sat down on the bottom step and watched her. His eyes narrowed, but they were squinty to begin with.

Angel's stomach tightened, but she picked up the banana and pulled the peel open. She took a bite and swallowed it. "Well?"

"Donnie."

"Donnie." Angel repeated the word. Her wary eyes trained on him; she then slowly took another bite from the banana. She was starving, but she'd be saving half of it for Jillian. "Thanks for the banana." She knew his eyes were trained on her mouth as she ate it, knew he was thinking of her sucking his dick. *Ugh. What a revolting thought.*

He didn't answer, but nodded once, his tongue coming out to slide salaciously over his lower lip. *Fucking pig,* Angel thought.

"What's your boss planning for me?" He shifted uncomfortably. "It won't change anything if you tell me," Angel coaxed.

"He said we're gonna have some fun with you then get your boyfriend to pay up."

"Do you believe him?" she asked, shaking her head. She wanted to tell him that if she were harmed, Alex wouldn't pay the ransom. "They won't let you have any fun, Donnie. Swanson is a greedy bastard. He and that big, fat pig will use me up before you get a chance. You know that, right?"

He pulled at the crotch of his dirty jeans, and Angel wanted to puke. She swallowed and set the banana down. She didn't have much time, and she had to make a move now.

Her arms lifted and she pulled her shirt up over her head and off then stood up. "If it's gonna happen, I'd rather it be with you," she said softly, taking a few steps toward him. "Do you want to be with me?" She inched her sweatpants down so the curve of her hips, her navel, and the top of her purple lace bikini panties peeked out.

"They'll kill me if I do," Donnie said, his eyes running up and down Angel's body. She was just glad Jillian was asleep.

"Why don't we be friends, Donnie? That way we both win. I let you fuck me, and you help me get away from them. I can tell by the way they talk to you, you're nothing to them. Swanson only cares about himself. Whatever promises he made, he won't keep."

She could tell he was conflicted. Conflicted and confused was good.

"We fuck, you get us out, and I get you a bunch of money. Think of the life you could have. What could you do with a million dollars, Donnie?" Angel's voice was filled with sex and temptation; she looked at him through half-lidded eyes.

"How 'bout you blow me, instead?" His eyes continued to ogle her, then landed on her breasts. Angel had no intention of fucking him, and she sure as shit wasn't going to suck him off. Conviction made her brave. She had to get him at a disadvantage. He had to believe she was going to do as he wanted.

"Come over here." Her words were low and sultry on purpose, though the man made her stomach turn.

Donnie got up quickly and walked toward her, his hand going to his belt to begin opening his pants en route.

Angel didn't stop to think. She whirled and connected a round kick to his jaw, making him stumble backward.

The man yelled. "You bitch! You're gonna pay for that."

She stood in a fighting stance, her feet wide apart and her arms up to protect her body, fists clenched. Angel's body was at an angle to Donnie's, her left side in front of her. She prepared herself to deliver the blow of her life.

"Moron. Did you fucking think I'd let you touch me?" Angel taunted. The noise startled Jillian awake, and the little girl started to wail loudly. "Nasty bastard."

"Anga!" she cried. "Anga!"

The man charged at Angel again, and she let him in close; close enough to get his arms around her waist, his fingers digging into her soft flesh. His breath was rancid, and his body smelled foul from sweat, cigarettes, and urine, but she couldn't turn her head away, though his odor made her want to gag. She had to keep her eyes on her target.

She had one chance, and only one. She brought her right arm back and rammed the heel of her hand up and hard into the tip of his nose with all the force she could muster. It was one of the first moves she learned in the self-defense classes she'd taken right after her rape in college. Donnie dropped like a stone, landing with a sick thud in a crumpled heap on the concrete floor. He never knew what hit him. The bones in his nose were shattered and shoved up into the frontal lobe of the brain, causing instant death.

Angel didn't have time to celebrate or even take a breath; she had to get them out of there while she had the chance. Her breath rushed out in a whoosh as she threw her shirt back on and followed it with her coat, silently thanking God that the men hadn't been smart enough to take it from her. *Ignorant assholes*, she thought.

The temperature in the basement dictated that Angel had left Jillian's coat on the whole time they were down there. She shoved the banana in her pocket and picked up the sandwich. It might not be safe to eat, she wasn't sure, but it joined the fruit inside her coat.

The plate was glass, and she dropped it on the concrete. It broke into five pieces, and she chose the one with the sharpest point and put it in the other pocket.

She picked up Jillian and ran up the stairs. "Hush, baby. We have to be quiet, okay? It's very important we are very quiet."

"Tay." Jillian nodded.

"We have to be brave, too. It's going to be okay."

At the top of the stairs, Angel's eyes flew around the room. The house was very old, the appliances had seen better days, and there were rust stains on the sink where water had leaked around the faucet. She raced to the back door and opened it. Outside, it was overcast and windy, trees surrounded the large clearing the house sat on. The trees blocked her view beyond, and she couldn't see the sun, so she had no idea what direction was which. There was one dirt tire path worn through the grass, but there was no way to know where it led or how far it was from a real road. Swanson would assume she would follow it. She looked around and headed for an old barn at the opposite end of the clearing, which was closely guarded by trees on two sides. Maybe she'd find something she could use for a weapon inside, if nothing else. Or, maybe there was a place inside she could hide Jillian.

Angel was torn. She could run, but to where? Getting lost in the woods would mean certain hypothermia and death, but after the dirt road leading out, the barn would be the next place they'd look for her. She pushed through the barn door and waited for her eyes to adjust to the darkness. The wood was weathered and splintering; the entire building was dilapidated almost to the point of falling down; a few small streams of light were coming in from two windows and a few cracks in the wood of the walls and roof.

Dangerous debris scattered the floor. She'd need to be careful where she stepped.

At least, the wind was less intrusive inside, and Angel put Jillian down gently. "Bean, I have to set you down for just a minute. I'm right here, though, okay? Hush now, sweet pea."

Jillian was shivering, so Angel zipped up her coat then quickly took stock of her surroundings. There were several old tools hanging on the walls and scattered around. A couple old pieces of equipment and a big seed wagon. Angel had seen them many times sitting in fields waiting to be filled with grain while farmers combined crops. This was wooden and very old. One of the wheels was flat, so it hadn't been used in years. This place had been deserted for decades. No one would come to find them here, unless they were looking, but she couldn't take Jillian into the woods and get lost.

She had to trust that Alex was coming to find them. Her decision made, she began her search. An old ice pick and a pitchfork were the most promising. The wooden handle on the pitchfork was broken and splintered; all of the paint was missing. Like everything else here, it was circa early thirties and forties. Angel picked them up, climbed up on the wagon, using the hitch and one of the tires as leverage; and tossed the two items inside. She jumped down and rushed to Jillian's side.

"Come on," she whispered. She lifted the little girl and carried her the few feet back to the wagon. "Bean, hold on tight. Wrap your legs around Angel's waist. It's going to be okay. I've got you." Angel repeated her path over the hitch and up the side of the wagon, stepping on the wheel. With Jillian plastered to the front of her torso, Angel knew she wouldn't be able to climb up and over. Her arms wouldn't have enough leverage, so she got down.

"Baby, you gotta get on piggy back. Grab around my neck." She sat down on her haunches, and after Jillian's arms were around her neck, she hoisted her up on her back. More adept on her third try, she climbed up quickly and had soon pulled herself and Jillian over the top of the wagon. It was dirty inside, and the dust made Jillian cough. Angel tried to wave the dust away from her face, but it was useless.

"Bean, sit down, okay?" Angel said softly. She put her finger to her lips to tell the little girl to be quiet. Angel stood in the wagon; the top of it was over her head. She stood on tiptoe and looked around the barn. There were glass windows on the sides opposite the doors, and one of them was broken. There were two large doors, used to bring farm equipment in or out, next to the regular door that she'd brought Jillian through. With both of them closed, she'd be able to hear if anyone came in. There was another wagon—the flatbed variety—at the back and it had something black lying on top of it. Angel knew it would be filthy, but it looked like a tarp that could be used as a cover.

She squatted down by Jillian. "I'll be right back," she said softly. "Stay here." Angel climbed out of the wagon, holding on with her arms then swinging her left leg up, she used it to pull up until she was sitting on top of the wagon. It was easily eight feet to the floor of the barn, but she hopped down then hurried over to the other wagon.

Lifting the edge slightly, she was assaulted with a horrible stench. She turned her head in revulsion. She gagged, coughing violently as her stomach lurched, and she lost the small amount of banana she'd eaten, vomiting on the barn floor. "What the fuck?" she muttered. Her eyes were watering from the stench and throwing up. The tarp was sticky and stiff, and Angel didn't want to think about why, but one thing was sure: they couldn't use it as a cover.

She left it and hurried back to Jillian. When she'd climbed back inside the wagon, she sat down beside her. The wagon was shaped like a funnel with what looked like a hinged door closure at the bottom, which served to empty the grain from the wagon. Angel and Jillian were at the mercy of the slope and sitting in the middle. Angel straightened her legs and used them for leverage to hold them up against the side and away from the pitchfork and ice pick, that wanted to slide down to the concave center as well. She pulled Jillian on her lap and took the banana out of her pocket. "Are you hungry?" she whispered.

Jillian shook her head, and Angel put it away.

"I'z scared of those mean mans." Sad blue eyes looked into Angel's face. "Is Mama coming?"

"No, baby. But Zander will." She wrapped her arms around Jillian and rested her chin against her head. It was slightly warmer in the wagon, huddled together as they were, but it was still chilly. "Zander will find us." Angel knew it in her soul; no doubt, Alex wouldn't stop until he found them. She just hoped it wasn't too late.

"When, Anga?" Her little voice was soft, as if she realized the need to keep as silent as possible. It was scary. They were still so close to Mark Swanson and his goons. Far from home free, but the smart thing to do was to hide—and wait. "When will Zander come?"

"I don't know for sure, Bean." Angel's faith in Alex was unshakable, and she would hold on to it, and the little girl on her lap, for dear life. "But he *will*. I promise."

*****

The phone finder app led Alex and Kyle to a sparsely populated area of the Ozark Mountains soth of Springfield and at least 300 miles southeast of Joplin. There wasn't much around, and as they'd gotten closer, the GPS lead to an unpaved path that carved through the woods, winding away from the road. It was apparent to both of them the road would lead directly to their objective, with little chance of an offshoot road to hide Alex's Audi, and driving in directly would mean losing their element of surprise.

The location posed several other problems. They'd have to walk in, so making a fast escape with Angel and Jillian would be impossible. There was no way of knowing the distance off any main road or how long it would take to walk in. It was getting dark, and the sooner they got in there, the better. And lastly, they'd only have one weapon each. They shoved what extra ammunition they could into their coat pockets, and Kyle slid his knife into his boot.

It was dreary, and though they had on coats and the stocking caps Kyle had brought, it was still cold. The hat was irritating Alex, rolled up as it was so his face wouldn't be covered. It itched and he pushed it off, discarding it impatiently. They followed along the road, though back under the cover of the trees. They moved swiftly, not speaking, adrenaline and determination keeping them warm and alert. When the roof of an old farmhouse came into view, Alex motioned for Kyle to continue as he was while he moved to the opposite side of the road.

Alex had been in touch with his parents, Becca, and the hospital while they were still driving. Cole was out of surgery, and though still in serious condition, was alive. It was a huge relief. Now, Alex's insides were on fire in anxious anticipation. His mind was sharp, his focus clear on what needed to be done. This place was so fucking secluded and deserted, the house in a serious state of disrepair; it wasn't likely anyone had been here in years. Alex was certain it was why Mark Swanson picked it. Maybe his family owned it, maybe the mob did. His promise to Standish dictated the need to find out.

The Camden County Sheriff's department had located the rented SUV abandoned in a wooded area two hours northeast of where they were now. At least, they'd found something, and it was being dusted for prints. They were on the hunt. Alex had received a call from Kenneth, and though he'd let it go to voicemail, it held valuable information. He was glad they were actually working the case, though his subconscious told him it would make things more difficult. In his gut, Alex knew it would be a fight to the death, and law enforcement involvement would create more questions and red tape.

Within a few hundred yards of the house, Alex could see no evidence of any vehicles.

"Fuck," he muttered. The phone finder led them in this direction, but the unincorporated roads made it uncertain at best. It was the general area, but what if this was just an old abandoned farmhouse? Or, what if they'd moved their hideout? This would have been a wild goose chase.

There was a barn on the property, and Alex pointed toward the barn, silently telling Kyle to check inside. Maybe the vehicles would be inside.

He would've never imagined he'd be faced with something this dangerous or desperate. Alex was decidedly calm. He was resolved. He'd leave with Angel and Jillian, or they'd all get killed. There was nothing in between those two options that he'd consider. It was all or nothing. It was the way he lived his life, the way his relationship with Angel had been from day one: all or nothing.

Leaning with his back against a tree, which hid him from view of the house, Alex breathed out through his nose and closed his eyes to center himself. His father's semi-automatic was comfortable in his right hand, and he wanted it to be a precaution, but he knew it was more. He didn't want to need it because the guns could be traced. The situation was too unknown to know what would be required, and what could comfortably be told to the authorities, but only a moron would go in without being armed. But, he'd keep it as clean as possible.

Alex watched Kyle go behind him in the direction of the barn before he made a crouched run toward the house. There was a covered porch, the walls screened-in on all sides. The screens were dirty, the house almost falling apart, the paint almost non-existent, worn away by decades of wind and weather. Hopefully, the filthy screens would inhibit a good view of anyone approaching through the yard. The yard that was little more than overgrown weeds.

Alex crept up the steps and pressed his back to the wall beside the door. He reached across and wiggled the doorknob. His heart was now thudding uncomfortably in his chest. Surprised to find the door open, he turned the knob slowly, careful to keep silent, then pushed the door open with his fingertips.

He looked in cautiously. There were no sounds. Not one. The place smelled foul—old and moldy.

The place was a complete dump, the furnishings out of date and run down. It was probably infested with vermin. If this had existed within in the city limits, it probably would have been condemned. Plaster was falling away from the slats on the ceilings and walls, and several of the lights were free-hanging bulbs that were rigged up. No, this wasn't a posh hideout.

Alex walked through the house, and though he found no one, there were ashtrays with fresh butts in them, dirty dishes piled in the sink, and a dirty fry pan and trash scattered around proved that people had been here recently. Very recently.

Alex noticed a half-open door off the kitchen, and it took effort to push it open because it scraped on the floor. The stairs led down, and Alex stopped as dread flooded him. This would be the basement in the video. This is where she was. But now, there was no sound.

"Angel?" Alex called softly. There was no answer. Would he find her downstairs? The video was taken in a basement. "Angel!" he called again, louder, panic clamping down on his heart and lungs. There was dim light coming up the stairs. He had to know either way, but his heart raced as he made his way cautiously down the stairs. He took three steps down and his eyes landed on the cot in the middle of the room. On the floor in front of it lay the lifeless body of a man. Alex had a brief moment of horror at seeing the still form until it registered that it wasn't Angel. Though he didn't make a sound, his free hand landed on his chest as his heart lurched.

Was this one of Swanson's men? And, how did he end up dead? Alex went down further so he was able to check around the square room and get a closer look at the body. He was a greasy, dirty man in his early twenties, his lifeless eyes staring blankly from his bony face. He looked almost emaciated, like he could have been an addict or ill.

Alex nudged the body with his foot, pushing him over to see what killed him. A trickle of blood coming from one nostril was the only visible injury. No sign of Angel. Where was she? Now, he was consumed with a new worry; how would he track her? What if Swanson had her phone, but Angel wasn't in the same place? His stomach tightened and his heart fell. He felt like the bottom dropped out from beneath him.

A sudden pain, intense and explosive, burst in his head and light flashed behind his eyes. Alex started to fall, his legs buckling beneath him as he fell to his knees then fully to the floor. His eyes blurred and everything went black.

*****

When Alex came to, he was sitting down, and his head lolled forward. He couldn't move. When his mind cleared, he registered that his feet were tied to the legs of a chair and his arms behind his back, were bound at the wrists. He couldn't move them at all; when he tried, ropes cut into his elbows, as well. He was immobilized.

His head throbbed so painfully, as if the top of it would fly off with each beat of his heart. His eyes fluttered and tried to focus; his ears registered someone yelling from the floor above him.

"Boss, she's got the brat; she couldn't have gone far." The voice was gruff and had an uneducated lilt. Alex blinked again. He was looking at his lap and trying to lift his head to search for the sound.

"Find her! *Now!*"

That voice, Alex recognized. Mark Swanson's voice came from the kitchen above him. And his words gave him hope. Angel was gone. She'd at least managed to escape the house. She had to be the one who killed the kid still lying on the floor where he'd fallen by the cot.

The chair he was attached to was positioned off to one side, the stairs directly in front of him. Alex shook his head to clear it even though it hurt like a son-of-a-bitch. He had to get out of here, and he had to find Angel and Jillian. The chair was wooden and, like everything else in the house, very old. It wasn't anchored to the floor. Alex wiggled his ass in the seat to determine if it was solid or if it had any give. It creaked, indicating it wasn't that strong, but even if he could stand up, the way his ankles were tied prevented him from being able to walk or back up enough to ram the chair into the cinderblock walls of the basement.

If he wanted it broken, he would have to tip the chair over and hope crashing it to the ground would be enough to shatter the wood. Logically, it would be better to wait until he was sure the second man left the house because the loud crash would alert those upstairs. His biceps and triceps bulged and strained as he tried to pull his hands free of the ropes, but there was little give. He grunted as he pulled harder, the ropes burning into his skin. "Fuck!" he murmured softly, frustration threatening to explode his heart.

Ten seconds after the front door to the house slammed, Mark Swanson was coming down the stairs, carrying Alex's gun. He was smiling sadistically, enjoying Alex's helpless position.

Alex glared at him viciously.

"Well, well, well," Swanson murmured, patting the barrel of the gun on the palm of his left hand. "I admit you surprised me, Avery."

"Then you're an idiot," Alex shot back sarcastically.

"You're hardly in a position to make insults."

"Fuck you," Alex spat.

Swanson lifted the gun and used the butt to deliver a vicious blow across Alex's jaw. His head snapped back with such force, the chair wobbled. Pain exploded again, his neck twisted, and he could taste the saltiness of blood in his mouth.

"See… If I were you, I'd cooperate."

Alex spit a mixture of blood and saliva on the floor. "It seems you've lost your bargaining chip." He gave a low chuckle that only served to infuriate Swanson further.

"My guy is going to find her, then I'm going to have a little fun with her."

It took effort, but Alex's mouth twisted mockingly. "Dream on, dumb ass. Isn't one dead body enough for you? Angel isn't exactly a damsel in distress."

Alex had to keep Swanson distracted, but his mind was flooded with concern for Angel. He could feign bravado, but he was scared shitless. He wondered if Kyle found her and Jillian, and if not, could she get away from the man Swanson had sent after her. He'd been knocked out from behind, so he hadn't seen him.

Swanson shook his head. "He's three times the size of this one." He nodded at the dead kid. "She won't stand a chance. And, I still have you."

"That's true. But, if you kill me, you'll never get a cent, you stupid son-of-a-bitch."

The other man huffed. "You have a big mouth for someone tied to a chair with a gun pointed at his head."

Alex didn't say anything, just kept his eyes locked on Swanson. He was bleeding and hurting, but there was no way in hell this fucker was going to win. If he died himself, he vowed he'd take Swanson with him.

Alex shrugged nonchalantly and cocked his head to one side. "Because, I still have the upper hand."

Swanson's eyes narrowed menacingly. "Really? How so?" His tone dripped with sarcasm and arrogance, obviously mocking Alex's statement.

Alex shook his head. "You don't get it. You need my money. You fucking *lost* the thing you had over me." He let a slow smile slide over his face. "Even if you kill me, *I win.*"

"When Dennis finds Angel, I'm going to fuck her right in front of you. Then I'll kill you both. Then I win."

Alex's heart began to hammer in his chest. Swanson could do what he wanted to him, but not to Angel. He would rather die than see something happen to her. "If you find her; if she doesn't drop your other thug. If I don't get loose and rip your goddamned head off." Alex's eyes never wavered as he said the words: his voice solid, stoic, convincing. "That's a lot of fucking 'ifs'." The other man bristled, and Alex drove his point home. "In case you missed it, you don't have the best luck when it comes to me."

Mark Swanson's face mottled with rage, turning a bright red. He still had Alex's gun, and he could easily hit him again, but Alex couldn't stop his taunting.

"Between the cops and Marvin Standish, you'll be hunted down like a dog." Swanson's eyes widened at the mention of Standish. "Oh, yeah, I guess I forgot to mention that. Who do you think told me where to find you?" Alex forced another sly smile. "He doesn't want you breathing. You'll either be whacked or be some big motherfucker's bitch behind bars." He laughed harshly, still taunting. "If I had my druthers, the latter would be my choice, I admit… However, I'm not all that optimistic."

Alex knew he was pushing the boundaries of what was safe, and if the other man came back with Angel in tow, they'd all be fucked. His bargaining power would be gone. "You need money. You know that or we wouldn't be here. The only way you survive is if we make a deal."

17

Consequences

ANGEL PULLED JILLIAN close to her body. She could tell from the lack of any light from the cracks in the wood, and the drop in temperature, that the sun had gone down. They were both cold and shaking. Angel had done her best to keep Jillian warm by opening her coat and plastering Jillian up against her chest, then zipping her own coat back up around the little girl. Jillian was asleep after eating the rest of the banana. They both had to go to the bathroom, and Angel had no choice but to risk a trip into the woods earlier but had made it back into the barn, and the wagon, without seeing anyone.

She was nodding off, but then startled when the door to the barn creaked. Instantly, her eyes were open, and she was at full attention. Someone was coming. Her heart sped up in panic, slamming painfully into her breastbone. She inhaled a shuddery breath, holding it as she listened to someone come in and walk around. A flashlight beam moved around, and Angel could see it when it hit high on the walls or the ceiling of the barn. Whoever it was wouldn't be able to see them inside the wagon unless they climbed up and looked into it. Hope bloomed inside her. Maybe it was

Alex. She wanted to jump up and look; she wanted to call his name, but she couldn't. In case it wasn't.

Her worst fears were confirmed less than thirty seconds later.

"Come on, girly," the gruff voice of the bigger of Swanson's goons called. Her heart sank and fear flooded through her. He wouldn't be as easy to take down as the skinny crackhead had been. And, her position inside the wagon, while it hid them from sight, left her at a disadvantage. He'd grab her and subdue her if he saw her climbing out. She couldn't move. "Dr. Hemming! You'll freeze out here. Think of the kid."

There was a grunt then the man yelled in pain. "Arghhhhh!"

The thud that followed indicated he'd fallen down. She froze in place, her ears straining to hear what was going on. Had he tripped?

"Stay down, you motherfucker," a male voice muttered. "Ugh!" he grunted.

Her eyes widened in surprise. Kyle? She recognized that voice.

There was another grunt followed by a few seconds of silence.

"Angel? Are you in here?" Kyle asked. "I said stay down!" he yelled loudly.

Angel thought she was dreaming. She stood up and grabbed the side of the wagon. Jillian was still strapped to her underneath her coat. She peered over the edge.

It was hard to see, but her eyes had grown accustomed to the darkness after hours in the barn, and Angel could make out Kyle's outline. One foot was pushing against something on the ground. The flashlight, still lit, laid on the ground next to the dark blob that would be the other man.

"Kyle?"

Kyle's eyes shot in the direction of her voice.

"Angel! Where are you? In the wagon? Are you okay?"

"Yes. We're cold but okay." She used her arms, but it would be hard, if not impossible, to climb out with Jillian attached as she was. "Thank God, you're here. Is that asshole incapacitated?"

"He has a knife in his back and a gun trained at his head, so I guess you could say that."

"Where's Alex? I can't climb out. I have to hand down Jillian first."

"He went to the house. I'll have to help you out. Give me a minute."

Angel was relieved Kyle was there, shocked he'd come with Alex but so thankful. She was also scared shitless Alex might be in that house alone with Mark Swanson. "Kyle, please hurry."

"Oh, fuck it," Kyle muttered. There was a low noise of him moving something then another grunt as he removed the knife. He considered his options. He couldn't leave with the possibility this man would get up and fight. He flipped the gun around, holding it by the barrel, and bashed it as hard as he could against the man's head. There was a sickening thud and a cracking sound. Kyle grimaced.

Within seconds, the gun was stowed, and he was climbing up and sitting on the edge of the wagon, one leg inside and the other still perched on the tire. "Come on," he commanded. His arms surrounded Angel and pulled her up until she was sitting next to him. He moved out of the wagon, and scooted back on the tire when both of his feet were in place. "Can you swing your other leg over?"

Angel unzipped her coat, peeling a sleeping Jillian from her chest. With the shared heat missing, Jillian stirred and Angel shivered. "Take her, Kyle." She quickly handed Jillian over then climbed down behind Kyle. Jillian's head settled onto Kyle's shoulder, but when Angel was on the ground, he handed her back to Angel.

"I have to do something with that." Kyle nodded to man on the dirt floor.

"Is he dead?"

"If we're lucky."

"Jesus, this is so surreal. We have to help Alex!" She was anxious.

"He sent me to the barn when he went to the house. When we got here, there were no cars. I saw them drive in and hid on the backside of this barn. There were only two of them. They went in then this asshole came out here."

"There were only three of them, so Swanson is the only one left."

"What happened to the third one?"

"He'd dead. I fought him." Kyle wasn't surprised at her calm strength, but he was in awe she could fight like that. "Let's go."

Kyle shook his head and touched Angel's arm. "Alex made me promise to get you out of here before I did anything else."

"Do you have a car?"

"Yes and no. We walked in. The element of surprise would've been lost if we drove in."

"How far away is it?"

"I'd say a good four or five miles out." They were now at the door to the barn, and Kyle was peering out. "I don't see any sign of Alex, but there is a light on in the house."

"Take Jillian out, Kyle. I can't have something happen to her. I'd never forgive myself."

"Angel, we'll all go. Come on."

"No!" she said frantically, shaking her head. "Someone has to help Alex." Her eyes flooded with tears and she choked up. "You don't know how ruthless Mark Swanson is! He takes pleasure in torturing people."

"Then you take Jillian out, and I'll go in for Alex."

"I don't know where to find the car; you have to do it."

Kyle put his hands on his hips and glanced up before looking back at her. "Angel, there is no way in hell I'm leaving you here. That's crazy."

Angel's hand reached out. "We can't argue about this; we have to do something! Now."

"Okay, well, this guy is toast, so you'll be safe in here with Jillian. I'll go."

She shoved Jillian back at Kyle. "No. I know the layout of the house. You don't. I can sneak up on him easier and faster than you can. Please, Kyle." Her eyes were pleading from her bruised face. "*Please.*" Her voice was laced with desperation.

He sighed. He could see her point, but it went against his better judgment to let her go in alone. If only they didn't have the kid to deal with. "What if we put her in the back of that old Cadillac?"

Angel shook her head adamantly. "No. That's the car they brought us here in. If he manages to get away from us, he'll take off with her in the backseat. I can't risk that, Kyle. Please! We're wasting time."

Kyle pulled the gun from his waistband, cocked it, and handed it to her. She took it automatically, but she didn't want to use it. "Kyle, we can't shoot him. I deal with this shit all the time, and we can't use guns."

"You can if it's self-defense."

Depended on the circumstances, her mind argued. The way the fucking laws were written, who knew what would happen. She couldn't shoot Mark Swanson in the back, but that would be the easiest way. "Okay. Thank you, Kyle." She touched his face with her empty hand.

She opened the door to the barn without another word and raced across the yard as fast as her legs would carry her. At the door to the house, she gripped the gun in both hands and pushed through it. Angel wasn't prepared when Mark Swanson charged up the stairs toward her. He was armed with a large handgun that she didn't remember seeing before. She raised the gun and tried to steady it with both hands. His was larger and more menacing than the one she'd trained on him, and it was pointed right at her. Adrenaline rushed through her veins.

"Stop right there."

Mark Swanson stopped abruptly; his eyes taking in the gun in Angel's hand; he smiled wickedly. Her hands were shaking and he saw that. She was small, and she barely eaten in almost a day and a half. She would be weak.

"Come now, Angel." He took another step toward her. "Let's be reasonable, before you get hurt." Anger welled up inside her as she lifted the gun higher. He'd beaten and threatened her repeatedly, and with no sign of Alex in sight, he had to have been hurt, or worse.

"I said stop!" she yelled. "Alex?" she called loudly. "Alex!"

"Downstairs," he called. That voice was even more beautiful then she remembered. Her breath left in a grateful rush at the sound of his voice. *Thank God.*

Swanson, starting toward her, still held the gun up in his hand and trained it at her. She didn't think, only reacted. Angel's fingers squeezed the trigger and a shot rang out, sending one bullet slamming into Mark Swanson's upper right chest. He staggered backward, looking stunned, and his arm holding the gun dropped to his side. His fingers relaxed and the large gun fell to the floor, clattering on the old tile floor of the kitchen.

"Angel!" Alex cried out in agony. "Oh, my God! Angel!"

She rushed forward and shoved Swanson with all her might. He stumbled backward, but didn't fall, though she did succeed in knocking the gun from his hand. "Downstairs," she commanded softly.

In the basement, Alex, still tied to the chair, was pulling on the ropes so hard they were cutting into him sharply. He could feel the blood start to ooze and run down from his wrist and onto his palms.

"Angel!" he shouted again, his voice full of anguish. He couldn't breathe; he didn't feel the pain as the ropes ripped away at his flesh. Finally, he pushed off with his foot causing the chair to topple backward. The wood cracked and splintered into several pieces. "Jesus Christ! Answer me!" He was on the floor, face to face with the blank eyes of the dead man lying in front of the cot, frantically trying to be free of the ropes that confined him. With his elbows no longer restrained, he was able to twist his hands free of the ropes, though more of his skin was ripped open. He scrambled into a sitting position to begin working on the ropes at his ankles, blood covering his hands and running in rivets down from the wounds just above his elbows and soaking his shirt. Splinters from the broken chair ripped into his hands, but all he could feel was the sickening beat of his own heart. "Angel!"

"I'm okay, Alex! Downstairs," she demanded again. "Now!"

Alex's breath rushed out and grateful tears blurred his vision. She was safe, but they weren't clear yet. Relief flooded through him, and his muscles trembled then sagged. A tear rolled from each eye as he watched Swanson stumbled down the stairs. Finally, Alex was free of all of the ropes and stood up, but he'd been tied in one position for so long, his legs and feet were asleep.

The right front of Swanson's shirt was soaked in blood, beginning to run downward to saturate his pants as well. It wouldn't be long and he'd be dead, based on the way he was bleeding. He slipped on the last couple stairs and stumbled forward.

All Alex saw was Angel. She was pale except for the angry bruise on her cheek and her black eye. Her hair was a mess, and her clothes and coat were covered in filth. She was the most beautiful thing he'd ever seen. He sucked in his breath and stepped forward. His legs were shaky, and electric tingles ran through the bottom of his feet and legs; it was almost painful, but he quickly got to his feet.

Swanson yelled and, turning, rushed toward Angel in a last effort to take the gun away from her. It happened in a flash, but it felt like slow-motion replay. In one move, Alex stepped forward, and without thinking and using both hands, gripped Mark Swanson by his head. Pulling in opposite directions, he snapped the man's neck. When Swanson fell between them, Alex reached out and took the gun from a stunned Angel. It was still hot from when she'd shot Swanson, so Alex quickly put on the safety.

Angel was shaking in shock, and Alex stepped over the dead man and enfolded her in his arms. She started crying into his chest, her arms tight around his waist. He pulled her as closely against him as he could with one arm, careful to keep the gun in his other hand safely behind his back. He could feel her heart thundering against his own, feel her shoulders shaking, and the warmth of her breath on his neck. He'd never been more thankful for anything in his life.

"You're okay, baby. I've got you." He closed his eyes and kissed her on the temple. The relief flooding through him brought tears to his eyes. "Jesus, God, I was so scared." His mouth was still against her head. "It's okay, babe. I have you."

"Aleeexxxx!" She was crying as if her heart was broken, clinging to him for dear life. His super, strong girl was falling apart. "Are you okay? Did that bastard hurt you?" she cried.

Alex almost laughed despite the situation. Was he okay? She was the one who'd been almost killed. His mouth found hers in a gentle kiss. "Yes. It's over, Angel."

"I was afraid I'd never see you again. Are Becca and Cole okay?" She was terrified of the answer, but she had to know.

"Becca is fine. She was in the convenience store, but Cole was shot." Angel pulled back, her mouth opening to speak. Alex shook his head once. "He's alive," he said before she could ask.

"Thank God." Her face crumpled again. Frustrated, angry tears filled her eyes. "I've never hated anyone as much as this bastard, Alex. He's hurt so many people."

"He won't anymore. But what did they do to you? Are you hurt?" His words stopped, his panicked eyes met hers, and both hands pushed her messy hair back then cupped both sides of her face.

Alex wanted to ask Angel if she'd been violated by Mark Swanson or the others. The question ate at him, twisting in his gut like a dull knife. He wanted to know only because he hated to think she'd gone through something so horrific. He worried if he did ask, she might think it would change the way he looked at her. He wouldn't be able to stand it if she thought it would change his feelings for her.

Angel read his thoughts and shook her head, sniffing and wiping away a single tear that managed to escape. "No. I'm okay, Alex."

He brushed his mouth on hers softly. Relief washed over him like a tidal wave, but still he didn't have the exact answer he was after. He didn't want to push her. "Good. Because I'd wake that cocksucker up and kill him all over again."

He brought her to him in a tight hug, and she laughed against his chest. His gentle hands found both sides of her face, and he kissed her again and again. He was elated and miserable, happy and heartbroken all at once. "I love you so much. I was so afraid."

"Alex, you're bleeding." She pulled back and examined his wrists, noting the blood, which was also seeping through his shirt at both elbows, and some of it was dried.

"I'm fine, it's from trying to get free of the ropes. I barely feel it. Where's Jillian?" His arms burning where the ropes had ripped into his skin, but his wrists were far worse.

"With Kyle," she said, her face turning into his neck as her hands slid from his arms back around his waist. "Outside. He killed the big one in the barn."

He wanted to hold her tighter, to kiss her, but they needed to move. Alex released her gently. "I guess we've all been busy. Is this Kyle's gun you used on Swanson?"

"Yes."

Alex's mouth tightened and anger exploded inside him, and his voice boomed at the same time he shoved it into the waistband of his jeans. "Why the fuck are you in here and not him? What was he thinking? I should castrate him!"

"It was my fault. I was familiar with the layout of the house, so I knew I'd be able to sneak in easier. We have no reason to be mad at him, Alex! We should be thankful he's here. I couldn't believe it when I heard his voice. What's he doing here?"

Alex was still furious, but her words put things in perspective. Kyle deserved his gratitude not his wrath. Angel was right, but still, he didn't agree with the choice, and Alex still wasn't sure he wouldn't confront Kyle later. "I needed help, and I knew he would help me. Allison called him for me."

"Makes sense. We both owe him a lot."

"I agree, but I'm still pissed he let you come in here. I need a small knife. Try to find one, but don't touch anything with your bare hands."

Angel nodded and found one in the kitchen, returning it to Alex. She watched him remove his shirt and wrap a part of it around the handle.

"What are you doing?"

"I don't know. *Fuck*! It depends if we're calling the cops or not. Either way, I don't feel comfortable leaving Kyle's bullet in this asshole's chest."

"Holy shit! Why wouldn't we tell the cops, Alex?" Angel's eyes flashed at him. "We're not criminals. And why can't we leave the bullet?"

Alex explained his meeting with Marvin Standish. "I promised I wouldn't implicate him."

"If he doesn't want to be implicated in dirty shit, I guess he shouldn't dabble in it, then," she pointed out, with barely veiled sarcasm.

Alex rolled his eyes. They were standing in the middle of this shitstorm and seconds away from the most thankful moment of their lives. "Are we arguing about this right now? We're alive, and I'd prefer not to go to prison or get whacked because I didn't keep my word! *If* you don't mind." The look he shot at her was incredulous.

Angel's mouth snapped shut.

Alex dialed Marvin Standish's personal number.

"Did you find what you were looking for?" Standish answered.

"Yes, but not where we thought. Are you connected to any property in the Ozark Mountains?"

"We could have associates that may but not directly, no. Why?"

"Because that's where we found the, um, package. It turned into quite a mess. I'll need to call someone, if it won't be a problem for you."

"What happened?"

"She was taken; I found her. Shit happened, and now it's over. It would be easier to tell the authorities the truth because it was self-defense, but I am a man of my word, so I needed to make sure you have no connection to the location before I do that."

"We're clear."

"Good."

When the call ended, he breathed out a sigh of relief. "That's that."

"I can't believe this is happening. We *killed* three people, and now you're BFFs with a mob boss?" She huffed, wondering if any of them would have some sort of traumatic repercussions later, forever emotionally scarred from any of this. Looking at Alex, he was solid as a rock, taking it all in stride. Kyle hadn't seemed any different, so time would tell.

Alex walked to Angel and put two strong arms on her shoulders. "It was pure survival instinct. We had no choice. As for Standish, I did what I had to do, and I would have done a lot more if it meant getting you back without getting hurt." His voice was hard, but his eyes were full of pain. She knew the torment he went through, and she knew the love that drove him. "I was in fucking hell!"

Angel nodded in understanding and touched a hand to his jaw then the injury on his temple. "I know. I understand. I would have done the same thing."

"Good. Go get Kyle. You don't need to watch this."

When Angel left to find Kyle, Alex crouched down to Mark Swanson's body and located Angel's iPhone in his left front pants pocket. Thankfully, it wasn't covered in blood. He took it and shoved it into his own pocket. He despised the bastard, and while he thought he'd take pleasure in killing him, he felt only relief that he wouldn't be able to torment them any longer. He didn't feel remorse, and he didn't feel pleasure. He felt nothing but relief.

No matter what, he would not allow someone who helped him to be implicated in this nasty mess. Sighing, he put the knife to Swanson's wound, praying the fucking bullet wasn't in too deep.

*****

It was just before dawn when they'd walked out of that hellhole. When Alex walked out of the house, Jillian, now awake, began struggling in Kyle's arms. She didn't know Kyle, but she knew Alex.

"Zander! Zander!" She put out her arms and went immediately into Alex's embrace, hugging his neck with all her might.

Alex chuckled. He had his coat back on, so the blood on his shirt wasn't showing. All four of them were dirty and looked worse for wear. "Hi, sweetheart." Alex kissed Jillian on the cheek, and Angel's heart swelled. Could he get any more amazing? He was like some modern-day knight in shining armor, only better. He was strong and responsible, and true, he didn't take any shit, but deep down, he was the most caring man she'd ever known. And one day, he'd make an incredible father.

"Anga said you'd come."

"She did?" Alex smiled. "Anga knows me pretty well."

Alex had carried Jillian with one arm—the child soon fell asleep on his shoulder—and his other hand was threaded with Angel's the entire walk out of the woods. There was some discussion between the three of them about how everything would be explained, and how much easier it would have been if the local sheriff wasn't involved. Then, they could've walked out and never mentioned it again. But, the authorities were searching for Angel and Jillian, so they would need an explanation about how Alex had managed to find and extricate them, where they had been held, and what contributed to the deaths of the perpetrators.

Once they reached the car, Angel called and reserved rooms at the same hotel where Alex's parents and Becca were staying, while Alex drove back to Springfield. It was decided they'd drop Kyle at the hotel, and Alex and Angel would meet Charles, Cora, Becca, and the authorities at the ER of the same hospital where Cole was being treated.

Becca had fallen apart when she'd been reunited with Jillian, and all of the women cried. Angel hugged her briefly, kissing Jillian's head and telling her they'd explain it all in the morning. Becca hugged Alex hard, thanking him again and again for Jillian's safe return.

Alex ruffled Jillian's hair and touched her soft cheek with one finger. "Zander, are you gonna ride horsies wit me and Anga?"

Alex looked at Angel, his expression full of questions. "Horses?"

"Just say yes," she instructed with a tired smile.

"Okay, sure. I'll ride horses, Bean."

Alex and Angel were enfolded in hugs from Alex's parents. Cole was awake, and would make a full recovery, though he would be in the hospital at least a week before he was well enough to fly back to Chicago. Allison and Josh had not accompanied his parents to Springfield.

Alex and Angel were treated for their injuries, and Jillian was also examined. It took another two long hours to make their statements. Alex told the truth about the rescue, but left Kyle's involvement completely out of it. He was on the verge of a record deal, and he didn't need his career ruined before it began because he'd risked his life and helped a friend in dire need. Also, there was no mention of Marvin Standish.

Finally, mid-morning, Alex and Angel were allowed to go back to the hotel, but the authorities requested they not leave the state for a few days while the investigation began.

They were quiet with each other because, as tired as they were, words seemed too much effort. They peeled off their filthy clothes, and Alex shoved them into one of those plastic bags the hotel provides for laundry and saved it for the police. The blood evidence would prove they'd both been bound and beaten. Their exhaustion was tangible in the way they barely spoke and how slowly they were moving. Alex had been given the belongings that were in the rental car Cole had been driving, so they had a few clean things. What they needed most was to get clean, get sleep, and love each other.

They took a warm shower together because Alex couldn't bear to let Angel out of his sight, but there had been no wild lovemaking. Instead, it was gentle kisses and reverent caresses, love words, and wave upon wave of reverent worshiping. Alex didn't intend to make love to Angel. Both of them were injured and exhausted, but once they were in the small space together, alone and surrounded by the warm steam, it was more a case of reaffirming they were together and safe, and were unable to help themselves.

Angel's hands slid up his soapy chest, and she heard his fast intake of breath as the soap ran into the open wounds on his arms and wrists. She wanted to kiss every inch of him, to take away any pain. She kissed his chest, and his hands fell to her waist. When she lifted her face to his, her mouth dropping open, he couldn't help but be aroused. Her soft touch, the obvious want in her dark brown eyes, made his heart dance and his dick twitch.

"Baby." His hands ran down her arms then around her body. Angel, feeling his thick, full arousal against her stomach, reached one hand down to close around his swollen flesh. Alex groaned against her mouth. "Angel, we don't have to…" It was said in an aching whisper.

"I want you. I was so scared I'd never get to feel your hands on my body again. I thought I'd never get to be with you like this. I think that was worse than dying."

"Oh, Angel," Alex moaned into her mouth and took it with his, at the same time lifting her up and against the wall of the shower. Her legs automatically wound around his waist, and she pressed her body tight against him.

"I wanted to take you into my mouth… pleasure you." She said the words between hungry kisses.

"That's not close enough," Alex responded. His mouth was after hers like he was starving and finally, he moved and guided the head of his cock into her body.

"Mmmmm…" Angel sighed as he filled her, and her body stretched to accommodate him.

"Fuck, I was going crazy. I was out of my fucking mind." His throat tightened even as he lost himself in Angel's warmth. Tears squeezed from beneath his closed eyelids; Angel could taste them on her lips when she kissed the side of his face. Her heart exploded.

"I love you, and we're together now. Just love me."

"I'll never let you go." His mouth found hers and would not leave it again until their passion was sated.

Alex was gentle, but the kisses were deeply passionate; the hungry touches, urgent and intense as emotions overflowed and hushed love words were mixed with tears and slow, desperate thrusts.

Only when Angel was shuddering against him and clenching around him, did Alex let himself come. He didn't want it to end, but his arms and legs were starting to shake from fatigue. They were both on the verge of collapse.

When they fell into bed, Alex pulled her onto his chest, and they curled around each other Alex still turned everything over in his mind; so much surreal shit in just two days. It was Monday, and maybe he'd ask Mrs. Dane to clear a few more days. His face was bruised, as was Angel's. He'd be able to hide the injuries on his wrists under his shirts. but not so to his face, so a few more days away would be needed.

His hand ran down her arm in a long caress. His heart ached knowing all she had gone through, and he was upset he hadn't been able to prevent it. He took her hand in his, silently rubbing his thumb over the top of her fingers, and brought it to his mouth, softly brushing his lips against her fingers. He loved touching her and hadn't stopped since they'd left that awful house; so thankful she was alive, and they were together.

"Angel?" He'd whispered into the dark created in the daylight by the pulled blinds. "I love you. No matter what. I want you, no matter what."

"I know," she whispered back. Alex closed his eyes slowly, his arm tightening around her gently.

"I've never been so tormented. I was in so much agony; I lost my humanity for a while. I came in there prepared to kill all of them. It didn't matter how many of them I had to face or what happened to me afterward. I've been in literal hell."

Angel turned her head and kissed his chest, running her open mouth back and forth softly. It was arousing, but this wasn't about sex, it was about love.

"I wanted to try to escape, but having Jillian with me made it more difficult. I didn't think I'd be able to get away with her, and I would have made whatever sacrifices to keep her safe. I knew you'd come for us."

Alex's heart hammered beneath Angel's ear. She could literally feel it beating, not just hear it thrumming. "Yes, Jillian's involvement made it worse. I bet she was terrified. I know you said they didn't hurt you, Angel, but I have to know. Did they…"

"It didn't come to that, Alex. They didn't touch me like that." Alex let out a breath, unaware he'd been holding it, when he finally heard the words he needed. "I promise, I'd tell you if they had."

"I thought you might bury it inside of yourself to spare me. High-powered psychologist status notwithstanding."

"It's moot, now. I may have before, but we promised we wouldn't have secrets."

His chest rose beneath her cheek as he sucked in a big breath. "Thank God. When I heard that gunshot, I felt like the earth had opened up and swallowed me whole. Then, when you came down the stairs behind that fucker, as horrible as it was, you were the most beautiful thing I'd ever seen. I was so grateful you were alive." Alex's voice shook with emotion, but a small laugh broke from his chest. "You leave me speechless. You're so brave, and unlike anyone I've ever known. Never a dull moment."

Angel sighed and closed her eyes, snuggling in, thankful she was back in Alex's arms where she belonged. "I missed you."

He pressed his lips to the damp hair on the top of her head. "Tell me about the horses." Alex was finally relaxed, his muscles blissfully uncoiled after the prior ten days of hell. He could feel sleep drawing him in.

"I promised Bean we'd go to Will and Ben's and ride the horses because her birthday got cancelled."

"Okay," Alex murmured. "We have to stay in the state anyway, so that works." The truth was, staying in the state was playing well into Alex's own plans to meet Angel's father. Now, more than ever, he wanted to meet Joseph Hemming. Not only did he want his permission to ask Angel to marry him, he also needed his help to convince her that her career path was way too dangerous. It would be too much to ask that Angel would acquiesce to his wishes, but maybe with her father's help, she would listen to reason.

"You're going to stay with me?"

"Yes. It will be a while before I let you out of my sight."

Angel smiled softly, love for this man overwhelming her heart. "I'll suffer through."

"You're stuck with me," Alex murmured, content.

Angel grinned wider, still with her eyes closed. "Good thing I like your peen, then." Exhausted as she was, she couldn't help but tease him. "Because, less than stellar peen has been a major dealbreaker for me in the past."

Alex chuckled, reminded again why this woman owned him. She was beautiful, brave, smart as a fucking whip, and funnier than hell. He kissed the top of Angel's head and pulled her closer. "At least, I've graduated from 'man banana'."

Angel giggled against his chest, her fingers gliding over the hard muscles and smooth skin.

His small laugh came out as a sigh. "You are so goddamned perfect."

18

The Plan

KYLE WAS FLYING back to Chicago; Alex and Angel had gone to the hospital to see Cole one last time. He was doing well, though he was feeling guilty about losing Angel and Jillian.

"You got shot, Cole. Seriously," Angel scoffed, grabbing his hand. "Why didn't I hear the shot?"

"I didn't hear it either. They had a silencer."

"Oh."

Alex filled Cole in about what went down. At least, he gave him the same story they'd told the police. Alex would tell him everything when they were both back in Chicago.

"Looks like I'm out of a job," Cole smiled up at his younger brother.

"I told you, we'll figure it out. With Bancroft gone, we'll have some restructuring to do. You've done a great job."

Becca lingered with Jillian in the waiting room until Angel and Alex left the room, then she went to say goodbye to Cole. Angel sensed something brewing there, and Alex looked pointedly at Angel when Becca breezed past them in the hospital hallway and into Cole's room.

"Will we be waiting long, do you think?"

Alex shrugged, looking fresh and happy despite the bruise on his temple. His jaw was clean and smooth, and he smelled delicious. He was dressed in designer jeans and an expensive Ralph Lauren sweatshirt.

"We're going to ride horses and do farm shit. Why are you dressed up?" Angel grinned, and he put his arm around her shoulders and pulled her close to the side of his body.

Alex laughed softly. "I borrowed the sweatshirt from my dad. He doesn't own anything without a label."

"Ugh," Angel let out an exaggerated groan. Angel had on jeans and a long sleeved T-shirt layered under her black hoodie with her coat over her arm. Her thick locks were pulled up into a high ponytail, and her Gucci sunglasses were propped on top of her head.

Alex flicked her sunglasses. "What's that? Those wouldn't be *Gucci*, would they?" he goaded.

"Yes, asshole. They are Gucci. A birthday gift from a patient."

"Mmm. Figures." She did have nice clothes; her car and apartment were the only extravagances he was aware of. The clothes were necessary for her job, and the apartment's location was practical for the same reason. She didn't waste money on frivolous things. They'd be disposing of the apartment soon, he hoped, and he was set on having another discussion about her job. "Speaking of birthdays; mine is coming up before Christmas. I'd like to take you out to dinner."

She looked up at him as they walked into the main floor waiting room where they'd agreed to meet Becca when she was finished saying goodbye to Cole. "Won't your parents want to spend the evening with you? We can all—"

Alex sat down and pulled Angel onto his lap, not giving a damn if anyone was watching. "They've had me for thirty-two birthdays. I want it to be you and me. Alone."

Angel's arm was around his shoulder, and his was clamped around the back of her hips as she sat in his lap. His eyes were serious as he looked up at her, so she didn't tease him again. "Okay."

He nodded and squeezed her hip and pulled on her arm until her mouth landed on his in a brief kiss. "Good."

Alex and Angel were still together, talking intimately, two of their hands threaded together, when Becca came out of the elevators, holding Jillian's hand, walking slowly to match her daughter's short gait. When her eyes landed on the couple, she rolled her eyes. "Get a room, why don't cha?" she spouted off, happiness lighting up her face. She was dressed similar to Angel, and Jillian was all decked out in jeans and a sweater.

"Get a room alld ready!" Jillian repeated her mother's words as best she could. A sixty-ish woman sitting to Alex's left laughed, and Angel's brow shot up as she jumped up from Alex's lap and bent to scoop the toddler up, both of them holding back laughter.

She put a hand to the front of her shirt. "Mommy meant let's vrroooom already. In Alex's fast car." She looked pointedly at Becca. "Right, Becs?"

"Oh, yeah." She pursed her lips and nodded wryly. "Yeah, right," she scoffed.

Kyle was taking a cab to the airport, and they'd said their goodbyes in the lobby before coming to the hospital. When they all piled into Alex's Audi, they took off for Joplin. Angel had promised Jillian, and she was anxious to see her dad. Alex seemed anxious to meet him as well, and it was to be expected. She'd met his entire family, so it was only natural for him to want to get to know hers. Her father was all she had, besides Will and Ben, so this would be good.

Alex inhaled deeply, and Angel glanced over at his strong profile. He had a nasty bruise and cut on his temple, held together by a butterfly bandage. Her own face was showing signs of abuse, her black eye beginning to turn an ugly yellowish-green, and the cheek on that same side was still swollen and bruised. They had been very lucky.

He seemed very contemplative. "What are you thinking about?"

Alex glanced at her; his eyebrows rose at her question. "Hmm?"

Clearly, she'd roused him from his thoughts. "Penny for your thoughts?"

"Just looking forward to the time off. Without the stress of worrying for while."

He reached for her hand, and she willingly gave it to him. He brought her hand to his thigh and pressed it into his denim-covered leg. Angel nodded. "Yes, me, too."

Becca was helping Jillian play with the headphones of her new iPod Shuffle in the backseat. Alex had soft music playing in the luxurious car, and she relaxed.

Alex wanted to talk to her about moving in with him and her job but felt that was better done when they were alone. Instead, he asked her about Joplin and her father.

"Was your dad happy we were coming down, or does he feel invaded?"

"No, he wants to meet you." Angel was turned enough so she could look at Alex but still hold his hand, her head resting against the black leather headrest. "I've told him about you."

"Uh oh."

Angel smiled. "Yes, what a horrible picture I've painted of you."

He lifted her hand and kissed the back of it. "Anything I should know?"

"I can't think of anything specific. I'm the only child; the only girl with these three men, and they're all pretty protective."

"As they should be. I respect that. Are you good at riding horses? Did you do it a lot?"

"There was one horse I particularly loved. Uncle Will bought her when I was seven, and I used to go home from school on the bus with Ben every night to ride her when the weather was nice, and many times when it wasn't so nice. Dad had this thing where I had to eat so many fruits and vegetables every day, and I used to pack carrots and apples in my lunch then save them. I bet it was 300 pounds of apples I didn't eat in those ten years."

The landscape got less wooded as the drive progressed. It was still green and hilly, but less so as they got closer to Joplin.

"So you kept going home with Ben? Into high school?"

Angel knew what he was asking and she shrugged. "I didn't have a ton of friends. I was the janitor's daughter, and that sort of had a stigma attached to it. Like I wasn't worthy of anyone. Ben never treated me that way."

Alex glanced in the rearview mirror, and both Becca and Jillian were sleeping soundly. Jillian's little head had lolled to one side, and her headphones were still stuck in her ears.

"Were you this gorgeous in high school?"

She looked at him and paused. "I was hideous. I had braces until I was almost seventeen, and flat-chested almost all the way through middle school, and no curves."

"I'm happy that changed, then."

Angel smiled. "I'm sure. I was a nerd. Total bookworm. I was after the scholarships."

"No singing, then?"

"Sure, I was in choir. And I had piano lessons from an old lady who lived three doors down from us. I used to go into the music room during lunch period and practice."

"Well, you're very talented, in any case."

"Did you and Kyle talk and plot how to get me back in the band?"

Alex glanced at her briefly, his mouth sliding up into the half-grin she loved. "No. Sorry, we were a little busy with other shit."

"Good."

Joplin was a moderately small town by Missouri standards and microscopic in comparison to Chicago. The population was about fifty thousand and not much happened there. There were some trucking firms and such, and a few factories; it had undergone some new developments in recent years and the high school had been completely rebuilt after that big tornado a few years earlier. From what her dad said, it was divided in two campuses now, and he was responsible for the janitorial staff at the ninth and tenth grade buildings.

As they drove through town toward the southwest side where Angel's father's house was located, Alex took it all in and tried to picture Angel's youth, so different from his own. He was privileged, his father's business already very profitable before he was even born. She'd had no mother. Her father struggled alone, she lived in this small town, and she could have gone to a community college and married a local man. That would have been easier. But, Angel would never choose easy. She'd accomplished so much.

"Are you familiar with that famous picture of Bonnie and Clyde? The one where he's holding her on a car? Well, there are a couple; another where she's got a gun pointed at him?"

"Yes, I think I saw it once in middle school," Alex replied. She'd called them Bonnie and Clyde when Swanson was lying dead at their feet. Was that what she was thinking about?

"There is a story about them killing two cops in Joplin in 1933. Afterward, when they left in a hurry, they left some of their stuff, which included a camera, and the Joplin Globe developed the film."

"Really? That's really interesting."

"My dad is really into history, so I've heard that story a hundred times. He'll probably tell you, too. It's about the only nefarious thing that ever happened here, and not nearly as dangerous as all of the shit that happens in Chicago. Turn left at the next light, then the third right."

Alex followed Angel's directions and made his way into a neighborhood of small houses that were probably built in the 1950s. A lot of wooden two stories with brick chimneys and huge trees lining the street. It was nice but modest.

"Should we stop at the store for groceries or anything? I don't want to feel like we're barging in."

"He knows we're coming. The house isn't what you're used to."

"Angel, stop. I'm sure it's great."

Her mind told her Alex wouldn't judge anyone based on money, but still, he came from money, and it was a little intimidating for him to see how humble the house was. Not that she was ashamed. She loved her father, and he had always provided for her, even if he'd had to go without himself.

"It's the white house second from the corner. My dad did the best he could with what he had."

"Honey, you don't have to defend anything." He parked the car and squeezed her hand. "Wake up, sleepy heads. We're here," Alex called into the backseat.

"What'd you do drive 200 miles per hour?" Becca asked. "It seems like we just left."

Alex pulled the radar detector down and put it in the glove compartment. His guns and Kyle's were safely stowed in the trunk. He'd have to get Kyle's back to him when they were back in Chicago.

"Not quite," Alex laughed.

Angel was getting out of the car quickly because her father came out onto the porch and down the stairs to meet them.

"Hi, Daddy!"

Alex watched her rush into the arms of a man in his late fifties. He was thin but with a small beer belly. He was dressed in his work uniform of light gray shirt atop dark grey pants.

"Hey, there's my baby girl!" Joseph Hemming said happily as he enfolded Angel in a big bear hug and lifted her off the ground.

By now, Alex, Becca, and Jillian had alighted from the car.

"Where'd are da horsies?" Jillian asked excitedly.

"Wait, sweetheart," Becca murmured.

When Joe released Angel, she threaded her arm through his and turned with him toward the others. "Daddy, I'd like you to meet Alexander Avery."

Alex walked forward and extended his hand.

"Hello, sir. It's nice to meet you."

"Hello. I'm Joe Hemming."

Angel was surprised by how fast her heart was beating. These were the two most important men in her life, and she desperately wanted them to adore each other.

"Angel's told me a lot about you."

"Well, if it's bad, she's lying," Joe said with a smile, his eyes narrowed on the injuries on Alex's and Angel's faces. He looked at his daughter. "What happened to your faces?" His voice was laced with concern. "Were you in a car accident?"

"I'll tell you about it tonight after we're settled in. Okay?"

He eyed Angel for a minute, gauging her response. He looked at Alex. "Was it something to do with those shady bastards she prosecutes?"

Alex met Angel's eyes, and he knew she wanted him to brush her father's question off but would not begin his relationship with Angel's father with a lie. Here was an ally in his argument. "Uh, yeah."

Joseph Hemming frowned and shook his head. "Angel, we need to talk about this."

"Later, Dad, please? Becca and Jillian are here."

He didn't look satisfied with his daughter's answer, but manners overruled and he stepped around his daughter to hug Becca. "Hi, Beckie Boo."

"Hi, Joe," Becca answered and hugged him back.

"And who is this beautiful princess?" He bent toward Jillian and got down on his haunches. He'd met Becca before and Jillian, too, but when Jillian was only 20 months old, and she wouldn't remember.

Jillian looked up at Becca. "This is Angel's daddy, baby. It's okay. Say hello."

"Iz Jeian," she said, her 'L's missing.

"Jillian! What a beautiful name. Can I have a hug?"

She nodded and went into his arms.

Alex's hand came to rest on the top of Angel's shoulder, and when he squeezed the muscle at the base of her neck, her arm snaked around his waist.

"Thank you for that nice hug."

"Can we see da horsies?"

"Sure! We're going to have a barbeque on the farm with the horses. Let's get your stuff inside the house, then we'll go."

Alex left Angel and went to the trunk. He wasn't sure what Angel had told her father about the past week, so he quickly took out his duffel, her gym bag, and Becca's one suitcase. The trunk closed before Angel's father came and lifted the suitcase.

"This way, Alex." He nodded toward the house. It was a nice, older home that had been maintained well. The hardwood floors were a bit worn, but it was clean and the paint was fresh.

It was a three-bedroom house, and he wondered about the sleeping arrangements. Though they were adults, he wasn't going to disrespect Angel's father by assuming they'd be sharing a room.

"Angel's old room is upstairs, as is the spare room. You can put all of the things in there."

Alex's eyes met Angel's. "Will you lead the way?"

She picked up her bag, preceding him up the stairs while Joe did some catching up with Becca. The spare room was decorated with an old white chenille bedspread, the bedroom set equally dated, though again, it was spotless. He set his duffel on the bed in the spare room.

Angel's eyebrow shot up. "Planning on bunking with Becca and Bean?"

He shook his head. "No, but, uh, I'm not sure where I'm bunking, but it's not with you. Is that your room?" He nodded in the direction of an open door that led into a room decorated in dark plum and white. It wasn't frilly like some of his high school girlfriend's rooms had been. Instead, it was understated and functional. Aside from a few posters, a bookshelf filled with young adult books, and a few picture frames, the room consisted of a dark wood bedframe, dresser, and matching desk. It was clear these were much newer and of good quality; evidence where Joseph Hemming's priorities lay. Alex's respect for the man was already solid because of the woman he had raised, but to see it with his own eyes added another dimension.

"Why?" she asked.

"Come on. Just…" Alex paused. He felt embarrassed having to explain himself, and certainly, this was the first time in his life it would even occur to him to sleep apart from his lover, regardless of where they were. "I don't want to be disrespectful. And I don't want him to think I disrespect his little girl."

Angel smiled softly, as she set her bag in the corner of her room. "He isn't ignorant, Alex. He doesn't think I'm a virgin; I promise. But, if what you do to me is disrespect me, then disrespect me some more." She nudged him playfully.

"Don't make it hard."

Angel giggled. "That's not what you usually say."

He laughed. "Stop. Please, don't argue." He bent to kiss her mouth. "I'll be suffering enough as is, but it's worth it."

She kissed him back. "You know how I hate to see you suffer," she whispered against his mouth.

"I'll find a way for you to make it up to me."

She giggled softly. "Promise?"

"Yes."

"I don't think my bed will hold Becca, Jillian, and me. I might have to get a sleeping bag."

"Is there a couch? I can sleep on that."

"Wow. Pinch me." Angel's tone was sardonic, but inside she was soaring. Alex really wanted her father to like him, and that meant the world to her.

Alex's hand curled around hers, and his forehead rested against hers. "I don't want to screw this up."

"I love you a whole lot."

"I know. I'm counting on that." He kissed her again, letting his tongue push inside her mouth and rub against hers in a sensually slow caress. When he pulled back, Alex sighed and nodded toward the stairs. "Let's go. I'm starving."

She cocked her head, one eyebrow shooting up as a devilish smile danced on her lips. Despite her bruises, she was so beautiful; it took his breath away. He was still holding her waist, and her hands wrapped around his forearms, careful not to hurt his wrists, though she had to touch him. "And?"

His white teeth flashed in a brilliant smile, and he looked down into her face. "And... *barbeque* sounds really good."

God, he was gorgeous. It was all she could do to keep her wits about her.

"Hmmph!" Angel snorted, biting her lip in an effort not to laugh her ass off. "Dad didn't say it was barbeque, ding-a-ling. He said it was *a* barbeque. Which means just meat. You know, *meat?*" She looked at him in mock coyness as she flirted with him. "Wonder if they'll have any sausage? Since you won't give me any, I mean."

Alex burst out laughing, and Angel couldn't stop herself from giggling. "Is ding-a-ling slang for sausage?"

"Nope. For man banana," she said, tongue-in-cheek.

He laughed even harder. Fuck, he'd missed her, and thankful couldn't touch how he felt.

*****

Later, they went in Joe's old Ford truck to William's farm, about ten miles west of Joplin. Alex and Joe sat in the front, Angel and Becca sat on either side of Jillian's car seat that had been moved from Alex's car into the back seat of the F150.

It was dusty and dirty inside, but her dad used it for fishing and camping trips. Alex still looked slightly out of place in his designer clothes and immaculately groomed hair. Angel had shoved her hair into a topknot on her head, and Becca's blonde locks were held back by a red and white bandana. Alex was relaxed and thoroughly enjoying the day.

The dirt lane of the farm was lined with trees, now losing their leaves as fall colors filled the landscape. A white fence replaced the trees about half way in, and there were four horses grazing in the pasture.

"Horsies!" Jillian screamed. "Horsies!"

All of the adults smiled.

"Do you want to ride one of those horses, sweetie?" Joe asked.

Jillian clapped her hands excitedly. "Yep! Zander said he'd ride wit us, too!"

Angel's father glanced at Alex and grinned. Joe had graying dark hair, and Alex could tell it used to be the same dark chestnut of his daughter's. She didn't look much like him in the face, other than the color of her eyes, so she must resemble her mother. Alex felt bad for the man. Looking at the face of his wife who left him all these years ago must have been difficult. Some men might have resented the child and not lavished love on her the way Joe had. It was obvious the sun rose and set on Angel.

The minute the truck stopped, another older man with a fluffy white beard stepped out of the large house. It was a ranch style and newer than Joe's house, dark brown with a lighter tan roof. Angel scrambled out of the truck and into his arms.

"Uncle Will!" she squealed.

"Will and Ben are like our family, and both those boys adore Angel. She was everyone's little girl," Joe explained.

"Even Ben? I thought he was her age."

Becca was unbuckling Jillian from the car seat. "Hurry, Mama! I want to pet the horsies!" The minute she was free of the confines, Jillian slid from the seat and hurried after Angel, not waiting for her mother.

"Careful!" Becca called after her. "Don't fall, Jill!" She followed Jillian and was soon greeted by William.

Joe and Alex remained in the truck for a moment. "Don't worry, son. Angel is head over heels for you. I can see it."

Alex smiled. "Yes, I guess it's natural curiosity, and I want to know what to expect when Ben gets here."

Joe nodded and opened his door. "Come on."

"Joe?" Alex asked to stop him. "I'd like to talk to you for a few minutes alone at some point. Would that be possible?"

Joe nodded knowingly. It hadn't been long since Angel had been telling him about Alex, but it was clear the two were smitten with each other. "Sure thing. We'll get the girls set up on the horses, and they can take a spin while the pig finishes on the barbeque."

Alex and Joe got out and walked the thirty yards to the house, which was surrounded by a lawn as manicured as if it were in the city. If it weren't for the pastures and cornfields, Alex would have sworn they were in one of the more modest suburbs in Chicago.

A slow smile slid across his face. "Angel said it might not be actual barbeque, but it smells delicious."

"Oh, no. We used to smoke whole pigs when Angel was growing up. Will knew she was coming home, so he wanted to surprise her. We'll pack some of the meat up to take back to my place. Nothing goes to waste, and that's what Angel likes."

"Yes, I know. I'll tell you about our first date later."

They approached the women and the other man.

"Uncle Will, this is Alexander Avery. He's my... um, he's my..." The word boyfriend could not describe the hunk of hotness that Alex was, and she couldn't introduce him as her lover.

Alex stepped up, offering his hand with a smile. "Just Alex is fine. And we've been seeing each other for several months."

William smiled graciously through the long beard. His teeth were yellowed, no doubt from years of smoking the pipe that stuck out of the pocket of his denim overalls. He looked somewhat like Alex had imagined "The Farmer in the Dell" looked when his mother had told him that story as a child. "Nice to meet you, Alex. Sorry it's so dusty out here. Those duds of yours are too nice for the likes of this place."

"They'll wash," he dismissed with a smile.

"Okay. I got beer and snacks out back."

Jillian was tugging on the leg of Angel's jeans ferociously and looking up at her. "Anga, pees can we go to the horsies?"

Angel looked at the men and shrugged. "Sorry! We have business to attend to."

"Okay, honey. I'll ring the bell when Ben gets here."

"Yes, do. How's he been?"

"He's got himself a girlfriend, finally. I think he's bringing her."

"Great! I can't wait to meet her." She picked up Jillian and perched the toddler on her hip. "Come on, monkey. Will, are the saddles and tack still in the same place?"

"Nothin's change around this old place," Will noted.

As they went away, William handed Alex and Joe a beer. There was a picnic table set up around the back of the house inside a three-sided covered porch. It had had several large windows with screens, and three of the eight were open. There was a wood-burning stove inside that kept it comfortable.

Alex liked it and made mental notes of the fire pit outside. The patio was lined with what looked like a native rock wall, and the fire pit was built in to one side. It was rustic and comfortable.

"This is a great place," Alex murmured.

"We want to know about you and our little girl," William said, grinning. He'd been checking the pig but came in and sat down at the table across from Joe and next to Alex.

Alex laughed. This was new to him. He'd never met any family of his previous relationships. The closest he came was when Whitney invited her parents to a benefit at the Museum of Natural History, which Avery gave a shitload of money to. He'd said hello and left Whitney to them. "Um, well, we met at a Home Depot, but we didn't speak."

"Really?"

"Yes. I had laryngitis and a girlfriend, so I couldn't pursue her. But I saw her and bam! She was beautiful, and I was pissed."

"So you were dating someone else?" Joe asked, concern filling his face.

Alex shifted, leaning both elbows on the table, his beer in one hand. "Well, I'm going to be completely honest because Angel means the world to me, and I want to tell you the truth. I'm not sure what she told you about my background, but I run a company for my family, but that wasn't my dream. My brother was supposed to take the reins, but he wasn't up to the task. I was at Juilliard."

"That's quite an accomplishment, young man," Joe said, and Will nodded. "Maybe you can play Angel's old piano for us later? It isn't much, but I keep it tuned."

"I'd love to." Alex cocked his head and smiled. "Now I'm responsible for much more. The company employs thousands of people, so I reconcile it is a greater calling, beyond what my family needed from me."

Both of the men were intent on what Alex was saying and didn't interrupt him.

"That said, I'm very focused, and when I first came into the business, I had a lot to learn and a lot to get my head around. When I dated women…" He paused and took a breath. "Well, let's just say I wasn't in it for love."

"I can understand."

"Yes, well, Angel was beautiful. I was stunned the first time I saw her, and she barely had any make-up on and she was wearing shorts and a T-shirt. Not typically my type."

Joe smiled a knowing smile.

"She sort of blossomed in college. She was always such a tomboy, but the first time she came home from Chicago, damn, what a change," William chuckled. "We took her to the VFW and all of the boys were stumbling over themselves. It was funny as hell."

"But you didn't meet?" Joe asked.

Alex told them the story of Whitney calling the show, and Darian being Angel's producer. "Darian kept telling me how amazing she was, but I had, if you'll believe it, this schoolmarm-ish picture in my head."

Joe and Will laughed at the obvious absurdity of Alex's 'vision'.

"I bet you got a surprise," Will said.

Alex nodded and smiled. "Yes. It was fate, I suppose, though I'd never been a believer in it. I called the show because I was intrigued just by her voice and her words as she counseled the callers. Darian arranged for us to meet, and I realized she was the elusive beauty from the Home Depot. I couldn't take my eyes off her, and for the first time in my life, I actively chased." His eyes were contemplative and his lips twitched at the corners. "She didn't make it easy."

Joe sat back and took a long pull on the longneck in his hand. "No, she wouldn't," he agreed with a grin.

The other two men laughed. "Did she beat you into submission? That's quite a shiner she had, and you're a little worse for wear."

"That's another story, which I have no problem telling you later." Alex didn't know how long the girls would be gone, and he needed to get to the point.

"But I can tell she loves you," William said. "She's glowing."

"I adore her. I'm head over heels in love," Alex admitted, a little embarrassed. "I've never said anything like that before, except to her and my own father. Both times, it's been about Angel."

"I can see that you do. I'm grateful that Angel has you, Alex," Joe said.

"I'm glad you feel that way…" He hesitated and met the other man's gaze unflinchingly. "Because I'd like your permission to propose to her. I promise I'll take care of her and keep her safe."

Joe looked at Alex seriously and placed a hand on his heart. "You're an honorable man, Alex. That's all I could ask for my little girl. Of course, I'll give my permission."

William was grinning from ear to ear. "This calls for something stronger than goddamned beer!" he said happily. "What's your poison?"

"Anything is fine." Alex sighed, and any apprehension he had left his chest. *Thank God.*

William got up and went into the house.

"When were you going to propose?"

"I have the ring, and I was hoping on my birthday. I'm going to take her to the restaurant where we had our first date."

"You're a class act, son. Welcome to the family." Joe reached out, and Alex gave him his hand. "I can't hug you or Angel will think something up." He nodded behind him to the pasture where the girls were riding two horses. Angel was riding a black stallion, and Becca was on a gray mare. Jillian sat in front of Angel, and she started to gallop. Jillian squealed happily. Alex watched the woman he loved; mesmerized at the many sides to her. She was magnificent, and she was his.

"Hey, Zander!" Angel called from the big pasture across the road. "Wanna come with us? We're going into the woods!"

"Go ahead, son," Joe said.

William brought out a bottle of Jack Daniels.

"Will, I'll have a drink when we get back," he told the older man then answered Angel. "Okay, babe!"

"Yay, Zander," Jillian hollered. "Zander! I want to ride wit Zander, Anga!"

"Meet me in the barn, Alex!" Angel called, turned her horse around, and took off at a run.

Alex looked at Joe apologetically, not sure the other man was finished with their conversation.

"When a woman asks you to meet her in the barn, you go." Joe winked at Alex.

Alex laughed and got up from the picnic table and started to leave.

"By the looks of things, you've got quite a way with the little one."

"She's a doll. I adore her."

"Then I'll expect some babies in the not-too-distant future."

"Yes, sir. That's the plan." Alex flashed a brilliant smile.

"Good plan."

19

The Man Who Has Everything

THE TIME WITH Angel's dad had been amazing. Things had gotten back to normal; they were both back to work, and Angel was doing her Friday night stint at the station. Kyle had contacted them both a couple of times and reiterated his wish that she come back to Archangel. Alex had to admit, he liked the idea more than her involvement with criminals on a day-to-day basis, but Angel wasn't so easy to convince. Besides, when they were married, would he want her traveling? He traveled enough for the two of them combined, and they'd never see each other. That was something they'd have to work out.

Cole was recovering nicely and would soon be back to work. For the time being, Alex would have him take Bancroft's place, with Wayne and Sid in place with him. Eventually, one of them would take over local security, and Cole would oversee it for Avery Enterprises as a whole. Charles couldn't be happier to have both his sons involved with the business. Alex was the right one to be at the helm, though, when it came to the money and longevity of the company.

Alex had brought a suit with him and had changed into it. It was his birthday; Angel was meeting him at his office, and they'd go to Tru together.

It was a Thursday night. He would have preferred it to be Friday, but that goddamned radio thing was in the way. Oh, well. It wouldn't be the first time he'd had to live on coffee and Excedrin after a late night with Angel. Tonight would be a late night. He planned on making love to her all night.

He'd showered and changed in the en-suite bathroom in his office, taking particular care with every detail. His mother and father knew of his plans. He inhaled deeply as he combed his hair, added a little gel, splashed on cologne, and brushed his perfect teeth. His jaw was newly shaved, and his hair newly cut. He buttoned up the very light lavender shirt he would wear with his black Armani suit. He'd chosen a silk tie with a subtle pattern in silver, black, and dark purple and a silk pocket square that exactly matched his shirt.

He slid on the tie and tied it after securing his cuffs with the engraved double "A" cuff links. He sucked in his breath again. He felt nervous. Things were good with Angel, though he still hadn't convinced her to move in with him. He'd even played the "we can donate your rent to charity" card, but that hadn't worked either. She was so independent, but they spent practically every night together, and it was bothersome. Both of them had some clothes now in residence at each other's apartments, and she had some things at his house. They spent most of the weekends there, and it was paradise. Only one thing would make it better. Well, maybe a couple of things. And he was hoping to get that ball rolling tonight.

The intercom buzzed on his desk. He glanced at his Rolex. It was only 5:30, and Angel wasn't due until 6 PM. He walked to his desk and pressed the intercom button.

"Yes, Mrs. Dane?"

"Sir, you have a visitor."

He pressed it again. "Send her in." He walked around the desk, and pulled the hand-carved mahogany ring box out of the drawer, and shoved it in his pants pocket. Fuck, he hoped Angel wouldn't see the bump in his pocket. He needed his jacket.

It buzzed again. His brow furrowed quizzically. "Yes?"

"It's not Dr. Hemming, sir."

He frowned harder. Maybe it was his mother or Allison, and maybe they wanted to surprise him. "It's okay, Mrs. Dane. Send whoever it is in."

"Yes, sir."

When Mrs. Dane opened the door, Alex was still standing behind his desk. He looked up, and his heart fell to his stomach. What the fuck was Whitney doing here?

She was all made up and carrying a gift wrapped in dark brown paper and a blue bow. She was dressed in a long black coat and leather gloves. He didn't register much else, other than her hair was around her face. She looked apprehensive, and he was fucking speechless.

"Alex! I didn't want to forget your birthday," she said, taking a few hesitant steps into his office.

"Uh…" He had a moment of panic. Angel was due any moment, and tonight of all nights, he didn't need this. "You're supposed to forget my birthday; we're not together anymore." He knew he sounded like a rude asshole, but goddamn it! This was the biggest night of his life, and she was about to fuck it up.

She looked taken aback, and her face fell. "I was just trying to be nice."

"Whitney, I don't know what I have to do to make you understand, but, to be blunt; I'm with someone else now. You and I will never happen again."

Her chin trembled as she walked the rest of the way in. "I brought you this." She set it on the desk. "I'll always care about you, Alex. Do you have to be such a prick to me? I'm trying to make peace between us."

He leaned, half-sitting, on the front edge of his desk and looked at her. "I'm not being a prick. You showed up here without calling, and I have plans tonight. To be clear, we *have* peace. I have closure. I'm sorry if you don't, but I'm not sure what else to do to help facilitate that for you. I wish you the best, but it's over between us. For good."

A tear fell on her cheek and rolled down. He sighed. He felt bad for her, but he had to get her out of there before Angel showed up.

"I can't accept the gift."

"It's nothing huge."

"It doesn't matter, Whitney. I don't want it."

"Alex, please—" she began, her voice breaking. She came forward, until just a couple of feet separated him. She was closer to him than the fucking chairs in front of his desk. "Don't you remember?"

He shook his head. "Whitney. Enough. I'm sorry, but it wouldn't be right for me to accept it. I'm expecting someone; I'm afraid I'm going to have to ask you to leave."

The buzzer on the intercom blasted, and he closed his eyes.

"You have to leave, Whitney. I'm sorry." The last thing he wanted was Angel to have visions in her head that involved him fucking anyone else tonight.

"Yes, Mrs. Dane?"

"Uh, I'm sorry to interrupt, but Dr. Hemming just arrived."

Shit! "I don't want to keep hurting you. You have to stop. I've moved on."

He had no choice. He couldn't keep Angel waiting, so he had to trust that she could handle seeing Whitney, and maybe if Whitney could see him with Angel, she'd get the fucking message once and for all. Words sure as hell hadn't worked. He walked behind his desk and leaned in to the intercom. "Send her in."

"Yes, sir."

The mahogany door opened, and Angel walked in. She was breathtaking, and he wished with all of his heart Whitney wasn't standing between them. Angel had on a softly sparkling, black cocktail dress, black silk stockings, and stiletto pumps. She carried a small, beaded clutch and a short cashmere coat over her arm.

"Hi, babe," Alex greeted her. "You look stunning."

He walked around and past Whitney, and took her in his arms, placing a brief kiss on her mouth. She was a bit shocked, and her eyes stayed open when he kissed her. Alex's eyes met them when he drew back. "She was just leaving," he said softly, his arm sliding around her waist to draw her into the office with him.

Angel's heart began pounding at finding Alex's ex standing in his office on his birthday. She stopped a few feet in, but when Alex came to her and kissed her, it became apparent he didn't invite the woman.

"Hello, Whitney," Angel said graciously. "I hope you've been well."

"Yes. I just wanted to bring Alex a birthday gift."

Angel nodded. "I understand," she said gently. She could see the other woman's pain, and she could afford to be compassionate. Alex was committed to her; of that, she had no doubt. His arm tightened around her waist.

"Whitney." Alex was becoming exasperated. "I've already said I can't accept it."

The blonde woman nodded, her head dropping to look at the floor. Angel could see the tears welling in her eyes and put a hand to Alex's chest. "It's okay, Alex." She met his eyes and nodded almost imperceptibly.

He was amazed by Angel's graciousness, but he still didn't want the gift.

"Well, then, thank you."

Whitney nodded and turned to leave. "Happy birthday, Alex."

Angel could see her heart was broken, and she felt a sudden deep sadness for the other woman. To have loved and lost this man was a great tragedy. To love him and not have his love in return would be worse than the deepest hell.

The psychologist in her had the urge to tell the Whitney she could certainly recommend a counselor for her to talk to, to help deal with this, but she knew it would sound condescending and bitchy. She decided it was better just to say nothing.

Once the door closed, Alex pulled Angel closer. "You're incredible. If Kyle brought you a gift on your birthday, I probably would want to beat him senseless."

Her hand ran down his tie, then she nuzzled his jaw with her nose. "I can afford to be understanding. I'm the one in your arms. You smell amazing. Happy birthday, lover."

His hands reached up, and he cupped her face, both thumbs rubbing softly along her cheekbones as he kissed her gently. They'd made love early that morning when Angel woke him up with soft kisses all over his body. She'd ended with taking him deep in her mouth and giving him more pleasure than he could take. He'd stopped her, pulled her on top of him, and they made love for an hour. They were both late for work, but neither of them regretted it.

His body stirred at the memory and at her nearness. He loved her beyond words. Tonight, he would pleasure her until she couldn't take any more. He pressed his erection into her hip, showing her, in no uncertain terms, what she did to him. His mouth ghosted over her lips, nudging, licking, and sucking gently.

"Mmmmm, Alex. Please don't start something we can't finish. I'm starving. I didn't eat lunch today so we could have that amazing cake tonight."

He smiled against her lips. "I want you. Every second when you're with me or when you're not; it doesn't matter."

"Me, too." She touched his jaw. "But, I don't have to walk around with a big old problem. Poor thing."

He remembered the ring box in his pocket, and the last thing he wanted was for her to feel two hard things pressing into her. He released her. "I'll get my jacket, and we can go."

Angel fingered the package's blue bow, curious about what was inside. "Are you going to open this?"

"No. I have no desire to even know what's inside," he called from the other room. "Donate it somewhere."

"You don't know what it is; so how can we donate it?"

"How the hell should I know? I'll have Mrs. Dane get rid of it."

"You should have seen her face when I walked in. She looked like a deer in the headlights. I wondered what was up."

Alex came back in, buttoning up his jacket as he walked toward her. "Mrs. Dane? She'd never met Whitney before. She wasn't allowed at my offices."

Angel cocked her head as Alex took her coat from her and held it for her to slide her arms into it. Her dress was a simple sheath, covered in an unobtrusive floral pattern made entirely out of clear sequins and crystals; understated elegance and class, as always. It shimmered softly.

"Hmmm. No women in your apartment or your office."

"Not before you."

Alex moved the curtain of her hair out of her collar once the coat was on and placed a hot, opened-mouth kiss on the cord of her neck, ending with a little soft sucking. It felt delicious and sent a shiver running through her. "You smell so wonderful. I want to eat you."

"Later," she said softly, smiling. She was so happy it threatened to burst from her.

"Count on it."

"Mmmm. So no offices, no apartment… no wonder she was brokenhearted."

"Forget about Whitney," Alex said as he shrugged into his own long, black overcoat on. Like Angel's, it was made of cashmere, and it was perfectly tailored to his tall, broad-shouldered frame. "I have."

"Alex," Angel admonished. "She's hurting. I've seen it a hundred times, and in this case, I have an intolerable case of empathy."

"Remember she called you and tried to fuck with your head. Did you forget that?"

Angel shook her head. "No, but love makes you do crazy, desperate things sometimes, doesn't it," she pointed out.

Alex couldn't argue. She was right; he'd been pushed to the limit when Mark Swanson took Angel, and yes, he would do it all over again. He'd do more. He nodded. "Yes, it's a recent revelation, but she needs to move on. I just want to concentrate on us tonight, okay? I have something important to discuss with you over dinner."

"Really?" Angel figured she knew what it was about, and so she feigned ignorance. She'd see what he had to say.

He guided her from the office with a hand on her lower back. Angel felt it comforting. They'd always been all over each other, but since the episode in Missouri, whenever they were together, he was constantly touching her, his possession of her screaming of all of those around. She loved it more than she cared to admit.

Angel was curious when Alex pressed the button for the lobby and not the garage. The elevator whizzed down to the black marble lobby level and dinged when the stainless steel doors opened. "Where are we going?" she asked in surprise. "Are we walking? I should have worn a longer coat."

"No, I love the short coat," Alex said suggestively. It was the same length as her dress, which was about four inches above her knees and left her long, black silk-covered legs, open to his view. He knew she'd dressed for his pleasure, not the weather.

Alex took her gloved hand in his and began the walk across the ornate, large courtyard that sat between the front of the sky-scraper and the street. There was a long, black limo waiting at the curb.

"I should have guessed."

Alex smiled. The uniformed driver saw them coming and was waiting with the back door open. "Good evening, Mr. Avery. Doctor Hemming," he greeted them. Alex allowed Angel to slide in ahead of him, and when he joined her, the door closed behind him.

It was the epitome of luxury, an expensive bottle of cham-pagne waited with two Waterford crystal flutes, the leather seats were comfortable and plush, warmed from underneath, and the partition between the driver and the back was discreetly closed.

Alex ignored the champagne and unbuttoned his coat, pulling Angel closer, his hand sliding up her thigh, his fingers squeezing her firm flesh beneath the whisper soft silk in gentle massaging motion.

"Mmm," Angel moaned as his mouth took hers, her body quickening as his hand slid beneath the hem of her dress.

"You're so beautiful," he said softly. "I'm the luckiest man alive." He meant every word. He loved her beyond reasoning, and he wanted her to the point of pain. After months together, he was just as hungry for her as he was on that first night together.

Angel squirmed under his probing touch, his fingers inching higher as he kissed her more deeply. She ripped at the belt of her coat, wanting to be closer. The thigh high-stockings she wore only fueled his desire more. She knew how to turn him on more than anyone he'd ever been with, but if she did nothing, if she wore a burlap sack, he'd be just as hungry.

When his fingers reached the place he was seeking, he didn't find soft silk or lace as he was expected, but her bare flesh, newly waxed and perfectly smooth. His cock was already huge and aching against the confines of his slacks, but blood pushed in almost to the point of pain.

"Jesus Christ," he groaned into her mouth. She was damp with desire, slippery smooth and his mind was filled with tasting her, bringing her to orgasm with his mouth, and then pushing his cock into her tight body over and over.

"Surprise," Angel whispered, her hands wild in the hair at his nape. She scooted down on the seat, more fully beneath him, and her hips arched up. "Happy birthday."

"I want—" the words ground out as he buried his face beneath the curtain of her hair, and his hips pushed his hardness into the soft flesh. His hand still between them, his fingers parted her flesh, and Angel gasped when he began a slow, soft circle on her clit.

"Uhhhh, I want, too. I want you inside me."

He wanted to take her right there. Her hands made short work of his buckle and zipper, freeing his pulsing cock. She was frantic beneath him, her hand around him urging him forward toward her body. Alex gave in to the hedonistic urge to let her slide the head along her folds, pressing forward when it came in contact with her clit. He knew it drove her nuts, and all was fair in their war of love. His breath rushed out at the pleasure of her hot flesh trying to suck him in.

"Oh, Angel. God," he panted. "Fuck, I wish we were having dinner in Denver."

She took his lower lip between her teeth and pulled gently. She couldn't help but smile as her mouth played with his. He seemed to be resisting.

"Fuck!" he grunted out as her hips surged again. He pulled back a little.

"Baby, there is not a thing on God's green earth I want more than you. But I made reservations at Tru, and we're almost there."

"Ugh…" Angel bemoaned the reality of it as the limo stopped. "Just a taste, please, Alex. Push inside. Please." It sounded like a plea. Her body was aching and open, needy and pulsing.

Alex's weight crashed down on her and pushed her fully back into the leather seats, his elbows coming to rest beside her head, his forearms under her shoulders, and his hands holding her head. He stared into her lust-filled eyes and knew his were equally dilated and hungry. She was so goddamned sexy. The sexiest thing he'd ever seen.

He would give her what she wanted, knowing it would leave them both aching and on fire during the meal. Even if he was capable of denying her, he didn't want to, but with everything the evening promised, it would make them even more sexually charged.

His hips moved, and the broad, round head of his cock slipped and slid against her wet lips. She was smooth as silk, and he slipped inside her without the aid of his hand or hers. Her fingers fisted in his hair, and her back arched, helping him slide deep inside her body.

"Uhhhh," Alex groaned as her hot tightness encompassed his length. His cock was pulsing, and she squeezed and clamped down around him in a series of intimate pulls. "Angel," he said softly before his mouth took hers passionately, and he pulled out, only to thrust in again, then again, then again.

It was starting to build fast, and he knew he'd come easily. She was just too fucking hot. He pulled out almost all the way and she whimpered in protest. He pushed in again, his stomach clenched. It felt so fucking amazing. Three more long, slow, thrusts and he was on the verge of coming.

"Babe, I gotta stop," he whispered breathlessly, burying his face into her neck. He pulled out. "I gotta stop."

"Uhhhh," Angel moaned. "Uhhhhhhhh."

Her body was jerking beneath him, and his arms pulled her tight. He kissed the side of her face then her temple.

"Jesus, Angel. You are so. Fucking. Hot! You're going to kill me!" His breath was coming out in heavy pants. "So amazing. I could die inside you and be happy about it."

He separated from her and pulled her into a sitting position.

"Mr. Avery, we've arrived at the destination."

Alex sat back and straightened his clothes, doubting he'd be able to achieve the polished perfection he'd done in his office. He pushed a button on the door. "Yes. Give us five minutes."

Angel pulled her dress down and took a compact out of her clutch. Her chest was heaving, and her hair was a little messy. She played with it and reapplied her dark red lipstick.

Alex ran his hands through both sides of his hair.

"Do I look fucked?" she asked.

Alex smiled, the corners of his lips just barely lifted. "You're fucking beautiful."

"So are you. You are the most beautiful man I've ever seen."

His smile widened. He didn't need compliments. He oozed confidence about everything in his life, but praise from Angel filled him with pride. She was so spectacular in so many ways; he felt his heart swell and his chest puff with pride.

He decided to leave his coat in the limo and pulled on the cuffs of his shirt, underneath the jacket of his suit, then reached out to caress her chin. "Thank you, sweetheart." He wanted to tell her how much he loved her, but that would come in an hour or so when he presented her with the ring in his pocket. "Are you ready?"

She nodded. Angel's gloves had ended up on the floor in front of her, and Alex bent to retrieve them but left them on top of his coat.

The door to the limo opened, Alex stepped out, offering Angel his hand, and she joined him. The restaurant had fewer people in front of it than it had the first time they'd come here. Alex whisked Angel inside, and soon her coat was securely checked.

"Good evening, Mr. Avery." The hostess, Karen, was the same one Angel remembered. "Dr. Hemming." She greeted them both with a smile.

"Hello, Karen," Alex answered.

"Everything is ready, sir."

Alex offered Angel his elbow, and the beautiful couple followed Karen into the restaurant. There wasn't anyone else dining. It was completely deserted. Angel's breath caught. Everywhere she looked—on all of the tables, on the bar—were large bouquets purple Canna Lilies, she now adored. "Alex," she breathed out. Candles were flickering everywhere and were the only light in the room. The effect was breathtakingly romantic.

"Do you like it?" He leaned in and kissed her on the temple.

"It's amazing. But it's your birthday. I mean—" she stopped, and shook her head, her eyes darting to his.

"Yes, I know. But giving you pleasure is the best gift I can have."

Her mouth closed and love filled her expression, and she shook her head again, this time in wonder of him. The opulent dark wood, sheer white curtains, and dark lavender velvet that covered the seats on the chairs were an amazing compliment to the vast array of the lilies, which were the stars of the rooms.

Angel squeezed his arm which rested beneath her hand, and his free one came up to cover hers. "This is unbelievable. Did you buy this restaurant, too?"

"Only for tonight. Do you *want* me to buy it?" He grinned, and she smiled back. "I can."

"Only you would ask me that, Alex. I love you," she said simply.

Karen stopped by a table. "Here you are." She smiled knowingly. "Davis will be with you momentarily."

"Thank you, Karen."

Usually the waiter would be there immediately to pull out the lady's chair, but Alex chose to do it himself. When Angel moved in front of him to sit down, he bent to her ear. "I know," he whispered brashly. His confidence was oozing, and Angel rolled her eyes and laughed softly as he took his seat across from her. The table was small, and he sat back, his fingers tented, and stared at her.

His deep green eyes sparkled, intense and burning, and locked onto hers.

The sommelier appeared as if by magic. His face was lit up like a Christmas tree, and he was carrying two crystal champagne flutes in one hand, his full head of snow-white hair as amazing as Angel remembered. He picked up the white linen napkin in front of Angel, unfurled it, and laid it gently in her lap. "Good evening, sir, madam!" he said enthusiastically.

His tuxedo was perfection. "Good evening, Davis," Angel murmured.

Pleasure flooded the man's features because she remembered his name. "It's a pleasure to see you again, Angeline."

"Thank you; you also."

Davis turned to Alex, who was still watching Angel. "Mr. Avery, the champagne is chilled to the perfect temperature. The 1995 Charles Heidsieck 'Blanc des Millénaires' is a wonderful vintage. Excellent choice. I couldn't recommend better." There were wine glasses and water goblets on the table above the silverware on the right of each plate. Davis deftly replaced the win glasses with the flutes.

Angel's lips lifted in a lopsided smile, her lips closed, and a dimple appeared in one cheek. Her heart was starting to thrum as Alex studied her. Even when others spoke to him, his eyes never left her. Her skin flushed as warmly as it had during the frantic session in the limo.

"I'll bring it right out. Would you like a few minutes, or would you like Dustin to bring the menus right away?" he asked.

"A few minutes, please, Davis." Alex's elbows rested on the chair arms, and his tented hands were close to his mouth; still, his eyes were trained on Angel.

"Very good, sir."

It wasn't lost on Angel that the sommelier and the waiter were the same they'd had on their first date.

"I'm sorry I didn't wear the half-naked dress," Angel murmured.

"This one is beautiful, too. You made up for the half-naked back by the lack of panties." His voice was low and intense, his body swelling at the thought.

Her mouth curved into a sly smile. "What do you get a man who has everything?"

"You could agree to move in with me."

Angel swallowed. She'd already decided to make that his gift, and it was amazing how in-sync they were. The truth was, she'd already decided to tell him she was ready to take that plunge, and she planned on telling him tonight.

"I could," she nodded.

Davis appeared and poured some champagne into Alex's glass. He took it and inhaled. It was nutty and lemony, fragrant and almost mouthwatering. He took a sip, and the flavor almost exploded in his mouth. It tasted buttery and utterly fantastic. "Excellent, Davis." Soon both glasses were filled, and they were inconspicuously alone once more.

"I can't believe you've done this. It's so expensive."

"Don't worry. Though the champagne is excellent, it's not as extravagant."

Angle picked her glass and took a sip. Her eyebrow went up. "It's lovely."

"Isn't it?" She knew he wasn't talking about the champagne, and she blushed.

"I'm talking about having this restaurant deserted. How did you manage it?"

"Easy. All I had to do was cover the receipts."

"Do you always get what you want?" Her eyes challenged, and her words teased.

"Why do you ask questions when you know the answer?" He was nonplussed and undeterred from the original conversation.

"So... you *could*," Alex prompted Angel to continue.

"Uh huh," Angel said offhandedly, taking another sip of the champagne. She could see him sit up a little straighter in his chair. It would be fun to taunt him, she resisted. It was his birthday, after all. "I decided it doesn't really make sense to have two apartments in the city."

"And?"

"And, I miss you. I don't sleep well without you. I like having you close."

Alex took a breath and smiled brightly. He wanted to kiss her but reached out and took her hand instead. His fingers closed around hers. "Finally." He squeezed her hand, and rubbed his hand over it.

Dustin came to the table, happy to see them. "Hello, and good evening." He opened a menu, and placed it in front of Angel, then repeated the action with Alex, then left them to peruse the menus.

"What about a variety, baby?" Alex asked. "So much of it looks very good."

"It's your birthday, so, of course, it's your choice. Anything but caviar."

He smiled. He'd never acquired a taste for the cold, salty fish eggs himself. "Careful what you promise. Is everything my choice tonight?"

"Pretty much." She smiled back. She loved him so much. Giving him the moon wouldn't be out of the question.

They decided on a tasting menu that include things like a crab and turnip appetizer, heirloom beet salad, prime beef rib eye on potato confit, seared foie gras, roasted duck breast, halibut glazed in truffle jus, mint and grape consommé, followed by the amazing bitter almond cake with the sweet milk chocolate ganache.

During the delicious meal, Dustin brought each course and cleared without much conversation. Davis appeared to refill their champagne glasses and bring another bottle when the first was gone. Everything tasted amazing.

"Angel, I wanted to talk to you about something."

"Beyond moving in?" She was intrigued as she reached for her champagne. Angel was feeling a little woozy from two and a half.

"Yes. Since it's my birthday, I hope you'll indulge me." Alex set his fork down on his plate.

"What is it?" She was wary, and it must be important for him to play the birthday card.

"I want to discuss your position with the D.A.'s office." Angel's head snapped up, and her mouth opened to protest, but Alex held his hand up to stop her. "After all of the shit we went through, I'd hoped you might want to choose a less dangerous career path."

Angel paused, considering her words carefully. "Alex," she began. "You know how much my work means to me."

He nodded and pushed his plate forward on the table. "I do, but I also know how much *you* mean to *me*."

His face showed heavy concern, and his brow was low over his amazing eyes. "Psychopaths like Mark Swanson don't happen every day."

"I realize that. Once was enough for me." His voice took on a harder tone.

Her heart fell. Was he saying he wouldn't be with her if she didn't change careers? "It's what I do. I help a lot of people."

"So, then, don't take the bad cases."

Angel shook her head in frustration, her brow crinkling. "How do I know which ones those are, exactly? Figuring out who is guilty, who are the nutcases, and who are homicidal is my part in it."

"I get it, Angel; I'm not a moron." Alex expected her pushback, and though part of him didn't want to discuss this during this dinner, it had to be settled. "But I have a vested interest in the outcome."

"Maybe you should have fucked me in the limo; it may be your only opportunity tonight," she said angrily.

Alex sighed heavily and downed his almost-full glass of champagne.

"Would you leave Avery and teach piano lessons if I asked?" Angel asked quietly, her eyes sad.

"No, but my job doesn't threaten my life."

"Will you leave me if I refuse? The truth, Alex." Her voice was tight and tears glazed over her dark brown eyes. He didn't want this evening to turn out like this, but this was important to him, to their relationship, and to the future of their family, were they to have one.

He looked at her steadily, a certain sadness falling over his handsome features. He shook his head. "Nothing will make me leave you."

Relief flooded over Angel, though she was hurt that he was even suggesting such a thing. She sucked in a shaky breath.

Alex didn't know if he should continue or not, but this was more important than any discussion they'd had to date. The gravity of it had weighed on him since their return from Joplin.

He signaled for Dustin. There was low music playing in the restaurant, and even though it was empty, he wanted to go into the lounge. It was more intimate, and he'd be able to sit closer to her and get his arms around her.

"We'd like dessert in the lounge, please. And please bring the champagne."

Alex pushed back from the table and stood: soon standing beside Angel's chair, he held out his hand and waited, watching the conflict pass over her features. He was sorry he'd even brought it up, but it was done, and it had to be dealt with.

She looked up at him with liquid eyes. Such beautiful eyes in such a stunning face.

"Please come with me," he requested softly.

She put her hand in his and stood. He bent to kiss her temple, inhaling the intoxicating smell of her perfume as his hand threaded through hers.

They followed Dustin into the lounge, which was filled with more candles and lilies. He lifted her hand and kissed the back of it, and she leaned into him.

Angel struggled with her convictions when faced with Alex's concern. She understood; he had a valid argument. She could stomp her feet all day long, pout and scream that he knew her career choice before they got in so deep, but everything had happened so fast, and it wouldn't change his perspective. Her mind was logical, and emotions aside, she knew how hard it was for Alex. He had solid control of everything in his life, yet he felt helpless. He'd been reduced to consorting with the Chicago mafia and spending millions because she wasn't open with him, and yet, here he was in front of her, loving her, asking her not to risk her life. He hadn't walked away, and that was huge. It was proof he loved her, proof he had changed at a base level. True, it was professional ethics to keep her cases secret, but was it more important than making this man happy? No. Nothing was more important than Alex. She had also changed.

He motioned for her to precede him into the same curved booth they'd shared the first time he'd touched his mouth to hers. Once she was seated, he joined her, his left arm curving around her hips and pulling her close, his right hand closing over hers and pulling it onto his thigh.

Dustin refilled the champagne flutes discretely, and withdrew, while Alex gaze held Angel's gaze.

"I get it, okay?" Alex said. His voice was low and intense, that beautiful voice which groaned her name when he came inside her. Her heart lurched. "I know your job is important to you, and I'm not going to be the asshole who asks you to stay at home and be the little woman. That isn't you. But this whole situation with Swanson scared the shit out of me and put it all in a different perspective. I have a shitload of money, and yes, women have been like a revolving door in my life, but I don't want that anymore. I want you. Nothing else."

"Alex," Angel's eyes closed, and a tear fell. His words were honest, sincere, and on the verge of profound. She felt each one as if it reached inside her chest and squeezed her heart.

"Don't put me through that. I can do anything. I can take anything on, but I can't lose you. I'll suffer it if it's the only way I can have you, but I'd rather not. I'd rather just enjoy every second with you."

Angel swallowed at the tightness in her throat. She wanted to speak, but it was difficult.

"I'm not asking you to stop counseling people, but I just don't want you working with these dirty lowlifes anymore. I love you, and I don't want to lose you." Her eyes filled up, and first one, then another fat tear tumbled down her face. "Even when you're crying, you're the most beautiful thing I've ever seen. Even when you're busting my balls and we're fighting like cats and dogs, there's nowhere else I'd rather be."

Angel put a hand to his mouth to stop his words. "Stop. You don't have to say any more. My job means a lot to me, but you mean more." Her voice trembled; her shaking hand traced his jaw. "I love you, Alex."

20

With Every Breath

ALEX KISSED HER soundly on the mouth, his hand going to the back of her head to hold it. He sighed in relief. He backed out of the booth and pulled her with him. There was soft music playing, and Angel wondered why.

"Do you want to dance?" she asked.

Alex shook his head. "No." He stood facing her, both of his hands holding hers. "I mean, yes. Any excuse to hold, you, but in a few minutes."

"I love you, Angel. Those words were hard for me to say before I met you, now they fill me up, and I want to shout them out. You make me very happy. You're all I could want. Almost."

"Almost?" She frowned a little bit. He was acting very strange.

"Yes, almost."

"Alex, what's wrong?"

"Not a thing. Everything is amazing. Thank you for saying I'm the most important thing in your life, because that's what you are to me." Alex drew in a deep breath, filling his lungs to capacity. This was a moment he never thought he'd be facing, but here it was, and it was the most important of his life so far.

"Angel." He looked down at their hands and rubbed his thumb over her empty ring finger.

"What is it, Alex? Whatever it is, just say it."

He looked up into her eyes. "I didn't believe in love until you. You are surprising, and brilliant, beautiful, and just everything to me. To say I love you is not enough. Seriously, I can't breathe, I love you so much. My life was good before you, but now it's brilliant. I don't ever want to be without you."

His heart was thundering in his chest, and he took her left hand and placed it over it, leaning his forehead against hers. "Feel that? That's what you do to me."

Her fingers curled into the fine Egyptian cotton of his shirt as the gravity of what was happening registered in her head and heart. Alex reached into his pocket for the ring box and opened it.

Her chin lifted, his words making her heart pound. She wanted his mouth on hers, to be closer than close. He gave her what she wanted; it was what he wanted, too, but the kiss was gentle and deep, his tongue moving with hers in a gentle ebb and flow, giving and taking. It was perfection.

Angel's breath left her chest when he pulled back. Alex couldn't help placing two more small kisses on her mouth. His heart and body quickened. He could just kiss her forever and be happy, but he had something to do first.

He took one step backward, went down on one knee, and took her left hand in his.

Angel's hand flew to her mouth, her own heart seizing in joy, and pain, and love. The moment was surreal, and she knew this was what the entire evening had been about. This was what all of the flowers and the empty restaurant were about, not his birthday. Was this really happening? She knew he loved her. He'd proven it over and over, but they'd only been together eight months, and he was who he was. Angel's soul was overwhelmed and so full of him she couldn't breathe, her chest and throat ached, and her eyes welled with tears.

"Oh my God."

Their eyes met and held.

"I never thought this moment would come. I never believed I'd want to spend my life with one person, or that I could love someone at all, let alone this much. I never thought I'd want to have children, but I want it with you. It's humbling to know that the perfect life I thought I had was a hollow existence. From the moment I saw you: I wanted you, from the moment I heard your voice, you intrigued me: and when I kissed you, I'd never been so consumed with desire. But more than all of that, I love you. I'll be miserable for the rest of my life if you're not with me for every breath I have left. Angeline Marie Hemming, will you marry me?"

By now, Angel was shaking, and silent happy tears dripped from her eyes. He was amazing and more of a man than any she had ever known. She might as well have been flying, so much happiness engulfed her, yet it was as if her heart was breaking. She loved him so much it hurt. "Yes," she said softly, nodding. "I love you, so much. So, yes, Alex."

He slid the ring on her finger, and she barely noticed more than it sparkled in the candlelight, and the white gold was cool against her skin. She didn't look at it: her eyes were riveted on Alex.

In an instant, he was on his feet, enfolding her in his arms and kissing her as if it were the last kiss they'd ever share. He lifted her up off the floor to bring their mouths level. Alex's strong arms held Angel tight, her soft form melting into his harder one. Their mouths fed on each other; their tongues began an intimate dance that couldn't be finished in their current location. He laughed softly against her mouth.

When the kiss ended, Alex hugged Angel tight, and her arms wrapped around his shoulders, her hands holding his head. A deep, relieved breath filled his lungs and caused her full breasts to flatten against his chest.

"Oh, babe," he said and placed a smaller kiss on her mouth as he lowered Angel to the ground. "I'm the luckiest bastard on the planet. Thank you for saying yes."

"Like I could refuse."

He pulled back just enough to look at her. "You could have."

"I don't think so."

His hands still on her hips, he twisted at the waist to look for Dustin. The young man flushed, discovered with Davis and Karen, watching the entire proposal. Alex smiled. They all had sappy looks on their faces but scrambled to compose themselves, embarrassed he'd caught them eavesdropping, and worried he'd be angry with them. Alex was too elated to be angry. He smiled brightly in their direction.

"I'd like a bottle of the champagne and the cake to go, please."

"Right away, sir." Davis, Karen, and Dustin said simultaneously, all three of them beaming.

Five minutes later, Alex and Angel were back in the limousine and on their way to Alex's apartment. There was palpable energy vibrating between them as Angel sat close to Alex, and his arm stretched across her lap to hold her opposite leg. They were as close as they could get, their hips and legs touching, Angel leaning into Alex. For the first time, Angel allowed herself to take a good look at the ring on her finger. The dark in the back of the car only allowed a limited view. She could see it was simple and good-sized, though not obnoxious. She sighed and laid her head on his broad shoulder.

"Do you like your ring?"

"It's too dark to really look at it, but I'm sure it's beautiful. Though, I don't need a huge ring." The fingers on her right hand ran over it, trying to feel the style. It was a solitaire and the band simple.

"I knew you'd feel that way, and believe me, I reined it in."

She shook her head. "I'm sure," she said wryly. "Though you reining it in is probably like buying a private island in the Bahamas for someone else."

"I did keep it reasonable. It's very representative of you, but I wanted the world to know, you're mine."

"I just want *you* to know," she said softly, and his hand squeezed her thigh possessively. "Kiss me, Alex."

"Wait a few minutes and we'll be home."

"I know you want to kiss me."

He smiled, this conversation reminiscent of a similar one the first night they were together. "Not until I can make love to you. Once I start, I'm not stopping all night."

"It's that whole orgasm thing again."

Alex laughed as she read his mind. "Yes."

"We should call Darian, and thank him for throwing us together."

"He knows. He'll be my best man, and we'll make him sing karaoke at the reception." The dimples in his handsome face made his smile all the more magnetic.

"I don't need a huge wedding, Alex. Something small with just our family and closest friends."

"I want to give you the best of everything. I want to give you the fairy tale. If anyone deserves it, it's you."

"But, I don't need any of the frou-frou stuff," Angel said seriously. "I just want you."

"You have me." Alex bent to kiss her mouth. "Always."

She wasn't cold. The limo had been warm when they got in, but Angel snuggled closer. "I'm... sort of stunned. It's so soon."

Alex leaned down and pressed his mouth into the hair above her temple. "I've been anxious for months but knew you'd balk if it was too soon."

"Did the kidnapping motivate you?"

He shook his head. "No. I purchased the ring before that."

Angel was content and euphoric, but she was also Angel, and she was ornery. She took the hand Alex was resting on her thigh and pushed it higher, over her bare hip and under her dress. "Did you forget about that? You were so serious during dinner."

Alex huffed with amusement, his hand squeezing her ass and his dick beginning to betray him. "I never forget that I want you. It's a constant ache. Stop it. You're being naughty."

"I can take care of that ache," she whispered, pulling one hand up and sucking one of his fingers into her mouth.

Instantly, his cock sprang to life, blood filling it in an instant, and he groaned. He pressed one of her hands into his erection that was pushing through the fine wool of his expensive slacks. Her fingers curled around his hard flesh, and she rubbed and pumped as best she could through the fabric.

"Fuck, Angel, please," he pleaded. His voice was low and velvet. "We're pulling up to the curb. Now I have a raging hard-on."

"I like your raging hard-ons," she teased.

Alex said nothing as the car stopped, but he quickly buttoned his overcoat, shooting Angel a sardonic look that said "You're gonna get it."

She smiled as his hand took hers, threading their fingers together. When the driver opened the door, Alex got out, pulling Angel behind him. He handed the driver a hundred-dollar bill.

"Thank you."

"Thank you, Mr. Avery. Will you need me any more tonight?"

"No, Darrell. Goodnight."

"Goodnight, sir. Dr. Hemming."

Alex motioned for Angel to precede him into the building but kept ahold of her hand. He swiped his fob in the elevator that would whisk them up to his penthouse then pressed Angel against the wall, unbuttoning his coat and pulling hers open.

She watched him intently, and her tongue slid salaciously over her full lower lip. His eyes burned into hers.

"Are you going to punish me for being naughty?" she teased, her voice a sensual caress, filled with invitation.

He moved closer until she could feel his hot breath on her face. He reached down and flattened his hands on the outside of her thighs and slid her dress up, burying his face in her neck, tasting and ghosting, his teeth nipping softly at her silky skin. She was covered in goose bumps, her body started to tremble.

"No." His hand moved to the secret place she wanted him to touch, and she gasped. Her heat almost burned him as her body arched, and her legs opened slightly, to give him easier access. He parted her flesh slowly, still running those delicious nibbles very slowly up and down her neck. She was hot and slick, with the perfect amount of wetness.

"Huhhhh," His breath rushed out in desire, uncaring that the elevator could open at any moment and someone might see them; consumed by the moment and the woman in front of him. He slowly pushed two fingers inside her, and she moaned his name, her eyes closing. He curled them upward and pressed the spot inside her he knew drove her crazy.

Her legs trembled, and he was satisfied he'd put her in the same state she'd left him in.

"Alex, God," Angel groaned, gripping his shoulders to keep from falling. "Ungggg."

"Yes, I know," he whispered urgently as he dragged his mouth over her jaw up to her mouth. "It feels so good, but it aches so fucking bad, doesn't it." His fingers rubbed back and forth inside her, not thrusting but pulsing against her G spot. His cock was twitching and throbbing in time with his pounding heartbeat. He was so turned on, he thought he'd burst. "I'm going to make that go on and on, Angel, for hours."

He kissed her, then his tongue ravaged the inside of her mouth, sucking her tongue deep into his mouth. He felt her fingers tug at his hair, and it only served to incite his desire more.

The elevator dinged as the floors passed, and finally, the doors opened. Angel moaned in protest as Alex removed his fingers, but his other arm remained around her waist as he pulled her from the elevator and into his apartment.

It didn't take long before their coats were on the floor in the foyer, her purse and his keys clattering on the sparkling marble tile. One light on the small table in the entryway was the only light beyond the cityscape glowing in through the large windows of his great room.

They were frenzied, hands on each other, the need between them raged, but Alex wanted to savor every touch. His mouth was on hers in a hungry kiss, both eager to get closer. They were wrapped up and clinging together; mouths gorging and indulgent, tongues laving, each sucking and nipping. Their kissing was always so electric; so amazing between them, it overwhelmed them both.

Alex ripped his mouth from hers, both of them panting, and Angel's hand gripped his head, trying to pull his mouth back to hers, her leg curled around his hip. Fuck, she was hotter than hell.

"Angel, I want you." His breath was heavy and hot, rushing in and out of his body. "So much."

"Then have me."

Alex wanted Angel to remember every second of this night. *He* wanted to remember every second, and he wouldn't rush it or fuck her in the foyer. He would make slow love to her and wring every modicum of pleasure from her until she was begging him to let her come.

He lifted her up, and automatically, her legs wrapped tightly around his waist, her dress was still pushed up enough to allow easy movement. His arms held her bare butt as he turned and walked with purpose up the stairs to his room.

He pushed open the door and laid her on the bed. Angel didn't want to let him go and reached up to kiss him. He gave in because he wanted to deny her nothing, but his fingers, soft on her jaw, he took control and slowed the kiss. When it broke, he took her hand and kissed the inside of her wrist with his open mouth, sucking slightly, his eyes burning into hers.

"I want to go slow, babe." Alex moved away to turn the stereo on. He'd planned for this, so the playlist of sexy songs had been compiled and began playing. The volume was low, but the Bose speakers flooded the room with sultry surround sound.

He stood and shed his clothes in front of her. She watched him, trying not to push her dress down or hide her nakedness. He looked down at her as his jacket and tie fell to the floor, and he began to unbutton his shirt. His breath caught in his chest. She still had on her stiletto heels; the whisper thin stockings, darker than her alabaster skin, were edged in lace, showing below bare thighs and bare... She took note of where his eyes were focused, and she spread her legs for him. His cock screamed, getting harder, feeling like the skin would split. Her eyes were full of want and love, sparkling in the dim light filtering in from the balcony doors. He liked how the low light outlined her body, allowing him to see her body and her gorgeous face, her hair splayed out in a dark halo around her head. *His* sexy Angel.

"Mmmm..." What a sensual picture she made.

Alex pushed his shoes off, the toe of one on the heel of the other, uncaring if he ruined them. Angel's eyes followed the movements of his hands as he unbuckled his belt and pushed his pants to the floor. His muscles were so magnificent. He was cut; his movements were lithe and beautiful. She couldn't tear her eyes away.

His shoulders were broad, his arms and thighs strong and defined, his abs tight and toned, the six-pack made sexier only by the trail of hair that led down the center and disappeared into the low waist of his boxer briefs. His erection was thick; full, and pushed to the side, barely contained inside his boxers, but he left them on.

He came to her, and her hands reached for him. He took her hand and pulled her up, unzipping her dress to push it off her shoulders; he kissed one softly. She smelled amazing, and his eyes closed. As much as his dick was aching, his heart was aching more. He loved her beyond words.

Angel's black lace bra was low on her full breasts, the scalloped edge barely covered the nipples, and he brushed his fingers, ever so softly, over the top swells. "Mmm..." he moaned against the skin of her shoulder then her neck. His fingers ached to touch her and moved over the firm flesh, still covered in lace. He cupped both breasts, his thumbs teasing Angel's already taut nipples. He could smell her desire, and it drove him mad.

He sighed against her as her hands moved over his ass then pushed into his briefs to squeeze the firm muscles there. "Angel... Jesus. It's never enough."

Her dress was in a rumpled pool around her waist, but he left it there and gently pushed her back against the pillows. "I know," she whispered. "I know, Alex."

Her fingers were light as they explored the hard curves and valleys of the muscles on his stomach, inching lower toward his cock, and they tightened beneath her ministrations. "Take these off," she murmured.

His hand grabbed her wrist, gently stopping her. "Don't touch me yet, babe. I want to take our time."

He was sitting on his knees between her spread legs, out of Angel's reach. Her hand rose toward him, at the same time Alex's hands slid up her thighs, pressing them open further. One hand inched higher, as his other moved to pull down one cup of her bra to close around the firm mound. "Fuck, you are so beautiful."

He bent to take the nipple in his mouth, the gentle sucking and flicking of his tongue, combined with his thumb gently brushing in torturous teasing brushes over her clit, made Angel arch and writhe beneath him.

He moved from one breast to the other, biting at her hard nipple through the black lace. "Alex," she called. "Please."

She was still vibrating from their time in the limo, and he seemed intent on torturing her. He moved slowly, relishing her body and worshiping it. His mouth moved lower, and she was wishing he'd removed her dress, but he moved below it, and soon, she forgot everything. Her fingers fisted in the sheets, and her head fell back as he rained soft, sucking kisses over her stomach, between her hipbones, and lower, his hand still inflicting the slow torture on her clit.

Finally, she felt his hot breath lower and couldn't help but raised her hips toward his mouth. The fact she was aching for his touch aroused Alex even more. He lay down on his stomach and laid one hand flat on her stomach between her navel and pubic mound, his other reached for her hand, threading through it and holding her tight. He started slow, blowing hot breath on her then using the tip of his tongue to move around her clitoris.

It was delicious and so torturous. "Mmmmm," she moaned and involuntarily arched again.

Alex couldn't take it. She tasted amazing, and her soft sighs and low moans were making him nuts. He pushed one, then two, fingers inside and started a slow pulse against her G-spot in time with the way his tongue pressed her clit. He couldn't help himself; he sucked the silken flesh into his mouth again with the pulses. He was a skilled lover, and he knew it, yet no other woman's pleasure had ever mattered more to him. He needed her pleasure like he needed his own.

He could feel her clench around his fingers, feel her clit start to pulse under his tongue, and he'd be damned if he could stop. He wanted her to come hard, and she did. Her whole body jerked and shuddered. He milked her orgasm, lightening his pressure but not letting up, his eyes watching her head thrash on the pillow, her body arch. She cried out his name.

"Alex, you have to stop." She jerked again, the aftershocks still rocking through her, and her clit was so sensitive, his touch almost hurt. "Uhhhh, Alex."

He inhaled and moved, crawling up and over her body to kiss her deeply. His heart leapt in his chest when her arms went instantly around his back and shoulders, her fingers almost clawing into his skin, and her legs wrapped around his hips.

She kissed his strong shoulder then his neck as he lay down beside her, his body still entwined with hers. They were facing each other, and Alex pushed her hair back and looked into her eyes.

"I will give you that ten times a day."

"Oh, Alex." Angel reached up to cup his face with her small hand. "You're so good to me. How could I ever doubt you?"

He covered the hand on his face with his, then turned and kissed her palm.

"I wasn't always like this. To be fair, when we met, this wasn't me. You changed me."

"You were always good."

He pulled Angel closer, wanting to kiss her. He was still rock hard, and he couldn't help pressing his hard flesh into her soft stomach.

"You make me better."

Angel pressed on his shoulder, silently communicating that she wanted him on his back. "Help me out of this," she requested softly.

She raised her arms, and Alex pushed the dress up and over her head until she was free of it. He dropped it softly to the carpet on the side of the bed, both hands coming to her hips, his thumbs rubbing over them. Angel reached behind her, unhooked her bra, and soon, the black lace joined the dress.

"Will you leave on the stockings and the shoes?" Alex questioned, a small smile gracing his sensuous mouth.

"I'll give you anything you want."

"I just want you," he said, repeating the words she said in the cab. The heat in his gaze intensified as his eyes roamed her body. His hands moved up to cup her full, high breasts, their round shape and rosy nipples so perfect. In his eyes, she was perfect.

Angel's features were soft with satisfaction and love, and her hand closed around his flesh, pulling and twisting his cock firmly. Alex closed his eyes and bit his lower lip.

She licked her palm to lubricate it and make the sensations more incredible for him. He moaned and began to breathe in shallow pants as she worked him. His eyes flew open and trained on her face. There was a drop of clear pre-cum leaking from the head of his penis, and she rubbed it around with her thumb. He bucked his hips underneath her, and she eased off on her touch.

"Angel?" he questioned. "Are you still sensitive?"

She shook her head and bent to take him in her mouth. He was long and wide, and it made it difficult to go as deep as she wanted, so she wrapped her hand around the base and moved it in time with her mouth, using her lips to cover her teeth.

"Uhhh, babe. That feels amazing," he groaned. Her hair hid her from him, and he pulled it back and up with both hands so he could see what she was doing to him. His stomach muscles tensed as his orgasm built. If he let himself, he would explode in her mouth at any moment. Angel's other hand wrapped around his scrotum, and she used the ring made by her index finger and thumb to pull it down and away from his body. Though he still felt ready to come, whatever she'd done gave him more control, and it could continue to build. She pressed on the hard flesh behind his balls with two fingers, and he gasped. It was the most incredible feeling he'd ever had; it was building beyond the point of where he'd normally come.

She pulled her mouth off to speak. "I want you to tell me if you're going to come, Alex. Don't come, but don't stop me until you are almost there."

"Fuck. Angel," he groaned when she started again. It was so intense; it almost hurt when he got closer and closer. A couple of minutes later, he couldn't take it another second.

"Babe. You gotta stop."

She kept a hand around him but sat up, wiping her mouth with her other hand.

"That was incredible."

"I'm not done." Angel lifted her body and guided him into her body, sinking slowly down until he was sheathed inside her. "Uhhh," she breathed.

Alex's eyes darkened. Her body was hot and tight around him, and Angel used inner muscles to hug him tighter as her hips began a slow rocking. She was so good to him. His cock was super sensitive, and her body seemed even tighter and hotter than she normally was: the sensations were incredible.

Alex knew he'd come without much more stimulation, but he wanted Angel to come with him, and he reached out to touch her, massaging between her legs and feeling his own body moving into hers.

Angel's head fell back as she rode him, her hips rocking and his beginning to rise to meet her.

"Kiss me, Angel," Alex commanded.

She fell forward, her mouth latching on to his as their pace increased. He was still touching her, but his other hand wound in her hair, and his tongue plundered inside the warm recesses of her mouth. His orgasm built and built, and despite his hardest efforts to stop himself from coming, he exploded inside her. "Fuuuuuck," he grunted, his body tingling and jerking violently, coming harder than he ever had in his life. He was shaking with the force of it, blood sending a hot flush beneath the skin of his face and chest.

He flipped Angel onto her back and pumped into her hard, increasing the pace of his fingers on her clit. She bit into the flesh of his bicep, but he didn't feel it. He eyes never left her face as he felt her begin to come. She didn't utter a sound as she fell over the edge. Alex finally stilled, physically exhausted, against her. He kissed the side of her face and traced her cheekbone with his thumb. Both of them were spent and breathing hard, covered in a fine veil of perspiration.

"I love you, Angel."

She hugged him tight. She could give some smartass response, but all she wanted to do was hold him and never let go. She turned her face into him. "I love you, too. So much."

Alex slid out of her but stayed above her, staring down into her face, a look of wonder on his face. "That was too damn incredible. Can it be my birthday every day?" A sly grin lifted one side of his mouth.

Angel smiled softly, a finger running down his face. He was the most handsome, beautiful man she'd ever seen, and it was hard to believe someone so incredible would want her and love her with the same ferocity she felt for him; yet, he did.

"Yes," she murmured softly.

"What was that?" he repeated, a gentle tease and smile in his voice. Alex softly nuzzled Angel's nose with his, tracing it with the tip.

"Mmmm," Angel protested with a soft poke to his ribs.

"Yes to moving in, yes to perpetual birthdays, yes to making love, and yes to marrying me, all in one day." His mouth began to play with hers, his heart so full it hurt.

How could she resist this man? He owned her—heart, body and soul—but she was a more than willing prisoner. "Okay, yes; to all of the above," she said seriously, the tip of her finger touching his lower lip.

"I don't think I've ever heard a more beautiful word," Alex said as he bent to claim her mouth in another passionate kiss.

Epilogue

"WE SHOULD GO in here," Becca said, stopping in front of a bridal shop on East Oak Street.

Angel should have been suspicious when Becca asked her to meet for drinks on Rush Street. She rarely came out to the downtown bar scene, and it was late Friday afternoon, and Becca suggested she come and hang out with Angel during her show. She'd never been in the studio when Angel was on air, so she thought it would be fun. Jillian was spending the weekend with her parents. Since Alex was traveling, Angel had agreed.

"Are you and Cole that serious already?" Angel shot her friend a mocking glance.

Becca rolled her eyes. She and Cole had been spending time together since they'd been back in Chicago, and he had fully recovered, but she knew Angel was teasing. "No. You're the one engaged, bitch," she shot back.

"So?" It was an early spring day, and it was beautiful outside. "We haven't even set a date."

Becca tugged on her arm. "So... you should at least look, Angel. You can't keep a man like Alex waiting forever."

"It's been four months since we got engaged, Becs. We've only known each other a year. Lay off."

Becca knew how long it had been, and she also knew Alex wanted to get married in the not-too-distant future. "I know, Angel, but what's the harm in looking? It could be fun. If I were engaged, I'd be buying every bridal magazine I could get my hands on! Aren't you anxious to marry Alex?"

"We're together, and we love each other. We don't need a piece of paper to be committed to each other. It won't change a thing." Becca tugged Angel closer to the entrance of the upscale exclusive shop. "Look. It says 'by appointment' only. Better luck next time, Becs."

Angel started moving back out the door, but Becca stopped her. "Well, maybe we have an appointment."

"What?"

Becca shrugged. She was dressed in designer jeans, tall black boots, and a leather jacket over a heavy cowl neck sweater, her blonde hair done up in a messy bun. The cool air had kissed both of the girls' faces with a healthy flush. "We have an appointment." Her head cocked to one side then the other, then she looked heavenward. "I made you an appointment."

"Presumptuous much?" Angel asked, astonished, still decked out in a classic black wool pencil skirt and fitted suit jacket, her favorite chartreuse blouse, and her black Prada pumps. She'd just left her office before meeting Becca.

"What are best friends for?"

"For overstepping their boundaries, apparently." Angel looked aghast.

"Look, Angel, last week, when we all went bowling, I watched Alex when I asked you about your wedding. He's anxious. He wants to get married. Why would you keep a man like that waiting?"

Angel paused and considered her friend's words.

"You love the guy. So what's the hold-up?"

"We don't want a huge wedding. This stuff is just a waste of money."

"Oh, my God. Shut up, and get your ass in here, pronto!" Becca insisted, opening the door and pointing inside. "Now." She cocked an eyebrow at Angel.

Angel stood planted in place. Becca nodded into the store, more exaggerated than before.

She wasn't sure why she hesitated, other than it seemed weird when she and Alex hadn't set a date. Allison and Cora had asked to take her bridal gown shopping just the week before, but she'd brushed off the invitation with an excuse about work.

"Angel, get your little ass in this store, already! It'll be fun. We've got a couple hours to kill."

Secretly, she wanted to look at gowns, but it went against her convictions that the wedding was about the love not the outward symbolism. More often than not, too much money went into pomp and circumstance when the real focus should be on the person you're marrying. She'd seen women get married purely for the wedding then live to regret it. Her heart was one hundred percent invested, though, and more than the dress, she was more interested in stunning Alex. That was what her wedding daydreams were about.

"This place looks too pricey. My dad will want to buy the gown, and he can't afford it here."

"Let's just look. What could it hurt?"

Angel chewed her lower lip before nodding. "Okay."

"Okay! Yay!" Becca's face lit up like the Fourth of July. She ushered Angel through the double doors.

A very chic, middle-aged woman, her dark hair pulled back in a sleek chignon, greeted them. She was wearing a simple cream-colored dress that was tailored to fit her like a glove. "Good afternoon, ladies. I'm Sonya. Which one of you is Angel?" she asked.

Her voice, the way she looked and walked, it was all beyond expensive.

The boutique had a few dresses in the windows and others on six headless mannequins around the entrance; the styles starkly different from each other.

"I'm Angel," she answered. "This is my *ex*-best friend Becca." She shot Becca a wry look and offered her hand to the woman.

The woman reached out and shook her hand, "Sorry?" she asked quizzically.

"Oh, don't mind her. She doesn't think she wants a wedding gown," Becca answered. "She thinks she's being coerced."

The woman's thin eyebrows shot up, and her fine features took on a shocked expression. "What? Every woman dreams of her wedding dress from the time she's a young girl!" she said incredulously. "Didn't you ever play dress-up in your mother's wedding dress?"

Becca's eyes visibly widened.

"Um..." Angel prickled. "My father burned it in an old oil barrel on a friend's farm when I was barely two years old." Her answer was abrupt and very, very honest. She looked the woman straight in the face without flinching. The same couldn't be said of Sonya. If she was shocked before, she was more so now. "Along with everything else she left behind when she took off."

The woman looked taken aback and apologetic. "I'm so sorry, Angel. I didn't know."

Angel shrugged, running her hands down the sheer sleeve of one of the gowns, admiring the intricate pattern of the lace. "You couldn't know. I'm sorry if I was short with you."

The moment was awkward, but Sonya had the two women follow her into a smaller room with mirrors on all three walls and a platform in the center. There were three dressing rooms on one side; the décor was a combination of blush, cream, and white. It was all very soft and subtly elegant. In the middle dressing room, they sat down on some upholstered, blush pink chairs around a small glass-topped table.

"Well," Sonya cleared her throat lightly. "Do you have a style in mind? Your figure is quite stunning. You can get away with wearing any type of gown you want."

"I have no clue, to be honest. I would imagine my fiancé would enjoy something somewhat fitted."

"What type of wedding are you having?"

"We haven't set a date or picked a venue. Maybe this is premature," Angel hedged. "Doesn't the dress usually come after all of that stuff is figured out?"

"Well, sometimes, but at other times, the venue and time of day the wedding is held is predicated by what gown is chosen."

"Expensive works," Becca piped up. "Her fiancé is Alexander Avery; perhaps you've heard of him? His family will expect something extravagant."

Angel was horrified and wanted to kick her friend under the table, except the clear glass tabletop wouldn't hide her action. "Becca!" she admonished instead.

"What?" Becca was nonplussed. "I didn't fuck up his name, did I?" She grinned.

Angel wanted to die of embarrassment, but the consultant just laughed. She felt her face flush.

Sonya reached out, patted Angel's hand with hers, and smiled. "Should we shop through the racks, or do you just want me to pull a few gowns for you to try on?"

"Um," Angel looked around the store. There were many, many beautiful dresses. "We can try a few that you choose." It wouldn't matter anyway since nothing would be purchased today.

"Excellent! I'll be right back. Do you have a color preference? White, ivory, champagne?"

Angel shook her head. She hadn't thought about it enough to get as far as color choice. "Whatever you feel would be best is fine." She smiled pensively, looking up at Sonya, who was smiling brightly.

"Don't worry, honey. I'll pick some beautiful gowns. Be right back."

Becca was flipping through one of the bridal magazines sitting on the table, and she glanced up at Angel. "What do you think of this one?" She shoved the open magazine toward Angel. The picture was of a woman on a chaise lounge, her extravagant gown pulled out behind her. It was a full and beautiful ball gown covered in tulle.

It was pretty, but not really Angel's taste. "She looks like a giant marshmallow."

Becca was exasperated. "Ugh! Angel. You are such a buzzkill."

"I think it's too soon, Becca. Alex and I haven't talked much about the wedding. We have time. Beyond that, I think I should invite Cora and Allison when I shop for a dress, don't you?"

Becca perked up. "We can call them."

"We're already here; there isn't time for them to get here."

Sonya came back into the room carrying three dress bags and hung them on the high hooks. "These are all sheathes or trumpet style so we won't need crinoline, but do you want a strapless bra?" she asked, looking up at Angel. She was bent over and unzipping the first bag.

This wasn't "official" in Angel's mind, so she dismissed the suggestion. "I think I'm fine just tucking my straps in, if necessary."

Sonya had Angel in and out of a dozen dresses within the hour, and Becca was playing with her phone, other than to look up each time Angel had on a new dress to give her opinion.

Angel tried a couple of ball gowns, but her original instinct about the fitted gowns seemed spot on. She was standing on the platform in the larger room lined with mirrors, looking at every detail of the gown. "I like this style, but I'm not sure." She studied herself in the mirror. It was a sweetheart neckline with cap sleeves, silk satin, and flared beneath the knees with silk chiffon ruffles. "I like the shape."

"Knock, knock!" Ally's happy voice broke in. Angel glanced in the direction of the door, and a smile split her face as Ally and Cora appeared.

Angel's lips formed a stunning smile. "Hey! Did Becca call you?" she asked in surprise, bending at the waist to reach down and hug each of them from her perch on the platform.

"Yes, and I'm so glad she did!" Cora returned. "Oh, Angel! You're going to be such a beautiful bride."

"Do you like this one? It's a little plain, don't you think?" Allison asked. Angel nodded.

"A little. I don't care for the sleeves."

Ally wrinkled her nose as she gave the gown another once-over. "I agree."

The two women sat down on a plush sofa behind the platform after they greeted Becca when Sonya returned with three more gowns. "Who's this?"

"This is Cora and Allison, my future mother and sister-in-law." Angel introduced them, feeling a bit of pleasure rush through her at being able to address them as such.

"Wonderful! I think we are getting closer! Are you ready, Angel?" She asked after she'd deposited the new dresses inside the dressing room.

Allison, Becca, and Cora were supportive of Angel's likes and dislikes but honest if they felt a particular gown wasn't right.

"Angel, I'd like to look in the couture designs," Cora mentioned, pointing to a room to the left.

Angel shook her head. "Um, my dad will want to purchase the dress, and I don't want it to be too extravagant."

"Nonsense. You're never too extravagant on your wedding gown. I never expected Alexander to get married, so we're going to knock his socks off. Charles and I will help with the gown."

"But—" Angel began, but Cora waved her objection away.

"Sonya, please." Cora's voice was quiet but commanding as she instructed the consultant. "The most beautiful you have, please. Designer or not, just bring out the most beautiful in the store."

Sonya went into the dressing room and returned carrying out five of the rejected dresses. "Yes, ma'am," she said, disappearing out of the room.

Angel stood there, grateful that Cora wanted to help and was willing to pay for the dress, but cash wasn't the issue. She could pay for it herself, but she knew her dad would want to give that to her.

"Cora, Alex and I have discussed it, and the important thing is just getting married. All the other stuff doesn't matter."

Cora's elbow was leaning on the back of the small sofa, and her right knee curled beneath her. She looked young and vibrant, a fresh pink hue kissed her skin. "Nonsense. Alex told me he wants only the best for you, darling."

Angel sighed. "But the best isn't always the most expensive."

"Let's just see a few, shall we?" Her request sounded indulgent, but Angel knew the consultant would bend to the purse strings and acquiesce.

"He's the best for me." She sounded cheesy even to herself. Becca reiterated with gusto.

Becca reiterated with gusto and made an over-exaggerated gagging motion, as if she were about to puke. "Excuse me while I vomit."

Angel's eyes widened, and she shot her a warning look.

"Alex would want you to have only the best, Angel," Ally interjected.

"Does he always get what he wants?" She and Alex had discussed it, and while she knew his position on giving her the "fairy tale", he understood that it wasn't the wedding that mattered to her. She didn't know how she got here. Becca and she were going to have dinner and drinks, and instead, she was defending her views on not going overboard on the wedding.

Allison huffed in amusement. "Now that you mention it, yes, and it's maddening."

Becca laughed. "Angel, just try some on. And, remember, less is more. He died when he saw you in that backless dress, remember?"

"When was that?" Ally asked.

"Their first date. You should have seen Alex's jaw drop. It was the only time I've ever seen him speechless."

"'Less is more means something else in this case, Becca."

"Why can't it be both?" she asked, rolling her eyes. "Angel, live a little."

"All humor aside, Angel. Alex loves you; he'll only get married once, and so will you. That said; let's knock him on his ass, shall we?" Ally's eyes danced with mischief as she grinned. "There are so few occasions where I get to witness him stumbling and stuttering, so give a girl a break." She smiled brightly.

"Please, just humor us, hmmm?" Cora's finely tweezed brow rose, and she smiled softly. "There's no harm in looking, is there?"

"I suppose, but honestly, I don't want Alex thinking it's about money, and I don't want to hurt my father."

Cora laughed. "Believe me, Angel. Alex realizes you don't care about money, and let your father pay part of it. He doesn't have to know he didn't pay for all of it."

"We're just looking now, anyway. I don't want to buy a dress until the date is set, so this is all a little premature."

Sonya returned and ushered Angel into the dressing room. Two other consultants appeared, each of them carrying three dresses. They deposited them on the hooks on the wall, removed any remaining that Angel had already tried on, save the one she currently wearing, and disappeared. It was a well-oiled machine.

The zippers were undone on the bags and several amazing gowns appeared. Angel was a little speechless at how beautiful some of them were, and she didn't want to fall in love with a dress her father couldn't afford, despite Cora's insistence she would help buy it.

Angel gasped at some of the exposed gowns dripping with designer labels and embellishments. Mark Zunino, Vera Wang, Oscar de la Renta, Vivian Westwood, Givenchy... Angel was speechless. "Holy shit," she said without thinking.

"These are breathtaking, Angel!" Becca said.

Cora and Ally were not so blown away, looking at the gowns with a more critical eye, though they did like three of the five.

Sonya shooed everyone out of the dressing room but Angel, and one by one, she helped Angel into each one. Angel's heart stopped when she put on a strapless Oscar de la Renta gown in stark white. It was fitted close to the body until just above the knee and, rather than covered in ruffles or a huge skirt, it flared out softly. It was made of silk shantung and organza with small hand-made embroidered flowers applied in almost complete concentration on the bodice that lessened until they were spaced about three inches apart at the hem. There was a detachable silk organza train. A small silk ribbon bow with a silver and crystal brooch on it at the center of the sweetheart neckline and a smattering of clear sequins on the hand-appliqued flowers. It was simply stunning.

Cora, Becca, and Ally all gasped out loud when Angel stepped out of the dressing room, lifting up the front of the dress and stepping up on the platform. Sonya took the train and puffed it out, so it lay down as it would when walking down the aisle. For once, Becca was speechless.

"Oh my God. Angel!" Ally cried.

Cora's hand went to her mouth, and her eyes welled with tears. It was exactly the reaction Angel would have wanted her own mother to have, if she'd have been in her life. "That's just breathtaking, Angel. It's perfect. Do you love it?"

Angel looked in the mirror from her perch on the platform, her hand ghosted, in amazed wonder, over the luxurious fabric that felt whisper soft. It was light as air and so beautiful.

"Wait!" Sonya said and rushed away, only to reappear a minute later. "Close your eyes."

She placed the matching veil on Angel's head.

"Oh my God," Becca breathed. "That's it, Angel."

"Yes, it's stunning," Cora murmured.

"So beautiful," Ally added.

"Can I open my eyes?" Angel asked anxiously. As much as she had protested, she was anxious to see the finished look.

"Yes."

When her eyes opened, Angel's heart stopped. Her throat swelled and tears threatened to overflow. Angel looked ethereal as she stared at herself in the big mirror. Her dark brown eyes were wide with stunned wonder, tears started to tumble from her eyes. She never thought she'd feel so emotional over a dress, but it was more the prospect of wearing this for Alex.

"Oh my God." The veil was the same fabric as the train with multiple layers, full at her head, then tapering out to one layer that was about six inches longer than the train. "I... can't breathe." She reached up and wiped a tear away, though she wanted to laugh. "It's gorgeous." She fingered the sheer organza of the veil. It had a fine edging of white silk thread and was completely devoid of embellishment other than the sparkling headpiece. "It's just so beautiful. I never imagined something like this."

"Gorgeous?" Ally was excited, her face flush and her hands clasping in front of her chest. "Alex is gonna lose it." Her eyebrows shot up, and she nodded her encouragement.

"*You're* gorgeous!" Sonya exclaimed.

"It's beyond imagining," Cora's eyes were tearing up as well. "My son will be so pleased, Angel."

"It's just perfect, Angel; though, you might like your hair up," Becca added.

Angel reached down and looked at the price tag. It was well over $12,000. "I love it, but it's way too expensive."

"Angel," Cora began, but Angel shook her head.

Angel half-turned toward her, still on the platform, and the beautiful gown twisted around her. Her hand raised a bit to stop her. "No, Cora. I just can't justify spending this kind of money on a dress." She wiped a tear away. "I'm sure when we get closer to the wedding, I can come in here and find something I love just as much for much less."

"Alex would want you to have it, Angel."

"I know he would." Her hands smoothed down the front of the dress over her hips, then she wiped away a stray tear that still trickled down her cheek. "He's all sorts of amazing that way, but really, it's not about the gown. It's about him."

Cora sighed, love filling her expression. "He's lucky to have you, Angel." She could see Angel genuinely loved Alex, and she couldn't want anything more for her youngest son. She got up and went to hug Angel tight. It was obvious she loved the gown, and she admired Angel very much. This was only further proof her son's fiancé' was not one of the bimbos after her son for his money or status.

"Can we at least mull it over?" Cora asked gently.

Angel hugged her back hard, closing her eyes. "It's so pretty, but it's just too much."

Cora pulled back and took a hold of both of Angel's hands. "Just think about it, honey."

"My brother will be knocked senseless. That alone should be reason enough to buy it," Ally added.

Angel smiled at all four of the other women beaming up at her. "Okay, I'll think about it." She said the words to placate the women in the room, but deep inside, she knew she wouldn't get this dress. It was breathtaking, all of the things little girl dreams were made of, and it would be amazing to have it... but she had Alex. Her heart swelled and burst, knowing that soon, he'd be her husband. He was hers. She was his. He proved it in every smoldering look, the sexy words he whispered, and when they made love, his possession screamed in every touch, every demanding kiss, and the way he took control of her body. She wouldn't have it any other way. That was Alex. It was at the core of who he was, and she didn't need anything beyond that.

*****

Alex sat up in bed, propped up on his muscular arms. His tanned torso was cut and strong, the bumps of his stomach muscles showed above the sheet as it fell low on his waist, and he ran a hand over the stubble on his jaw. The weather was amazing, and the resort was five-star, located at Agios Ioannis Diakoftis on the eastern coast of the Mykonos. The bungalow was private, the service top-notch; everything first class. Cooks, valets, housekeepers, all so discreet, they didn't even know they were there, other than the food that miraculously appeared, or the bed that was made in the mornings or turned down at night.

He'd promised never to keep secrets from Angel, but surprises were the exception. This was a surprise all right, but somehow he'd managed to pull it off. He'd had her assistant cancel all of her appointments for three weeks, and had Becca, Allison, and his mother shop and pack a bag for her filled with an assortment of sundresses, shorts, tops, bikinis, flip-flops and lingerie from Entice. Alex told Darian the radio show would have to be reruns for three weeks. His best friend wasn't happy about that until Alex spilled his guts. Then everything was miraculously fine. Satisfaction had settled over him the moment the car pulled up beside the private jet on the tarmac at O'Hare. To give her credit, she didn't protest too much. A little at first when he whisked her into the back of the limo outside her office building on Wednesday night, but once he'd told her he was taking her to Greece for a holiday together and started kissing her senseless, she had no choice but to shut up.

The open French doors led out to a covered porch, the steps leading directly out to the beautiful, white sandy beach and the pristine aquamarine water; the sloping hills beyond the lagoon green and lush. It was glorious. Alex sucked in a deep breath as the soft breeze blew through the bedroom, scratched his stomach, and glanced outside. There was a private, freshwater pool, mere yards off of the beach, surrounded by a red-stained teakwood deck, off-set with a stone patio. A private linen cabana was situated on the deck a bit away from the pool. It was all so magnificent. A perfect private oasis.

Alex smiled at a sleeping Angel, naked and wrapped in nothing but a sheet. Her face was serene, and the eight-hour time difference called for a nap when they arrived three days before. Now the jet lag was finally under control, but the beauty of the whole situation allowed them to make love until the wee hours of the morning and sleep as long as they wanted, which was exactly what they had done. The lifestyle of relaxation was addictive. It was late afternoon. They'd gone walking through a local village, had lunch at a local restaurant, made love upon their return, then drifted off to sleep in each other's arms.

He lay back down beside the woman who consumed his heart, turned onto his side, tucking one arm under his pillow, and stared into Angel's beautiful face. She was so beautiful, serene in her repose. A new glow on her skin from the hours spent on the beach the day before only made her more breathtaking. Her engagement ring glinted elegantly on her finger. He needed to touch her, and his hand reached out to brush her hair back behind her ear.

Angel stirred, her long black lashes fluttering open lazily, then closing again as a small smile curved her luscious mouth, and as her fingers closed around his wrist. "Mmmm..." she breathed, scooting closer to his body. She lifted her chin and kissed his chest.

"Do you know how much I love you?" he asked softly. "If I could do nothing more than watch you sleep for the rest of my life, I'd be happy."

Angel smiled again. "I never thought Alex Avery, womanizer extraordinaire, would turn out to be such a romantic," Angel teased, nuzzling into the skin of his neck.

"Answer the question," he commanded softly, his fingers making delicious circles on the skin of her arm and shoulder before sliding around her back.

Angel wrapped an arm around his waist. "Of course, I do, silly." She pulled back just enough to stare into his beautiful dark green eyes. The look on his face was serious. The little crinkle appeared above her nose. "Why are you asking me that?"

"Just making sure." His hand slid up and over her hip, down the slope of her waist, and over her ribcage making his cock twitch and start to swell. "Being with you is like nothing I've ever felt."

Angel swallowed. His intense expression gave her pause. It was the first time since they'd arrived in this beautiful place that he'd been this serious. "Are you okay?"

"Yeah, babe. I'm good. Better than good. Sometimes, I'm still a little shell-shocked by you."

"Okay. It overwhelms me sometimes, too. My heart hurts with how much I love you." Her eyes searched his, and her throat tightened. In spite of their teasing banter, or maybe because of it, he was the love of her life and there was no disputing it.

Alex's arms tightened around her, and pulled her close, and his head swooped to take her mouth in a hungry kiss. Soon their tongues were laving, and he was pressing Angel back onto the bed, his erection leaving her in no doubt of his desire.

"Baby, do you want to take a bath with me?" she asked. Her breath was hot on the skin of his bare shoulder as her fingers skittered over the solid planes of his body.

Alex had wanted to talk to her, but it could wait a few more minutes. His love and desire was once again taking over, but he nodded and rose from the bed, bending to slide his arms underneath and around his fiancée. Alex carried a still sheet-wrapped Angel into the large and luxurious bathroom, and sat her on the edge of the big Jacuzzi bathtub. Though the suites were meant for couples, the bathtub was more like a hot tub and could easily hold four people. He was naked, and Angel watched him bend to turn on the water and adjust it. Though she saw him naked on a daily basis now, she couldn't help but admire the way the muscles moved beneath his smooth skin, enjoying the small amount of soft dark hair on his chest as it tapered down his belly. His cock was huge and so engorged, she could see it pulsing.

"I'm one lucky bitch," Angel murmured, a teasing lilt to her voice. Alex smirked, and his breath came out in a huff.

"It's a good thing I'm not conceited," he returned, meeting her eyes and reaching out to gently tug the sheet from around her nude form. His expression mirrored his happiness, his white teeth showing in his now tanned face. Angel remembered the first time she saw him about a year ago. He'd been tan like this, as well.

"Have you been here before, Alex?"

He shook his head. "No. Not this resort. I've been to Greece a few times. I love it here."

"Yes, it's pretty." Angel turned and slid into the tub. Alex soon followed her into the steaming water. There was room to sit across from each other, but Alex reached for Angel and brought her close, kissing her deeply while pulling her legs around him in one movement. She ended up on her knees, her arms wrapped around his shoulders as his cock bobbed against her. The water was hot, but her flesh was hotter. Alex wanted to bury himself deep within her, but he wanted to make love with her, not fuck. This was important. He'd never loved another woman, but loving Angel felt like his life force.

She ground her hips into his at the same moment she bent to kiss his mouth. Alex groaned against her, the sound muted by the sound of the water still rushing into the tub. Her hands pulled and tugged at his hair as their mouths moved with each other. My God, he thought, his heart throbbing as much as his body. He couldn't get enough of this woman. He'd never be able to get enough.

"Uhhh… Do you think making love this much is obscene?" she whispered against his mouth as his body pushed into hers. "Uhhh…" she gasped.

"No. It's never enough," he grunted.

Angel bent her head and sucked his earlobe into her mouth, biting it softly. "I suppose this is what it will be like being newlyweds," she whispered.

Alex's hands were on her hips, pulling her forward, in order to move back and forth on him. It felt amazing, and he liked having free access to her breasts, neck, and mouth.

They were passionate, forgetting the running water, even as it spilled over the side of the tub, as they moved together. When Alex finally spilled into her body, Angel was gasping and jerking with the force of her own lovemaking.

They were both breathless, their arms still tight around each other, placing kisses on each other's shoulders. Alex breathed out and placed an open-mouthed kiss on her cheek then her temple. His body still fully sheathed inside hers, he held her tight but moved back to look into her face.

"Do you want to be newlyweds here, baby?"

She laid her head down on his shoulder, still relishing the feel of him inside her. She nodded. "Yes, I love this place. I like when it's just you and me."

Alex's hand reached up to thread in the hair on the back of Angel's head. It was damp, the tips of the tendrils completely saturated.

"I do, too. So, I have one more surprise for you."

She looked incredulous. "I don't need more surprises, Alex."

"I know. You don't need much, but I like doing things for you. Will you let me? Without arguing?"

"Well—"

Alex's eyebrows shot up and his head moved to one side, though he was still looking into her face. "Uh! No arguing."

Angel nodded. He asked so little of her, and he gave so much. "Okay."

"Good." He reached toward the side of the tub and turned off the water. There were already puddles alongside it, but more sloshed over when he braced his arms on the tub's edge and hoisted himself and Angel up and out of the tub in one motion.

After Angel and Alex separated and dried off, he bent to kiss her softly on the mouth. "Will you meet me on the beach at sunset?"

"Do you want to go for a walk before dinner?" Angel wrapped one of the large white towels around her small form as she looked up at him.

"No." His eyes were intent.

"No?" she asked, curious what he meant. "We just had a bath. You don't want to go into the ocean, do you?"

"No."

Her eyebrow cocked, and she leaned against the vanity. It was clear to Alex, she was getting impatient.

"It's the surprise. Just go with it, please?" He smiled a brilliant smile that no woman could resist.

Angel nodded, following him back into the bedroom, and watched him throw on some khaki shorts and a T-shirt. "You stop being so sexy, already. That may have worked well for you in the past... and it still does. It's not fair, so quit it." Alex chuckled and walked toward the door. Her mouth fell open then she bit her lip. "Wait. Where are you going?" *What was he up to?*

Alex laughed lightly. "Babe. Stop. I'll meet you in a couple hours."

"You're not going to hop a flight back and desert me here, are you?"

Alex shoved his wallet and phone in his pockets then pushed his feet into flip-flops. He shook his head wryly and walked to her; taking her head between his hands, he bent to brush her lips lightly while swatting her on the ass with an open hand. "Be good. I'll see you then."

"Alex!" Angel called, but he was gone, leaving her standing in the middle of the suite, perplexed.

*****

Angel had chosen a soft coral sundress and her hair was piled up in soft curls on top of her head. She looked at herself in the mirror. Did she look different? Her whole life had changed. She had sublet her apartment and was living with Alex full time. She still worked with the D.A.'s office, however, but only as a consultant to help the assigned clinical psychologist interpret the personality tests. She was whisked off to Greece for three weeks, and rather than yell and scream at Alex for not discussing it with her first, she was over-whelmed by how amazing he was. She was head over heels in love and happier than she'd ever been.

She smiled softly at her reflection, taking out a soft coral lip gloss and began unscrewing it. She shook her head. Unreal. The bungalow was one of several lined up on the beach, and because they never saw a single soul, Angel was surprised when someone began knocking on the door. It wasn't as if they even used keys, so why would Alex be knocking?

"I'm coming!" She ran quickly to the door. There were a few feminine voices on the other side, so she peered through the peephole but it was black. *What the hell?*

"Anga! Y'open the door!"

Was that Jillian?

Angel opened the door, and standing on the front porch was a very excited Jillian, Becca, Ally and Cora.

Her mouth fell open in astonishment. "What are you doing here?" she asked, dumbfounded.

Jillian threw herself at Angel, hugging her legs with both arms, and Angel put a hand down to her face as the child looked up at her.

"Weez is gettin' marrdied!" Jillian's face was pink with excitement, her blue eyes dancing in her round little face.

"What?" Angel looked up at the other women. Ally and Becca were smiling, dressed in light aquamarine, linen sundresses. Cora had a wistful look on her face, also dressed for the beach in an elegant chiffon dress that hit just below her knees in a slightly darker shade. They were all perfectly made up, but barefoot. Jillian's hair was full of baby's breath, and her dress was white linen dotted with small flowers in the same shade of aquamarine as Becca and Ally's dresses. She looked like an angel.

"Weez is gettin' marrdied!" she said again happily, jumping up and down.

When it finally dawned on Angel what was going on, she was still speechless.

"Are you okay?" Becca asked in concern, putting an arm around her Angel. Her friend had a stunned look on her face as her eyes went from her face, to Ally, to Cora. "Angel, breathe!"

Cora walked toward her and put a hand to her cheek. "Don't be angry with Alex, darling. He's been planning this for a couple of months. He wanted to surprise you."

Angel's eyes blurred. "On the beach at sunset?" It was all very romantic and not something she'd expect, even as loving as he'd become. An iron band slapped around her chest as her lungs froze.

Ally nodded.

Angel's heart threatened to explode, the tightness in her throat almost unbearable. "I'm just surprised."

"We can throw a big party in Chicago next month," Cora said.

"Um..." Angel's legs were shaky. "I don't have anything to wear. What about my father? As much as I love Alex, I can't get married without my dad."

"He knew that sweetheart," Joe said from the doorway.

"Oh, my God! Daddy!" Angel exclaimed, her hand going to her chest.

"I would have kicked both of your asses if I'd have missed this."

He was carrying a white gown bag from the bridal shop and laid it across a chair, then came forward and enfolded his daughter in his arms. Angel melted into him, feeling a emotional. "I can't believe this." Everything was so overwhelming. Even for someone who usually had a strong hold on her emotions. Ever since she'd met Alex, it was as if he'd brought all of her emotional walls crumbling down. "I'm so glad you're here."

Her father hugged her tight. "Come on now. You don't want to keep that fine young man waiting." He wiped her tears away as the others looked on. Angel gave him a luminous smile, her heart felt like it was shattering with happiness.

"Anga! Why is you crying?" Jillian tugged on her dress. "Don't you wanna marrdy Zander?"

Angel nodded. "Yes. I want to marry Zander. Very much."

"Tay! Let's go!" Jillian started to spin around, fascinated by how her dress twirled around her.

"Let's get the show on the road, shall we?" her father asked, his brown eyes meeting hers. He kissed Angel's cheek and backed away. "Okay. Meet you out back when you're ready."

After he left, the women burst out in a bunch of excited screams, and Angel hugged them all in a big group hug.

"Let's get you into this, shall we?" Cora asked happily.

"This is what the appointment was about? Sneaky bitches." She laughed.

"Yes! Oh my God! Alex was relentless!" Ally exclaimed. "He wouldn't stop bugging me! Then afterward, he wanted to know what you'd chosen. I wanted to fucking smack him!"

"Allison!" Cora admonished.

"What? It's true." Ally grimaced with wide eyes only for Angel to see.

"Did you all come together?"

"Yes. Alex sent the jet back to get us. A stop in Joplin first, then we all piled on in Chicago. Jillian has been like a jumping bean. We've been on the other side of the island since yesterday."

"Incredible."

It wasn't long before they had Angel into her dress. It was as beautiful as she remembered; even more so. The crystal that adorned the bow between her breasts had been replaced by a sparkling, antique diamond broach. Angel gasped when she saw it.

"This is really beautiful." Her fingers delicately touched the intricate design.

"It was Charles' grandmother's. It's very old. Alex used to love looking at it sparkle when he was a baby, so she put it away for him. He wanted you to have it today, Angel."

Angel blinked at the tears burning the back of her eyes. She didn't want to cry and ruin her newly re-applied make-up. Not before Alex saw her. She changed the subject to help her get a grip. "How does the gown fit so perfectly?"

Becca answered. "Sonya is very efficient. That, and I smuggled in that strapless dress you wore to the breast cancer fundraiser last year. That fitted one?"

"You guys are quite a crew."

"Wow!" Jillian said, buzzing around Angel when Becca was putting the veil on her head.

"Isn't Angel beautiful, sweets?" Becca asked the little one. Jillian nodded. "Bootifoo!" she agreed.

"It's a little much for the beach, isn't it?" Angel asked. She was on cloud nine, her face hurt from smiling at the same time as tears choked her up.

"Maybe, but it's not too much for my brother," Ally answered.

Angel inhaled deeply, nodding. Ally was right. Nothing was too much for Alex.

After one last look in the mirror, they were ushering her out through the double doors in the bedroom onto the deck around the pool. The sun was just turning the sky a brilliant coral that faded into dark lavender. The water was turning darker as night fell, but the sun reflecting across it made it sparkle.

She could see Alex's silhouette on the beach, his hands in his pockets. He was enveloped in shadow, so she couldn't see his face or how he was dressed; he was too far away. Cole and Darian stood next to him, and Joe and Charles were waiting for the women.

Outside, four hotel staff were waiting by the cabana, their arms laden with the purple Canna Lilies that had become a symbol of Alex and Angel. Jillian was handed one on a shorter stem, then three each, bound with white silk ribbon, were given to Becca and Ally. With a full bouquet of purple lilies, white orchids, and freesias firmly in one hand, Angel put her left arm through her father's right.

"Ready?" Joe asked, his eyes glowing love. Angel wasn't sure, but she could swear he was tearing up, and she leaned in to kiss his cheek.

"Yes."

The hurricane lamps were lit, and two rows had been placed down the beach to where Alex waited.

She couldn't help but choke up as Charles kissed her cheek. "You look stunning. I never thought I'd see this day. Thank you, sweetheart."

"For what?"

"For making Alex believe in love."

"Everyone is so wonderful. I'm going to cry." Angel's voice cracked on the last word.

"Happy tears," Cora said, her own eyes welling up.

Charles took Cora's hand and tucked it in his arm after they both kissed Angel on the cheek and then turned and walked across the sand.

Angel watched them go then looked down at her father's feet. "Everyone's barefoot. Even the men?"

Joe smiled. "Yes. I thought it was silly at first, but it seems appropriate."

Ally walked in front of Becca, who had Jillian by the hand.

"Are Uncle Will and Ben here?"

"Yes, and Alex's friend, Darian. Otherwise, just the family."

Angel nodded, swallowing. "That is the family." She didn't need a huge wedding. This would be better than she could have ever imagined.

"Are you scared?" Her father murmured the question so only Angel could hear. There was a lone violinist playing classical music as the girls walked toward the others on the beach.

Angel suddenly felt calm. She shook her head. "No. After what happened between you and Mom, I didn't think I'd ever want to get married. I didn't think I'd trust anyone that much, but I trust Alex."

"I do, too."

Angel squeezed her father's arm, and her feet sank into the satin-soft sand as they stepped off the deck. This was the first step into the rest of her life with the man of every woman's dreams. She laughed to herself. Yes, he was every woman's dream, and she was marrying him.

The sun was in her eyes, so Alex, Cole, and the minister were mostly in shadow until they got right in front of them. Alex's hair was still a bit damp and slicked back, and he was dressed to kill in a black suit over a crisp white shirt and black silk tie. He looked impeccable. She glanced down, and just as expected, his feet were as bare as everyone else's.

When Angel approached Alex, and her father kissed her on the cheek his heart stopped. Angel handed her bouquet to Becca he reached for both of her hands.

She was going to start crying, so she tried hard to tease him.

"There's still time for a pre-nup, you know." Her voice trembled, and Alex knew she was struggling for control. His beautiful, strong Angel was as fragile as the finest glass. And she needed him in ways she'd never needed anyone else. That knowledge filled him up to bursting.

"Why? Are you afraid I'm going to steal all your money?" A smile tugged at the corners of his beautiful mouth as mischief lurked in his eyes.

A small, tearful laugh burst from her, and she squeezed his hands.

Alex thought she was the most stunning thing he'd ever seen, and it was hard to believe he even existed before meeting her. "You're so beautiful. I'm the luckiest man on earth."

She smiled brightly, lifting her tear-filled, luminous eyes to his. Alex's own throat was tight, and his eyes burned. He loved her so fucking much, he couldn't even breathe, and she was all he would ever want.

"Surprised?" He smiled softly, rubbing his thumbs over the tops of her hands.

"You are *so gonna get it* later," she said, her voice, though cracking, was amused.

Alex laughed softly, his eyes unable to look away from Angel's face, but his eyebrow cocked in amusement. "Promise?"

"Oh, I *promise.*"

"Me, too."

After Angel handed her bouquet to Becca, Alex took both of her hands in his and kissed the inside of her left wrist, his mouth open and caressing. Their eyes locked, and it seemed like they were all alone on this beach, and the entire planet.

Everyone watched the couple in silence, and it was as if time stopped.

"I love you, so much," she said in a soft, trembling voice. The tears she was holding back finally broke free to tumble down her cheeks. "I can't believe how much."

Alex thought the tears only made her more beautiful, she'd wrapped around his heart from the very first time he'd laid eyes on her. A hundred years wouldn't change it. "I love you, more. *I promise...* I love you, more."

Other Books by Kahlen Aymes

All titles available in all eBook formats and paperback.

After Dark Series
1. *Angel After Dark*
2. *Confessions After Dark*
3. *Promises After Dark*

The Remembrance Trilogy
Prequel—*Before Ryan Was Mine* (Publishing 12-16-14)
1. *The Future of Our Past*
2. *Don't Forget to Remember Me*
3. *A Love Like This*

Coming in 2015
UnTouch Me (Stand Alone Novel)
The FAMOUS Novel Series

Stalk Kahlen

Facebook: https://www.facebook.com/kahlen.aymes.author
Twitter: @Kahlen_Aymes
Find her on Pinterest, Instagram, YouTube and Goodreads.

Visit Kahlen's website for Merchandise, Signed books, Julia's
Recipes, Missing Scenes, Events, Kahlen's Blog, and Playlists:
KahlenAymes.com

For news on new releases, contests, appearances, and
excerpts; subscribe to her
newsletter: http://eepurl.com/RuW4X

Request an ebook autograph at:
http://www.authorgraph.com/authors/Kahlen_Aymes

Rights Information: McIntosh & Otis Literary, Inc. 353
Lexington Avenue • New York, NY 10016 • Tel: 1-212-687-
7400 • Fax: 1-212-687-6894 • Email:
info@mcintoshandotis.com